STATE OF GRACE

A NOVEL

Also by the author:

Cold Hands

STATE OF GRACE
A NOVEL

Joseph Pintauro

Times
BOOKS

The lyric that appears on page 91 is from "Carolina in My
Mind" by James Taylor © 1969, 1971 by Blackwood
Music Inc., and Country Road Music. Used by permission.

Published by TIMES BOOKS, a division of
The New York Times Book Co., Inc.
Three Park Avenue, New York, N.Y. 10016

Published simultaneously in Canada by
Fitzhenry & Whiteside, Ltd., Toronto

Library of Congress Cataloging in Publication Data

Pintauro, Joseph.
    State of grace.

    I. Title.
PS3566.I56S7   1983   813'.54   82–50047
ISBN 0–8129–1020–6

Manufactured in the United States of America

83 84 85 86 87 5 4 3 2 1

For Anthony Pintauro

Woe to him who would not be true, even though to be false were salvation.

—Herman Melville,
from the sermon on Jonah in Moby Dick

STATE OF
GRACE
A NOVEL

Chapter One

H E STEPPED OUT OF LIGHT onto a dirty white tile floor, into the dark vestibule, into odors of moldy linoleum and oil-painted tenement walls. No names over the buzzers. The front door had been ripped off by the landlord. Brown paint made the first floor a tunnel of glossy darkness, except where light descended the stairwell, softly inviting him upward. He walked toward the light. His lowered eyes could not keep out the sounds coming from behind the doors, noises avalanching down the stairwell as he took his first step. Babies crying, people arguing. *"Who pockets the money? Me? Who sits and waits for you to mind him so I could take a crap? Haggh?"* Radio voices, the voices of television, cartoon music, salsa. He could envision the apartments: worn floors, dusty chifforobes, small bedrooms jammed with oversized furniture, walls crowded with religious symbols, agonized Christs, dolorous Madonnas with hearts pierced, darkly lit devotional candles, St. Vincent pointing to fire in his chest, St. Rocco pointing to his bleeding knee, St. Lucy holding two eyes on a saucer; graveyard standards, wax flowers, palms, holy pictures, crucifixes, of wood, of plastic, of fake gold.

Clattery, shrill Spanish; Yiddish, softly, behind doors. He ignored the door of Madeline Corey near the landing. He'd stop there on his way out to give her one of the two hosts in the solid-gold case near his heart.

As he breezed up to the second floor, he caught that floral odor coming from his cassock, of funeral parlors mixed with underarm odor (three wake rosaries that week), and cassocks absorb odors —incense, sweat, hospital smells. But the worst were the odors of funerals. So many people had died in his arms in his years as a priest. That part was beautiful. It was their helplessness later that broke his heart: the powder, the makeup, lifeless feet stuffed into new shoes, tuxedos, ballroom dresses, high heels, wedding gowns, smiles waxed into the faces of cadavers; bodies empty of spirit, the dead, lying on display like marble dolls on wilting flowers.

Fresh coffee perked somewhere on the second floor. He rose through its odor as through fog, corned beef, cabbage, and chicken soup—odors that linger like homeless ghosts in tenement stairwells, ghosts afraid to leave, fighting one another, getting old together, hiding from the light. He burst through them, two steps at a time, upward, till he reached the landing of the fifth floor, where the fresh smell of latex paint welcomed him, and the newly painted, pale-blue door of Mrs. Caccavale.

He knocked gently. The door opened, revealing candle flame. The old woman wore a white handkerchief on her head out of respect for the Blessed Sacrament. Italian sauce bubbled on a stove that took up half the kitchen. He stepped onto the clean, waxed yellow floor inlaid with red and blue teapots and cups. The old woman loved to clean, but dust filled the plastic roses out of her reach in a wall sconce. An oversized kitchen set was squeezed against the window, trapping two muscular chrome chairs against the radiator. The tabletop was slick gray Formica in the disturbing pattern of crushed velvet.

She ushered the priest into the bedroom where her son Dominic sat up in bed, blinded by sunlight. The room glowed; the white sheets gave off radiance. Behind the man's head was an old crucifix from Sicily, a black wooden cross upon which the white bisque figure of Christ was nailed. Christ's hair and beard were of black horsehair. His bruises were of rouge, rubbed into the chalky skin. His wounds were painted over with nail polish. Tom took from his pocket an aspergillum, an object like a tiny silver fountain pen, containing holy water. He unscrewed the top and sprinkled the man, who turned to him with blank eyes. The communion that the middle-aged priest was carrying was not for Dominic. Dominic was forbidden to receive communion. Monsignor Granger, the pastor of St. Barnabas', had deemed him unfit years ago. The white round wafer, the living presence of Jesus Christ, could not be given to someone who couldn't comprehend the miracle of transubstantiation. Granger was strict when it came to that sacrament. A half-dozen children each year were kept from receiving First Holy Communion because they failed the communion test. And Dominic Caccavale, fifty years old, didn't even know his name.

"Dominigeel." The old woman shook her son. *"Il prete sta ca,"* she shouted in dialect Italian. "The priest is here. *Look.*" She shook the man, as though he would suddenly wake up from his lifetime stupor and say: Where am I? The old woman, tiny, in her black dress and stockings, never gave up hope that her oldest son would receive his First Holy Communion. The poor man's head jerked. He stared blankly into the sun, oblivious of his mother. Tom turned and went into the kitchen. The old woman followed defeatedly. She placed the candle on the crushed-velvet tabletop.

"You want to confess first?" Tom whispered.

"No." She shook her head and knelt to receive the wafer. Tom took it out of its gold case, making the sign of the cross before her face. "May the body and blood of our Lord Jesus Christ preserve your soul into life everlasting." He placed the glowing white host upon her waiting tongue. Immediately, she closed her mouth and stood. She opened the door for Tom to leave and with lowered eyes she waited for him to pass into the hallway. But Tom paused.

"Signora, no more on Sunday." She stared up, wide-eyed. "Too *busy* on Sunday," Tom added. She continued to stare, not responding. Something seemed to be caught in her throat. Her lips pressed together against their will, as though she hadn't swallowed her communion. "You feel all right, signora?" Tom asked. The woman's fearful eyes widened the more. Suddenly she swallowed in a loud clack, and her eyes narrowed with anger. She turned away from Tom in an expression of embarrassment and resentment. Tom slowly realized that the woman was saving the host in her mouth for Dominic, so that after Tom left, she could give it to her son. It was out in the open. She knew it and blushed. The old woman stood against the window and spoke with deliberate disrespect.

"*Satisfatto?*" she asked. "You *make* me sin. The *priest,*" she said, trembling. "I have to touch the God with my fingers. But it's not my fault. Blessed Mother, help me." Rigid from holding her secret, she crumpled into the kitchen chair, but her eyes courageously returned to Tom's, surrendered to the emotions that pressed behind them, letting the tears come without shame. She strained her neck to keep her head from bowing. She wouldn't turn away her burning eyes. "All right if I put a coat hanger up me and pull him out before he was born? Eh, like they used to do? Eh, Fodda?" Her head shook nervously. The veins of her temples swelled. "You *spit* on the ones who do that, but now that I had my animal, you say he's not good enough for Jesus?" Her eyes squeezed. "You. *You* scare my boy when you come. *You,* the *priest.*" She buried her face in her hands and cried with abandon.

Tom couldn't leave while the old woman wept. He drifted awkwardly back to the threshold of Dominic's room. Dominic was looking blankly through the dust that swirled in its own tiny universe before his eyes. "Dominic?" Tom called in a whisper. The man's eyes whirled in his head. He jerked his head in Tom's direction, startled, but not comprehending. There was an intense odor in the room, of Lysol, which had not succeeded in masking another odor, an intestinal odor.

Tom's eyes lifted. Out the window, in the distance, he could see the spike of the Chrysler Building rising above Manhattan, pointing toward heaven, but he'd rather have lost his eyes in a tree, a shimmering maple or an elm.

Mrs. Caccavale had stopped crying. He walked toward her. The woman's eyes were raw. She grabbed his hand and kissed it.

"I sorry, Podre." Her tears wet his hand.

"I . . . have more communion with me," Tom whispered.

"Huh?" The old woman blinked, looking up at him. "Communion? For Dominigeel, Fodda?" The old woman pulled herself up on Tom's arm. "You *saw* he was smart? He's a fox. He tries to fool you, but he's *smart,* Dominigeel." She laughed through tears.

Tom squeezed out a smile and went back to the sunny bedroom and the tossing head of Dominic. "Dominigeel." Tom called him by the name his mother used. "Are you sorry for your sins, Dominigeel?" The head tossed. The face grimaced in an expression of discomfort. "I absolve you," Tom said as he blessed the man. "In the name of the Father and the Son and the Holy Spirit." Tom was sweating. Not only against Granger's orders, but also against the prescriptions of the Church, he was administering the sacraments of Penance and Holy Eucharist to a totally uncomprehending creature. Had the old woman intimidated him? Or was it simply that he refused to believe that Christ would consider Himself defiled to enter the body of Dominic Caccavale, who was, after all, human.

Giving the man communion to ease the old lady's pain seemed right, though Tom knew many priests would disagree with what he was about to do. Guiltily, he opened the gold communion case and broke in half the communion intended for Madeline Corey. He made the sign of the cross before Dominic's swirling eyes. The man's mouth was turned down, as though he were going to cry. "May the body and blood of our Lord Jesus Christ keep your soul, now and into eternity." Dominic's head jerked away. "Open," Tom encouraged. "Eat, Dominigeel. *Mangia.*" Tom inserted the white half-wafer between the man's upper lip and tongue. Dominic chewed limply with a pained expression. Then he startled Tom with a deep, resonant tone: "Ugggggahh-hhaaaaaa."

The old lady squeezed between Dominic and Tom. "Swalla. Dominigeel?" She shook her son gently. *"Swalla."* She patted his back. "No be scareda da priest." Dominic groaned again, louder, and jerked back so violently it surprised even his mother.

"Whadda y'all excited? *Swalla.*" Her voice grew tougher. His eyes bulged; his face reddened. "Swalla!" she screamed. "Dominigeel . . . "

Without warning a glistening mass of phlegm flew out of Dominic's mouth and landed in a pool on the sheet between his legs. Tom recognized three opaque white particles of the Holy Communion.

"Signora!" Tom turned helplessly to Mrs. Caccavale, who backed away in horror. *"Debbiamo . . . debbiamo mangiare,"* Tom shouted at her. "We must eat it. The host . . ."

The woman shrank farther toward the doorway, as though she didn't hear Tom, as though she were witnessing a punishment from God. Tom knew he had to pick out the white particles. Clearly, this was an indignity to the Sacrament that he had caused, for there in the phlegm of Dominic Caccavale was Christ himself, his divinity, his humanity, his body and his blood. Tom fingered the mess, pulling up one of the white particles, putting it into his own mouth and swallowing it. He picked out the second piece, the third, and did the same.

He felt faint. He wanted out—the hallway, the sun.

"When you come back?" the old woman called after him. "Podre . . . " But he didn't turn; he couldn't answer. He pulled open the hallway door, welcoming the paint odor, the dark, the cool stairwell. He flew downstairs, through old ghosts, down, past Madeline Corey's door, until he saw the sun like a box of light glowing at the end of the hallway. He ran toward it. He stepped into it, squinting, finding himself in a sea of September sunlight, safe in the streets of Brooklyn.

It took effort to bend his legs at the knees. He felt shaky, wooden. He couldn't move fast enough. He kept his eyes down, pretending he was on the sidewalks of his hometown, near the Thames River of Connecticut, where Irish-Americans of a high class spent weekends sailing tiny boats. But his lowered eyes couldn't stop the machines in the noisy wire factory on Meeker Avenue, nor the traffic roaring forty feet overhead on the Brooklyn-Queens Expressway.

"Fahder, eh, Father."

As he rounded the corner, some kids playing stickball called out. They were what he needed. They were his children in the profoundest of ways, and he had promised himself to make the world new for them. He knew he would never be a father in the physical sense, and the loss of that, the isolation of it, made him long to embrace the young, to give them his time, his blood, his life. But their wonderful faces couldn't dissolve the drab, cold feeling that had overcome him in Dominic Caccavale's bedroom, a smothered feeling as though his lungs had frozen, a feeling of physical despair that he had first felt a year ago, in Peru. His emotions scrambled to pull themselves out of the familiar pit. He was forty-one years old, ten years a priest, and he knew that despair was the deepest, most dangerous sin for one who had set his life aside for God.

He opened his cassock at the top and slowed down. The cool wind evaporated his sweat. He gulped at the wind and welcomed the sun on his face.

"Yoo-hoo. Father Sheehan." Kitty Brady, a chubby white-haired woman, ran toward him in high heels, her breasts and hips bouncing, waving a letter. "Kevin's been made a chief petty officer." Her pearls swung as she ran, squealing with joy. Her bright face drew a smile out of him. "I'm so excited I can hardly breathe, Father."

"Great for you, Kitty." Could she know that her face was pulling him out of a terrible mood? He wished the whole world were made up of Kitty Bradys. She kept up with his big strides, chattering alongside him, her buttocks bouncing all the way to the bread store. As she turned into the doorway, she shouted back, shaking a chubby finger at him, "You get some sun, Father. You hear? You're white as milk." He smiled gratefully and threw her a good-bye with his chin.

He wished he could live in the streets, with the people. He felt secure with them; he could navigate around them.

"Eh, Fodder." One of the altar boys licking an ice appeared on a skateboard behind him and threw an arm over his shoulder. "Hey, I'm tall as you."

"Oh, yeah?" Tom practiced his Brooklynese.

"Father Tom!" A little fellow jumped in their path. "I got my altar boy prayers memorized."

"You ready to take the plunge, Raimondo?"

"Yeah."

"Okay. Tuesday after novena we'll test you."

They disappeared behind him like leaves in a wind. A word or two, a slight touch, was enough for them.

It was that way in Peru, too. Unexpected memories of Peru always gave him an ache of loneliness. The sweet dust of rainless Lima, that inorganic earth, suggested a purity that Brooklyn couldn't imitate. In Lima's dryness, life and death were sisters.

Padrecito, Padrecito, the children of Lima would call as they followed. To them he was a Pied Piper, an enchanter, drawing crowds wherever he went, but it wasn't music or magic he dispensed, it was simply food and medicine. He had life to offer them, physical life, the kind of salvation that they could pick from his fingertips like cherries off a tree, and their choruses, when he passed, filled him with an abiding sense of himself that was more validating than the orders he received from the bishop's consecrating hands at his ordination. At certain moments he dared to know the thrill of Christ himself, gathering the people around him, in the name of the Father.

The streets of Brooklyn, though friendly, seemed almost empty in comparison to Lima. There, humanity flowed, overabundantly, in a great whirlpool. Was he sorry about coming back to the States? It had seemed right when he wrote to the North American bishops.

Dear Excellency:

I am a citizen of the United States, formerly a Jesuit of the Canadian Province who was incardinated into the Diocese of Lima, where I have worked all of my priesthood. I have obtained the permission of Right Reverend Monsignor Eduardo DeSilva to offer my services

*to a North American diocese for two years. I speak Spanish fluently
and some Italian. Please contact me if there is a place in your
organization.*

In Christ,

Rev. Thomas Sheehan

He pulled open the inner doors of the vestibule of St. Barnabas'
and entered its vast body. Baptisms were over. The lofty space
was bathed in the florid hues of stained glass. Stale traces of
incense blended with the old varnish of the pews. He tried to
ignore the obscene, muscular architecture of the church, its fat,
fake-marble pillars, its melodramatic arches. He missed the small
elegant Jesuit chapels of his seminary days, of dark wood and blue
stained glass, but the places of worship he loved best were in Peru,
where altars sprang out of meadows, in barrios, on dusty hilltops
before thousands of people.

He walked down the middle aisle, glancing up at the great
dome, which was a blue that no real sky could ever be, chalk blue,
complete with gilded clouds and angels. The Blessed Virgin Mary
was central, caught in a kind of suction that was pulling her up
toward the sun which was bursting beyond, as if she were the
very axis of the mammoth church. Tom advanced under the giant
Byzantine cross, upon which hung Christ, larger than life, looking down. He unlatched the altar gates and stepped up to the great
red Persian rug laid out like a jewel on the white marble floor.
The rug ran up six marble steps, ending at the main altar, from
which there rose spires of real white marble carved with bas-
reliefs of the Twelve Apostles. Three stained-glass windows
dominated the sanctuary, the middle window depicting Christ on
the cross; the other two depicting the crucifixions of Dismus the
good thief and the despairing thief. On the walls beneath the
three windows, in gothic letters, were painted the words: *This day
thou shalt be with me in Paradise.*

As Tom climbed to the main altar, he noticed a form moving
swiftly across the doorway of the sacristy, the small room where
priests vest before mass. The key was in the tabernacle door. Tom
must have left it there. He turned it, opened the door, and

genuflected. He breathed a sigh of relief to see that the vessels were undisturbed. Suddenly, a drawer slammed in the sacristy, so loud that the smack echoed throughout the church.

"Father, would you kindly hold still up there? I am coming to talk to you," the wheezing voice of Monsignor Granger rang from the sacristy. Tom held still before the tabernacle, watching Granger out the corner of his eye, moving briskly about.

Granger loved his own motion. His every gesture was a deliberate expression of his authority. He and his cape filled the spaces of church and rectory whenever possible. Granger kept busy *being* the monsignor, the pastor, in the titular sense, for when it came to real work, he left most of it to Tom. The sixty-four-year-old monsignor walked like a potbellied ballet dancer, as though he were putting on a demonstration of coordination. His cape was part of the dance. It caught up to him when he stopped, and when he turned, it twisted round his body. He would throw his arms up, to force the cape behind him, and the confused fabric would collapse in a heap at his heels as he genuflected.

Granger marched up the altar steps to Tom's side, where he genuflected profoundly to the open tabernacle. He then stood, stretched an arm rudely in front of Tom, and slammed the golden door shut, causing a gunshot to ring in the church. He dangled the key before Tom's eyes. "This," he whispered vehemently, "belongs in the *safe,* not in its lock where any Puerto Rican junkie can find it."

Tom looked at him coldly, genuflected, and turned to leave. "I'll be inside if you want to talk to me."

"Wait a minute." The monsignor grabbed Tom's sleeve. Granger had baby skin laced with capillaries. He was afflicted with a thermal sensitivity that caused his face to flush at the slightest emotion. "Mrs. Caccavale just called to find out when Dominic is to receive his Holy Communion again."

"Oh."

"Have you been giving that man communion?"

"Today was the first time."

"You betrayed that poor woman. You made me look like an ogre for upholding the rubrics."

"Monsignor . . . "

"I forbid you to try this stunt with Dominic Caccavale again. Do you understand that, Father Sheehan?" His voice was a wheeze, like the roar of a faraway stadium. He released Tom's cassock and snapped the key in his fist with hurt glowing in his face. He genuflected into his hidden sea of purple, then spun around. "We have a guest for dinner," he said with a measure of forgiveness in his tone. "He's waiting for us in the dining room." Pulling his cassock up over his shoes, then looking down, Monsignor Granger stepped out over the marble precipice, then floated down the marble stairs smoothly as a swan, his cape, like water, trickling behind him.

Granger was right about the key. It bothered Tom that he was absentminded enough to have left it there. He took out Madeline Corey's half wafer, which he had intended to return to the ciborium. He consumed it, begging forgiveness from Christ for putting the sacrament into his mouth so tight with anger. He walked down the marble stairs, genuflected, and went into the sacristy.

Tom followed the helpless cape into the wailing tunnel, a construction of corrugated steel, like a covered bridge, that connected the church to the second floor of the rectory. Granger had designed it, with thick purple and yellow glass tiles inlaid into its floor to give the industrial-looking structure a liturgical feeling. The effect, in the daytime, was of walking on squares of light. They called it the wailing tunnel because during storms the noise of the wind scrapping the scalloped edges of steel was ear-piercing. But even in fair weather, the mere pressure of walking caused the corrugated sheets to rattle so loudly that the trip was like a walk through a platoon of drummers. Tom followed in Granger's thundering footsteps, half hypnotized as the cape flickered over the alternating purple and yellow squares. It unfurled behind the futile efforts of Granger's hands to catch it, but when he opened the door to the rectory, it returned to its master's body like a magnet, hugging him, disappearing with him into the dark of the rectory, behind the great steel door.

The rectory was extremely dark, so that as Tom entered on

the second floor, his eyes had to adjust. The only windows in the building were on the third floor, where the priests had their living quarters. The second floor was windowless: a windowless dining room, a windowless kitchen, and a money-counting room. The first floor, also windowless, was full of parish offices and meeting rooms. The only apertures on the first and second floors were bathroom exhausts. Granger had had the rectory built to be burglarproof in 1956 when the old rectory was destroyed to make room for the Brooklyn-Queens Expressway. The new rectory had to be squeezed closer to the church. So it was built narrower and higher, like a silo, which he connected to the church by the wailing tunnel. The rectory's exterior was gray brick, an unsuccessful attempt to match the church's massive blocks of granite.

All the rectory walls were entirely covered in dark-green vinyl, imitation Florentine leather. Vinyl, Granger reasoned, could be washed, saving money on painting. And washed they were, once a month; and the floors and furniture were vacuumed twice a day. A vacuum cleaner always seemed to be humming somewhere in the building. The floors were forest-green wall-to-wall carpeting throughout. Ceilings were a lighter shade of green and were shadow-boxed to give off indirect fluorescent illumination. It was impossible to see the stairs. All the lamps throughout the rectory were Chinese, with silk lampshades and low-wattage bulbs.

Crucifixes were everywhere, the Bauhaus type, like those in Cistercian monasteries; the drapes were of polished cotton, maroon and gray stripes, matching most of the chairs in the rectory. Central air conditioning had been installed throughout, and the system was kept running nonstop from April to October. Sounds of frigid air blowing out of ceiling gratings were constant. To conserve the precious cold, windows were not to be opened, as if Granger wanted it cold enough to wear his cape at all times. It was a house rule that cassocks were to be worn always. Granger never wanted to see one of his priests out of clerical garb.

Tom let the great steel door click behind him. He could see into the dining room, where a strange monsignor, Granger's guest, stood smoking a cigarette. The man caught Tom's entrance with a quick eye. He was taller than Granger and obviously well built beneath the black tent of his cassock, big-shouldered, paunchless, his dazzling white crew-cut contrasting sharply with his ruddy but unwrinkled skin. The man had the blackest eyebrows Tom had ever seen. They arched sharply over light-brown, almost amber-colored eyes, giving his face a kind of charcoal-drawn quality, like a cartoon character from *Terry and the Pirates* —square jaw, deeply dimpled chin, and those huge, chameleon eyebrows of Mephistopheles. The blue glow of a black, closely shaven beard was visible in his skin. Tom took him for an Irishman, until Granger introduced them.

"Tom Sheehan, our resident Jesuit. Monsignor Ronald Kruug."

"Nice to meet you, Monsignor Kruug." Tom smiled. Black hairs covered each finger of the hand that reached for Tom's. When Kruug lifted his cigarette to his mouth, a silky black wave of hair showed, running down the side of his hand like a horse's mane. His smile was benign, glowing and kind, exorcising the gloom of the rectory.

"Well, it's very nice to meet *you*, Father." He winked jovially at Tom. "Arthur and I are classmates."

"You don't have to apologize for it," Granger said dryly as he walked into the dining room.

"When Monsignor Granger told me he had a real live Jesuit living here, I almost doubted him. How did Arthur earn such a prestigious curate, I asked myself?"

"Monsignor, sorry to interupt. If you'll excuse me, I've got to wash my hands," Tom said, trying to soften his abruptness.

"Certainly," Kruug replied, a bit slighted, turning away as Tom rushed to the stairs.

Tom habitually pushed a foot deeply into each step because the rug was stretched and it slipped underfoot.

In the bathroom, he washed and filled a glass with water and threw two aspirins into his mouth. He came out, swallowing, dialing the phone.

"Hullo." The tiny voice answered on the first ring.

"This is Father Sheehan, Madeline."

"You were sposta come, Father."

"I got sidetracked, Madeline. Will you forgive me?"

"The kids said you came in the building."

"Yes, I did, but I got involved. I'll come later, around seven. May I?"

"I jus' gave myself the needle. Make it a little later?"

"I have confessions later, Madeline."

"Is it Saturday today?"

"No. It's Sunday, but we have a Labor Day Breakfast tomorrow for the Policemen's Benevolent Association."

"Tomorrow's Labor Day already?"

"Yes."

"God help me."

"Suppose I come tomorrow, say after lunch? Then we can have our little talk. Will that do?"

"Whatever you say, Father," the woman said sleepily.

"Thank you, Madeline. Good-bye."

Deirdre rang the dinner buzzer. Tom didn't eat meat, so the prospect of Sunday roast beef didn't appeal to him. He pulled out a bottle of Scotch. He twisted off the cork and lifted the bottle to his lips, letting the liquid fill his mouth, flushing his teeth. His eyes caught themselves in the window, eyes as gray as the northern light that illuminated them. He liked his face, thank God. He wondered what kept it serene. He focused through his reflection to the underbelly of the expressway, which stood like a pregnant dinosaur over the rectory. The narrow Metropolitan Avenue exit was causing a truck to scream, braking to avoid the barrier. Twice Tom had been awakened by police in the middle of the night to give the last rites to a driver who hadn't cleared the barrier.

He had intended to spit out the Scotch, but when the buzzer signaling dinner sounded the second time, he swallowed it.

"Bless us, oh Lord, and these Thy gifts," Granger whispered, "which we have received from Thy bounty, through Christ our Lord. Amen."

Tom sat down at the wide side of the table, between the two monsignors, who were stretching right hands over the platter of carved roast beef, blessing it in the sign of the cross. Granger offered the platter to Kruug, who had to stand to receive it. Granger's face wore the deliberate expression of polite annoyance, his eyelids half closed, eyebrows raised.

"Kevin Brady was made chief petty officer." Tom made an effort to sound cheerful.

"Very nice," Granger responded. "I must call his mother . . . what's her name?"

"Kitty."

"Yes. Catherine McLoughlin Brady." Granger expressed his all-knowingness at every opportunity. Tom watched as Kruug lifted a rare slice of meat over his shiny white porcelain dish. The slice slipped, smacking the dish and splashing a drop of blood onto Kruug's cassock. He busied himself cleaning it with his napkin. Tom rescued the heavy platter, passing it to Granger, who spoke out once again. "You know, don't you, that Dominic Caccavale is a vegetable, incapable of an act of love."

"That would mean Dominic was also incapable of sin," Tom said with a smile.

"So is a fish," Granger retorted.

"Arthur, correct me if I'm wrong," Kruug interrupted innocently, "but in church earlier I saw no altar facing the people. Are you still pretending Vatican II never occurred?" Kruug had a naturally coarse voice, but he could dignify it for Granger.

"You know, Kruug," Granger, chewing, said with mock politeness, "I often have this dream that it is twenty years ago, 1959, inside St. Peter's Basilica, and the bleachers on both sides collapse under two thousand visiting bishops, all clad in white, feet over miters as the roof caves in on the whole Catholic Church . . . " Kruug laughed, but Granger wasn't finished. " . . . and those twisted Bernini columns break in half as I shout: 'Good God, has King Kong unleashed nuclear havoc on this congregation?' And a bored-to-death God drawls out from the clouds, 'It's only John the Twenty-third having himself a party.' Then I see the old wop from his balcony opening his window.

He's yelling, 'Let in the fresh air.' And what flew in, Ronnie? Eh?" Kruug shrugged in ignorance. "A huge black vulture with a ribbon in its beak that reads in the vernacular: 'For the Pope who threw out the baby with the bathwater.' "

Kruug laughed with generous candor. "Enough, Arthur."

"That baby is hostage somewhere, Kruug."

"All right."

"You feel the loss of him more than I, and don't pretend you don't."

Kruug closed his eyes to Granger and turned to Tom.

"How has the council affected your priesthood in Peru, Father?"

"I'm afraid I got left behind in the changes. Though it doesn't matter much in Peru. The poor people there decided for themselves long ago what a priest is. It would take more than a council to change their minds."

"Oh?" The monsignor leaned toward Tom. "Then tell me, what have the people of Peru decided that we are?"

"We are what we do, Monsignor." Tom smiled to show no disrespect.

"What *do* we do, Father, for example?"

"In Peru, Monsignor, the people don't read scriptures, just like most people here. Their idea of a priest materializes when we give them something to eat. So we share our nourishment, food, medicine, drink, shelter. We respect their myths. We try to take their fear of life away so that they have something to celebrate, something to thank God for. Or else, Monsignor, why do they need to come to church?"

"Yes." Kruug's eyes softened. He leaned back, visibly impressed. Kruug dipped his napkin into his water. He rubbed the spot on his cassock.

"What is it I smell?" Granger asked loudly, sniffing the air. "Is it Scotch? I smell Scotch." Tom's face pinkened.

"Does blood stain?" Kruug hurled the question into the air.

"Blood doesn't show on black," Granger said quickly.

"Father"—Kruug turned back to Tom—"Arthur tells me you're from the Canadian Province?"

"Upper Canadian."

"Yet you requested duty in diocesan parishes down here."

"I'm not a teacher," Tom said simply. "I'm used to cities. Social work with the underprivileged is all I know, really." Granger smothered a burp.

"But how'd you wind up studying in Canada, someone from Connecticut?" Kruug asked.

"How'd you know I was from Connecticut?" Tom asked.

Kruug abruptly stopped chewing. Granger's eyes shot up from his dish.

"Arthur, did you mention it to me?" Kruug asked, blinking.

"Why would I have?" Granger's eyes juggled both men, then shot back down as he cut his meat with annoyance, taking a sip of water and glancing paranoidly over his glass.

Again Kruug turned to Tom. "So I take it, Father, you had enough of the missions and Peru. Why, may I wonder?"

"Changes. It's hard to explain."

"I'll bet," Granger mumbled as he swallowed.

"I'm sorry, Monsignor." Tom turned to him. "I don't understand your comment."

"I'll *bet*, I'll *bet*, Father, that's what I said. I'll bet it's hard to explain the *changes* in Peru." Granger was shaking a little, smiling, half embarrassed.

"I was beginning to miss the United States. . . . " Tom was grabbing for words. "My friends had left Peru."

"Lay friends?" Kruug asked.

"No," Tom answered, a little annoyed by the interrogation. "One friend really, a priest that left. . . . "

"Left the *priesthood?*" Granger asked, chewing.

"Yes." Tom's stomach hurt.

"A Jesuit?" Kruug asked.

"No. He was not a Jesuit." Tom stared into the centerpiece of flowers. Instantaneously, white flashes of light burst, internally, and behind the light, little scenes appeared in his mind. He saw a funeral on the beach near the Pacific in Peru. A young dead priest was being buried in his cassock. The face was Tom's. The cassock was Tom's. His hair was longer, the way Tom kept it then. The young priest was Tom. That's why he was no longer in Peru. How could he explain to Kruug and Granger that he had gotten older down there, that he had found himself totally alone, and no longer who he was? He had become a new man overnight, a stranger, a loner.

"Kruug, I need you to hear my confession later." Granger shocked the two clerics with his out-of-the-blue request.

Kruug smiled, as if Granger had made a joke, but when Granger blushed, Kruug quickly took his smile back. "Sure, Artie, I'll hear your confession."

"Penance is a wonderful sacrament. I see no shame in respecting it. I haven't been to confession in three weeks." Granger's baby skin went from red to reddish blue.

Tom tried to alleviate Granger's discomfort. "I haven't been to confession in six *months,*" Tom said with a smile.

But Granger refused the help. He dropped his fork on his dish in pretended shock. "You mean you were able to keep your hands off yourself for six months?" Granger asked melodramatically.

Kruug's face went slightly pale. Tom reached for his water, knocking the glass over. Granger continued chewing with his eyes on the spill. "Well, *answer,*" Granger said through his meat.

"Granger, stop this," Kruug commanded gently.

"No. Let him *answer* me," Granger insisted.

Tom held on to a smile, to keep the possible joke in force, as he shoved his napkin under the tablecloth, under the water spot. But he couldn't keep the smile; it slipped off his face. "I'm not getting this. What do you want me to tell you?"

"Have you remained in the state of grace since your last confession?" Granger said, popping a piece of buttered bread into his mouth.

"I'm pretty sure I've been in the state of grace since I went into the seminary." Tom felt his own face warming now.

Granger blinked theatrically. "An *uninterrupted* state of grace?" Granger asked, looking straight at Tom. "That's over twenty years now, Father. Twenty years of no internal consent to lascivious thoughts? No little touches?"

"No consent. No little touches," Tom responded, hating himself for letting Granger bait him into a sin of pride. Kruug's awed eyes heated the side of Tom's face.

Granger stuck a rare piece of meat into his mouth with ironic satisfaction and chewed slowly, curling his lip. His eyes tried to seem amused, but they were unsuccessful. Jealousy crept into them. "Well then," Granger went on, speaking and chewing, "if you've managed to keep your priestly vows, you should get down on your knees and thank Him. Thank Him, yes." He chewed on in spite of his hurt. "Thank Him for the grace He has clearly denied to other priests, who sadly . . . fall." He was low on air, wheezing again, chewing and trying to breathe at the same time. His face grew so fully red it seemed about to burst. But he wouldn't quit. "I would not be so cocksure of that grace if I were you. Celibacy was not meant to be an athletic feat . . . a vow of stubbornness. It's not a marathon." Granger suddenly sucked in air.

Kruug jumped out of his chair. "Spit out the meat, for heaven's sake, Artie."

"Huh?" Granger looked up at his friend in surprise. He force-swallowed the huge piece of meat. "Sit down, for God's sake, Kruug. What the hell are you worried about?"

Tom stood, pushing his chair behind him, and started for the door. "Excuse me. I have something to take care of." He entered the dark stairwell and ran up, pushing deep into the loose rug.

"Pride precedes the fall," Granger sang out from his chair. "Remember that, Jesuit."

"Then God help us and God forgive us both," Tom called back.

"Speak for yourself," Granger continued in his singsong.

Tom stopped dead on the stairs. In a staggering impulse to bring his rage back down, he turned and began to retrace his steps, hardly knowing why. He slowly floated down the staircase and entered the dining room like a ghost.

"What . . . " Both monsignors were taken aback when he reappeared. Granger pushed back his chair in alarm.

"Shouldn't we be ashamed?" Tom looked down at them.

"Oh, come now." Granger smiled. "We've been teasing you."

"Three grown men sitting here, in our black skirts," Tom said almost calmly, "talking about masturbation. Three priests, while there's a world full of pissed-off, betrayed people on the other side of these walls, stacked in tenements, one on top of the other like living corpses. The sacraments don't soften their lives. When was the last time you climbed those stairs, Granger?"

"Oh, my dear Father Sheehan, save your sermon for your government. Mail it to our President or to those business people across the river in those shiny skyscrapers, but spare me this humorless evangelism. I did my share of climbing stairs."

Kruug stood. "Gentlemen, why don't we either sit down to have our dessert, civilly, or part company?"

Tom paused, then turned and flew up the stairs to his quarters, slamming the door behind him. *Damn, you are a fool, Tom Sheehan!* He paced. Granger was the devil tempting him. It was so bizarre: another priest, tempting him. Granger embodied all that Tom feared becoming. And yet, he felt no immunity from Granger's disease. Already Granger's bitterness was not unlike his own.

It had grown humid that evening and it was uncomfortable during confessions. Granger and Kruug had finished by eight, but Tom was still there at nine. His last penitent was a young woman with a speech impediment.

"Mey boifren dreisa giss mee widis tong."

"He tries to kiss you?" Tom whispered.

"Yeah. Widis tong. Mey boifren."

"I see. Is there anything else?"

"No, Faahdah." She paused. "Deyah onnerstannn mee?"

"Yes. Certainly."

"Thaan, whadai ssseai?"

"You said your boyfriend tries to kiss you with his tongue; and I think you worry too much about it."

"Huh ughhuh, huhah," she laughed. "Uhreelee?"

"Yes."

"Meee . . . ouy loykue ou, Faahdah."

"You what?"

"Loyk ya. Ouy . . ."

"You like me?"

"Yaah. De de . . . awdah breests, dey, dey, navah dawk ta mee beefawr."

"Well, that's wrong of them. God made them priests for you. Didn't He?"

"Oym loyk a . . . aireebawdee yellts, deep douun. Uhreelee."

"I didn't get that."

"Oym loyke airreebawdee yelts, deep douuwn."

"Deep down, you're like everybody else?"

"Yaah."

"I'm sure any person could tell, if they gave you half a chance."

"Bahht dey downnn't."

He was silent, not knowing what to say.

She caught herself from crying, sniffled and cleared her throat. "Ohm sauree."

"You know, you don't have to have sins to come to confession. You can come anytime to talk if you like, and if I'm not here, then ring the bell at any other rectory, and find another priest you'd like to talk to. Will you promise me that?"

"Aoy prahmis."

"Good."

"Faahdah?"

"Yes?"

"Daaang kue."

"You're welcome."

He gave her her penance and absolution, then waited to hear her footsteps leaving the church. When the doors of the vestibule banged behind her, Tom stood up. He took off his purple stole, folded it, and stuck it into his deep cassock pocket. Then he opened his confessional door and stepped into the quiet and empty church. Walking up the middle aisle, he focused on the three sanctuary windows which glowed in the aftermath of the sunset. The church was, in all that light, anything but boring. All its garish muscles were curtained in darkness, leaving the windows floating in a void. Christ was crucified on a gnarled tree that rose out of a miniature countryside into a purple sky smeared with red, darker than blood. The crucified body was sharply outlined in black, hanging limp from pinned hands, spiked through the palms. His knees were bent and weak, His hair dark and wet. His wounds glowed like rubies.

Tom made fists. It was commonly said that Christ was nailed through the wrists because His weight would have pulled His hands through the nails. But there were those who held that Christ *was* crucified through the palms, while His feet were nailed down-sloping, allowing Him to stretch up, alternating the pressure. This was, in fact, the ingenious torture of the cross, that the pull of the victim's outstretched arms would inhibit his lungs; he couldn't exhale unless he stood up straight. But then the pressure of the nails in his feet would become too much. The torturous rising and falling eventually ceased with asphyxiation and death. Tom could never look up at that center window without pulling in a breath.

The church felt cool in comparison to the confession box. (Only Granger's confessional was air-conditioned.) Tom's cassock was drenched. Sweat rolled down inside the plastic collar. He longed for air. He decided to climb the fire escape of the school, to watch the sunset and smoke a cigarette. He felt for his matches as he pressed against the large south door of the church.

He crossed the hot schoolyard in a warm breeze and began his way up the clanging fire escape, five stories to the roof of the school. He had gone up there once before, the week he arrived from Peru. It had been near midnight on Christmas Eve, and in the snow he had surveyed his appointment for the first time, vested for midnight mass—alb, stole and biretta.

He saw a vision up there that night, not a real vision of course, but one he encouraged. He saw his past stretching in a long recognizable trail behind him, and he was standing at its precipice teetering over all Brooklyn and Manhattan, under the roar of low jets trying to land at La Guardia through the snow.

Now the heat was almost unbearable. He wasn't expecting visions this time. He just wanted to cool off, high above the hot asphalt, and when he reached the top, the roof dropped out from under him into darkness. It was like stepping up into the sky. The horizon in the west was solid gold, except where the sun had left a smear of rust and rose. Stars dotted the eastern horizon. Another sunny day tomorrow. The end of summer. Labor Day.

He lit his cigarette, sucking in the sharp nicotine. The rush kicked open his lungs. His neck and shoulders began to relax. His temples throbbed. He blew out the smoke in a giant mushroom over Manhattan. He pulled out the hard white plastic collar, sending his hand inside his cassock to brush the wetness from his chest. The cool air rushing in gave him goosebumps.

He loved the cigarette. He could never give it up. Nicotine and Scotch were his rewards. He peered around his drifting mushroom of cigarette smoke, at Manhattan sparkling in the distance. Its shimmering orange and silver lights outnumbered the stars. The Twin Towers glittering to the left, Empire State to the right: earmarks of the new Rome, luminous in the oncoming blackness. A dazzling new world was giving birth to nightlife, to concerts, nightclubs, limousines, women in high heels.

He took another drag, squinting at the moving lights of the silent planes. He didn't know the world. The people in those planes, for instance—they were pursuing ideas totally different from his, individuals, each a nation of one, people with selfish goals he never dreamed of, people who could never understand his choices, what he was doing, what the Catholic Church was doing, or who that bearded man was, nailed to a tree, the almost nude thirty-three-year-old man, pushing up on His impaled feet. What do those women in high heels know of suffering? What do the people behind those shining skyscraper windows know of the heart of a priest?

He took another deep drag on his cigarette, savoring it after two hours of abstinence. His body felt more comfortable now, exhausted but relaxed. He felt a chill, recalling Granger's words describing his chastity: *marathon, athletic, a vow of stubbornness*. And then, a feeling as if something were moving deep inside him, like a beast too large to pass through the narrow channel of his throat. He turned to the fire escape.

He felt sorry for the beast and himself as he made his way down, slowly, toward the schoolyard, then slowly across its warm concrete to the rectory. As he climbed the dark rectory stairs, he admitted that he hated the terrible security of Granger's castle. He was climbing deeper and deeper, up, toward his room, up, into Granger's windowless air-conditioned tower, toward a soft-pink, twenty-five-watt light bulb glowing through a silk lampshade—higher and higher, into the artificial cold, like an upside-down snail, retreating toward its own dead end, like Jonah, being swallowed by the whale.

Chapter Two

B Y ELEVEN-THIRTY THAT NIGHT, the Brooklyn-Queens Expressway had grown quiet except for the hydraulic screams of the big trucks outside his window trying to stop for the Metropolitan Avenue exit. He hadn't prayed his breviary in a long time. He stood in the dark with his back to the wall. The room was no longer unfamiliar. Brooklyn was no longer new. He was now part of it, fixed to it. Peru had slipped out of his hands, like an eel, leaving his fingers pinched, fingernail to fingernail, with nothing more grasped than the slime of its tail.

He peeled down his bedcovers in the dark. Then he stripped, letting his clothes drop to the rug. He threw his shorts toward the laundry bag, then sat on the hard mattress. He pointed his feet under the icy sheets, trying to enjoy the cold on his legs and back. He pulled the turquoise summer blanket up to his chin.

The bed was too high and too short. He had made a habit of placing the soles of his feet flat against the footboard, then slipping his heels off the mattress. This meant that his head pressed against the headboard, causing his knees to rise. He kept his hands folded on his chest, though it made him feel as though he were laid out. But after all the months of experimentation, he found it the only position that allowed him to fall asleep.

He contemplated the closed, motionless drapes. He listened for the whir of the electric clock and the cold air blowing through the vent. The room was otherwise silent, except for the noises pressing on the window from the outside world. Sometimes he put himself to sleep trying to decipher those outside sounds. His ears stretched for meanings beyond the traffic, over the river. Sometimes he imagined that Manhattan was moaning, like a chained giant on its back. Sometimes the noises came from the Brooklyn streets. The clang of a garbage-pail cover would start him wondering whether the rats or garbage mongers had knocked it off. Sometimes Tom imagined he could hear smoke-stacks, like vertical cannons shooting toward heaven. He imagined the toxic whiteness ascending into the moonlight, as though its purpose were to fill up the vastness of space. He tried to think of its beauty, to turn it into something else. A storybook blizzard, on its way to the moon.

Why did snow keep popping into his thoughts? Snow so pure, so holy. He opened his legs, letting his heels find the cool fresh corners of the sheets. In Peru he had elevated cold to the realms of the exquisite—a glorious nostalgic northern rarity. But Granger's air conditioning was not that kind of northern cold. Granger's cold lacked light. It lacked purity. It was forced through an oily machine, filtered through fiberglass. The air conditioning turned the absurd, vinyl-lined palace into a re-frigerated mausoleum that sealed out life and noise. But the expressway noises vibrated against his window anyway. He thanked God for that.

When he squeezed his eyes shut, to sleep, the radiance of the sheets penetrated his lids, so that even in the dark, glowing in his mind, there was snow again, so very deep and so fine, the kind that lifts with wind, gently burning the nostrils, actually reaching the lungs, touching ozone and oxygen to the bloodstream. Snow in the blood, snow in the brain, in the mind, where it could be felt as well as imagined, whiteness in the mind, stretching for distances, soft as cream.

Was the northern place his mind was drifting toward in the past year, the place where his friend from Peru, Philip Behan, might have gone? Pure as the childhood place where Santa lived? Too cold for children to follow, except the few who die, who become angels. He drifted to the sound of sleigh bells and laughter, pulling him northward. But then he dreamed that he woke to find his room covered in black wool—walls, ceiling, floors, furniture; only his face sticking out of the blankets was not black. Another person was in the room. He couldn't see the person, but he could hear the breathing. His eyes flew out of his head like birds searching every corner, flying between the ceiling and his body from wall to wall, but they couldn't uncover the creature who was in the room with him. He wanted a door out, but he knew even if his birds found one, his body couldn't move toward it. He was paralyzed.

That was usual. He had had this dream before. He even knew who it was hiding somewhere behind the black wool, waiting to emerge from behind its folds. He would have to lie there and wait for it all to happen. He knew who it was.

His ears tried to cling to the real noises of the trucks on the expressway, life going on outside his dream, but he couldn't scale the dream's walls. His volition was functional. He was aware. But he had no power to move his body, so much as to blink an eye. He was powerless to save himself from this dream, in which nature was going to exact her payment for being abused and ignored by him. This dream was the price he had to pay for his chastity, the punishment for his celibacy. These were the most anguished moments of his priesthood and the worst temptations of his life.

Snickers from the darkness confirmed the presence he feared. His teeth started grinding. He pressed his head against the headboard until his collarbone touched it and his knees locked, making his legs so rigid that his thigh muscles swelled and stood up thick as loaves of bread, hard as marble. And though, as usual, he would try to call out for help, very little sound would escape from behind his clenched teeth. His screams were internal. They were never allowed to enter the air outside his body.

Nnnnngggggg. Ngggggggg . . . His intention was to call to Kruug in the room next to his, or even to Granger, anybody who might hear, as the snickering figure moved closer to him, coming into his light. Ruthie Rassmussen, licking a vanilla ice cream cone, the most beautiful cheerleader Waterford ever had. It was always she who came to him in these dreams. She had learned just what to do. She would throw back her long blond hair with confidence; she would smile, knowing how it gave a porcelain shine to her perfect chin. She knew her wet, red lips would stretch to even greater perfection when she smiled. Her teeth were white as a toothpaste ad. She would hold off contacting his eyes, knowing he could dismiss her with a glance. She had been tricked before by the power of his gray-blue eyes, their authority. So she concentrated on his feet instead, as she simply took the black blanket from under his chin, with its black sheets, and peeled them down, revealing the hair on his chest, down past the shock of black genital hair, his penis, over the trembling immensely swollen thighs, the bumps of his knees; down the sharp shinbones, past the ankles, over the feet, revealing the whiteness of a priest to the room, letting the black bedcovers fall to the floor.

Tom begged God to help him, for Jesus to intervene. But nothing stopped her from lifting herself onto the bed and sitting on the sharp shinbone of his leg, below his knee, as if she were riding a pony. He could feel she was not wearing panties. She tongued her melting ice cream nonchalantly. It steamed and melted so fast that drops trickled down her arm, falling off at her elbow onto him. He could feel the wetness of her vagina pressing on his shinbone. She rocked gently, masturbating herself, making noises on the fast-melting ball of ice cream. She wouldn't look into his eyes, staring at his penis instead. He begged St. Ignatius and St. Francis of Assisi to protect the chastity he had vowed to keep for Christ, for there was no doubt who it really was in Ruthie Rassmussen's form tempting him to break his vow. He recalled the admonitions of Thomas à Kempis that he had read in the seminary daily: that the devil would concentrate his best powers on the purest of heart and ignore those who had already fallen.

So he worked hard, especially in those dreams that accompanied all his nocturnal emissions, not to cooperate with the unavoidable pleasure. But this time Ruthie had worked her way farther up his leg than ever before. She was using his kneecap to masturbate, moaning, and clucking away on the melting ice cream. In panic his mind raced up to the ceiling in search of his birds, to help him look down at his white, helpless body. He saw that his penis was still soft, wrinkled, lying white and tiny in its black nest. But then she slid up higher until his kneecap was lodged between her buttocks and her vagina was touching the swollen muscle of his thigh. Suddenly she jammed herself onto the muscle, taking it inside her, fitting tightly onto it like a glove, as though the muscle had broken through his skin and was lifting, springing out of its tissue sac wet and red, like the muscles in those anatomy charts, larger by far than any penis, yet shaped like one. She descended full upon it. *"Ahhh."* She tricked him, riding the muscle torturously, but it *felt* to him as if it were his penis, and he was on the verge of exploding—when she stopped, holding perfectly still, suspended above him, waiting for him to make the next move. He hung there breathless, wanting to reach back and grab the headboard with his hands, but he couldn't. Finally, Ruthie dared address his eyes, moving her body ever so slightly, careful not to push him over the edge. She reached down and scraped his nipples with her red fingernails. "Now grab your cock and jerk it off," she whispered. "Get it over with." Her voice echoed as if electronically amplified. It resounded through large speakers. She pleaded into the ice-cream-cone microphone, blabbering words into the melting cream, licking loudly, while he tried to outshout her with Ave Marias and Pater Nosters in Latin. He knew his body was going to have to let go of weeks of backed-up semen and prostatic fluid, while trying to avoid the inevitable orgasm that accompanied it. But there must be no doubt afterward that he hadn't cooperated with the sensuality, that he hadn't committed the mortal sin of cooperation.

Ruthie's patience, as he hovered on the brink of ejaculation, seemed eternal. Drops of her ice cream drummed on his stomach, mingling with his sweat, trickling into his genital hair. The powers he was holding back in his groin wanted out, but he refused to assist the ejaculation. His ears reached for traffic sounds outside the walls of the dream. He caught them, but the sounds of trucks on the expressway had no power to pull him out. "Finish yourself off," she bubbled into her ice cream.

"*You* do it. Please, Ruthie," he pleaded. "Please . . ."

"Unh-uh," Ruthie said as she moved ever so slightly up and down the muscle, traveling only an inch at a time. Up an inch. Another inch. Down all the way. Up again.

He grabbed his penis. His knuckles scraped her pubic hair. His hand rubbed up, down, up, down, as she groaned, leaning forward and pressing her clitoris against his rapidly moving knuckles. The expressway noise was turning into a screech, a long loud skid. "Fuck me," she shouted over the noise. "Fuck," she commanded.

"Noooo." His throat opened. His voice was coming out now. "Nooo . . ." He arched his back, thrusting his penis full up into her.

She smiled, coming down hard on it, fucking fast; then, at the moment he was about to come, she slipped off him quickly, hovering over him, waiting. "Get back on, get on," he screamed.

"No. Jerk yourself off. Jerk yourself off." Then, jerking himself once, twice, he came in a burst, shooting his come up under the umbrella of her hands. The screeching truck stopped. Silence. Then an enormous explosion, so loud that it blew down the walls of his dream. The curtains flew up, and glass blew in upon him, all over the bed. Color returned to the room. Ruthie disintegrated, then disappeared. He was awake, blinking at a red glow of fire outside the broken window. He smelled gasoline—a gasoline truck had hit the Metropolitan Avenue divider. He lifted his hand to his head, his hand sprayed with glass and semen.

"*Help.*" He was hearing the tiny muffled cries coming from inside the truck. Or were they *his* cries, echoing from afar, from out of his departing dream?

"No," he whispered. Those were definitely the screams of a trapped man. Tom had been lying there several minutes listening, thinking how the screams of children are ordinary and the screams of women pitiful, but how the screams of a man cannot be compared to anything else in the world. A shrill alarm went off miles away. He heard the emergency horns of the chemical plant. Fire engines, police sirens.

Why wasn't he jumping up? Why was he lying there with his sticky hand pressed on his forehead, blinking up at shadows of fire on his ceiling? Was it because the cries for help had stopped? Was it because he thought he was still dreaming? Or was he lying there stubbornly, in some curious act of rebellion?

The rectory buzzer rang loudly in his room, because he was the priest on duty. The buzz surprised him. Still, he did not sit up. Some driver was probably burning high above the streets, while his unknowing loved ones were sleeping somewhere, maybe in the Midwest or down South, blond-haired sons and daughters. Or maybe he was a young driver, leaving behind a girlfriend. Maybe he was a loner, like Philip Behan in Peru, obsessed with motion, velocity, who drove because he was in a contest with Time, an insomniac, a man in flight. Maybe he had hit the divider in some voluntary way, to stop it all; or perhaps God had willed the tragedy in order to wake Tom up. But that would be an awful God. No. The trucker had nothing to do with him. Why must every tragedy have something to do with him? When would it be that human pain had nothing to do with him?

The buzzer rang for the second time. This time Tom threw aside his covers and stood up, a little dizzy, cold in his nudity. His nose was blocked. He groped for the light switch with his left hand and for a towel with his right.

The gasoline truck was charred by the time Tom and the two policemen got there. The cab was covered in carbon and foam, impaled upon the divider. The rest of the truck was scattered all over the roadway. Flares held up traffic on both sides. The door of the cab had been pried open. Anxious firemen and police separated, making a pathway, as Tom approached. The body was sitting up straight, the head back, the entire form charred. There was no way of telling the man's age. No features, no silhouette. A wedding band showed on his left hand. As Tom rose up on the step, his disgust bottomed, his trembling deteriorating into a strange calm. The smell of holy oils came up as he pressed his thumb into the silver container. Suddenly, he recalled the prescription in Canon Law that priests are not to use holy oils on burn victims. Tom gently went ahead and made the sign of the cross on the man's forehead anyway, speaking the short form of absolution and Extreme Unction in Latin. *Ego te absolvo ab omnibus peccatis et censuris.* Now what? He felt useless.

It was not enough what he had done. As he walked away from the truck, Tom felt embarrassed by the cruelty of God, ashamed of his own cruelty and inhumanity for being afraid to share the man's ugly misfortune. He felt the aloneness of the charred dead man, the aloneness of every man and woman on the earth. He felt himself a coward, a failure, for in spite of all his ideals and his zeal, he hadn't been able to alter the cruelty of the situation in the slightest.

"A terrible thing. Terrible," the policeman muttered for the fifth time as he let Tom out of the patrol car in front of the rectory.

When Tom reentered his room, the frightening thought occurred to him that for the first time in his priesthood he might no longer be in the state of grace. He not only cooperated with the dream, but why also hadn't he gone immediately to help the man in the burning truck?

He tore off his cassock and flung it behind him. Then he ripped off the contoured bedsheet, sending broken glass back toward the window. He fell upon the hard blue-satin mattress with one leg hanging off, the toe of his black shoe touching the floor. He grabbed his pillow and beat it over the floor once, twice, to shake off any remaining glass, then buried his face in it. He coughed, to clear his throat, but then several more coughs blew up from his lungs into the pillow and in a moment he realized he was crying. There was a strange self-forgiveness in it, an odd pity mingled in—a surrender, but to what?

He was himself and he was not himself. The answer, the world had changed. In recent years it seemed that, although his cells continued to reproduce themselves as always, they were not reassembling in their former patterns. The young eager priest had been replaced by a new, darkly older man.

From the very first minute that he had decided he would be a priest, lying in his adolescent bed on the second floor of old Mrs. Sharskey's two-family house in Waterford, Connecticut, his intention had never faltered. He had been watching the shadows of Mrs. Sharskey's elm brushing the window screen that night. It had been like falling in love. His calling to give his life to God had come in the form of a burning need, a painful wish to love with every iota of his being, as Christ had loved the world, enough to die for it, to embrace it, such love that could laugh at death—God's love, God's laughter. He had wanted to know the cavalier power of that laughter, the confidence of it, its surety. He desired its conquering audacity. That kind of laughter and that kind of love would be his life. Who wouldn't envy such a life? What more could a grown man be? He understood that sexual abstinence would be absolutely necessary. He had no idea how he would manage it but he would. He'd see it through day by day, with God's grace. He felt it was an easy trade-off in the face of such passion, such unbridled emotion and boundless courage as would be a priest's. He let his heart rise up in that darkness, with the words of the Prayer of St. Francis of Assisi, which he had memorized: *Lord, make me an instrument of Thy peace. Where there is hatred, let me sow love. Where there is doubt, faith. Where there is despair, hope. Where there is darkness, light.* Yes. One man can save the world. It had been done before. Christ had. Others might.

As the elm brushed his upstairs window screen he would whisper the entire Prayer of St. Francis over and over, letting his spirit loose with every word, to fly up through the flat tar roof into windless realms.

On the other side of the wall, Tom heard the ring and clatter of clothes hangers. Monsignor Kruug's closet had opened. The electric clock said three-forty. The monsignor must have grabbed for that royal-blue smoking robe that Granger left in the closet for guests.

Tom was not surprised by the gentle knock on his door. In the bedsprings' vibrations he had felt Kruug approaching. Kruug waited for a response; Tom didn't make a sound. He had forgotten to bolt the door. He hoped Kruug had the good sense not to walk in. But he heard the squeak of the knob turning, and a javelin of light shot across the rug to the wall. Tom could see the elongated shadow.

"Tom? Uh, Tom?" Kruug flicked the wall switch, flooding the room with overhead light, catching Tom sprawled across the blue satin mattress of the bed, the toe of one shoe touching the floor, the black trousers strangulating his legs, his eyes red. Kruug looked on, stunned, recalling the time he had run over a twelve-point buck in Montauk, a great deer that had frozen in his headlights. Blood on his bumper. The animal's strange squealing.

Tom untwisted himself immediately, sitting up, facing Kruug.

Fear and tension were in his eyes. Still, he was such a handsome man, Kruug thought, such a blend of assertiveness and humility. But Kruug also felt guilty, as though he had uncovered a rape. Tom was the trapped unicorn. He hoped that the Jesuit couldn't detect his fascination with the scene. He *was* curious, but he had also ached when he heard Tom's crying through the wall. If what Tom had revealed at table was true, about his unbroken chastity, then the Jesuit from Peru was one of an almost extinct breed. And this one's eyes burned like icy gray flames, like the eyes of a mystic who had just turned away from a glimpse of God.

Kruug wondered how he himself appeared to the Jesuit, dressed in Granger's silly, slick blue smoking robe, which made chills run up his bare arms.

Tom stood. "Will you kindly excuse me, Monsignor?" he asked in a deep voice with a sniffle. He pulled open the dresser drawer and grabbed a handkerchief.

"Obviously we both are awake. I heard you . . . "

"I'm quite fine, thank you." Tom slammed the drawer closed.

Kruug stood there, hardly breathing. Then he spoke. "I thought you might care to talk about your situation here."

"No, thank you."

Kruug didn't move. "You know," the monsignor said carefully, "Granger is a good priest, a good man, Tom. He sought laughs in the seminary for his eccentricities, and unfortunately, he got them. In his head he still hears an approving audience. But his friends are almost all dead now, and he doesn't know how awful he sounds to the younger men."

"I understand. And I appreciate your defending him. But I'm really very tired, Monsignor."

"Okay, Tom, I'll see you tomorrow."

Just as Kruug was about to close the door, Tom thought of a way that the already awakened monsignor might help ease his pain. "Monsignor, would you hear my confession?"

"Of course," Kruug responded with surprise, pressing forward. "No, in your room, please. I'll be there in a moment."

Tom stepped into his bathroom, closing the door behind him. He took a sip out of a large bottle of cherry-red mouthwash. He spit the red liquid into the sink, splashed cold water on his face, and soaped up with a new bar of soap. Even as he dried, there remained a stubborn trace of the sacramental oils on his thumb. He flung the towel at the bed and threw on his cassock. With eyes still red and his face damp and cool, he walked into the rose light of Kruug's small room.

Kruug pushed closed the door behind Tom, and in the breeze Tom caught the smell of dust, of furniture polish, and the sweet odor of clean sheets. Kruug tucked his violet stole under the blue robe and fell backward into a deep, nubby, dark-green club chair. Tom knelt into the chair's mushrooming dust and leaned clasped hands against the wide arm, as if it were a prie-dieu. He cast his eyes away from Kruug's hairy chest, which puffed out in gray balls from under his elaborate frock. "In the name of the Father and the Son and the Holy Spirit." Silence that had reigned in the room undisturbed for so long was put to flight by Tom's whispers.

"Bless me, Father, for I have sinned. My last confession was six months ago. Since that time I . . . I . . . " Tom was blocked, distracted.

"You're tired. Take your time," Kruug whispered. Kruug's breath smelled like cooked mushrooms. His underarms were giving off a goat odor, mixed with ginger, as though he had just splashed himself with after-shave.

"I should have prepared . . . before confessing," Tom apologized.

"It's fine. It's fine. We're floating here in the middle of the night. We've got all the time in the world."

Tom stared at the leather-inlaid drum table. Kruug's eyes lifted slowly, sneaking a glance up at the tired face. The Jesuit's black cassock made his thick brown hair seem all the richer, shiny, like the winter coat of a chestnut mare. His eyes were pale gray, in the low light, almost blue. And his eyelashes moved like dark brushes, very dark, soft as mink. Tom's chin was ever so slightly pockmarked. The scents of gasoline and burned incense, cigarette smoke and dried perspiration, were on the Jesuit's cassock. There was also the fragrance of his just-washed face. It produced a sudden vision in Kruug's mind, of his ordination day thirty-three years ago, in the Cathedral of St. John, when right after the bishop had made them priests by that rare and special sacrament, he and his classmates flooded the oak-and-stained-glass sacristy, dressed in long, flowing white albs, like a flock of huge white birds assembling, opening, as it were, their wings to one another, embracing, blessing one another for joy in what the bishop had just given to them with a few rare words, annointing and consecrating their white hands, making them worthy to touch the gold vessels. As they flooded that tiny sacristy room with their whiteness, loosening the maniturgiums, unbinding their hands of those white cotton ribbons that had tied them in a position of prayer, that odor of the holy oils rose from their palms, filling the place, the very odor of oil that Kruug now detected on the Jesuit. It made him want to leap up and embrace the young priest kneeling inches away. But then came the Jesuit's spiced-cherry breath.

"Monsignor, I feel that I'm getting into trouble here."

"All right, son, how do you mean? Mental trouble?"

"No, not specifically mental . . . "

"Mental and spiritual combined?"

"I'm trying to find a starting point." Tom wished Kruug would let him speak for himself.

"You do have sins?"

"I'm sorry?"

"I say, do you have specific sins to confess?"

"First I was hoping I could just . . . "

"To talk? I understand. I'm listening. Go ahead."

Tom shifted on his knees, wishing he could pour out his heart, but the monsignor was obviously too jumpy for that. A silence followed in which the monsignor breathed loudly, loosening his robe and clearing his throat. "You're finding it difficult here with Granger, aren't you?"

"Yes, but that's not it, Monsignor."

"I don't understand why a Jesuit would want to work in a diocese."

"City work reminds me of Peru."

"Then you miss Peru?"

"Certain people, yes." Tom felt the overwhelming sadness of having to say those words.

"On the other hand, you're a Jesuit and you've stuck yourself here away from your own kind. Don't you want to work for your province?"

"I broke with the Jesuits, Monsignor. It's a long story. They'd have me back perhaps but I want to get back to being American, the kind from the States. This country is in moral trouble. I want to catch up on what is happening to my own people."

"Have you been back to Connecticut yet?"

"No," Tom said, a little startled.

"Why not?"

"My folks are dead."

"You have no friends there at all?"

"I'm forty-one years old, Monsignor. I left there as a kid."

"But you *must* go back."

"Must I?" Tom asked with surprise. "Why?"

"Well, it's like Peru. You speak of both with a kind of constriction in your voice." Tom was shocked by the monsignor's presumption.

"Monsignor, I know. I appreciate what you're trying to do, but this is not what I came in here for."

"Maybe you ought, then, to just state your sins," Kruug said in a slightly offended voice.

"First, I have neglected to pray."

"Do you mean the Divine Office?"

"Yes, Monsignor. And I cooperated with an orgasm."

"You'll have to explain that one."

"I was having a wet dream, and I helped it along. There was volition, I think. It's not very important."

"Well, you might have dreamed the volition, you know. I've had that experience."

"I would like to confess it anyway," Tom said with the slightest impatience.

"Of course."

Tom didn't want the confession to turn into a personal exchange. He would settle for just the peace of mind of knowing he was in the state of grace so he could fall asleep and wake up ready to pray the mass.

"And I would like to place before God the sin of despair."

Kruug shifted uncomfortably in the deep chair. "Despair? Dear God. What form does it *take,* this despair?"

"What *form?* I . . . my belief . . . is suspended, in God, in the Divine Plan."

"But that's natural, isn't it?"

"It is not natural for me," Tom said quietly.

"To me, despair is a total giving up of all hope, not a momentary thing," Kruug offered.

"Mine often feels permanent."

"What form of *action* does this permanent giving up of hope take, Father?"

Tom understood that the monsignor was trying to minimize the sin, but why couldn't he just accept it? Kruug was still waiting for Tom to answer his question.

"What do you mean by action?" Tom asked with noticeable exasperation.

"I mean, what *action* accompanied this giving up of hope? Was it a sinful action?"

"Monsignor . . . it's . . . it's a *feeling.* You know what I mean?"

"Precisely. It's a feeling, like depression. But it's not a *sin* to be depressed, now is it, Father?"

"No," Tom answered with a sigh. There was a beat of silence. Tom tried to reassemble the words to describe his next sin. "I'd also like to confess that tonight . . . I . . . "

"You what? Go on."

"A gasoline truck exploded right near the building. Did you hear it, Monsignor?"

"I saw the glow in the schoolyard."

"Did you hear the driver calling?"

"No." Kruug arched a thick black brow dramatically.

"Well, I *did* hear him," Tom continued, "and I . . . I refused to get up out of bed."

Kruug kept his cheek to Tom and stared at the drum table. "You refused? You mean you were lying there, in bed?"

"Yes."

"And you merely *continued* lying there?"

"Yes."

"So, what was wrong with that?"

"I feel guilty of negligence . . . in a man's death, and guilty of withholding the sacraments from him."

"But you went on the call. I heard you go."

"It was too late."

"Yes, but was *that* the efficient cause of this man's death, your lateness?" Kruug leaned forward like a coach on a warm-up bench. "Let me put it this way: What commandment did you break?"

Tom pulled back from the mushroom odor. "What *commandment?*"

"Yes, what commandment would you say you broke?"

"Thou shalt not kill?" Tom was aware of the extreme answer. "Do you realize how scrupulous this all sounds to me?"

"Yes, I do, but the feeling I have *is* of killing. So why don't you just let me confess it the way my conscience tells me to? With all due respect, it's your job to accept that." Tom couldn't keep a sharpness out of his voice.

"Listen to me," Kruug demanded in a complete change of tone. "You are the penitent. Don't try to impose your system on mine. Okay?" Tom didn't answer. "Now . . . was this tonight?"

Kruug tried with difficulty to ease his voice back to its original tones.

"Yes. Tonight." Tom accidentally swallowed the words.

"I meant the nocturnal emission."

"That was tonight too."

"Were you asleep, before the explosion?"

"Yes."

"And were you by any chance having that dream, that wet dream?" Kruug seemed uncomfortable with the expression "wet dream."

"Yes. I was having that dream." Tom had developed a cramp in the back of his neck.

"Now, are there any other sins you wish to confess?" Kruug asked.

"Yes." Tom hesitated. "But now, I, I . . . forget."

"Take your time. Were they grievous sins?"

"I can't remember what they were."

"They aren't likely to be grievous."

"How would you know that, Monsignor?"

"At table tonight you said you felt you had been in the state of grace since you entered the seminary. Now if that was true, and I assume it was . . . "

"It was true." Tom so regretted that statement at table.

"Then could it be that since dinner twenty years of behavior reversed itself? You see what I'm trying to say?"

"I'm afraid I don't."

"You're being *too hard* on yourself. Either you're undergoing some very untypical nervousness or you are terribly, terribly naive," Kruug said gently. His hand was gripping the nubby green chair. "Don't you realize this?" Tom kept silent. "A man in despair doesn't come to confession. Does a man in despair believe in sin? Does he?"

"Give me a minute, Monsignor. I'm drawing a blank here." Tom felt trapped. It was all so pointless. He shaped fists into a pedestal for his forehead, then let his head sink down slowly to rest on it. He was sweating. He wanted to stand and simply walk out the door. Instead, he escaped inwardly. He unleashed his mind, letting it fly back. He thought of air, of the ocean, of blue-black hills slowly moving on the water. Whales in the Pacific, and the raw clean smell of the ocean off the coast of Peru. *Yoo Haaaaaagh Yoooooo.* Screams of joy echoed like whispers in his memory as the ocean lifted two men on the same surfboard. He and his friend Philip, heaved upward by an ocean that seemed intent upon presenting them both to the very moon. He saw it now as he never had, from a distance, two faraway men standing atop a wildly bucking ocean, while their laughter rose out of them, expanding like vibrational rings, into the calm night sky, up into space, laughter, on a journey into the pure, clean nowhere. Then the shotgun crack blowing out from inside the wave's curl, the sudden thunderburst, loud as a cannon. Then silence, except for the high juicy song of something slicing the mirror of sea. He could hear Philip's voice inside his head as though his old friend had slipped into Kruug's room and whispered into his ear: *You've got to find the laughter in everything, Tom. That's where the grace is.* How he wished it were Philip Behan sitting in Granger's green nubby chair.

"Father?" Kruug called gently.

Tom lifted his head slowly. "Yes, Monsignor," he responded as politely as he could, forcing as much air as he could into his lungs.

"You're sorry for all your sins, aren't you? Even the ones you can't remember?"

"Yes. And I apologize for being so difficult."

"Don't apologize. Why don't we simply make an Act of Contrition for all the sins of your life? There are excellent reasons for your upset. You are a rare priest, the old-fashioned kind. I don't think there are a dozen young priests in this diocese, or this world, who know what a nocturnal emission *is* anymore. Chastity is a lost dream. We're in a time of subjective morality. But before you get snobby about it, remember there are others struggling like you. I managed to keep my celibacy and chastity intact too. That's *my* kind of loving God, and I think it's a much harder gift to give Him than marriage is. When you meditate on the perfection of that gift, the temptation often goes away. All right, son?"

"I thank you, Monsignor."

" 'Oh, my God . . . ' "

"Oh, my God, I am heartily sorry for having offended Thee . . . " Tom closed his eyes and obediently recited the Act of Contrition. But Kruug delayed in the absolution, to stare at the priest's closed eyes, to watch the radiant face, to bask in the sweet breath and the resonant words of his contrition.

Kruug knew he hadn't come off well with the Jesuit. He had tried too hard. He had gambled that Tom would feel better about him later, like a mother who appreciates her child's crayon Valentine, however misshapen. He got another whiff of the young man's cassock. A curate's cassock should stink that way, he thought to himself. The cassock was not a prom dress. It was the uniform of an infantryman in the army of Christ, a soldier at the front lines. Yes, it's better a cassock should stink, he thought, better than that dry-cleaning odor on fastidious, dilettante priests who changed their cassocks the way women change dresses. The cassock was armor, a black shell that has to repel not only the devil, but all the hate and envy of the world, all the pain of the dying, all the anger of the neglected. Because it *was* a battlefield, the secular world, and any priest who did not come home from those streets tired and soiled with war was a coward, a deserter.

Kruug realized with a start that Tom had finished his Act of Contrition. The Jesuit's head was up. His eyes were opened, waiting. The face was paler, but the eyes burning strangely vibrant in the low light seemed icy blue now. Kruug was embarrassed. "Excuse me." He turned to speak the words, releasing Tom's eyes, and upon the last word of absolution, the impatient silence flew back into the room, hungrily reclaiming it. Tom stood, and Kruug cast his eyes downward.

When the door latch clicked into place, the monsignor let his arm drop to the floor, falling back relieved, exhausted. He lifted his eyes to the ceiling, praying in his mind, apologizing to God for lying to Tom about his chastity, especially in the sacrament of Penance, for Kruug had lost his purity a long, long time ago, and many times over, through the habitual sin of masturbation, and he asked God to forgive him for that lie and to help him not to be jealous of the strong and principled Jesuit, whose cherry-flavored breath still hovered in the room.

Just before the first light of dawn, Tom heard a click in his sleep. He opened his eyes upon his own reclining shadow on the green wall. Light had entered the room from behind. Disoriented, he looked to the crucifix over his bed. Christ was still there, looking down placidly.

"Tom." The voice whipped his head around. Kruug was turning on the lamp. The door was closed.

"Monsignor . . ." Tom sprang up.

"I . . . I didn't want to knock or call from the hall because Granger might have heard."

"What's the matter?"

"I've been talking to the bishop on the phone; he's a friend. . . ."

"At this hour?"

"Yes, about your situation here."

"What situation?"

"You're tired and you're angry, and you sound very depressed to me. When was the last time you drove a car, or drank a beer with a younger priest? There's a priest in Montauk, a curate with me, who needs your example. Why waste your time and your soul in this place? Come out to Montauk, to Stella Maris."

"Wait a minute." Tom put his hand to his head. "You're getting ahead of me here."

"I want you to let me go into Granger right now and tell him I want you the hell out of here by tomorrow morning."

"Are you kidding?" Tom almost laughed as he threw on his cassock. "I'm a little worn out, Monsignor, but good Lord, I hope you didn't imply to the bishop that I'm cracking up here."

"That's just the tool I'll use on Granger."

"The *tool?*"

"That's right."

"Now wait a minute, wait a minute, Monsignor. You are overlooking the fact that I've got responsibilities here."

"There's a priest assigned to me who can't work, and you know something else?"

"What?"

Kruug smiled. "You are dying to get out of here."

"Oh, really?"

"Come on, Tom. Stop wasting our time. I bungled all tongue-tied in confession but now I'm saying something real. Be decent enough to admit it. I'm a busy man. I can't hang around this place to help you." Tom stared. "Give me your sick-call list. Write down the names of the people who need attention, and let's get you the hell out of here." Tom walked across the floor, stunned. "Granger's a sick man. You've given him enough. Do you honestly want to impale your priesthood on the spire of St. Barnabas'?"

"Shhh." Tom hushed him gently. Kruug took the admonition with a knowing smile. "There are *people,* names, faces, I'd be letting down. I'd be terrible to disappear on them."

"You know what they call me at the Chancery?"

"No."

"The priest doctor. The bishop supports me in anything I do for the welfare of a priest, and there is one thing I know for certain: You need out. *Quam primum.* Trust me. After breakfast I have to leave for two weeks' vacation. My sister expects me in Virginia, so I have only a couple of hours to work on this thing. Give me the green light to go in to Granger; I'll have you out inside of twenty-four hours. I'll have an immediate replacement, someone who can handle him."

Madeline Corey shot into Tom's mind, and the girl in confession. He turned away. "But the people . . . "

"The people are everywhere, Tom." Kruug's eyes were tender. "Give me the list."

"Why are you doing this?" Tom asked with some irritation.

"I don't like what I see here." Kruug's eyes moved with alarmed sincerity. "Granger's gotten worse. The bishop hoped you'd shape him up; instead, it's ruining you. You're in a tough time of your priesthood, and this is the last place to go through that kind of thing. Are you hearing me? I don't care how someone like you wound up here; I just want you out before this place pulverizes you. You want it, too."

Tom opened his mouth to protest, but nothing came out. He had underestimated this monsignor.

"Stella Maris? That's your parish?" Tom said.

"It's on the ocean. The ocean has power, you know."

"In Montauk, you say?"

"Correct. We have deer on the beach, and eagles that fly above the gulls. When I come back from vacation, the first thing I'll do is to ferry you across the Sound to Connecticut. It's time you went home. You'll be surrounded by water on all sides. Water reflects heaven, you know."

Tom sat down on the edge of his bed and rubbed his head in disbelief. "You would go in and wake Granger right now?" he asked, incredulous.

"Darn tootin'. He's got the six anyway."

"What if he refuses?"

"Just you choose between two words—yes and no. Say no, I'll go back to my room. Say yes, and you're home free. It's your choice. You know what's happening. You're capable of acting."

Tom looked coldly into Kruug's eyes as the monsignor looked coldly back, waiting, standing tall in his purple-trimmed cassock open at the neck. There was no lunacy in the man's eyes, though there was shrewdness. And in his own heart, Tom had no trouble understanding what he wanted. He had known it for months.

"Yes," Tom said with a little shudder. "My answer would be yes if I really had to choose between your two words."

Kruug straightened his back. "Then go to bed, and whisper your good-byes to this place." The monsignor turned out the lamp and slipped out of the room, leaving Tom sitting on his bed, in the darkness.

Tom rose and listened through the ringing dark for the faint knock upon Granger's door. The thrill of leaving St. Barnabas' surprised him with its suddenness. He walked to his door and put an ear to the sounds in the hallway.

"Artie. Artie. It's me, Ronnie."

Granger opened. "What the hell do you want?"

"Get inside. We've got to talk." Then Granger's door closed.

Tom stepped barefoot onto the green rug of the hallway, hiding in a shadow near the dimly lit Chinese lamp.

"What?" Granger shouted. "Are you crazy?" Granger's muffled voice rang in the predawn stillness. Tom dared to move closer. "Tell him to write to the bishop for a transfer if he wants one," Granger yelled.

"He'll write the bishop after the fact," Kruug said.

"After *what* fact?"

"Of his leaving tomorrow."

"You're out of your mind." Tom heard a glass fall. "Leave it," Granger yelled. "The nerve of you waking me up."

"Artie, listen . . . "

"The bishop hasn't given you authority to go around to his parishes plucking curates out."

"He has, in an emergency."

"Bullcrap."

"It's true."

"You're a guest in my house. Who the *hell* do you think you are?"

"Artie, this place is getting the boy nervous."

"Don't give me this 'boy' stuff. It's been getting *me* nervous for twenty-one years. How do you expect me to function here without a curate?"

"He's cracking."

"I'm not going to get into a tug-of-war with you over the Jesuit, Ronnie."

"You don't even *like* the man."

"I never liked any curate. Good grief! Marriage instructions, altar boys, sick calls. I'll have a heart attack trying to make ends meet around here."

"I'll see that you get a top-notch replacement."

"I said nooooo," Granger shouted in a long note. "How dare you . . . eat here and sleep here . . . as a guest, and all the while . . . you're playing . . . sneaky doctor games."

Granger's breathing was strained.

"Don't insult me, Artie."

"Then don't you make me . . . sick . . . to my stomach." Silence. "Where's my medicine? Where's my spray?" Tom could hear loud inhalations. There was a pause.

"He's a Jesuit, Artie. He's not ours. I can walk out of here with him tonight if I want to." A cabinet door slammed, glasses clinked.

"What are you going to tell the bishop?" Tom inched closer.

"I'll tell the bishop he's cracking up. It's simple."

"Oh, so now you're the diocesan psychiatrist, not the jail warden. Did you tell the Jesuit he's going to have to live with that freak Buoncuore? Does he know what that nut *did?*" Granger's nose was closed.

"Arthur . . . Arthur, look at me now. You're not listening. You're going to be responsible for a small tragedy here if you don't insist that the Jesuit take a rest immediately. You'll have a mess here, I promise you, and you'll have to answer to his superiors as well as to your own bishop. Now why don't you wise up and make it easy for yourself?"

"You are so full of shit," Granger said idly.

"What's happening to your priesthood, Artie?"

"Worry about your own priesthood, Ronnie."

"You lose curates too frequently. Your name is mud in the seminary; they'd rather have cancer than be assigned here. They call it the ice palace. The jebbie stayed a whole damned year. That's six months longer than any of them."

"Oh, God in heaven! Look at you, trying to make me believe I'm a monster so you can have him."

"*Have* him?"

"Yes, to play cuddly priest doctor with an overscrupulous ex-Jesuit. You were a sucker for that type in the seminary; I remember you."

"He's a tired man."

"He's a *scroup,*" Granger screamed.

"Shhh. He certainly isn't."

"A scroup! Yes, he is. And a proud one. You should be shaving down his pride instead of coming in here and puffing him up more."

"He's a good old-fashioned priest, Artie. Have you read his dossier? He was one of the best down there in Peru. He built houses for the poor with his own hands. He delivered babies out of dirt holes." There was another silence.

"You're a Judas," Granger hissed with final, shocked understanding. "What a fool I was."

"What the hell are you talking about?"

"His dossier. How'd you see it? Huh, Kruug?" Granger shouted.

"I . . . wait a minute now, Artie."

"You knew he was from Connecticut. How, Ronnie?"

"Artie, don't put me in a spot."

"The bishop sent you here to spy on me, didn't he?"

"That is *not* what is really happening, Artie."

"You're shafting me." Granger's voice was cracking.

"No," Kruug said firmly. There was silence, then softly, sobs. "Now don't get this way on me, Artie."

Granger was weeping. "You damned viper, Ronnie. You came here to make trouble for me."

"No. I swear I'll cover for you."

"How can I *know* you will?"

"It's the jebbie I want. Not you."

"Swear on the crucifix you'll cover me with the bishop, that you won't mention my asthma, or . . . "

"I swear."

"Hand on the crucifix."

"No mention of asthma. No negative reports whatsoever."

"I want him out of here after his mass in the morning." Granger's voice recovered. "I don't want to see his face *ever.* No words of good-bye. *Out.*"

"No words. No faces."

"You love this, don't you, Kruug? Fix the little blackbird's broken wings. You salivate for these opportunities. When you talk to the bishop," Granger said, clearing his throat, "tell him, in my heart, somewhere deep down, the priesthood is safe, it's good. . . . "

"Artie, you're one of the finest . . . "

"Now just get out. Please. Just go, Ronnie."

Kruug was in the hallway, closing Granger's door behind him. He saw Tom. "Did you hear?" Kruug threw a whisper down the hall.

"Some," Tom answered guiltily.

Kruug grabbed Tom's arm, pulling him into the guestroom and closing the door. He looked at Tom with nervous, dancing eyes and a tight smile. A pallor cramped the skin around his mouth. "I did what had to be done to get you out of here with no red tape." In his nervousness, Kruug squeezed Tom's arm so tightly it hurt. "I lied a bit. God forgive me. I had to say you were cracking."

"How did you see my dossier?" Tom asked.

"I saw it at the Chancery."

Tom felt a sudden fear of Kruug's abilities. "Is his asthma the reason for this air conditioning?"

"Yes."

"Why didn't he tell me?"

"He tries to keep it a secret. The bishop knows. Don't worry. He'll never take this place away from him."

"And who is this Buoncuore? What's *his* problem?"

"Who, Gene? You'll like Gene. He needs someone like you to give him a good example." Kruug grabbed up a pen and pencil and pulled his address book out of his suitcase and flipped pages. "Buoncuore won't have much good to say about me, though." He laughed.

"He won't?"

"No. I goad him. He's the direct opposite of you. He needs some of your spirituality. You need some of his irreverence."

"Why did Granger call him a nut?"

"Gene *is* a nut. Does that scare you?"

"It could."

"Well, forget it. Being likable is Buoncuore's number-one preoccupation. Now, here's my sister's number in Virginia, in case you need me. I'll be gone two weeks. And here's the Long Island Railroad number." He wrote. "And this is the bus number. The bus is more comfortable. You'll need a reservation for that. You have money?"

"Yes."

Kruug was so typically North American. He was one of those priests that blended sensuality, sentimentality, and shrewdness, while somehow maintaining a truly naive belief in God and the Commandments. He was strict and ruthless, totally priest, totally human, and manipulative in the extreme. Yet, Tom felt he could deal with the man, perhaps even like him. There was a nonintellectual power to Kruug that promised safety and predictability. And as long as Kruug was on Tom's side, he could tolerate the man. Yes. He had let himself be seduced for his own good. He was using Kruug; they both knew it. It was true he was losing his people, but he couldn't let himself think of that. He promised himself he would write. He could come back perhaps. Montauk was a mere hundred miles away. He accepted the slip of paper that Kruug was handing him.

"This was very fast, Monsignor," he warned.

"I know. Don't worry. When I come back, you take your vacation, you hear? That's an improvement right there, isn't it? The rest we'll play by ear. I like you very much, Tom."

Tom held out his hand. "I suppose I should say thanks. But . . . "

Kruug accepted the outstretched hand. "But what? You changing your mind?" Tom didn't answer. "Go to sleep and stop aggravating. It's done, my boy. You're better off. Now's the time for a little of that old-fashioned faith."

"I'll give it a try." Tom cracked a smile.

Kruug consciously registered the Jesuit's grateful expression in his memory. Later, on the long car ride to his sister's, he would recall it as he meditated on the wonders of destiny working, knowing that God doesn't allow Himself to be fooled, not even by priests.

Chapter Three

TOM DIZZILY RAISED HIS BEAUTIFUL gold-and-silver chalice at mass, giving thanks, although he had to fight off feelings of guilt. He prayed for equilibrium, for the return of his love of his own being. At the memento for the dead, he whispered the names of Alice and Frank Sheehan; at the memento for the living, Monsignors Granger and Kruug, the mysterious curate at Stella Maris whose name was Gene Buoncuore, Madeline Corey, and Kevin and Kitty Brady.

In his short sermon to the faithful, he made no mention of his departure. At the communion he ingested the Godhead hungrily with the prayer that he be helped to transcend the failings of his humanity. After mass he grabbed his chalice case by its black strap, turned his back on the sacristy, and walked quietly through the wailing tunnel for the last time.

He knocked on Granger's door. "May I come in, Monsignor?" No response. The door seemed to open a few inches on its own. Tom pushed in to catch Granger falling into a sheet-covered chaise. The pastor clutched a very wrinkled handkerchief to his nose. He quickly grabbed an inhalator off the end table and buried it in his cloak. He threw one foot up on the chaise and busied his eyes, covering his ankle with the edges of the black cape. Plastic rolldowns covered the bookshelves. The room was

rugless, immaculate but bleak as a garage. Granger looked up at
the Jesuit as if to say, Well, speak.

"I came in to say that I'm sorry."

"Don't lie to me, Sheehan."

"Beg pardon?"

"You're not the least bit sorry. I'm the sorry one."

"There's no need for you to be sorry, Monsignor."

"Are you forgiving me?" Granger laughed with pain. "God,
isn't it amazing how cruel human goodness can be?" He put the
inhalator back on the table with a thud and stood up, walking
toward his closed venetian blinds, tightening his cape around him.
He remained facing the closed blinds, catching drips from his nose
with the handkerchief.

"Too bad you didn't have the guts to do this thing on your
own. You had only to talk to me, you know. You didn't need
Kruug."

"I intended no insult."

"Because you're such a *good* man, Father Sheehan, eh?" Tom
wisely didn't answer the sarcastic question. Granger turned to
show his hurt. "Even now you don't hear me, do you? You say
to yourself, 'He's old, cantankerous, troublesome.'" Granger
turned back to the blinds, lifting one a half inch, peering out.
"The light shines right through Tom, doesn't it?" Then, in a new
voice: "You should enjoy Monsignor Kruug. Like you, he is a
good and moral man. That should be cozy." Granger's mouth was
turned down, like a child about to cry. "My last curate said it
was bad luck to leave a parish without the blessing of the pastor.
Do you subscribe to that superstition?"

"Yes," Tom lied.

"Does that mean you would like my blessing, Father?"

"Yes, I would."

"Then kneel," Granger said with shocking gentleness. Tom
sank to his knees. "Good-bye, Tom," Granger whispered, in such
a way it gave Tom a chill. Placing both hands solidly on the
Jesuit's head, then raising his right hand, he spoke the words the
old-fashioned way, making the sign of the cross: *"Benedicat vos
omnipotentens Deus. Pater, et Filius . . . "*

Tom packed a suitcase, then brought communion to Madeline Corey. He wore his black raincoat with the collar buttoned at the neck so his clerical collar would not show. He carried his bag and chalice case. He passed Granger's garbage pails on the way back, imagining the pressure of eyes on his back, eyes from behind one narrow slit in those venetian blinds.

Cabs flew by in flocks on Meeker Avenue, taking shortcuts to the bridge to Manhattan. He lifted his arm; several stopped. He leaped into one and closed the door. "Lexington Avenue and Forty-fourth Street." He checked for his wallet. It was there, but not his keys—he'd left them on the dining table for Granger. For the moment, there were no keys in his life, none whatever, and it pleased him.

There was no time to spare. The bus would leave at two-thirty. He closed his eyes and let his hands fall at his sides. He didn't want to glance back at those Brooklyn streets. He wouldn't like it if someone familiar caught his eye and waved to him. He wouldn't be able to wave back to someone he might never see again. *Why?* he asked himself. They had been his people, his only rightful loves. "Good-bye," he whispered through the dirty taxi glass. "Forgive my cowardice. Forgive my selfishness."

The bus was parked on the west side of Lexington Avenue before the post office. *Montauk* was printed in big black type over its windshield. As Tom crossed the avenue, large puffs of rain clouds moved rapidly west over his head. The skyscrapers in the bus windshield began to bend out of shape, in moving patterns. The bus was pulling away.

"Wait," Tom cried out, running into its path, raising his chalice case and suitcase.

"What the hell are you trying to do out there?" The driver was a stout woman with a blond pixie haircut. Tom stepped up to her. His hand went to his neck, reminding him that his raincoat was hiding his clerical collar.

"I have a reservation," he panted, reaching into his back pocket for his wallet. "I'm sorry I'm late."

The driver closed the doors behind him and picked up her clipboard. Cars beeped, urging her to proceed.

"Sheehan is the name."

"Thomas?"

"That's correct."

"We waited eleven minutes for you."

"I'm very sorry." Tom unbuttoned the top of his raincoat. She noticed his white collar and looked away, pressing the gas pedal.

"Fourteen dollars, please."

Tom paid her and started down the aisle of the moving bus. There were no empty seats, except one on his right upon which rested a hemp shopping bag with a leather handle. It said *Barbados*. A coffee pot and silverware, tied in a roll like asparagus, were stuffed into it, next to a bumpy Irish knit. A woman was asleep next to the bag, her head against the window glass.

"Excuse me." Tom touched his chalice case to the seat. She stirred, looking up. Realizing there were no other seats, she quickly pulled the heavy hemp bag over to her, letting it down between her legs. She stuffed her skirt under her thigh, uncovering the seam in the seat that marked his territory, and he sat down into a vague cloud of tea rose perfume. She had obviously come a distance; her tired eyes told that. In the overhead rack Tom noticed framing sticks and folded canvas—a painter, he guessed. She was wearing a dark-purple cotton dress with tiny violets printed all over it, an antique dress, and over it a short-sleeved violet-gray sweater. A single strand of pearls rounded her neck, and her ears were pierced with almost invisible gold earrings, thin as silk thread. A blue satin ribbon was falling out of a loose honey-colored braid which rested on her shoulder like a loaf of soft bread.

He was so used to people needing him, making demands, that he forgot how nice it felt at times to be among strangers who had no rights to him. He was sitting closer to a pretty woman than he had in years, in such privacy, such immunity.

He began to have an erection, and it made him angry. He tried to think of something beautiful, the Trappist monastery in Chile, and those wild Chilean horses that roamed the plains in the outskirts. But it was Terrence Sullivan who came to mind instead, asking that classic question of Father Swain in Moral Theology class.

"Father, say you're on your way to the dentist, in a vehicle of public transportation, and there's only one seat left, next to a, well, say next to a . . . "

"Pretty woman?" Father Swain offered with a smile.

"More or less, Father, yes."

"Go on, Terrence."

"Father, may I sit down?"

"But you *are* sitting, Mr. Sullivan."

"I mean on the vehicle of public transportation, Father." The class laughed.

"Well, are your legs tired?" Father Swain asked in gentle sarcasm.

"Well yes, they are, say, Father. Very." Terrence smiled.

"Then sit down for heaven's sake, Mr. Sullivan." More laughter.

"All right then, Father. You're sitting there, say, and you find after a while you're getting an . . . an . . . "

"An erection."

"Exactly, Father."

"Well," Father Swain said, walking to the blackboard. "Could you not jump up and leave this vehicle of public transportation?"

"I could, Father," Terrence answered.

"But then you'd encounter another woman on the next vehicle. They populate half the world, Terrence."

"That's very true, Father. And I have an awful toothache."

"Wouldn't it simply be better to close your eyes, fold your arms in your lap, and recite the litany to the Blessed Virgin Mary until you reached your destination?"

"I could do that, Father. Yes."

"I suggest that you do, Mr. Sullivan, or else next time we'll

have to send you to the dentist in an armored car. Won't we?"
The class roared for a full minute.

Seminarians were healthy as peasants in those days, wearing
cassocks over dungarees, sporting clean faces and bright, healthy
eyes, willing to laugh at anything, all hopeful, all proud of the
gift they were giving of their lives. *Ad majorem Dei gloriam.* All
for the honor and glory of God. Some much too serious, some
crazily mischievous, but all pure-intentioned, trying constantly
to understand the burning mystery of God. Warmed by their
memory, Tom crossed his forearms over his lap and leaned back,
safe inside the echo of Father Swain's words, that there was no
obligation on his part to get up and out of his seat nor to move
away from the strange woman who unknowingly was causing
him sexual excitement. He relaxed in the soft growling of his
lungs, falling back into his cave of visions, cozy and assured that
Noldin-Schmitt, who wrote the moral theology text, and Father
Swain, who taught it, and the entire seminary agreed that it was
all right for him to be sitting right where he was. He thought
of Dominic Caccavale and the ghosts of Brooklyn hallways, and
then, as the bus bumped along, he opened a new frontier for his
thoughts. He drifted into a cushiony roller-coaster ride, up, into
that friendly darkness called sleep. His legs slowly spread apart.
His thighs flattened. His body was letting go of itself, falling. All
buses and trains must have been unconsciously designed after
Noah's Ark, he thought, with all their double seats. Was there
a dove overhead, flying with an olive branch in its beak?

He opened his eyes and caught her looking at him. Her eyes
were the color of her sweater. With the nervous fingers of one
hand she searched for the loose ribbon. She wore a small ring on
her small finger, a child's ring with a small pink stone. Then the
other hand rushed up, ten fingers in search of the ribbon, thin,
long fingers trembling, finally finding the end of the thing,
yanking it down, entwining it rapidly in her hand, curling it in
her palm, into her fist, out of sight.

He stretched up to free his undershorts, pretending he was
checking for his wallet; then, closing his eyes again, he let the

past year drop away into the wake of the bus and allowed his mind to unclutter itself for what lay ahead. He felt like one of the scouts that Moses sent ahead to the Promised Land. He was Caleb, on the eve of a new nation, the first man on the brink of a new world, falling asleep on cliffs overhanging the future.

Sharp sounds of horns opened his eyes. He had sprawled into her seat, and she was gone. He blinked at silver-blue tunnel lights shining into the window. The bus was stopped behind hundreds of immobilized taillights, under the East River. He pulled himself up and caught sight of her at the front of the bus, talking feverishly to the driver.

She was taller than he had imagined. Her soft braid was on the verge of coming undone entirely. The tunnel lights etherealized her body. She was not *too* thin, as he had previously thought. When she put a hand on her hip and stooped to look back out the rear window, he could see she had her straw bag and one other shopping bag with her. Her pocketbook was slung over her shoulder, and her face showed fright. She stepped down as if to leave the bus, but a transit policeman pushed her back, calling out beyond her to the driver.

"Hey, you can't let your people out."

"I can't put them in chains either."

"I'm feeling very claustrophobic," she said pleadingly to the guard. "The exhaust fumes . . . "

"Don't worry, lady."

"How long will it be?" she asked.

"Not long."

"What happened?"

"Lady, I don't know. What can I tell ya?"

"Then how do you know it won't take long?"

"Huh?"

Another guard passed them, running at top speed on the ramp, wearing a gas mask.

"Do you realize we are breathing in this carbon monoxide?"

"Close your door and keep this one inside," the guard ordered the driver.

"I want to walk out of the tunnel." She jumped into the bus doorway, keeping it open with her body. "How far is the exit?" She was obviously willing to leave her things now.

"You're in the middle of the *tunnel* here, lady. Now get back up there."

"But I feel like I'm going to get sick."

"Will you get her back *inside?*" the guard yelled, lifting her, pushing her up the step. "If you walk in these fumes, you'll really get sick." The driver closed the doors, shutting them inside.

"Young lady, sit down, for God's sake," a well-dressed older woman passenger called out from the backseat.

The younger woman's eyes widened. She reached for a seat handle and pulled herself back toward Tom. The other passengers ignored her, too concerned with the situation. Tom stood to let her by. He was sweating. He removed his jacket. She crawled in, lifting her legs over the hemp bag.

The transit cop was not aware that he had moved close to her window, speaking to another officer who carried a two-way radio. "She's in the fuckin' middle of the tunnel and she wants me to let her walk." He giggled, unaware that his voice was reaching her through the glass. Tom reached past her and banged his fist on the window. The transit cop turned in surprise and peered into the bus.

"Would you prefer to change seats?" Tom asked.

"No," she said angrily.

The guard softly punched the window. "Do I look like I'm *dyin'* out here?" he yelled, spreading his arms and smiling.

"You're already dead," she murmured.

"Take a deep breath," Tom ordered her.

"Of carbon monoxide?"

"You need to relax." She turned away from him. "We're not going to die." He smiled. "Breathe. Take the bad with the good," Tom said with a grin.

She gave him one brief look and turned away from him. She wrapped the blue ribbon around her finger, dropped it, pressed her palms to her thighs, and took in several breaths. Then she looked at him, seeming possibly on the verge of tears. "Thanks for banging on the window, for trying to help. I wasn't . . . "

"You're welcome." He was nervous, too, jumping the gun.

She turned back to the window. A beat of time passed. She took several more deep breaths. A full minute passed before she spoke: "Are you a minister?"

"I'm a priest."

"Catholic?"

"Yes."

"Forgive my ignorance."

"It's okay."

"My grandparents were Quakers," she said, staring at the inert red taillights, "but I, and my parents, never observed anything. What would you call us?"

"Nothing?" Tom offered with a smile.

She turned and looked at him with an expression of mild shock. *"Nothing?"*

"Well, I meant as far as your practice."

"You make it sound so empty. My father was a painter, a *wonderful* painter. That's certainly *something.*"

"I'm sure he was," Tom said, surprised at himself for offending her.

"He *loved* nature. He understood light. He worshiped life and every power in it."

"Maybe he was a pantheist?"

"The pan part, yes, but he wasn't a Theist, if there is such a word." Her eyelash fluttered involuntarily, as one eyelid quivered.

"But you said he worshiped everything." He wasn't thinking about what he was saying. He was only trying to lure her mind away from the traffic.

"I don't think he'd agree that he worshiped at all. I didn't mean the word *worship* in that way."

"How did you use the word?"

"Well, for one thing, to describe when someone loves another an awful lot, excessively, like . . . 'She worshiped him beyond belief.' " She was embarrassed. Her mind was not off the tunnel; she was still slightly pale.

"I don't believe a human being *can* love excessively," Tom said casually.

"I meant totally, compulsively, obsessively."

"What are we talking about?" Tom smiled broadly at her; she blinked.

"Worship."

"Oh." He nodded. "Right. And I was put off by your use of the word *love*."

"How did I use the word?" she asked.

"I think you said love '*excessively*,' and I questioned how that could ever be, how a love can be excessive." He smiled.

She was taking him deeply seriously, and he was enjoying it.

"Well, what we *call* love," she said impatiently, "is the most boring word of the past two decades." Her color was coming back.

"Love? The most boring word?" Tom smiled.

"Definitely the most boring word, because we can't escape the cliché, and in reality we're never really talking about it." She stopped suddenly, looking at him, studying him. "Catholic priests still can't marry, right?"

He recovered from the toughness of the question, answering it boldly: "Yes. We don't marry."

"You mean you *can't*." He shrugged in semi-agreement. "Well, then," she turned, "we're talking about two different things."

"How are we talking about two different things?" He smiled. The bus had started moving.

"Your life deals with divine love, or something. I was referring to people *pairing*—human love."

"Priests understand human love."

"I'm sure they do—in their own way."

"They do in your way, too."

"In *my* way? What is *my* way?" She smiled.

"Your way? I guess I don't know, really. Do I?" He smiled back.

Her color was returning.

He decided to terminate the discussion, but first he had to let her know one more thing. "Roman Catholic priests, we give up sexual love, okay? But we understand human love."

She blinked, examining his eyes. "Why would a normal man want to give it up? I don't see that part. Perhaps I shouldn't ask."

"I *had* to give it up, true," he said, trying to keep a thread of impatience out of his voice. "It's the custom, the requirement. But I felt consonant with the requirement."

"Yes, well, that's what I mean. How could you feel *consonant*, as you put it?"

"Well . . . " He looked away. "It's extremely complicated for someone who isn't Catholic to understand."

"I shouldn't force you to talk about it."

"You're not forcing me."

" 'Force' was a bad word. I'm sorry." She looked at her hands, then out the window. She turned back to him, flipping her braid behind her. Her teeth showed perfect in a smile. "You were very valiant, anyway, for banging on the window."

He turned to look at her, believing that the smile was genuine. Her earrings were catching light again from somewhere. "That's what the priesthood is for," he said softly.

"We need more of it."

"Thanks. I agree." He smiled, though he was still uneasy with her.

"We're moving."

The two of them watched the flow of red lights until the bus emerged from the tunnel. The rain had stopped. There was even some sun. The bus stopped at the toll, then started uphill over the bridge into Long Island City.

The sun was fully shining in Queens, though the asphalt was wet. She closed her eyes when they passed the factories and billboards, resting her head against the window glass the way she had when he first laid eyes on her. Her eyelids were tranquil. Her lashes were almost black, different from her hair color; her chin and jaw, symmetrical. She was still quite young. He could see blue veins through her skin at her temples. Women in Peru, even the rich women, were ruddier, chubbier. She was really a quite perfect, a quite delicately beautiful woman. He didn't remember North American women that way. The road rose, lifting the bus above the horizon. Suddenly there were fields of early pumpkins, woods of lindens and oaks. He could see ragweed and sumac, ailanthus trees, goldenrod, and blue thistle. His eyes drank in the maples and all the meadow weeds of his childhood in Connecticut.

Now the bus was doing seventy along the white roadway toward Montauk Point. She had fallen asleep while the bus sailed into sunny, blue-green expanses of sod farms, barns, and tree nurseries. He noticed that her hand was turned over in her lap, half opened. How badly her mind must have wanted to vacate her body. He hoped that in her dreams she was resolving the horrors of the Queens Midtown Tunnel.

He stood quietly, unzipping the black suitcase over her head, taking out his breviary. He sat down, softly, and started reading. In monasteries the monks chanted it together. A priest in the world had to read it alone. But with her beside him, dreaming her own private dreams as they flew over the white sun-drenched highway, he felt he had company. He was reading the psalms of David, poetry that had been written long before Christ, prayers Christ himself read as a young man. He was distracted by only one thought, one that occurred to him many times: how it would be to work on a friendship with a woman.

He read for an hour. Just as he finished the last hymn of Compline —*Oh, God, keep me as the apple of Your eye, hide me in the shadow of Your wing*— the bus took a sharp turn into Watermill Village. He propped his companion up. She blinked at the striped vegetable-stand awnings, the silvery clouds to the south reflecting water, beyond the potato field.

"My goodness, where are we?" She stood up, hardly awake, squeezing past his knees into the aisle. She went forward, talked with the driver, then returned, sliding back in past Tom's knees. "I get off at the yellow blinking light. My only question is: How do I do it with all this stuff?"

"Can I help?"

"Yes, but then how do I lug it to my rental, which is a half mile from the highway?" She was not as formal as before, talking as if he were an old friend.

"Are there cabs available?"

"Not if it's the way I remember it."

"It's my first time out here," Tom apologized.

"Well, it's been eighteen years for me, so we're almost in the same boat." Her eyes were scanning the overhead rack and looking out the windshield for the yellow light.

"You moving out here?" Tom asked, following her eyes.

"Uh, no. No," she said uncomfortably. "I'm renting a place for the winter. There's so much stuff because I paint, and I gave up my apartment." She stooped to see out the windshield. "This is where the trouble starts. Getting off."

"You'll have to help," she said as the bus slowed down. "What is this?" She read a street sign.

"Bridgehampton," the driver called.

"Is this it?" Tom asked, standing.

"No," she said, straightening. "Next, I think." She worried him a little. It was the look in her face.

"Do you have a pencil?" Tom asked, a little uncomfortably.

"Huh?" She turned in unconscious annoyance; then, realizing what he'd said, she unzipped her portfolio, sticking her arm deep inside, while he fumbled, looking for a piece of paper in his wallet.

"I think I need a piece of paper, too," he said.

She stuck her arm back down into the portfolio, then pulled her arm out, handing him a green-and-black fountain pen and a torn sheet of white paper. "It writes thin," she warned.

Thomas Sheehan S.J.
Stella Maris
Montauk

He folded it and gave the pen and paper back to her. "The phone's listed. Now if you get stranded, I can drive back to help you. I think there's a parish car where I'm going."

She stuck the paper in her wallet purse, snapping it shut and flipping it into her straw bag, standing up suddenly, forcing him to stand. He pulled his thick clerical suitcase out of the rack so she could get the rest of her things.

The late sun filled the back window. When the yellow blinking light appeared up ahead, the bus slowed down, coming to a stop before a real estate shack. The driver opened the doors, put on the brake, stood up, and helped Tom hand her things out to her: folded canvases, the sticks, the portfolio, the shopping bags, the silver, a gooseneck lamp, clock-radio; the percolator fell apart, bouncing down the steps. She gathered up the parts as Tom brought out a drawstring sack, placing everything neatly at the roadside.

"My name is Katelyn Snow," she said, reaching for Tom's hand.

"Nice to meet you."

"That it?" the driver asked, jumping into her seat and looking back into the bus.

"I think so," Tom said, jumping back inside. As he waved, the door closed, separating them. The bus distanced them as he watched her standing there with a coffee pot in hand, looking about confusedly.

Chapter Four

THE SOUND OF THE BUS DIED around the curve. Now birds twittered. Above her head a clicking noise, the blinking yellow traffic light. A fine wind hummed through the telephone wires. She paused, looking both ways for a telephone booth, but there were only field cedars and meadows full of shocking blue chicory. She hadn't experienced so much space and silence in a long time. She dragged her things, crushing the roadside thistle, making her way toward the real estate shack. A sign in the window said CLOSED. She decided to hide everything at the back of the shack, laying it all down flat in the tall grass so that it couldn't be seen. She'd have to walk to the Pritchard shack. She couldn't wait to see it again.

She slung her large straw pocketbook over her shoulder and stepped onto the asphalt of Sagg Main Street, following the telephone wires toward the ocean. She estimated it would take a half hour. She walked slowly, letting the late sun entertain her as it sprayed light across the fields, which lay hot and newly plowed, under hovering mists. In the east, a mass of orange powder was cascading downward out of the sky as if a colossal broom had just swept centuries of dust off the porches of heaven onto the spent, early cornfields. By the time she reached the little cemetery which split the road in two, a strong sea breeze had brought the ocean to her ears. She turned left onto Gibson, past grazing horses, then left again, onto the dune road. Here late cornfields appeared summery and green in the rising steam. The sun had become a large orange ball by then, but by the time she reached the shack, it had turned bluish red, glowing cold and low over a hill of young winter wheat.

The shack had once been the pump house of the Pritchard farm. Now the property had been divided off, although a vestigial water pump still stood next to the building. There was a front door, nailed shut, and there was a picture window boarded up with plywood. A row of frail multicolored gladiolas did nothing to set the place off. It was not as she remembered. The white paint was worn off, and the cedar shingles had turned a damp dark brown.

From the back, the place looked new. The cedars had grown up, hugging the shack on three sides, hugging the roof with large shoulders. A pine tree, twice the height of the place, shaded it on the other side. A long row of lilac bushes and privet made the yard private on the ocean side, while a hill of blond winter wheat loomed up behind the place like an illumination, sheltering it from the north and west. She stepped onto the cedar deck, and a dog started barking from a nearby pen, a black Labrador, whining and leaping at the chicken wire. She did her best to ignore him, pulling open the screen door, turning the knob of the inner door. It was locked. Two surfboards leaned against the house, and there were bulging suitcases next to them. Mr. Pritchard had said the door would be open and the key would be on the table.

The setting sun had turned the window into a molten sheet of yellow fire. She had to cup her eyes to see inside. Woodburning stove, 1940s drapery fabric, dirty dishes in the sink, a large messy bed. No key on the kitchen table. "Damn," she said aloud, stepping back on the deck. "Hush, you," she called to the dog. He calmed down, wagging his tail. The lease read Tuesday, September 7, but she had never expected the place to be occupied to the very last minute. "Well, they'd better be out by midnight," she said to the dog, turning away. An unopened box of Spic and

Span and a brand-new sponge mop leaned against the wall. She hoped that meant they were going to clean.

There were still a few hours left to the Labor Day holiday. Summer was still in effect, although the setting point of the sun indicated its imminent demise. She was disappointed, but felt bad for the people who had to take their surfboards and go.

She cooed to the dog as she left, walking toward the noise of the ocean, down Peters Pond Road, next to the fallen water tower between two potato fields. The ocean was boiling rough.

She longed to feel the warm sand with bare feet, to sit before the white, unruly water, but she was hungry. So she turned back toward the blue sun and the Topping farm, walking under fat sunburned maples, smelling honeysuckle and drying camomile. The very dust of the road smelled clean, lying soft as talcum around the tree trunks, pulverized by the hot summer. Horses grazed on both sides of the road as she walked. There was a riding academy nearby. Things had changed, but not unbeautifully. She could set an easel in any direction and there was something to paint.

She marched briskly, like a girl on her way to school, over the Bridgehampton bridge, with her straw bag over one shoulder, past swans and bush daisies growing wild among raspberries. She turned right at Ocean Road and walked past the umbrellaed farm stand stacked with corn and jars full of madly colored snapdragons, onward past dahlia and gladiola gardens, past farms rimmed by bowed giant sunflowers. She checked to be sure she had her wallet and her lease.

When she reached the monument on Montauk Highway, she found that Muller's Meat Market and Grocery had been turned into a large restaurant called Melon. She entered.

The place was noisy and crowded with New York City people. She sat down near a large window and ordered a salad, a glass of wine, and a glass of water. She ate quietly and slowly, finishing her food as the evening came on. The place was emptying out, so she ordered a cup of tea in order just to remain and watch the light die. When the tea came, she warmed her hands around the cup, noticing the automobile headlights softly going on. She sensed autumn in the purples and sepias of the twilight. People weren't wearing sweaters yet, but the sounds and scents in the cozy room were not of summer. By the calendar autumn was two weeks away, but anyone could tell by the tension of westbound traffic that summer had gone.

She bowed her head, staring into the traffic lights, touching her lips to her steaming cup. In a month fireplaces would be lit. Woodburning stoves would be started, and smoke would rise from the backs of horses in the morning.

Much *had* changed. It was never so busy, never so many cars. Still, the big lands were there. The long sweep of wind was still there. And the strange light, like the painters' light of Holland, the soft light of the French countryside, that light was right outside her window. She wondered if the real estate people could change that, too. Yes, she decided, of course they could. At that moment the streetlamps came alive, giving her a chill. And then, as if she had held the thought far off until now, the fact that her father was buried in Springs, so nearby, made her swallow hard. Thoughts of him had been hiding deep inside all day. Now, those streetlamps, softly going on, pried the lid off her memory. She was born in a rented cottage on Parsonage Lane, in an oasis of horse chestnut trees. From her window seat she could watch the Polish farmers driving their tractors into the barns behind their house. He hated the dark, her father.

On cloudy days he used to take her in that silly Spanish roadster of his, literally chasing after light, over dunes or through fields to find some clearing or water's edge to catch the sun before it slipped under the world.

She recalled his face so sharply. His crystalline amber eyes, his swarthy sun-browned face, blond eyebrows and lashes, wild yellow hair peppered with white, teeth always showing in an unconscious smile. "Daddy," she whispered into her cup, allowing the sentimentality of it. He had died when she was only twelve. Now she was about to return to those moments she had spent with him, but this time as a painter herself. She wanted to see what he had seen, to paint what he had painted, to know him that way. Once he had promised her a green sky.

"There, Katelyn," he said, pointing, "when that red stuff goes away, there's where the sky'll turn green." She sat on his knee, staring up into the scooped-out space which blinded her with horizontal rays that shot to her across the dark Wainscott earth, dark green, gray, damp colors; and when the rude pinkness disappeared and the farmlands dropped into an even darker sea of jade, that's when, just as he'd promised, the sky turned green, green as a lime ice cream soda, frosty green, from midocean to the far north. "Do you see it, Katelyn? Huh? Not blue, is it? It's sure as hell green. Tell me you see the green."

"I *see* it. Yes." That the sky was truly green frightened her, but she didn't let him know.

And one somber November evening, after days and days of rain, he found her sniffling, sitting on the window seat, looking out to the just-fallen night. She loved school, but was so lonely afterward. "You wanna go to a place where it's still daylight?" her father asked.

"Yes," she answered arrogantly, not believing him. He wrapped her up warmly and, against her mother's objections, he carried her out in the dark to the open Spanish roadster which had no windshield and no top whatever. He had no license; he drove the car illegally, trusting he couldn't be seen in the fields between the highway and the ocean. The old car had often been rained into, and there were still puddles on its rusty floor. The left mudguard was so loose that it flapped in the wind when they took off.

He ordered her to kneel on the seat and to lock her arms around his neck so the wind wouldn't knock her over. They were speeding almost madly down dirt roads, dwarfed by seven-foot-high winter wheat on either side, and when they turned into the cornfields, the wind tore at their hair, and the dry stalks screamed and whistled at the same time. He opened his mouth into the wind, yelling at her to look back at this color or ahead to that. His short gray hair made his yellow eyes electric. His red beard and silvery-blond eyebrows made him so terribly handsome. His skin was dark brown from painting outdoors all summer, and the tough yellow hairs on his arms curled up into little balls of spun gold.

He was right. It wasn't night there. All that winter wheat surrounding them radiated like an ocean of yellow light; the wheat must have been catching stray illumination from under the clouds, because it burned in spots even yellower. He yelled into the wind for her to see the neon line that quivered, hot and white, where the flannel sky met the wheat line. All this from the moving car. The speed filled her chest and the roadster's vibrations tickled her knees, going up through the bones of her legs, burning a hole right through her body and out of her mouth. She endured the rough pinch of his beard rather than loosen her grip on his neck. She could bounce out of the roadster any minute, like a beach ball, into the dusty wake.

Suddenly Peters Pond Road ran down to the Atlantic Ocean, which lay flat a quarter mile ahead. The dusty road split the farmlands in half. He pressed the accelerator to the floor, and they screeched downward at such a noisy speed that the car flushed hawks, red-winged blackbirds, and swallows on both sides, and the mudguard flapped like a broken wing. Sandwiched between the cloud blanket and the earth, they flew, squeezing out finally, up into the light, onto the wide sandy beach, into the last moment of day.

She refused to loosen her grip on his neck when they got out of the car. She loved him. Because he had kept his promise. She wanted to take the daylight home to that awful maroon-and-gray-wallpapered living room with its shabby dark-blue velvet chairs. She would lock all the windows and doors and trap the light inside forever. She was going to be a painter too. She knew it as he walked with her in his arms, cheek to cheek, talking every minute, never stopping. She was too young to understand all he used to say, but she held on to his words like fistfuls of confetti, tightly, in her little hands. Then, each night, alone in her bed, she would fling them up to the dark and watch them float down, like many-colored stars, onto her bedspread.

"Hey, see that? A mommie pheasant. Ain't she nice? Will ya hug me, honeybunch? Ouuuuu. You're strong. Now would ya gimme a kiss? C'mon. Ya love me, honey?"

He was the boat and she was the sailor. His hand was warm

and big, fat as a pillow under her legs, and she clung to his neck as if it were the ship's mast, catching his words with her mouth, breathing his breath, sweet with the odor of Chesterfield cigarettes.

"Ya like Potato Beach? Looka this flower. Ya make tea outta this. An' looka. Purple thistles, and here's a snapdragon. Now watch the dragon snap. See? Grrr. And here's a raspberry flower and here's a joe pie weed. Now let's take your hat off . . . 'n' this here scarf. There, dontcha feel that nice air in your hair? Ain't it almost summertime again, Katelyn darlin'? Didn't I show you a green sky? Didn't I show you day in the nighttime? Ya love me?"

Katelyn put down her teacup and pulled her sunglasses out of her straw bag. She put them on immediately to cover up her eyes, then opened her wallet with a snap.

"Waiter. Check, please?"

A corner of the recently folded white paper showed out of its leather sleeve. She pulled at it, opening it up.

Thomas Sheehan S. J.
Stella Maris
Montauk

Chapter Five

THE TAXI HAD LEFT TOM and his black suitcase on the cliffside road about two hundred feet above the Atlantic. A simple chain draped itself across a pebbled driveway, and a black arrow at his feet directed him downward. He stepped over the chain and followed the driveway down through tall pines. As he walked on a tilt, he could see luxurious homes hanging off the cliffs, partly hidden in vegetation, but Tom couldn't see the church or rectory until he reached the bottom, where the grounds opened into a hilly lawn overhanging the water. A stone church stood on his right, and a clapboard flat-roofed rectory on his left. He walked toward the white gravestone between the two buildings, solitary and tilted back in the close-cut grass. The inscription faced the water: *God is in the soul and the soul is in God, as the sea is in the fish and the fish is in the sea. St. Catherine of Siena.* At first glance, the church appeared to be one of those enormous European structures, but its size was only an illusion. It was actually miniature, probably capable of seating no more than one hundred people. But what it lacked in stature, it made up in its detail, such as the finest dark-blue stained-glass windows that Tom had ever seen.

The rectory could not have been a more inappropriate companion. It seemed constructed of spare parts, a clapboard boathouse with farmhouse windows, a front door of solid, thick glass that must have come from a bank or industrial building, complete with a glass cylinder for a handle and a lock at its base. All but the glass door was covered with white glossy deck paint. Cement pots filled with pink geraniums and languishing bloomed-out petunias did not help the building to come together in any way. There was no garage, and barely parking space for a half-dozen cars, but a breathtaking vision of the Atlantic Ocean spread out beyond it all, giving the illusion from any point that with a few giant steps one could be in Portugal. *Who are the parishioners of this cliffside parish?* Tom wondered. *Where do they come from? How do they get here? Where do they park their cars?*

Tom set down his black suitcase and wandered down toward the water. He passed through pines and beach roses, coming out at the white dunes. One moment's look at the ocean from that level brought to mind Peru. But the feeling of eyes upon him made him turn back up the grade. He climbed the steep rectory stairs to the back door, where he searched for a bell.

A short, blue-eyed woman in a black dress opened the door before he could ring. She was about fifty-five. Her face was a leaf that had grown in the dark—tender, wrinkled, pale. Her hair seemed dyed, a reddish color that did not complement her skin. Either something terrible had happened to her a moment ago, or the woman's expression was permanently fixed by an old disaster. The young girl had stayed behind in her face, frozen there, in a stubborn, suspicious expression. She wore no makeup, though her eyebrows were severely plucked. The black dress and the dyed hair seemed signals of a war between austerity and vanity that was going on inside her. Tom couldn't tell if the woman was hiding her sexuality or displaying it. The thick-heeled black work shoes made her seem either an old, shy nun or a young beauty ruined by incarceration.

"I'm Father Sheehan."

"I'm Muriel McClintock. Welcome," she said with a smile and a tilt of her head.

"Well, thank you, Muriel."

"Come in and I'll show you your room, unless you're hungry. Are you hungry?"

"No. Thank you." Tom looked down and carefully stepped up.

"Because if you are, I'll make an exception." There was an indefinable familiarity in her tone.

"You'll make a what?" Tom asked innocently.

"I'll make you something to *eat*." She emphasized the word *eat*. "Normally, you prepare your own snacks here."

"Oh. Okay."

"So do you want something to cat?" Wide, serious eyes, eyes that never blinked, waited his answer.

"No, thank you, Muriel. I would like to pay a visit to the church." A vague sadness started breaking up her face. "If I may," Tom added.

"Of course you may," she said. As if slighted, she turned and walked to the sink, stooped to pull a pot out from a drawer, pressed the drawer back with her ankle, and turned on the water faucet.

He left his bags with her in the kitchen and turned to the back steps, surprised to find the vast Atlantic at his feet. From the frail wooden stairs, the lawn seemed about to fall into the ocean. Its grassy knolls rose and tilted awkwardly, throwing him off balance. The shaky banister didn't help. He fastened his eyes to the clothesline and the small zinnia garden on his way down.

It took strength to pull open the heavy oak sacristy door. He walked slowly inside through the sacristy into the church. An old-fashioned marble altar rail with ornate brass gates was there, and no sign of a portable altar. This seemed strange in the light of Kruug's criticism of Granger.

Tom unlatched the brass gates of the altar rail and walked the middle aisle under the dome, which depicted the Blessed Virgin Mary's assumption into heaven out of the sea. She was flying upward like a rocket, through the center of a whirlpool, spinning as if she were inside a tornado of water, being sucked from the ocean floor into the sky. Tom looked up at the soles of her feet, imagining himself on the bottom. Whitecaps and waves were painted around the rim of the dome, and the eerie, dark-blue light of the blue stained glass made him feel truly under the sea.

Tom could feel each boom of surf vibrating through the cliffs. Near the Pacific, in Peru, there was a little stone hut that he and his friend Philip Behan used. Stella Maris Church smelled like that hut, of earth and stone and salt.

He was tired, not just from the bus ride, but from the year at St. Barnabas'. As he fell into a pew, his body surprised him, sagging with exhaustion. Above the altar, words jumped out at him in Latin: *Spiritus Dei ferebatur super aquas. Genesis 1:2.* And the Spirit of God moved over the waters. Where am I? he asked himself, surprised by his own question. His life had become such that it really didn't matter where he had come from anymore. He wished he could be everywhere at once, like God, so that there would be no place left to say good-bye to. He tried to say a few words of prayer, to send a message aloft, but he didn't have the spirit. Instead, he longed for darkness, not the kind one gets by closing his eyes, but for a sea of blackness in which the mind is loose to chart off new boundaries. The church did have one confession booth, behind him, in the rear. Its archways were draped with plum-colored velvet. It was dark in there. He felt foolish about his impulse to go and stand inside the booth, but he obeyed it in spite of himself, walking to the confessional and, with a little courage, pulling aside the deep velvet and stepping into the infinite dark.

There, facing the curtain, he listened for his own breath and let his eyes remain open, seeing nothing. He gave in to the floating feeling, wishing his body could follow his mind up, into the limitless darkness in search of new visions, new hopes. The woman on the bus appeared, her face and hair as wide as a galaxy overhead. An attractive woman. Yes. No harm admitting that. Beautiful, with her smile, her kind eyes. *How old and familiar woman is to the world. Yet women will remain always new to me.* Yes.

Her name was Snow. The word appeared white, disintegrating into a thousand flakes floating downward, touching his face. Cool. He imagined enlargements of frost crystals, complex, symmetrical, like symbols fallen from the heaven beyond heaven, lighting on his eyes. Goosebumps lifted the hair on his arms. He heard a click. A draft had entered the church. The curtain moved.

He leaned forward, placing his eye into the tiny slit of light, seeing into the church. No one. Sunset had turned the blue stained-glass windows into monstrous purple jewels. Tom leaned back into his darkness. Kruug had not lied. The ocean *was* close enough to hear. He stretched once again to see through the curtain space, but caught only the Blessed Virgin Mary standing above the main altar. She seemed to hover there, dressed in folds of blue and cream, standing barefoot on the head of the serpent, smiling down, offering the insides of her hands, palms turned to the world, like the woman on the bus, except that the statue focused intently upon him, unflinchingly, steadily, with unfathomable caring. *"Mary, Mother of God, help me."* He could hear his own whispers in the little box. *"I need you closer to me, Blessed Virgin."*

The large oak door of the sacristy slammed closed. Tom pulled back. Someone was in the church. He didn't want to be caught behind the confessional curtain. He heard footsteps, soft, squeaky, then through the slit he caught sight of a priest, a tall black-haired man, younger than himself, walking across the sanctuary. The priest wore a black cassock; his feet were sneakered in white. White trousers flashed under the black folds, and over his shoulder he carried what Tom made out to be a water ski, its gleaming steel keel facing up. The priest looked about suspiciously as he unhinged the seat of the sedilia, the bench that seats the celebrants of high mass. He placed the ski carefully inside. Tom's breathing was too loud but he couldn't control it. He stepped back deeper into the box and the floor squeaked. The priest in the white sneakers straightened up, startled, letting the seat cover slam with a crack that sent dust swirling into the sunbeams over his head. Tom dreaded the man's finding him in an empty confessional, on the penitents' side. He stopped breathing entirely behind the velvet curtain as the dark-haired priest approached to investigate, walking slowly up to the confessional facing the curtain. Tom could not help seeing the man's eyes clearly through the slit, dark as ripe olives, the quick eyes of a hurdle jumper, unrelaxed and alert. His hair was so black it made his olive skin seem pale. He was exactly Tom's height, and the skin around the man's eyes was darker than the rest of his face, like a Turk's, but a sharp nose and chin brought to mind one of those old oil–painted Florentine princes. His neck and shoulders were thick, yet he was trim. His eyebrows were sharply silken and black, and though he was closely shaved, the bluish shadow of his beard was evident. *He must be Buoncuore,* Tom thought, relieved that the priest was walking away. When the heavy sacristy door closed with a thud, the ringing silence of the church returned, and Tom came out from behind the curtain.

"There are no keys to the rooms here," Muriel told Tom in the kitchen. "You lock your door from the inside. There's a phone in the hallway and one in Monsignor's room. You can ask for a private phone when he gets back. The other one isn't allowed one, but you're not in his category. Kindly tell me in advance if you're in or out for a meal so I can take something out of the freezer." Her eyes refused to stay with his very long; she seemed to be reading her words from a card.

The thick glass front door slammed, vibrating the frail windows. Muriel's eyes widened. "Watch out. Here he comes," she whispered with sudden intimacy.

"Who?" Tom bent to her.

"Buoncuore." Her lungs made the sound.

The wooden floors creaked under the hallway rug. Then the same priest Tom had just seen appeared in the kitchen doorway. This time the man's eyes caught onto Tom's, holding for several seconds, but he continued down the hall without speaking and disappeared softly behind his door, which closed with a tiny click. Muriel's smile confused him.

"Why didn't you introduce us?" Tom asked.

"Why didn't you introduce yourself?" she asked back with ready indignation. Her smile dissolved into an expression of wonderment as if the vision of the priest had entertained her. It was as if a zebra had just entered her house, not a man, as if a four-legged beast had just walked in on her rug in the hallway. She turned and carried her amusement into the kitchen.

That evening Tom ate alone in the dining room. Later, he lay down in his room and fell asleep. Around ten the phone rang in the hallway, waking him. Two rings. Then it stopped. He gradually became conscious of having a headache, so he lifted himself from the bed and pushed groggily into the bathroom, feeling for a wall switch. When he flipped it, the white-tiled bathroom caved in on his eyes. One whole wall was mirror. His entire body was reflected. With his hand shading his eyes and trying to ignore his image, he pulled open the medicine-cabinet door. The wall mirror made the room twice its size, hospital-like; it smelled of Lysol and pine. No aspirin. He was thirsty for something sweet, like orange juice or soda pop. He washed his face and walked back to the bedroom, drying off. He reached for the doorknob to the hallway but whispers stopped him.

"Where'd you get the shit this time, Zimmie, from that creep doctor in Kings County? What's his name? Yes, I'm gonna rat on him; he's killing you." A pause. "Oh, yeah? And what happens to your kids if you cash in your chips? Tomorrow you call the center." Pause. "Because you've *got* no one else, Zimmie. I'm out of it, I told you." Pause. "Easy. Easy. Go ahead and cry." Pause. "Who, me? Sure, I pray for you. That's all I got to do all day."

Tom caught himself listening and immediately went back into the bathroom. Minutes later, he opened the hallway door, peeked into its emptiness, and stepped out. He tiptoed barefoot on the rug toward the dark kitchen. A moonlit window shone near the refrigerator, guiding him inside. He felt for a light switch, but had no luck this time, so he walked cautiously on the waxed linoleum into the middle of the room. Just as his fingers found the refrigerator handle, a voice sprang out of the dark behind him.

"Somebody's in this room with you, Father."

Tom yanked the refrigerator door open. Its light caught Buoncuore leaning against the counter, drinking milk, his bare feet crossed, dressed in a bathrobe.

"Gene Buoncuore." The man's hand reached out. Tom reached and squeezed it. Buoncuore had power to spare.

"Tom Sheehan."

"I figured." The black-eyed priest looked down at his own bare feet. Tom turned and found apple juice in the refrigerator. Gene reached for a glass and handed it to him.

"Thanks."

"What did you think of Princess Brillo?" Gene asked as Tom poured.

"Who?"

"Muriel McClintock." He pronounced her name with mock precision.

"She's . . . interesting."

"Uh huh," Gene said, swallowing some milk.

"She seemed a little on edge, or was it my imagination?" Tom asked.

"Muriel likes the edge. Don't mind Muriel. The boss thinks she's a sweetheart, so don't ever knock her."

"Then here's to sweet Muriel McClintock and Montauk." Tom lifted his glass.

Buoncuore held back. "Unh-huh. Here's to *you*, jebbie. Welcome."

"Thanks." When Tom closed the refrigerator door, the moon's easy light expanded the room.

Tom liked Gene's voice. His Brooklyn accent reminded him of the Corey kids and the altar boys of St. Barnabas'.

"How'd you know I was a Jesuit?" Tom asked.

"Kruug warned me and Muriel this morning by phone." Gene smiled for a few steady seconds. "What did he tell you about *me?*" Gene asked, lifting milk to his lips.

"Nothing much." Tom shrugged.

"Surprising."

"Just something about your not being able to work."

"I figured." Buoncuore looked out the window. "Actually my faculties are suspended."

"Oh?"

"Can't say mass. Can't hear confessions. Can't see my people. They phone me from Brooklyn. I just got a call."

"So you're not officially stationed here?" Tom asked.

"Stationed? Nothing so mild. I'm in custody, you might say. I'm a criminal doing time here with the priest doctor." He smiled. "That's what they call Kruug."

"He seems like an okay enough guy."

"He's Kruug. There's nothing to compare him to." Gene pushed away from the counter. "Did Kruug fill you in on what crime I committed? Or are you wondering?" Gene said over-defensively.

"Not interested," Tom said, taking his last gulp of juice. He put down his glass and smiled at Gene, smacking his lips a little arrogantly. Gene held the Jesuit's eyes. Tom let him have them without a blink.

"Answer me something, jebbie."

"Shoot."

"Were you in that church today when I stashed the water ski in the sedilia?"

Tom hesitated. "Yes, I was."

"Standing in the confession box?"

"Right."

"Do I have to put you under the seal to keep you from spilling the beans about that water ski? How do I get you to keep your mouth shut?"

"By promising you won't ask me what I was doing standing in the confession box." Tom smiled.

"It's a deal." Buoncuore showed a row of white teeth. "Now I'm curious. What the hell *were* you doing there?"

"Unh-uh." Tom threw out his right hand. Buoncuore grabbed it. The door clicked open in the hallway, throwing a javelin of light onto the rug. Gene tiptoed to the doorway. Then the light disappeared.

"It was Muriel." Gene gestured with his head. "Answer me something else now."

"What?" Tom folded his arms.

"What're we drinking milk in the dark for when there's a whole hour of Labor Day left to celebrate out there?"

"Beats me," Tom shrugged.

"C'mon. I'll buy you a drink at the Trail's End."

"Do we wear our suits and collars?"

"I do," Gene said with a smirk, "and Muriel checks."

It said TRAIL'S END RESTAURANT in red neon across the roof of a simple white-shingled house. Aquamarine trim on door and windows jumped out, seemingly also electrified. Night had descended behind the place like a musky velvet curtain that had fallen on summer. Stray headlights sneaked under the curtain escaping the oncoming winter.

There was one large room with a bar and upright piano. Tables and chairs were the kitchen type, painted a 1930s shade of pea green. A potted palm stood in each corner, and yellow crepe paper streamers crisscrossed overhead. Only one customer was in the place, an old woman at the bar, sitting cross-legged on a black bamboo stool, dressed in a tight leopard-print dress. She clicked open the wood frame of a fake-zebra pocketbook. A blue butane flame lit the tip of her cigarette. She sucked until a red glow formed, then, dropping the lighter and bag on the bar, she lifted one hand to catch the stray hairs of her upsweep, while her other hand lifted the glass to her lips, way back, so that the olive rolled into her mouth.

"Good evening, Fathers," the bartender said softly, coming toward them with glasses of water.

The woman turned, her drunken eyes missing them as they went to a table near a window.

"We have roast duck, Long Island baked potatoes . . . "

"Just a beer, please," Buoncuore said.

"Happy New Year," the woman shouted, sliding off her stool, walking shakily toward the screen door and pulling it open.

Tom asked for a Scotch and water.

"And happy . . . " She slammed the screen door behind her. "Happy Labor Day." Her voice sank as she addressed the whole

town which stretched out below her. "All you poor slavin'
motherfuckers. All I got to keep me warm this winter is a
goddam cigarette lighter. How d'ya like that?"

"Is Montauk really the end of a trail?" Tom asked with a
smile.

"It's the end of a long peninsula with the Atlantic Ocean on
all sides, except where all those headlights are going, to New
York City. Europe's over there." Buoncuore pointed. "Brazil's
that way, and over there's Connecticut, a ferry hop."

"I was brought up in Waterford."

"Well, the ferry takes you right next to Waterford, to New
London," Gene offered.

"I know." Tom stared, drifting in his mind. He saw himself
in sweat socks, brown corduroys, and soft moccasins. He smelled
yellow stuffing and roast chicken on the stove of the Sheehan
apartment on Elm, not far from the five-and-dime where his
mom worked.

"You okay?" Buoncuore asked.

"Sure," Tom answered, looking into his glass of water. "With
all these summer people leaving, is there going to be any work
for us in Montauk?"

"St. Theresa's is the real parish here. Stella Maris is just a toy.
Some rich woman built it in the thirties as her private chapel.
Now she's buried there, looking out to the ocean. Bequeathed it
to the diocese. The highway's too dangerous for parking cars. The
place is a white elephant, something the bishop threw to Kruug
till some big pastor dies. But Kruug's so gung-ho, he wants to
turn the place into St. Peter's."

"What are our duties?"

"Me? To sit on my hands. You've got the First Holy Communion class of St. Theresa's on Friday. You give the kids their test.
Blake is on vacation."

"Then what?" Tom asked.

"You relax till Kruug comes back."

"He wants me to take a vacation."

"Hold him to it."

The bartender put down their drinks.

"Cheers."

"What's your opinion of Kruug?" Tom asked cautiously, touching Gene's beer glass.

Buoncuore sipped, wiped his lips, then shook his head. "You're asking the wrong guy."

"Why's that?"

"He thinks he's a healer. He sees me as his diseased patient, and we can never negotiate around these preformed definitions of his. He comes down on me like a tough reformer, obsessive about my wearing the black suit and collar. Did you know he's a retired Navy Chaplain?"

"No." Tom looked up in surprise.

"Oh, yeah. He leaves his door open to check if I'm in my 'priestly uniform' when I go out. Discipline is my medicine. He's got Muriel on my back, which insults me more than anything. Now you, you can wear a clown outfit as far as he's concerned, but me, this is my treatment because I'm a bad priest. The conservatives are coming back in hordes. Sometimes I ignore them both and walk out dressed the way I feel like. But now he found out about my boat and my water-skiing the other day, so he's going to tighten the screws."

"You own a boat?"

"A seventeen-foot lapstrake with a forty-five horse." Gene smiled.

"Are you some kind of water-ski champ?"

Gene laughed. "The kids in Brooklyn gave me this ski two years ago because once in a sermon I said I used to dream of being a water-ski star."

"Did you really?"

"Well, yeah." He laughed. "But I was fourteen. So here I had this water ski with my initials carved into it, fifteen years too late, but I figured: Let me try the damn thing out. I bought a boat cheap and I used to fool around over by the Throgs Neck Bridge with the parish kids. When I came here, I said what the hell, and I drove the damn thing through Shinnecock, into Sag Harbor, all the way here, and docked it. Kruug nearly had a heart attack when he found out. He's ordered me to get rid of it." Buoncuore wore an odd smile. The man was prone to mischief. No doubt about that. "I hide the ski in the sedilia. He sits on it at high mass and doesn't even know it."

"But don't you need a partner to water-ski? Who drives the boat?"

"It drives itself."

"Of course you're kidding."

"No. I fix the rudder, throw her into high, and jump into the water."

"But . . . "

"I go around in a big circle." Buoncuore's eyes flashed bashfully. His grin widened. He loved adventure.

"But, how does the boat stop itself? Isn't it dangerous? You . . . you're pulling my leg."

"Of course I am." Buoncuore laughed. "No. I pay the dock boy to drive the boat." Tom shook his head and took a sip of his drink.

"But you're not going to continue this skiing under the circumstances?"

"Why not?"

"You intend to keep it up?"

"Sure I do." Buoncuore's smile weakened.

"Then you ought to hide that ski somewhere else."

"No. He'd see it in the car. If I leave it in the boat, it gets ripped off. The marina won't take responsibility. If I bring it into the rectory, Muriel will scream like something in a tree." Gene leaned over the table, closer to Tom. "I wasn't born to sit on my ass. My father is a businessman, you know? But his father was a bricklayer. Look at my hands. Do these look like they were designed to be sat on?" When he leaned back, his smile melted into seriousness. He grabbed Tom's plastic drink stirrer.

"Maybe we'll have an early winter." Tom tried to lighten up Gene.

"What the hell does that mean?"

"You can't ski on ice." Tom smiled.

Buoncuore didn't appreciate the little joke. He drank the rest of his beer and reached for his wallet. "Let's beat it." Tom slugged down his Scotch.

When the two were out on the wooden porch of the restaurant, Tom grabbed Gene's jacket sleeve. Gene, already one step below Tom, turned with a bewildered expression.

"Whatsamatta?" The hurdle jumper's eyes danced.

"I'm sorry," Tom whispered.

Gene pretended surprise. "For what?"

"For being so glib in there. I was only trying to be funny like you, but I don't have your talent, obviously."

A dimple appeared at the corner of Buoncuore's mouth. The anger in his eyes dissolved. "How would you like to see the lights of your hometown?" He jingled the car keys. Tom looked at his watch.

"Sure."

"Here." Gene dumped the keys in his hand. "You drive."

It was midnight and still the western horizon seemed to smolder from the long-burned-out day. The moon threw rude silver across the waters. Gene pointed down at his little boat. Its name, *Pssst!*, was painted on the stern above a yellow lightning-like bolt, the kind in the Captain Marvel comics. A clean white outboard tilted out of the water, and two red gas tanks, connected by a chain, were locked to the mahogany seat.

"See that yellow string of lights way out there?" Gene pointed. "That's Connecticut."

Tom squinted, imagining cool midnight on Waterford's quiet streets. "I shouldn't put off going," he said wistfully.

"Let's go tomorrow."

Tom looked at Gene. "Is there any problem with your going?"

"Not if I wear my black suit."

"Well then, maybe later on in the week we'll go."

"Terrific." Gene looked up to the stars. "You know what my favorite vestment is . . . that a priest wears?"

"The alb?" Tom guessed, pulling his eyes away from the lights of Connecticut.

"A T-shirt."

"*A T-shirt?*"

"Yes. You take all the copes and cassocks away from us priests, the black suits, black rabats, and we're left standing there in T-shirts just like every other poor jerk. We're part of the people again. Some of the younger priests are into the black. They say it gives us identity. Well, I don't know what identity's got to do with work. People know who you are by what you give them to remember you by. Right? Besides, I don't know what's expected of me when I'm supposed to look so different from John Doe."

"You should have known Moonghost," Tom said softly.

"Moonghost? That's a person?"

"He was a friend of mine in Peru who wore a white cassock all the time."

"A priest?"

"Yes. At night it made him shine like a ghost, floating through the barrios in that white cassock. The Indians called him Fantasma, El Fantasma de la Luna, the ghost from the moon. Others called him Espirituluna, moon spirit. I just called him Philip."

"He was a gent like us?"

"Oh, yes. But that cassock helped make him more."

"You miss Peru, don't you?" Gene asked, examining the Jesuit's eyes.

"I don't know," Tom said with a shrug and a wrinkling brow.

"This fellow with the white cassock, where's he now?"

"He's not in Peru anymore." Tom's eyes dropped down to the two red gas tanks in Gene's boat. "Are you proposing that we go to Connecticut in this *canoe?*" Tom clearly wanted the subject changed.

"Those lights are deceiving. It's a two-hour hop—by ferry." Gene looked right into the moon and spoke. "I think I'd really like the work in one of those barrios. But I'd settle for just being able to go back to Brooklyn." When Gene's eyes came down, he was surprised to catch the Jesuit looking at him. "What are you starin' at?" he asked.

"Somebody I wish I had a few solutions for."

"Nice. Nice sentiment, Sheehan. For that you get Montauk's

grand tour tomorrow. Is that a deal?"

"Deal."

Gene pulled him by the arm toward the car. He got into the driver's seat but didn't turn the key, sitting motionless, looking through the moon-streaked windshield.

"Why do they call it Labor Day?" he asked in a tired voice.

"Guess it's a free day for the work force." Tom shrugged.

"Sounds like a Russian idea." He paused. "Good-bye, summer. Hate to see you go, although I don't know why that is." He turned the key.

"Why *is* it?" Tom asked as the engine roared.

Gene switched on the headlights. "I don't know. Since I was a kid . . . maybe it's going back to school . . . it's just like the world is doing to you what everybody else does, making you think you've got something, then taking it away from you. Labor Day must be the law of the universe." The car moved slowly backward.

"Probably *is* the law of the universe," Tom said without conviction.

"Then why are *we* asked to give so much and never take anything back?" Gene's deep anger showed.

"I don't know," Tom answered.

Gene put the car into drive. "They should change the name of Labor Day. Call it something else. I'm bored with Labor Days." Gene spoke as if he were alone, in an almost inaudible tone.

The car rolled slowly over the stones in the lot, then turned smoothly left, onto the silver asphalt, zooming uphill away from the bay, toward the ocean.

At noontime the next day they picnicked for lunch in a dune bowl under the radar ear six miles east of Stella Maris. Stripped to the waist, they sat on towels, cross-legged and squinting into the intense light. The ocean stretched below them, like a long blue giant lying facedown. After they had oiled their bodies and eaten their last pieces of fruit, a silence enveloped them, an assumption of intimacy, a kind of instinctive cooperation with each other's privacy. But Tom cheated when Gene closed his eyes. He watched him lying in the sun, his hurdle jumper's pupils moving rapidly under his lids.

That night Gene took the parish car and didn't return until very late. The next morning, when Tom finished his mass, he noticed that Gene and the car were gone again. Tom spent the day in his room. After dinner, he walked down to the ocean's edge, in his cassock. Night was coming on fast.

From the beach, Montauk appeared, a heavenly city at night. Single-engine planes floated over the ocean, twinkling and blinking, while the radio of a fishing boat sent the voice of James Taylor up to the stars.

In my mind I'm gone to Carolina . . .

When Tom climbed back, up through pines onto the lawn, the rectory appeared like a long ghost ship, glowing white on pale-blue grass in the dark.

His bedroom was dark. He didn't bother to turn on a light. He checked the lock, double-bolting himself inside. Moonlight strayed in from behind the drapes. He walked to the window and leaned upon its frame. Now Barbra Streisand was singing over the ocean. He closed his eyes in the dark. He saw the room without seeing: the high single bed, its blue coverlet, the blond wooden crucifix, the pin-dotted wallpaper. But it was not the soft booms of the Atlantic he heard. It was the great western ocean, the Pacific, crashing far away in his mind. He took from his wallet a folded slip of paper, which he opened as if he could read in the darkness. He had its contents memorized. He rubbed his thumb softly over the words:

He said he longed for short, snowy days and long nights. He said he desired the killing cold, the kind that purifies the air and kills the mosquitoes. He wanted loneliness, to work by himself, and to read at night in a chair, by incandescent light.

Tom left the paper and his wallet on the windowsill and let himself fall down on his bed. The Pacific was louder now. He could imagine its horizons, its cold, dark-green color at that time of year when migrations of seals and whales convene to meet the coolness of the Humboldt Current, as it rises, northward, up from the Antarctic. So immense, so bountiful, was the silence of those sea villages in those days, Pisco, Punta Hermosa, places so unlike the little village of Montauk with its videogame rooms, its busy motels and pizza parlors. He saw the pure-white guano islands, and the glittering city of Lima, the mission of Christ the King, its dusty quadrangle with its few gnarled umbrella trees for shade. Head House, the priests called it. Soup kitchen, infirmary, dining rooms, offices and garages, and priests' quarters on the second floor.

His first six months of priesthood were more difficult than his time with Granger. Peru was a place of extremes, of change, of earthquakes and magic. Tom spent ten hours a day manning a switchboard in a dismal plaster room over a garage, typing reports and letters for a superior he saw only minutes each day. He spent his free time praying the Divine Office, meditating, and looking half fearfully out the windows to the distant hills where the poor waited to be served—Río Rimac, San Agustín, and the San Martín *barriadas.* He tried to get to know some of the priests who came to the common room. Although they were of various orders, they were friendly enough, but veteran missioners were independent creatures, even with their own kind. One priest, an Australian they called Moonghost, rarely even appeared at the common room. Tom knew of him from stories the Indians at Head House had told. El Fantasma de la Luna, they called him. Ghost of the Moon. Some of the elegant Limeños called him Espirituluna, but all the English-speaking priests called him Moonghost.

Rumors circulated constantly about the Australian. The Head House housekeeper, Marta, said he had magical powers because he prayed to the sun god, and the gods of the Indians that were not Christian. Jealous priests said he kept a woman in a stone house at the ocean and that he had had a child with her. But Marta swore on El Señor de los Temblores that she knew it wasn't true, that he was blessed of God because he never needed sleep; he was the saint of the open eyes, an angel walking on the earth. At night, she said, one could see him in the *barriadas* in his white cassock, luring the poor children out of their shanties. They would pet his white cassock as though it were the skin of a rare holy beast, and he would let them snatch packets of sugar from his hands.

When Tom asked Monsignor DeSilva, the diocesan superior of Head House, about Moonghost, the monsignor spoke almost as passionately. The rich, the poor, the Spanish, the Indians— Moonghost could speak their language. He stayed away from other priests, preferring to work alone. He was once of the Columban Order, but now he took his orders directly from Rome. His superior was no less than the Pope himself. He was one of the most independent missioners in the Catholic Church.

Tom soon began waking at dawn to watch Moonghost's jeep rattle into the quadrangle from wherever the priest had spent the night. Marta said sometimes he went too far away, because he returned to the quadrangle with an empty tank of gas. After a number of months Tom had developed the habit of waking in time to catch his returning. The gas station was near his window. Some mornings, through the slits in the shutter, he saw the man drenched in sweat, his white cassock open at the chest, his eyes reflecting the pink light of dawn.

One morning the jeep backfired under the window. Tom jumped up and banged open the shutters. Below stood the Australian, looking up and lighting a cigarette. Tom could see that the yellow mission bus had taken the jeep's place, blocking the pump.

"Morning." The Australian looked up worriedly at Tom. "Hope this heap didn't wake you."

"Oh, no, Father. Not at all. I . . . my name is Tom Sheehan." He couldn't believe he was talking to Marta's very Fantasma.

"Don't I see you manipulating those shutters every morning? I do try to keep this heap quiet."

"No trouble, Father."

"Do I *wake* you?"

"I depend on it. Honestly."

"You do?" The Australian reacted shyly.

"Or else I'd sleep till noon." Tom laughed.

The priest held a finger to his lips to remind Tom that others were asleep. "You drink coffee?"

"Absolutely," Tom whispered.

"I'll fix you a cup," the Australian said, walking off.

Tom closed the shutters, finding it impossible to get them back into their proper positions. He didn't know what Moonghost meant, whether Tom was to join him or if the man intended to come back with the coffee. Tom jumped into his black pants anyway, forgetting his underwear. He put an arm through one sleeve of his cassock and ran barefoot down the stairs, into the dusty quadrangle. He zippered up his pants as he followed the man in the white cassock toward the common room.

It was a large screened-in area, quite dusty and unkempt. Two shabby red velvet couches sat on either side of a low table piled with American and Spanish-language magazines.

"It's odd that they call you Moonghost," Tom said, hoping the man wouldn't be offended.

"It's because I'm a night creature." The man smiled, looking carefully at Tom. "My name's only Behan, by the way, Philip Behan." He stretched out a large brown hand, catching Tom's eyes and holding them for just a second. Moonghost scooped coffee into the coffeemaker. "Sit," he ordered. Tom sank into the red couch as Moonghost worked at the counter. "Milk? Sugar?" Moonghost asked.

"No, thanks," Tom answered. It fascinated him to watch the priest. The man was in excellent physical shape. Tom guessed him to be in his mid-forties. His hands were so big that objects became miniature when he touched them. He was monklike in the way he picked up functional objects and put them down, in a respecting way that validated them. He twirled the cover onto the milk jar and placed it back in the refrigerator, offered Tom a cup with its handle facing out, then dropped into the center of the opposite couch facing Tom. The Australian pulled his cassock up, revealing white cotton trousers underneath, very wrinkled, but very clean. At last, his eyes held still.

"You jebbies don't wear whites, do you?" Moonghost gulped coffee, then put his cup down among the magazines. He threw his feet up on a pile of papers and stretched his hands behind his neck.

"Jesuits wear white in Africa, I think," Tom answered.

"I only like 'em 'cause you can wash 'em. It feels good to put on everything clean. You can't wash black gabardine."

"True." Tom smiled.

"I have a jebbie-style white I can give to you, if you'd like it."

"You do?" Tom knew he would be embarrassed to wear the white cassock.

"Too tight in my shoulders. Be glad to let you have it."

"Do you really mean it?" Tom acted enthusiastic, but he really wanted a way out.

"Do I *mean* it? What the hell you think I'm sayin' it for?" Moonghost smiled with a little annoyance.

Tom tried to laugh. "We'll look like two popes walking around here," Tom said.

"I can't bother with how I look to others," Moonghost responded rather flatly. He swallowed the last of his coffee and was up for a fresh cup.

"More?" he asked Tom.

"No, thanks." Tom hadn't had his first sip. He drank as Moonghost shuffled around the dusty floor behind him. Tom enjoyed being close to the legendary man, but it also made him anxious. When Moonghost fell before him again into the opposite couch, Tom noticed the gray curling as his hair was drying. The man's eyes were quite blue. Thick white eyelashes sharpened their color. But the eyes were peering intently at Tom. He wanted to shrink. He knew his face was pale. Even in summer when he lifeguarded back home, his skin had never taken on that dark tan, and his dark hair always made him seem whiter.

What Moonghost saw, though, was a good-looking young man with a naiveté and a sense of humor that were refreshing, whose hair was so richly brown it forced one to think of chestnut mares. The Jesuit had long legs. Thick, athletic knees showed through his black cassock, and his wide wrists were wrapped in dark hair which showed out the cuffs of his sleeves.

"Why do you work at night?" Tom asked.

"Because I'm an insomniac," Philip answered simply. "I do work in the day mostly. It's not always work with me."

"Where do you go at night when you come home with an empty gas tank?" Tom smiled mischievously.

"That's a secret." Moonghost looked away.

"You have a woman and child somewhere in the jungle, they say," Tom dared to throw the rumor up.

"There *is* something out there, actually, but it's not animal." The man blushed, but he was obviously enjoying Tom.

"Let me guess," Tom interrupted. "It's a temple."

"Good heavens, no."

"A shack?"

"Where are you from? And stop acting so American before I change my mind about you."

"I'm from a place called Connecticut." Tom smiled, a little embarrassed.

"Well, I'm from a haunt in New South Wales called Broken Hill. And what of Peru? Are you at home here?"

"Frankly, I'm not in love with it."

"That's sad."

"Really?"

"Yes, because Peru can be deeply loved if she is right for you. Peru is like Eden after the fall, always scrambling to rise after a confusion. But she seems never to lose everything. There are hints that paradise did exist somewhere near here. One or two condors, with their ten-foot wingspans, still rule the place like gods overhead, immune to the *terremotos*."

"*Terremotos?*"

"Earthquakes. They are a part of life here. You will rarely see lightning, and rarely rain; it is a desert place. Trees are strangers here, but the dryness is sweet. You can learn from it. Death is not sticky here."

"Not sticky?"

"You'll see." His eyes went to the door. "Death and life are close friends here. They say that dust and breath are lovers in this part of Peru. There is no enmity between life and death here."

"You speak like a poet."

"Thank you."

"*¿Quales son sus escritores favoritos en español?*" He surprised Tom with Spanish.

"*San Juan de la Cruz, Cervantes,*" Tom answered. "*¿Y usted?*"

"I like this new writer, Gabriel Garcia Marquez." He smiled. "And Pablo Neruda, the Chilean poet, among others. About time they sent an American who speaks Spanish." Moonghost looked hard at the Jesuit and gently bit his lip. "Are you one of those people who needs his eight hours?" he asked cautiously.

"Not necessarily." Tom tried to hide a certain growing excitement. "Why?"

"Well, I don't know. Some night, perhaps, you'd like to come ride with me, and see the mystery for yourself."

"Are you serious?"

"My God, man! Stop being so incredulous. Yes. And I promise no temples, only that it would be a hell of a drive."

"Well, I'm definitely game." Tom tried to sound not too eager.

"Next day you'll be a little tired."

"All I have to do is answer phones." Tom shrugged.

"Let's say eight then?"

By eight-fifteen they were locking horns with a west wind. The sun had melted to their right, and on their left a monstrous white transparent moon was climbing, like a spirit, over the wall of the earth to peer down at its tiny gardens. Tom clung to the roll bar, because the road seemed to have dropped out in the sunset's glare. It felt like flying, into an icy pink-and-yellow horizon. Tom fastened his eyes to the giant white moon.

One could detect the fresh dryness of another day in the wind. It came from afar. Tom sensed wildness, an occult energy in the treeless landscape, and felt queasy to be borne so swiftly into the savage infinity of the horizon. He clung to the roll bar as his cassock flapped violently against his body, whipping around his legs like a black flag flying, while the snowy moon hung close enough to his cheek to burn it. He was glad to be enveloped in all that black fabric. Its weightiness anchored him against the noisy wind, engulfed him safely in darkness. *That is why a priest wears black,* thought Tom, *to anchor him in the infinite.*

He clung to the roll bar with one hand, to the windshield with the other, while his eyes ate up distances and the changing light. Purply, dark night arrived rapidly, turning his mind into an amphitheater of blue and iridescent green. He closed his eyes and saw his blood circulating, pink and lavender inside him. Occasionally, he drifted to sleep, but the wind kept slapping him awake.

By midnight the colors had all died inside him, and the jeep came to a stop. The moon, now small and sharp as a light bulb overhead, turned the land gray and the ocean silver. Waves boomed ominously nearby. Moonghost walked toward a stone building that stood next to a flagpole. He opened its rusty iron door and pushed inside. A piece of material came flying out of the dark, hitting Tom in the face. It was a bathing suit. Then out came a huge white tongue, ten feet long, gleaming like a spaceship coming into the moonlight. Moonghost was under the thing, holding it aloft, pointing it toward the sky.

"What is it?" Tom fell back in surprise.

"A surfboard." Moonghost dropped it on the grass. "Put on your suit, mate."

Tom obeyed, going into the dark stone building to do so, while Moonghost raised a white flag up on the pole. He stripped in the cold dark place, putting on the suit with disappointment. He hadn't even decided if he wanted to swim at this hour in the strange Pacific; Moonghost might have forewarned him. He was a good swimmer, but he had never surfed. He felt on edge and at the mercy of the energetic Australian who had turned out to be quite human after all.

"Do you surf?" Moonghost asked matter-of-factly as they

walked toward the thundering ocean.

"No. I'll watch," Tom said solidly.

"Oh, I'm sorry you feel that way," Moonghost answered. "I won't be long then. I'll join you back here." He entered the water without hesitation, leaving Tom watching on the shore. The man and his board breasted the crumbling whiteness and soon he was on his knees, paddling through flanks of foam into flat, open water, into the silver path of the moon.

What am I doing on this beach? Tom asked himself, suddenly annoyed by his isolation. Here he felt more lost than when answering phones back at the Head House. Peru was incomprehensible; he couldn't grasp the place. Geography was one of his blindnesses, and he felt utterly lost on the strange coastline. Tom made the Australian the focus of his annoyance, although it wasn't easy to spot a man in all that shimmering water. The holy man whom they nicknamed Moonghost turned out to be nothing more than a tall Aussie jock named Philip, who had just made Tom a captive witness to his prowess with a surfboard. Was this what he was losing sleep for?

He walked dejectedly toward a string of rocks shaped like whales and walruses crawling up to the yellow cliffs beyond the sand. The cliffs' vegetation shone metallic, bluish in the hard light. Then in the distance, something white sprung out of the water, startling him. It was the surfboard, flying up like a leaf, catching moonlight. A thrashing figure swam to it, and in no time the man and the board were coming out of the water, toward the rocks. Man and board seemed a propeller, spinning, then disappearing, as they sank to the sand.

When Tom reached them, Moonghost was lying on top of the board with his hands locked behind his neck.

"Hello." His heart pounded visibly inside his chest as water ran off him like quicksilver. "It's daylight, for want of a better word." He squinted at the moon.

"Yes, it's very bright now."

"Wouldn't that make you more comfortable about trying to surf?" Moonghost said seriously, sitting up.

"I couldn't. I'm kind of disoriented, actually."

"I'll bet we can give you a ride without getting you wet. Seriously. C'mon, I'll not get more than two drops on you." Moonghost stood up, grabbing the board and carrying it down toward the water. He slammed the board flat onto the wet sand, then called to Tom to come kneel upon it.

"No, thanks." Tom held back with folded arms.

"I'll lift you *both*—you and the board—onto the water."

"What then?"

"Then you'll kneel up front, here, and I'll fall on the rear and paddle us out a short way. We turn. We stand and come back. It's easy."

"What if I'm exceptionally clumsy?" Tom came forward and looked down at the board.

"I'll be holding you. You just stand rigid and still, and I'll hold you like this, by your shoulders, from behind, so's I can steer your weight. You won't get dunked. How's that for a promise?"

Tom examined the man's eager face, and then surprising himself, he said, "Let's have a go at it."

He stepped onto the board, sending its keel deep into the sand. He knelt as Moonghost directed. Then the big Australian dug his fingers into the sand, tunneling the board until he was able to grip it at the other side, lifting Tom and the board, almost miraculously. Tom, still kneeling, was now cradled against Moonghost's chest as he struggled to carry man and board into the water. Then beyond the breakers, gently, he let them down upon the water. The icy wetness came up around Tom's thighs as Moonghost slid onto the back of the board. Waves socked Tom in his crotch, soaking his suit.

Moonghost paddled into the wind, and the cold water sprayed up on Tom's chest and face. The taste of salt was strong, intense. The freshness of raw sea opened his sinuses. Tom smiled gamely, trying to focus on the horizon, but it tilted; it fell and rose, making him unsteady.

"Move back," Moonghost shouted over the wind. Tom slid his knees back a few inches, then his hands. "Good," Moonghost shouted. The voice from behind comforted him. He needed to know he wasn't alone in all that openness.

Then the horizon seemed to be encircling them, but no, it was actually they who were turning, into a position to catch a wave. Tom looked to the yellow cliffs. They were very much farther away than he expected. If anything went wrong, he knew he was out of shape to swim that distance. His heart beat faster. Slight panic. For some reason he didn't understand, he was lifting off his knees, as if to run away.

"Don't *do* that," Moonghost called out. "You hear me?"

"Don't do what?" Tom yelled to the sky.

"Don't lift. Just relax."

"Of course."

"Now slide one foot up from under you, flat on the board." Tom moved his right foot up. "When I say *stand,*" Moonghost yelled, "I'll want you to stand up, very simply, with ease. Okay?" Tom felt a wave swell under them.

The tip of the board came up, then slapped down as a wave passed through them. Another swell lifted, this time higher. Now the tip of the board hung five, six, seven feet over the water. "Stand. *Stand,*" Moonghost shouted. Tom brought his other foot up next to its mate and straightened his knees, slowly unfolding. "We're doing it," Moonghost cried, grabbing Tom's shoulders from behind. "Now hold stiff." The wind was to their backs, but Tom couldn't feel it because they were moving faster than the wind. Instead, the warmth of the land was hitting him in the face. His soles were tingling with vibrations, as the board sliced the water, holding stable within it, continuously faster and faster. Tom blinked away the wind. He was feeling new power, a lightness, and a kind of physical liberation that was totally unfamiliar. He might have been flying, a creature from afar, shot out of another world. Impetuously, he opened his arms, like the Christ of the picture cards, flying into the warmth of beach air, arms outstretched, Christ of the Andes, coming home to embrace His world.

"Tom." Moonghost interrupted. "Can you lean to your right? Let me have your arm; we'll bring the board to a stop."

In an instant, as if the whole ocean had turned upside down upon him, Tom was plunked into the churning whiteness. His feet hit solid ground. Soon he was walking toward shore, laughing and demanding another try.

They had four long rides, and the last time out they had the luck to spot whales in a school, gleaming soft and black, like shining hills at their feet, rising and falling through the water.

In the jeep on their way back, Moonghost handed his breviary and a small flashlight to Tom, and in the tiny beam he read Matins out loud: *Sun and moon, bless the Lord. Every shower and dew, all you winds, fire and heat, frost and chill, bless the Lord. Ice and snow, bless Him; light and darkness, bless Him. Let all the earth and all the heavens bless the Lord.* When Tom finished, they were in a capsule of stillness, a kind of hurricane eye.

"Why'd you become a priest?" Tom asked.

"To ensure my salvation," Moonghost said without taking his eyes off the road.

"Do you believe it is easier, really, being a priest, to save one's soul?"

"Well, if we get to heaven, it's a matter of degrees there anyway, isn't it?"

"I guess so," Tom answered dreamily. "Do you really think it's a *place,* heaven, as in Dante?"

"Well, I think it would be foolish to take one man's opinion on it." Moonghost smiled. "But yes, I think it can be called a place. It is wherever God *is.* Where is He? Up? In those galaxies? I think heaven could be here, right under our feet. Is He in the stars? Is He Inti, the sun god? Is He in our minds, like the Holy Spirit? He might be in the sea. Maybe He changes place, unsure whether He should come forward and become part of what we have become. Maybe He's a woman."

"With that kind of a theology, I find it amazing that you're still a priest, that you're even Catholic, in fact."

"Why? The Church is still young. Would you rather that all has been revealed? That there's no more for us to wonder about, to imagine, to ponder?" He took his eyes off the road momentarily to look up. The moon outshone the stars. "It wasn't to embrace the past that I became a priest. It was to find the future. Even as a kid, I lived for what was hidden, for what lay ahead, unrevealed. I was a wild one." He laughed. "Loved motion, loved velocity. You know, like now. I don't relish sleep, would rather move. I'm addicted to motion now. It makes me breathe. I must have shark's blood. I could never return to normal rest." He laughed with some embarrassment. "My spiritual director in the seminary told me I was a soul in flight. 'Well, if I'm in *flight,* then I'm a bird,' I laughed. Well, he didn't think that was funny. He warned me I'd collapse one day. He kept watching for it. Then he asked me who my model was, my favorite saint. 'The Holy Spirit,' I told him, 'because He was in essence the *wind.'* 'Be more concrete,' the old buzzard demanded. Well, what could I tell him? I said, *'You,* Father, for example. You're my model.' Well, he squinted and leaned toward me and hissed like Dracula, 'Never, never make a living priest your hero, because he can fail, and if he fails, he'll drag you and your faith down with him.' " Moonghost shuddered. "God rest him. He never did much for me, that one."

"*Do* you have a favorite saint?" Tom asked.

"I wouldn't slight one of them for the world." Moonghost laughed. "Although you might say Buddha or Inti, or any of the gods much more interesting to deal with. I'm a Catholic politically, but in my soul I don't know what you'd call me. Seeker of God, perhaps. My parents were born Christians, but they became Marxist atheists. *My* rebellion was to become Roman Catholic. Well, they were appalled." He grinned. "A strange couple by American standards. Both medical doctors. They wanted me to study medicine. Actually, I shouldn't ridicule them. I'm quite proud. They took care of the aborigines. They used to be hunted down like animals, you know. Still are, believe it or not. It happens in South America, too. Killed for pleasure, for real estate. I'm sure I took my example from the good doctors, but they were so funereal about their calling, while I was finding the revolutionary doctrines of the Church as exciting as a magic-carpet ride."

"What doctrines, specifically?"

"Christ's idea of making bread holy; that was clever. Why become a doctor when you can save lives by simply feeding people? But you can also topple governments with bread, can't you?"

"Still, why'd you become a *priest?* Why not a social worker, a politician?"

"I was also in love, you see, with the idea of the Christian God. Christ. Infatuated beyond recovery with His cunning, His audacity. And I wanted to serve His dream. I longed to dispense His bread, to complete His vision, to renew the world. Oh, I'd often ask myself: Is this all *true?* The virgin birth, angels, heaven, hell —is any of this *real?*"

"You developed some kind of certitude, I hope."

"Not necessarily. The mind goes from thought to thought, you know, from view to view. Does anyone really know what he believes? It's easier to know what you'd *like* to believe."

"Then how did you ever decide you should become a priest?"

"Faith." He laughed. "It's a leap, you know, a gamble. It's not certitude. I mean, heaven's not going to sweep you off your feet. You have to leap after things like that. It teaches you nerve, anyway, which is an indispensable virtue in Peru. Here, every day is the last day of the world."

"Yeah. Like dancing on a tightrope."

"But it's worth it, isn't it? What good would it do us to gamble on its all being a boring hoax? What would we gain? This way, at least, the wretched are given dignity, and we are given a dream." The blue eyes held still for a moment.

Peru started changing that very minute for Tom. He felt safe in an odd way, in an exotic new world, and freshly awed. Doubts lifted away like scales; questions remained unanswered, but they were unimportant now. He pulled in deep, relieving breaths, as though air were filling parts of his lungs for the first time, while ahead twinkled a glamorous city, surrounded by hills overflowing with poverty, hills of sorrow and love. The wind and the moon were at their backs, and their faces were in shadow. Their eyes became cameras boxed in darkness, each man safe in his own silence, grateful to have experienced the night together, glad not to be alone for once.

"I would give my right arm . . . " Tom said into the emptiness.

"Beg pardon?"

" . . . to work with someone like you."

More silence. Then Moonghost responded: "Ask DeSilva to assign you to me."

"Are you serious?"

"Try it, and let me know what happens. I should be very interested."

"He's pulling your leg," DeSilva said in shock the next afternoon. "He works with no one."

"I think you're wrong, Monsignor."

"No. No, no. It's impossible. He knows the Jesuits here dislike him, as does Maryknoll. They call him 'the Pope's puppet' because he came out of the Opus Dei movement. The Church is split all over Latin America. The left despises him. He's considered an extremist. He's even been called a papal spy."

Tom laughed. "But he is nothing of the sort. He's a sort of mystic."

"I'm his spiritual director. Don't you think I know? But he has enemies in the Church, and out."

"Then help me, dammit!" Tom shocked DeSilva.

"I am not a Jesuit. I have no authority with you. How can I help you?"

Tom engaged the monsignor's eyes and let loose the hurt behind his own. "Monsignor, I hated Peru until yesterday," he said with difficulty.

"Huh? What do you mean, until yesterday?"

"For six months, Monsignor, I've sat in that stuffy switchboard room over the garages, wondering why I am a priest and how the hell I'm going to last here. I feel ashamed and wasted. I gave my life to work in the missions. And now this man wants to teach me something, and you say I've offended the right, or the left. Hell!"

"The Jesuits will give you work soon enough." De Silva groaned with soft sincerity. "But you would literally have to quit your order to work with Behan, because to even vaguely suggest it will make them paranoid. Believe me. You'll wind up being transferred to some school to teach mathematics."

"Then I'll quit."

DeSilva showed outrage. "What? Tom, are you losing your senses?"

"I'm serious."

"Sit down. Please."

"Monsignor, don't try to talk me out of this. Please don't."

"But these are dangerous words, impetuous words. You would lose the years you put into your order and be considered a renegade. One day, you'll want to go back to your own. I've seen it happen."

"Request incardination for me," Tom said bluntly, "into the Diocese of Lima."

"Huh? You would no longer be a Jesuit."

"Talk to the cardinal."

"God help us!"

"I'll write to my provincial saying it is a matter of conscience that I do this. They've got to respect that. You will be my spiritual director."

"Wait, wait, wait." DeSilva looked up in wonderment at the young Jesuit. "You would go through all this just to work with Philip Behan? Why?"

Tom didn't know what to say. The truth was strange, elusive, deep. "Because it is a grave matter. A very grave matter, Monsignor." DeSilva's eyes narrowed.

"All right," DeSilva said carefully. "Give me a chance to talk to Behan, and give yourself a week. Think this over. Then, if you both still want it, I will go to the cardinal." DeSilva's expression was grim. "However, let me warn you. If you get to first base, the Jesuits will not take you back with open arms. You must be prepared to promise yourself to Peru forever."

"They tell me forever doesn't exist in Peru, Monsignor." Tom smiled.

"We shall see," DeSilva said, falling into his chair. "Now go back to your telephones and wait till you hear from me."

Tom lay awake that night, both scared and proud of his daring.

The liaison between him and Moonghost seemed more important than anything he had ever longed for in his life, except, of course, the priesthood itself. Why was he so desperate for it? He was feeling something totally new, totally wonderful, a feeling almost as strange and wonderful as his very love of God.

DeSilva worked the miracle. But the missionary orders in the vicinity did not like it. DeSilva publicly became Tom's defender, and privately his spiritual adviser. Tom continued to wear his Jesuit cassock and was still considered a Jesuit, but his commitment to Peru quickly brought him a popularity among Limeños in and out of the *barriadas* that no Jesuit ever had had before in that city. After his first year, the cardinal made him an extraordinary gift of an expensive silver chalice with an ancient node of Aztec gold that bore the smile of the sun god Inti. The cup had belonged to an old Spanish bishop of the diocese who had died that year.

Dies y Noche, Day and Night, the poor people called the pair of priests because one's cassock was white and the other's black, and a whole different world opened to Tom because of Moonghost. Businessmen, social workers, communists, as well as Christian Democrats—they all responded to Tom's disarming openness, giving him his way, and he had the talent to motivate them individually. His secret was that he gave them something back for their effort, a true interest in their lives. He never spoke English in their presence. The cardinal soon learned what a treasure he had in Tom.

Every noon the two priests met and showered at Head House, then opened their soup kitchen for the barrio children. They worked with a team of carpenters to build *fabricas,* shelters of scrap wood and tar paper. After supper, they met with committees, dropped in on the paper scavengers to help press the day's catch into cardboard. Moonghost had taught Tom to operate a sewing machine; Tom organized classes. The two priests still drove to the ocean, except on those sleepless nights when Moonghost walked off his insomnia through the silent barrios, throwing cellophane-wrapped goodies into open windows, like a ghost of good, walking in the desolate streets to force the face of agony to smile in the dark.

The small, saintly, graying Monsignor DeSilva was a good spiritual director to both men. "Learn what you can from him," he constantly advised Tom. "But be careful not to ignore other priests, especially Jesuits. You must reverse their distrust. Give them the chance to see what you do." Over the years Tom found himself too busy to put DeSilva's advice into action.

Eight years went by this way, and winter was ending in Peru. Tom had convinced the cardinal that something finally had to be done about the high toll of infant deaths and took up constructing a barracks infirmary. He worked with doctors and architects, while Moonghost worked closely with the cardinal's niece, raising money.

The two busy priests hardly saw one another. Sometimes, late at night, Tom would knock on Moonghost's door, but Behan always answered that he was meditating. That rang false and worried Tom. There were other signs. Marta, carrying a tray of food, called Tom into the quadrangle one night. "*Padrecito*."

"*¿Por qué El Fantasma de la Luna* no come?" she asked. "Why isn't he eating?" Tom reassured her and went directly again to knock on Philip's door.

"Yes?" Moonghost answered briskly, though he usually just opened.

"It's Tom."

" 'Fraid it'll have to wait, Tom."

"Marta says you're not eating."

"I'm *fasting*. Don't worry, mate, I promise I won't die on you. I'm really quite fine."

The next night at a shelter party given by the cardinal's niece, Tom was shocked when Philip entered with an expression that seemed to mix the extremes of sadness and fatigue, as though something had invaded his soul and defeated it. Near the end of the meeting, Philip didn't even manage a smile as he excused himself.

Later, when Tom entered the quadrangle, he saw his lights go out and decided Moonghost was at last giving in to sleep.

It turned out to be a foolish presumption, because the next morning Tom found Moonghost's door wide open and the place empty, the bare mattress folded in the corner, drawers and closet open and empty, except for the white cassock dangling from a hanger over his pair of old work boots. His breviary was left on the table, stacked in four volumes.

Tom ran across the quadrangle to DeSilva's office. He burst past the usual people waiting to see the monsignor in the early morning. He opened the big black door without knocking. DeSilva turned in shock, holding a white cup away from his lips. His guest ran out.

"Where's Behan?" Tom asked when the door was closed.

"I beg your pardon?"

"Where'd he go? Behan."

DeSilva stared at Tom, who waited with a pained expression for an answer. "He didn't want you to know . . . that he was leaving the priesthood."

"Huh? Who's leaving the priesthood?"

"Philip."

"Philip? No. He would've talked to me. He would've . . ."

"He didn't want to, obviously."

"But Philip would've *talked* to me!"

"What was he going to say, Tom? Lie to you?"

"He left *you* to lie to me? Is that better? Philip did that?"

DeSilva, noticing the pallor and the shock in Tom's face, started to fold up physically. "Philip was not afraid to tell you the truth." DeSilva sank into his chair, as if he thought he would never stand again. He placed his elbow on the chair's arm and rested his face in his hand. "I forbade him to let you know about it. I was afraid you'd follow him, afraid I'd lose you both."

Tom backed away from DeSilva. *"What?* Do you think I would do such a thing?"

"You admired him. Admit it, Tom."

"Monsignor, you're foolish to think I'm so weak. I am a priest by my volition. I renew my vows every day. I am *free . . .* " Tom couldn't continue. A new thought had invaded his mental process: the four volumes of the breviary Philip had left behind. "Philip. Philip . . . he . . . " Tom looked up pleadingly. "You mean he really gave up being a priest?"

DeSilva sighed. "He wrote to Rome for laicization with dispensations, and they denied his request. So he decided to leave without their blessing as soon as the infirmary was done."

"He left . . . the *priesthood?*" The truth was finding its way in small jolts to untouched parts of Tom's brain. If he had heard the news from anyone less than DeSilva, he wouldn't have believed it. There was no refuge. Philip Behan, the man they called Moonghost, the tall invulnerable Australian, had left the priesthood like a thief in the night, never giving his friend a chance to talk to him about it.

"Why didn't he confide in me?"

"I begged him not to."

"But that was so foolish. I might have helped him."

"Perhaps you could have." DeSilva spoke through the hand that cupped his face. "You're right. I am the fool."

For the next month Tom threw himself into the completion of the infant-shelter project, working obsessively. When it was finished, he drove to the ocean. He surfed, but he felt he was wasting his time. It was so adolescent, so redundant.

One morning he slept until noon, broke all his appointments, and had Marta bring up his meals. That was the day he composed the difficult letters to northeastern dioceses of the United States.

The first response was from the Diocese of Brooklyn:

> . . . *I have been instructed to inform you that the archbishop would be pleased to have your assistance in the parish of St. Barnabas, 75 Metropolitan Avenue, Brooklyn. The pastor there is the Right Reverend Arthur Lucas Granger.*
>
> *We await the letter of release from Monsignor Eduardo DeSilva, cosigned by His Excellency . . .*

Tom packed immediately and walked into DeSilva's office. DeSilva said nothing after reading the letter Tom handed to him.

"Will you get the Cardinal's signature and mail it to them?" Tom asked flatly.

"Must you leave this very minute?"

"Juan-José is waiting to drive me to the airport. He'll bring back your jeep." Tom offered his hand, but the monsignor froze, his eyes glazed over.

"Will you be back?"

"I doubt it."

"Tom, please."

"I really can't discuss anything, Monsignor. I'm feeling very bad."

"Allow me to give you my blessing?"

Tom could not bear the thought of kneeling before DeSilva. "No," he said resolutely, looking away.

"You are too hard on me."

"I can't help it." The monsignor raised his right hand in spite of Tom's wish and made the sign of the cross before his face. Tom rudely interrupted the words of the blessing. "Where'd he go, Monsignor?"

"Pardon?"

"Do you have any idea where he went? Australia?"

DeSilva looked dejected. "I can't say." Tom opened the door. "Wait, please," DeSilva called.

"Huh?" Tom stepped back inside.

"The night before he left"—he pulled open his desk drawer all the way and lifted a paper out—"he came in here and spoke. I wrote it down, some of it, the moment he left, because I found it beautiful, especially this." He held out the paper.

Tom took it and read: *He said he longed for short, snowy days and long nights. He said he desired the killing cold, the kind that purifies the air and kills the mosquitoes. He wanted loneliness, to work by himself and to read at night in a chair, by incandescent light.*

"May I have this?"

"Please."

"Good-bye, Monsignor," Tom said, folding the paper into his wallet. He turned and slowly walked out.

He jumped into the driver's seat of the jeep next to Juan-José. He turned the key and looked up around the quadrangle, to the gas pump, to the common room, to his shutters. He wondered at the changes that would come when he was gone. He could almost see a sudden vacuum of energy in the quadrangle. Sunshine filled it, but in the distance clouds prevented the sun from touching the hills. They remained black and gray, as if they belonged to yesterday.

Chapter Six

A BUOY BELL CLANGED. Tom and Gene leaned over the ferry railing to see it, but the bell was lost somewhere in the white water. It was foggy. The invisible Orient Point lighthouse groaned so deeply that it made their lungs tingle. The ferry floated like a zeppelin, sideways.

There was only one other passenger on the upper deck, a young woman who held her infant wrapped in a white knitted blanket with long fringes. The blanket seemed to glow annoyingly, forcing the woman to squint away from the sky while shielding the baby's eyes. Tom turned his back to them and sniffed the salt air. The boat was moving toward his birthplace, but also toward that cemetery outside of New London, toward that treeless stretch of flat land with its regulation-size gravestones and its unrelenting sky.

Gene handed him a Styrofoam cup of coffee. "I'm sick of people staring at this suit and collar. I feel like I'm wearing stripes and a number."

"They don't even know you exist," Tom said casually.

"I'd rather walk around looking like a Fuller Brush man or a plumber." Tom looked away, realizing that what Gene wore was inordinately important to him.

"Why don't you just take off the jacket and be done with it?"

Tom said. "Kruug and Muriel aren't peering around corners."

"Kruug's spies are probably watching."

"You're not serious."

"I wouldn't be surprised if he paid a couple of local cops to check on my quarantine."

"Huh? What quarantine?"

"Oh, he's forbidden me to go west of the radio towers."

"The ones we went past today?" Tom asked in mild alarm.

"Yep." Gene smiled. "Don't worry. If we get caught I'll use you as an excuse." Gene's smile metamorphosed into embarrassment. He tried a laugh. "When I was a kid, at Easter, I got all dressed up in this glen plaid suit and fedora from Mays department store. We'd visit my cousins in Staten Island, but I couldn't play in those stiff clothes. So when I got home, I put on jeans and went straight up to the big guys and bet them a quarter I could jump off the Cross Bay Bridge. I love falling. This friend of mine, Epstein, a Jewish kid, we used to steal from our mothers' pocketbooks and go to Coney Island for all the dangerous rides — the Cyclone, the Bobsled. Then we'd have to climb the el to get the train back home without paying, jumping the third rail, because we'd used our carfare on the Whip."

"Did the big guys take your bet?"

"Damn straight they did. And I won. But I turned so blue I nearly passed out. It was only April, and I had to swim half a mile to get to shore. Cold, but I earned a quarter, and a pile of buddies."

Tom was relieved to hear the self-adulation in the priest's voice.

"Remember those old retreats in the seminary? I'm sure you jebbies got them, where they'd warn you about the quote, unquote, loneliness of the priesthood, and in the same breath, they told you not to make any close friendships?"

"Yes." Tom laughed. There was a beat of silence and an uncomfortable lull.

Gene looked down at the water and spoke calmly. "Did *you* know what you were doing when you agreed to a lifetime of chastity and celibacy?" The question didn't catch Tom off guard;

somehow he expected something like it. He leaned on the railing, moving forward. He looked down at his hands, deliberately pausing as if to think. "If you never had a relationship with a woman," Gene went on, "this one theologian says, then you couldn't know what you were giving up; therefore, you were lacking in 'due discretion.' And that invalidates marriages, so it must also invalidate ordinations."

"You *are* a troublemaker." Tom shook his head and tried to find it funny.

"Come on, would you do it over again if you had the chance?"

"Become a priest again?"

"Yeah. Or would you run like hell?" Gene asked. "Do you mind my asking these personal questions?"

"I don't think so." Tom looked back down at his hands, wondering why he was lying.

"Well?"

"If I didn't have to put in all those years in the seminary again. Yes. I think I would become a priest again."

"Why?"

"I don't really know, Gene, and that's the truth." Tom looked away, knowing he was disappointing Gene. Then in a light-hearted, half-sad voice, he turned back. "Do you remember those drawings in those old black meditation books, of all the saved souls marching through an opening in the clouds, toward the immense light of heaven? It was so simple to be a priest in those days. You were Johnny Appleseed, or you were Merlin, you saved people with the touch of a wand. Every head you sprinkled had the right to get on that line and walk into that incredible light. It's not so easy anymore, is it, Gene? If I were a kid today, I don't know what I'd want to be. But in those days I *made* the choice, and I'll stand by it. Make it good, no matter what. I don't want to be a quitter, Gene." Gene kept his eyes on the milky horizon.

On land the sun seemed to find openings, illuminating the wide streets of Waterford and those big houses to which Tom had once delivered mail on Christmas holidays. A quiet, almost deadly silence permeated the streets. Tom expected it. That was Waterford.

They drove along Pequot, as if floating, through chiffonlike mists rolling in from the riverbank, where Tom and his mother had used to feed swans when he was very little.

"And there's the beach club. I worked there as a lifeguard."

Gene pulled up to the low wall at the club entrance. "Don't you want to get out and look around?" Gene asked.

Tom opened the door obediently and stepped out. He felt ridiculous, in his shiny black dress shoes and black socks, walking in sand. He moved toward a pyramid of white lawn chairs to see if they were the very ones he used to have to paint each spring. When he touched the finish, it jolted him back in time.

Gene stepped up behind him. "Where to next?"

Tom had no desire to touch base with Elm Street, to look up at the second-story apartment of Mrs. Sharskey's two-family house, where he had lived. As a boy he resented the old lady for owning the place. He wanted it to be the Sheehans', but the Sheehans never could afford such things.

"Did you hear me?" Gene asked.

"I'm sorry."

"What were you thinking about?"

"Oh. Mrs. Sharskey."

"Who?"

"Our landlady. Sweet old gnome who lived under us in her dark apartment near the cellar stairs. She was carved out of hickory, an elf, or a good witch in a fairy tale, who watched my father and me through the crack in her door as we came down the back stairs to stoke her coal furnace in her cellar. We got a discount in our rent for that. It was a small two-family on Elm. Coal was cheap as dirt. We kept the place warm as an oven."

"Can't we visit her?"

"She's surely dead. She was an old lady then."

"What about where your folks are buried, the cemetery?" Gene asked.

"I'd rather go back to Stella Maris."

"We didn't even have lunch."

"Let's eat on Long Island."

"But we have to wait for the two-o'clock ferry anyway."

"Okay. Okay."

They wound up in a place called Chuck's on Pequot, a marina restaurant surrounded by dark Polaroid glass. Gene had a bowl of chowder. Tom wanted no food. A Scotch, however, sharpened his spirits. He was relieved that the trip was near its end, grateful for Gene's silence.

"How come you don't want to visit the cemetery?" Gene asked sheepishly, examining Tom over his coffee. Tom shook his head without answering. "You're the boss." Gene looked away.

"Let's go." Tom stood.

"Hey. Sit down a minute," Gene protested. "I just started my coffee."

Tom sank back into his chair and tapped his fingers on the table, fully aware of Gene's sympathetic expression. Tom hated holding still. It was as if a huge beast were gaining on him and were going to devour him.

"What is the main issue here?" Gene asked softly. "Say it in a sentence or two."

Tom appreciated Gene's effort even as he resented it. Gene was one of those priests who probably had real strength for helping others but none for himself, and at that moment his eyes possessed such indisuptable caring that Tom reached into himself for an honest answer to Gene's question.

"I just feel ashamed," Tom said with noticeable agony.

"Ashamed?"

"Yes. I've been lying to myself for years."

"How?"

"Telling myself that it was good here."

"What's the truth?" Gene asked.

"The truth is that it wasn't good here, Gene," Tom said with a twinkle of hurt, looking out the dark windows. "It was good in Canada, the seminary. It was good in Peru. But it was just rotten here too much of the time."

"It's that way for kids sometimes." Gene smiled.

"I didn't live in one of those big houses."

"So you were a poor Irish kid."

"That's not it." Tom looked out to a sailboat coming in. "Poor wasn't the rough part. The rough part was those two, whose graves I don't want to visit."

"You afraid?" Gene sipped.

"Yes. I'm afraid."

"Of what?" Gene sipped again.

"Of going there and looking down and finding how glad I am they're not around anymore."

"I see. Which one bugs you the most?"

"Huh? God, what a question!"

"Your father?"

"My father?" Tom's eyes smiled sadly through the tinted glass. "He was one of those silent Irishmen you couldn't have a conversation with longer than two sentences. He opened up only once and that was to pick a fight with me. He was a cabinetmaker. He had this long mahogany toolbox with a thick steel handle covered with leather. He built it for himself, a beautiful thing, maybe a hundred pounds with the tools inside. He couldn't drive a car. Refused to learn, so he had to lug this thing wherever he went. He wasn't a big man. One night at the kitchen table, I'm talking about how all the seniors in my high school are sending in applications for law school and engineering, and my mother says to him, 'You know, Frank, the novitiate is just a trial period so that they could decide if they really want the priesthood or not.' Well, he just stands up and leaves the room. But he comes back with the toolbox and drops it in the middle of the floor just like it was a box of matches. The room bounces; cups fall off their hooks; and my mother, who is pale by now, orders me to leave the house. 'Do you want to be a common plasterer or a carpenter like me, with calluses on your hands and shoulders? Would you like to carry a thing like that?' He's screaming. 'Pick it up. Pick it up.' *No.* I didn't budge. 'We can't afford no such thing as a trial period. Do you hear that? Your mother has the mind of a fairy princess. She's turned you into a lollipop. But you're only the son of a poor man.' I could feel his jealousy, his anger. I got up to walk out. He yelled at me as I went down the stairs. 'If you get itchy between your legs, you'll be carryin' a toolbox like this all your life. When you crave a woman, you'll pay with calluses and a broken back. You'll keep that thing inside your pants if you know what's good for you.' He slammed the door and I walked out under the big elm in front of Mrs. Sharskey's. I walked the streets till midnight. There had never been any defect in my desire to give my life to God. I loved the thought of the priesthood more than anything else in the world. Still, in the novitiate, his words used to haunt me at night. Sometimes I'd ask myself, where would I go if I left? Was I persevering for God's sake or was it because of that awful toolbox? His voice kept me awake sometimes. Even now I'm hearing it. He was the only person in the world who ever succeeded in making me feel like a hypocrite. He spoiled my trust of my own motives, like a hungry brat eating the roses off my birthday cake."

"Phew!" Gene wiped sweat from his brow. "Is that all you had on your mind this trip?" Gene's facetious question brought Tom's eyes back.

"You satisfied now?"

"You being sarcastic?"

"I don't let people play shrink with me usually." Tom spoke with a firm eye on Gene.

"Why'd you let me?"

"I heard you on the phone with Zimmie. I envied him."

Gene's face lit up. "Good."

Tom's eyes flew down.

"I'm finished with my coffee," Gene said, standing.

It was darker, colder on the way back. The two priests stood at the ferry railing, Gene silently admiring his companion's strained face. Lines of age marked Tom's eyes; yet they remained clear and candid as a boy's. A certain innocence was still evident in them, a willingness to step aside for the inevitable, a humility. In the restaurant he had let some hard facts surface. He had showed fear, yet he hadn't run from Gene's questions or thrown up elaborate defenses. He had allowed himself to be seen into.

"I needed someone like you to show up in my life." Gene forced offhandedness into his tone and grimaced toward the vague horizon.

"Good." Tom's voice was almost inaudible. Something told Gene it was time for some silence, to let air between them, but he was too impatient to test the Jesuit's impressions of him, so he risked squeezing in a few more words.

"What's a Jesuit doing slumming with diocesans? Tell me the truth, Sheehan."

"Oh, I'm a doughboy at heart," Tom laughed, ducking the question and looking away. On the shore, two white horses ran playfully, out of the fog, nipping each other's necks. They caught Gene's eye.

Then *Block Island* floated by, in large black letters painted on a ferry. People stood on its deck, motionless, staring back at them, eerie in their inaction. Gene noticed Tom's fascination with them and waited until the boat was out of sight to speak again.

"You ever going back to Peru?"

"I could."

"Shouldn't I have asked?"

"Ask," Tom said simply.

"You think you will? Go back?"

"Well, there's trouble in Latin America now. They need help. Worker priests may come back. I hear there's a few in Poland. Some in prisons. The people need leadership everywhere. How many people die each week of starvation? The world is in terrible shape."

"I'd love to team up with you on something like that." Tom offered no comment, and yet Gene knew Tom had heard. "You know what was going through my mind on the way over?"

"What?"

"That you and I should make a pact."

"A pact?"

"Yes. I think we could use one another. I saw that in the restaurant today."

"What did you see?"

"I helped you face a few things."

"True."

"So, I simply figured we'd agree . . . to take care of one another that way, in various ways . . . in the immediate future."

"Take care of one another?"

"Look *after* one another. Friends. Like you and the Moonghost guy."

"But why would we need a pact to do that? It can't be avoided anyway. We're thrown together in the same rectory." Gene stared. "Well, aren't we?" Tom was casual.

Gene swallowed hard. "You're right." He pretended boyishly to be interested in the water.

"If anybody *doesn't* need a pact, it's us," Tom said dryly.

Gene smiled to hide the hurt. "I don't think you see what I mean."

"Okay. Try me again," Tom said with a trace of exasperation. It was the whole day that had wearied him, and yet he was quite conscious of backing away from Gene. He couldn't hide it.

"No. I got my answer." Gene straightened up and looked around, telling himself that he *had* gotten his answer. Gene had always dreamed of finding another priest to team up with intimately, to relate to. A cosmology of two, it was called, in something he had read once. One is doom; three or more spreads too thin. Two is the magic number. Other priests before Tom had backed off from the vaguest suggestion of it. But Tom was head and shoulders more sensitive than any of them. Maybe Kruug had tainted Tom's mind about Gene.

Tom put an arm around Gene. Gene moved swiftly out from under it.

"Hey, Gene."

"No, no, no. Don't do that. Don't say anything." Gene talked to his hands.

"What did I say? What's just happened?"

"There's nothing to worry about here."

"Fine," Tom said simply. "I said, *'Fine.'* Did you hear that? Gene? Look at me."

"I must be crazy."

"I'm saying *yes,* I'll make this pact. Whatever you want."

"No. I must be slipping."

"You're not slipping, Gene. You asked a simple question and I'm giving you a simple answer. *Yes.* I didn't intend to let you down. Don't make me feel bad now."

"I think I have to go to the men's room."

"Wait." Tom held him. "I insist you tell me what you're thinking. Don't drop this on me and leave."

"Okay. I'm thinking you're all the same, a bunch of stiffs who think you've earned exemption from feeling anything human."

"God! I hope that's not true."

"You're like all the rest, Tom. You've got juice for the faithful —plenty for the people. You all court the people like a bunch of salmon swimming upriver, shooting the good word all over their eggs, but you couldn't . . . "

"I couldn't what?"

"You can't love one person. You couldn't even pretend to. You're saving it all for the hereafter."

Tom felt the words, but he had no answer. They were too solid-seeming.

"Okay. I'll try to understand. I'll . . . "

"I'm upset. I'm shooting my mouth off and I just want to go to the john now. Okay?" He pulled away from Tom and disappeared behind the glass enclosure into the interior of the ferry.

In the car, Gene laughed stiffly, forcing small talk and telling jokes that dwindled quickly into silence. But when they passed the radio towers at Napeague, Gene spoke up in a fresh, solid tone. "Kruug warned you about me, didn't he?"

"Kruug told me nothing, except that you'd probably not talk favorably about him."

"Will you give me a chance to explain my version of what happened?"

"What *happened?* But it's wholly unnecessary, because Kruug didn't address that."

Gene paid no attention. "DeGroot, he was a friend of my pastor. Okay? Used to come to dinner a lot from the Newark Diocese. And one night I hit him. I . . . I actually hit him with my fist. I punched him in the mouth, in the face."

"Gene, you don't have to."

"People never repeat to others what the sonofabitch did to *me.* He picked me out, to destroy me, and I swear this to God. He used to smile at me when nobody was looking. I hated it and I showed it. Or he would wear this look of disgust. He was making *faces* at me behind the pastor's back, like a crazy man. I could ignore anything, but one night when we were eating supper, whatever I tried to say, he'd, like, interrupt it. So instead of shutting up, I made it a point to talk right through it. Well, all of a sudden he pulls away from the table and asks for his coat. My pastor says: 'What happened?' 'Don't expect me to return until you get rid of this bore,' he says. My pastor says: 'Take it easy calling names here.' " Tom watched Gene's pained face. " 'Get my *coat,*' DeGroot screams like some countess. The boss, ass-kisser that he is, runs for his coat. DeGroot, in the meantime, turns and he *smiles* at me, with this calm look of satisfaction. 'What do you want from me?' I begged him outright. 'Nothing, jocko,' he says. 'People like you disgust me,' he says with this sneer. 'Come back here, you sissy,' I yelled. My adrenaline is pumping like crazy. 'Turn around,' I screamed like I was the Pope. But he keeps going. And there was this bowl of fruit on the table, so I pick up a pear and I fling it and I hit him squish in the back of his head. 'Call the police,' he screams like someone who was shot. My pastor comes back in. 'He's *violent.*' He points to me. 'I'm putting him in jail,' he yells. But wait. When my pastor runs out of the room to call for help, you know what this sonofabitch *does?* He folds his arms and giggles. 'Keep screwing yourself, jocko.' Jesus, help me. I lunge at him: 'What do you have against me?' I yell, and he laughs, 'I know your type, Buoncuore.' I yell back, 'My type? My type?' I hit him in the nose. In the mouth, okay? Once, twice. Blood starts. The housekeeper runs in. I push him against the mirror. It falls. It cracks. She screams." Gene was hyperventilating.

"Easy." Tom put a hand on Gene's shoulder.

"Next day he gets a group of non-Catholic lawyers to file suit against me. You believe that sonofabitch? The bishop suspends me, takes away my faculties? They tell my parishioners I'm on sabbatical? Now who's gonna steal bingo money to rehabilitate my addicts? Huh? Other priests can't tell the pimps from the junkies. Who's gonna make breakfast for my old people? Who's gonna keep Zimmie from cutting his wrists? You tell me, jebbie."

"Gene. I'm sorry." He let Gene have all the pain of his eyes.

"Next time you back off of me, ask *me* what kind of man I am," Gene said with terrible hurt in his voice.

"I'm sorry. I apologize."

"I don't *want* your sympathy. I want nothing. I'm just tired of your lies, all of you."

"No one told me any of this, Gene. I swear to you. That's not what made me back off."

"Oh, yeah? What did?" Gene turned a tough face to Tom.

Tom's mouth was poised for an answer, but his brain couldn't produce one. "I . . . I don't know."

Gene drove the car down the pebbled grade of Stella Maris and stopped hard in front of the rectory's glass door. "Tell Muriel I'm out for dinner," he said without looking at Tom.

"You going to give us a chance to finish this conversation?" Tom asked as he opened the car door.

"Not tonight," Gene answered stiffly.

"Thanks," Tom said, getting out. "I look forward to it, whenever you say." Tom waved in a rain of pebbles as Gene spun the wheels, driving the car back up the grade. Gene didn't wave. He just zoomed up to the highway, then turned right, going east onto the smooth asphalt.

Chapter Seven

I T WAS NEAR NOON when Tom finished testing the First
Communion class of St. Theresa's. Six boys and eight girls
hung on to his cassock, like huge bells. He virtually dragged
them up the steep pebbled drive to Old Montauk highway where
their bus should have been waiting.

He smiled down at them, envious of their parents, wanting to
touch each different-colored head, wanting to gather all their
willing eyes. He made tiny steps for their sakes. And it was the
very moment that they all looked up to him at once, as he cooed
down cautions, that the blurred face of a woman passed in the
backseat of a taxi. He realized she might have waved.

After waiting much too long for the St. Theresa school bus,
Tom herded the children back down to the rectory and tele-
phoned the parish.

"Heaven help us, and the pastor's on a sick call," the
housekeeper said, taking the matter very seriously. "Did the
driver know he was *supposed* to come back to you?"

"I had presumed so."

"Oh, dear, can't you wait there a bit, Father?"

"Why don't I try fitting them into our parish car? Would you
take care of them?"

"Why certainly, Father."

"Then expect us any minute." Tom hung up and returned to the children.

One little girl had wet her pants, and that had made the others nervous. There were murmurings of pain as Tom closed the back door of the parish car, squeezing them on top of one another. One started to cry; one was punching.

"Hey, mister," Tom called out to the sky, "wanna buy a carful of clucking little chickens? I got some fat ones here." There was immediate silence, then such a burst of laughter from the group that Tom had to hold his ears as he jumped into the driver's seat. One of them punched him in the head. It was like driving a truckload of geese downhill. The children went wild with glee, squealing and cackling all the way past Miss Jane's Auto Body.

Tom wrenched his neck to look twice at a woman near the red phone booth, tapping her thigh with a newspaper folded like a stick as she paced. She looked right at Tom. He put on the brakes with such force that most of his precious cargo tumbled onto his neck. She started across the street to his window. It was hard to believe she was the same woman who had had difficulty in the Queens Midtown Tunnel.

Her smile was full of frank and undisguised friendship. She wore a bright, intelligent expression. The sun had touched her cheeks. Her hair was tightly braided and swept up, shining upon her head. Her fine gold earrings twinkled almost invisibly. Seeing her bare, fragile neck gave him a certain feeling in his knees, a weakness, like one gets from lifting a newborn baby. He enjoyed watching her cross the street in her translucent dress. It was a sheer white cotton dress, simple as a country apron, with wide shoulder straps that seemed stitched by hand. Her shoes were straw wedgies that had seen a little wear.

"Is it you?" She peeked inside. "Are they all yours? Hi, children."

"Who are you?" one child called out defiantly.

"Yeahhh." They crowded the window.

"They belong to St. Theresa's," Tom said.

"You're all terrific." She reached in to shake a few hands.

"Just had their holy communion test," Tom said.

"Did they all *pass?*" she asked with deliberate emphasis. Tom hesitated in the awesome silence.

"As a matter of fact, they *all* passed," he said. A chorus of screams flew out of the car. "How are *you?*" Tom asked above the din.

"Much less shook up." She laughed, blushing a little.

"What brings you to Montauk?"

She pointed to an encircled want ad from the paper: *Van $200. Sacrifice. Miss Jane's Auto Body.*

"That's it over there, I think." She pointed to a dirty white very scratched van that had a big "$200" painted in red over its finish. "I may buy it, if this Jane ever comes back from lunch." She caught Tom's eyes. "By the way, I owe you enormous gratitude for what you did on that bus. I was a madwoman."

"Nonsense." Tom touched her arm warmly.

"How's Stella Maris?"

"It's good."

"Could that be Miss Jane? Yes, I think it's her." She straightened and ran. "I'm glad we ran into one another again. I'll be in touch."

"*Do.*" Tom started pulling away. "Take care."

She seemed such a different woman than before, walking away briskly in that lovely dress.

Tom felt uncomfortable sitting alone in the dining room when Muriel entered wearing her usual expression. He didn't bother to explain his lateness. Over her black dress she wore a wrinkled red organdy apron with an iris sewn on as a pocket. A large red bow was tied just above her buttocks. She balanced a tray with a large lobster on top, and several brands of salad dressings, a bowl full of torn lettuce, slices of white bread, a stick of Hotel Bar butter, and a jar of mayonnaise. Tom stared at the creature, whose claws were still bound by thick blue rubber bands. There were lemon wedges everywhere. It was not the time to tell Muriel he didn't eat lobster.

"You cooked lobster for lunch!" he exclaimed.

"It was cooked when I bought it," Muriel answered frankly, putting down the bread and butter. "Monsignor likes his lobsters cold."

"It's *cold.* I see."

"Yes, and delicious cold," she said briskly as she went through the kitchen door. "I have Tab, Diet Pepsi, or water."

"Water, please, Muriel," Tom said, staring down at the lobster. The phone rang as Muriel reentered, her eyes now rolling with annoyance. She went into the hallway. "Stella Maris."

Tom took the lemon slices and squeezed them over his lettuce.

"The men in this house are all called Father," Tom heard Muriel say as he patted butter to bread. "Is it an emergency? He's eating his lunch."

"Wait," Tom jumped up, going toward her. "I'll take it." He coaxed the receiver out of her hand and, still holding his napkin, put the phone to his ear. "This is Father Sheehan." Muriel lingered in the hallway.

"This is Katelyn Snow."

"Who?"

"You know. Just now."

"Of course. I'm sorry."

"I think I offended the person who answered the phone."

"Who, Muriel? She's a good egg." Tom winked at Muriel, who took off her apron but did not move out of the hallway.

"Did you buy the van?"

"Miss Jane won't accept my check."

"No?"

Behind Tom the all-glass front door banged, making the entire building shake. Muriel moved toward the kitchen as Gene breezed behind.

"Hi," he said softly.

"Hi," Tom responded, cupping the phone.

"You said you were out for lunch," Muriel called to Gene as he passed the kitchen door.

"I am," Gene muttered, closing himself behind his door.

"Am I calling at a bad time?" Katelyn asked.

"No. *No,*" Tom said emphatically. "It's just that . . . Now let's see. If I call a local bank, might that help?"

"I think if you showed up in your white collar that would do it."

"Really? Should I come now?"

"Would you?"

"Okay. Stay put." Tom hung up and went to knock on Gene's door, but held back his hand, deciding not to risk it until there was time to talk. He went into the dining room and took his bowl and his dish with the lobster on it to the kitchen door. He kicked it gently open. Muriel didn't turn. She kept busy wiping the already sparkling clean sink with a pink sponge.

"Is she a parishioner?" Muriel asked point-blank. Tom took a few seconds to appraise Muriel.

"Is who a parishioner?" Tom asked gently.

"The one on the phone."

"No. She's not a parishioner, Muriel," Tom answered, setting his dish down on the countertop.

"Monsignor Kruug wouldn't stand for that, you know."

"He wouldn't stand for what?"

"Having lunch interrupted." She turned her eyes away.

"Well, I don't like lobster as much as he does."

"What *do* you like? I meant to ask you." She softened with such speed that it amazed him.

"Vegetables," he said, turning. "Mostly vegetables. Thanks, Muriel." He pushed through the kitchen door into the hallway, and then out the heavy glass door into the sunlight.

Miss Jane was a very fat, jolly black woman. "Ah didn' say she weren' trustworthy, Reverend. I jes' said I ain' 'ceptin' no check from no New York bank. You ask the other merchants and you git the same answer." Miss Jane had a constant smile, as if she knew everything in the world was a joke, including herself. She had enormous breasts which bounced inside her black stretchy pullover. Her tentlike jeans were covered with grease.

"But it's only a two-hundred-dollar check. I guarantee you she isn't going anywhere," Tom explained.

"Neither is the van." Miss Jane laughed, pointing at her mechanic's smile.

"But I can vouch for this woman," Tom pleaded. "I'm from Stella Maris."

"What value is that?" Miss Jane asked with an amused twinkle.

"Well, I've known this woman over a year," Tom lied.

"Who's gonna vouch for *you?*" Miss Jane giggled at her own joke. "They gonna vouch for each other," she yelled over to her mechanic, who threw her back a loud laugh. They were all smiling for some unknown reason, including Katelyn.

"Do you know Father Buoncuore?" Tom asked.

"What's that?"

"Monsignor Kruug?"

"Now you bring the monsignor down here, and I'll take the woman's check."

"He's away on vacation."

"These two ain't worth a wooden nickel," Miss Jane screamed with laughter. "If it wasn' for thieves, you wouldn' be in your business, right, Father?" she said, trying to be serious.

"I don't know . . ."

"And if it wasn' for thieves, I could take that check and you could take that van. But you are in that business. That mean they *is* thieves, and that's why I cain't take no New York check and you cain't have that van." She howled at herself.

"There's your answer." Tom sighed, turning to Katelyn.

"Gimme that check," Miss Jane said suddenly. "But you cain't take no van right now. She gotta go to Riverhead, to Motor Vehicle, an' git her plates."

"I'll do it tomorrow," Katelyn said enthusiastically, writing out the check.

"Meantime, I'll have Grease here double-check that ole engine. You hear that, Grease?" Miss Jane whacked the mechanic on his bony behind. He straightened up and shook his head, laughing at Miss Jane. "Git goin', before I change mah mind." She shooed Tom and Katelyn and brought the check inside to her cash register.

Katelyn walked Tom to the parish car, then held out her hand.

"I'm going to wrack my brain for how to make all this up to you, Father Sheehan. I don't usually throw myself on people, but I'm not sorry I did this time. You've been so kind." Her skin was peachy, healthier than it was on the bus.

"Why don't you come to Stella Maris? You can call a cab from there."

"But why?"

"It'd be more civilized than waiting at a curb. Someone might think you're hitchhiking."

"Then I'd have a ride." She smiled.

"Okay then, hitchhiker." He opened the door of the passenger side. "Get in." She paused, then obeyed. He slammed the door and rushed around the car, jumping in on the driver's side, turning the ignition key. They took off.

Tom was pleased with himself. He was feeling luxury in the company of a woman, such fine easiness. He resolved to try not to be nervous with her.

"Let's go to Riverhead right now and get your plates. Why not?"

"I couldn't put you through that," she demurred.

"I have nothing else to do. It would be terribly expensive by cab, and it'll mean you'll have your van tomorrow." She examined him.

"Do you mean it?"

"I'll change into my suit." He pressed the accelerator.

She found him dramatically more confident than on the bus. He took up more room now. His shoulders were large, his arms long, and he ravaged space with them. She felt a vague physical attraction for the Church, something she had never felt even remotely before, and a fascination with him.

He banged drawers looking for a shirt while she waited outside in the rectory office opposite Muriel's room near the front door. He was making noise, surprised at his nervousness. He checked his hair in the mirror, then stepped out into the hall, stopping at the kitchen door.

"She's waiting for you in the small office," Muriel said.

"I know she is. Thank you."

"Will you be back for dinner?" she asked blankly.

"Yes. Yes, of course."

Tom walked toward the small office door, opened it, and suddenly, seeing Katelyn sitting there, trapped by oversized oak furniture, he was embarrassed. She stood up, seeming quite relieved to see him. But he had forgotten to tell Gene he was using the car.

"Excuse me. I'll just be another minute."

She turned impatiently, throwing her eyes out the window. The knots in the maple paneling seemed like hundreds of eyes; and the crucifix struck her as ghastly. Above it were framed the words:

He who desires true rest and happiness must raise his hopes from things that perish and decay and place them in the Word of God, so that clinging to that which abides forever, he may also, together with it, abide forever.

Little handpainted bluebirds flying into the corners with ribbons in their beaks didn't make the statement less intimidating. She examined the pale wash of the bluebirds' breasts. It was good brushwork, but she stepped back from the words, as if they had the power to ensnare her. She opened the door and stepped into the dark hallway, into the odors of floor wax and rug cleaner, and pressed herself against the glass front door. But Gene Buoncuore pulled the door from under her.

"Excuse me," she said, trying to step around him. His beautiful eyes burned into hers, those startling dark eyes in their tired sockets.

"Gene," Tom called out, coming near. Tom introduced them. "I'm taking the car for a few hours."

"Sure. Sure," Gene said softly.

"We've got to talk later," Tom said.

"Sure. Don't worry about anything."

She leaned back in the passenger seat, hugging herself as they zigzagged down the highway. Small hills lifted them so high that the entire sky filled the windshield; then the ocean, flat and infinite beneath them. "Why do Catholics depict Jesus that way, nailed to a cross? I find that so shocking."

"It's all in how you look at it," Tom stalled.

"The cross was a form of execution, wasn't it, like an electric chair?"

"Well, yes. But . . . "

"I just find it pushy, like some of those awful newspaper headlines. I can't imagine children being brought up normally with that kind of thing in their lives every day. I feel sorry for Catholic children."

"I can understand how you feel," Tom offered, "but . . . "

"I was finding it hard to stay in the room with it. This may be offending you, but I can't help it."

"Well, the cross is not for every day, for every minute. It's invisible to me by now, taken for granted, I guess." His eyes went out the window. "At rare moments I suppose the cross provides some of us with a strange dark comfort. I hope you never need it."

"What do you mean by comfort?"

"Just that some people have crosses of their own they're suffering on every day, and if the world is ignoring them, well, that's a pain worse than death. They could grow to hate themselves and hate those who don't suffer. But the cross gives recognition to their anger. It's as if Christ is nailed up there saying: 'Look here. I *know* this pain; it doesn't separate you from history or from the rest of us. If anything, it connects you to Me, and I am God.' "

"Wouldn't it be better if He offered them some solution?"

"Well, His Church is His solution. My life is part of His solution."

"Oh, I see." She looked down, then out at the low dunes. She decided to keep quiet, remembering once when she was a girl how the crows had waited hours in a circle for a wounded gull to die; and when he refused to, they killed him. She shook the thought away and looked ahead.

Old Montauk Highway flattened into a freeway, cutting at sea level through the dunes of Napeague, westward through little villages toward the blinking light in Sagaponac where Katelyn had gotten off the bus that first day. There was still no sign of autumn on the roadsides. The clam bars were open and the breeze was dry as a desert wind. They sped along silently until she murmured somewhat sadly: "Oh, damn."

Tom turned to find her laughing. "What're you laughing at?"

"Me."

"What about you?"

"I was thinking about the Queens Midtown Tunnel."

"Yes?"

"And what I must have looked like to you trying to get off that bus."

"What was funny about it?"

"Oh, I'm just laughing out of embarrassment, I guess."

"That was a tough day."

"I had forgotten about your seeing me that crazed. Few people have." She grinned. "It was the hardest thing to do, actually, getting myself out here physically. It was like throwing myself out of an airplane, with my suitcase, electric clock, my pantyhose —not the way a sane woman does it. I leaped. But I'm here, where it's important for me to be right now. And all those summer people are back to work, leaving us the whole beautiful place just the way it was a long time ago."

She brought her legs up on the seat, Indian-style, one knee pointing toward Tom and the other toward the windshield, making a bowl of her skirt. She rested her palms on her thighs. He watched her staring dreamily ahead, erect and silent. He leaned back, letting one hand drop from the wheel. He increased the speed until they were zooming, cutting the dunes of Napeague in half, ocean on their left, bays on their right, and the sun in the middle. Gene's quarantine radio towers floated silently by on their right, and wind filled the car with thunder so loud, conversation was impossible. He would glance at her now and then, but she kept staring straight ahead, shading her eyes from the sun.

"Listen, do I have to call you *Father?*" she asked, trying to roll up the window so she could hear his answer.

"Obviously you don't want to," he yelled.
"It forces me into something."
"Then call me Tom."
"Thank you."

It took an hour for them to register the van and to obtain plates. Katelyn seemed worried as she wrote out her check. A mid-September day, it was hot as July. She was sweating more than he. When they stepped out into the parking lot, Tom removed his collar and jacket. She noticed the length of his arms and the dark hair that ran down, gathering around his wrists. His intellect might deny his sexuality, she thought, but his body does not.

They drove on the back roads with the sun to their backs, keeping silence until she turned to look out her window at the passing farmland. The wind was lifting the hair off her neck, and her arm rested outside the car. She looked sleepily to the distance as if finally feeling safe enough to let a hurt escape.

"I just had to give up the apartment; the increase made it impossible for me. I didn't have the strength to look for another place. I brought my daughter, Lizzie, to her grandma in North Carolina. She'll go to school there for a year. She hates me for doing it to her, and I don't blame her, but you have to think fast when September hits."

"You from North Carolina?"

"No. That's my husband's mother."

"You're married?"

"I'm divorced." Her voice tightened on the word. She looked out the window again. "Does that make me a loose woman in your eyes?"

"No." Tom shrugged.

"I'm the one who asked for the divorce. One of the hard parts of that was getting back into the business world. *Work.*" She mocked the word with a laugh. "I *hated* it. I became an art director for an advertising agency. In all fairness, I'd have hated any job. I just wasn't used to that sort of thing. The money wasn't fair, and it was on the ten thousandth floor of one of those all-glass buildings around Times Square. My copywriter and I used to close the drapes in his office because the clouds coming toward us would terrify us. He was a sweet middle-aged guy with high-tuition kids, so he couldn't afford taxicabs. He had a phobia of subways, which is what helped me to freak out, I'm sure, in the Midtown Tunnel, because he pumped me with hair-raising stories every morning, of the horror it was for him to get to work. One tranquilizer at eight to get him on the train; one at four in the office to get him home. Well, one morning I'm drinking coffee in my office, reading in the newspaper how seventeen nuclear bombs are pointed at New York City from various countries. Well, I swear on my honor at that very moment the general alarm goes off in the entire building. In about three minutes, six thousand people jam the stairwell. We're all cramped, no movement downward. Someone tried to climb down like a monkey along the banisters and he fell. Screams came up. It was the *Titanic*. Stampedes. People out for themselves. A dozen fire trucks waited to greet us. You should have seen the mess we all looked like. Was it nuclear holocaust? No. Just a copy machine smoking on the fortieth floor. I was so upset I jumped into a cab and scared the hell out of Lizzie when I burst into the apartment. I quick locked myself in the bathroom so she couldn't see me crying, and the next morning . . . " She took a deep breath. "In the mail came a big rent increase, and just like that I decided to come here. Home. I mean really home, where I was brought up, where I was born. Also, for years I ached to paint, the way my father did. He never made any money. Now his works cost so much I can't afford any of them. And he was broke all his life. I don't know why I should want to copy that, except for the feeling I get when I pretend I'm using his eyes. He painted all these fields and fences, these suns, light of every kind. Being in the same studio with his stuff was like standing on a planet that had a hundred suns, rising and setting every moment of the day. My mother hated them."

He kept trying to watch her mouth as she talked. He wouldn't dare interrupt her for fear his voice would disintegrate her visions. She was seeing across the farms. She had gone far off.

"You're fulfilling a specific need, coming out here. It's not running away."

"Oh, I *am* running away." She laughed. "Why deny it? Although this place has tricked me by changing so much. But the light hasn't changed, thank heaven. There are still farms, and the shack I've rented, it's nearly the same. Migrants lived in it when I was a kid. I wonder what it costs in the summer. Probably seven thousand a month."

"What else hasn't changed?" he joked.

"Well . . . " She looked sadly south. "The ocean hasn't. No one's filled it in yet. It has the power to swallow things up. The land hasn't got that power. The land is stuck with whatever they do to it . . . and they're *doing* it. Nevertheless," she said, inhaling deeply, "I'm here till May, when the rents go back up. My daughter will be through with school then, and I'll have a lot of paintings finished."

"To sell?"

"No," she said with slight embarrassment. "Let me show you Potato Beach," she changed the subject. "What a mysterious place that is. My father went there all the time to paint the old wooden water tower. Well, last evening I went there, and it's about to turn into Hollywood. Architecture? Shapes? Houses stretching their necks to get a look at the ocean. God! Where did the foxes go? And the pheasants? Still, if you put your hands to the sides of your eyes to block out the new houses, and you look down the dirt road straight to the ocean, you see it the way it was before you were born, and that makes you breathe for a minute."

She leaned back, placing her palms on the car roof and staring at her hands. "That's enough," she said. She was talking too sad, in horizontal strokes. She had to get vertical again. She focused on her fingernails. Should she spend time the next day shaping them or painting them? Neither. She would file them short and scrub them clean. Then she would go to Potato Beach and swim in the ocean until her hair filled up with sand. Then she'd rinse it with the hose at the shack, and shower in the outdoor shower using that shampoo and lots of conditioner, keeping her hair wet a long time. That was her secret. Then she'd put one tiny drop of baby oil on her palm and run her hands through her hair, then rub almond balm and icewater on her skin. Then she'd sit in the shade. She hated sweating under creams. But she needed a little color, so she would lie back in the wizened old wicker chair for fifteen minutes on the deck in the sun, then she would unzip her sleeping bag and throw it on the grass in the shadows of the cedars. She'd wear her white terry bathrobe and air-bathe in the shade.

As they sped eastward into the warm September afternoon, she realized that she hadn't felt so indulgent, so sleepily secure, in a very long time.

"Tom?"

"Uh huh."

"Why are you going through all this trouble for me?"

"It's helping you, isn't it?"

"Yes, and I appreciate it. But why?"

"Have you ever heard of the disinterested love?" He smiled coyly. She laughed.

"Don't tell me if it's going to hurt."

"It's a Zen concept, and a Hebrew one, too. It's called *caritas* in Latin, which means 'caring.' *Agape* the Greeks called it, as opposed to *eros.*" Her smile diminished as he continued. "It's also called the love of friendship; I mean, it pertains to the good of the beloved, not one's own interest or . . . or satisfaction, not in one's own pleasure."

She leaned forward to see his eyes. "You're telling me this seriously? That you're giving me the *disinterested* love?" His eyes made her think of the Virgin Islands and pale-blue Jell-o.

"Yes," he said.

She leaned back, looking out the window. He was chauffeuring her around, giving her uptight lessons in charity, which she almost resented. But she was amazed by his eyes as the car passed into shade. They were pale gray, the color of a cloudy day, the color of air, of rain, silver puddles reflecting the sky. They made him seem almost off the ground.

"I don't believe in *eros*. I don't *think* I do," she said, letting her head rock in false relaxation.

"You don't?"

"No. I think it's all *agape*. Or nothing."

"Really?"

"Yes. *Eros* is merely part of *agape*. Don't you think?"

"I hadn't thought . . . "

"It leads to confusion to put them into opposition," she mocked him.

He couldn't remember the last time a woman had tried to tell him something, a woman presuming there was something she could teach him. He held back a laugh.

"You strike me as a man who needs a more oceanic idea of love."

"What do you mean, oceanic?" he asked a little distrustfully.

"Wide, all-embracing."

"Very interesting." He smiled, genuinely amused. She was quite a bit younger now. "What have you got in that paper bag?" he asked, changing the subject.

"A thirty-five-dollar flashlight. That's because I mistook a marine supply in Montauk for your regular old-fashioned hardware store. It floats." She pulled it out and showed it to him. It was made of black rubber with a yellow head. She threw it aimlessly to the backseat. "In Montauk, everything has to float. But all I wanted was something to help me find my door."

She was falling together like pieces of a large, simple puzzle. Listening to her talk freely that way, aimless, as if she had known him a long time, oddly liberated him from her while making him feel closer. She almost could have been someone out of his past. Long Island was having a good effect on her. Her eyes were healthier. She wore a calmer smile now. He followed her gaze beyond the newly plowed farmland that rolled away from them toward the light mysteriously hovering over the ocean, illuminating the bottoms of the clouds.

Where there was no construction, the countryside was plush and beautiful. Still, the place was too self-occupied to satisfy what he was searching for: a time that already was, when there were no questions about the future, when things were made to last a long time, when choices had power, when the foundations of future decades were all in place and one walked out each morning from his bed into a solid, shining world which waited whole and ready for him.

The solid white highway line curved dangerously to the left as they entered the village of Watermill, the very same curve that had waked her on the bus that first day.

She stepped out of the car before her shack like a dancer, then held still, looking up with closed eyes, sniffing the air. "Listen," she commanded. He turned off the engine. The ocean rumbled and hissed.

"Nice sound, isn't it?"

His eyes scanned the landscape. The area was flat and open, different from the cliffs of Montauk, except for the sharp hill behind the shack which rose at an odd angle, almost against gravity. When she turned, the wind pulled her skirt and smoothed her brow. When she reached into the car window for her license plates, he took her wrist.

"Let me take the plates to Miss Jane and deliver the van here tomorrow." She stared at him incredulously.

"You're kidding."

"I'd love doing it," he assured her.

"Well . . . " She shrugged. "Fine. Would you like to have lunch here then?"

"Sure," he answered. She held out her hand.

"Thank you. I can't tell you how much your company has done for me." Her hand felt so unexpectedly delicate that his forearm muscles quickened, as if to catch it in midair.

Chapter Eight

THE NEXT MORNING TOM WORKED on the telephone, talking with every agency listed in the Suffolk County directory that could help the people of Stella Maris. He also called some of the names on the skimpy parish list to introduce himself. He called Riverhead for a list of the county's migrant camps, the Human Rights Commission, and the NAACP of Suffolk County. He wrote letters to Madeline Corey, Kitty Brady, and the Altar Boy Society of St. Barnabas. Then he got dressed to pick up the van at Miss Jane's Auto Body.

On his way out he knocked on Gene's door. "Gene? It's Tom." No response. He turned the knob and gently pressed in. Shoes were scattered; sneakers with laces tied, lying where they had been kicked off; every picture on the wall askew. White towels were thrown on the floor, and the white shades were drawn, though the curtains were flung over the rods to let in light. The room seemed a big locker in which Gene's energy had exploded. The wallpaper was printed with rosebuds and vertical stripes of lace, but most of it was covered with photographs, clippings, and newspaper ads push-pinned to the walls: musclemen, prizefighters, a giant lily, a Georgia O'Keeffe morning glory poster. A large photo of the mud men of Africa, all nude, except for their Napoleonic hats decorated with seashells. On the inside of the door was a travel poster showing eight people water-skiing in a pyramid, carrying a banner that read CYPRESS GARDENS. A blue-and-gold varsity sweater hung there, the cardigan type, with *Gene* embroidered over the pocket. Marlboro cigarette packs spilled out on the dresser; Alka-Seltzer foils and cigarette butts filled the ashtray. The bedspread was a moth-eaten woolen flag in giant panels of red, white, and green.

"Pigsty." Muriel's voice behind Tom made him jump. He whipped around. "Buoncuore doesn't want anybody to clean it."

Tom pulled Gene's door shut, throwing himself into the dark hallway with Muriel. The glare of the glass front door was suddenly miraculous.

"He's breaking his quarantine," Muriel said. Her arms were folded. She stood resting her weight on one leg.

"What quarantine?" Tom asked, pretending ignorance.

"He's not allowed past those radio towers."

"Who says so?"

"Monsignor Kruug. Don't worry, it won't apply to you."

"Why should I be treated differently?"

She looked at him warily. "May I make a suggestion, Father? Wait till Monsignor comes back from vacation before you take sides. Don't trust anyone too easily."

"Including you?" She smiled. Tom smelled nicotine on her breath. "Muriel, do you ever take a break, to visit friends or relatives?"

"I use my time off to buy groceries, Father."

"Why would you take on the extra work of worrying about where Father Buoncuore goes? Where did you find out that he's breaking his quarantine?"

"I beg your pardon?" She stared at Tom, taken aback. "I . . . I check the odometer on the parish car," she said, growing wan. Tom would bet she was lying. He wondered if Muriel could possibly be informed by a local cop as Gene suspected.

"The odometer in the parish car doesn't work," Tom gambled to test her.

Muriel gave him a long look of utter shock and walked toward her room and the glare of the front door. She opened her door, silhouetted in the blinding light, and turned back to him. He couldn't see her face. "You must despise me," she said, "if you'd lie just to test me, Father. And if you found I was lying, you'd condemn me, wouldn't you? But you don't condemn yourself for lying to pull a cheap trick on me."

"I didn't lie," Tom answered weakly, knowing he was wrong.

"Then you're a double liar, Father, because the odometer is not broken. Are you in for lunch?"

"No. I . . . "

"Dinner?"

"I don't think so."

She pushed into her room, then hesitated. "Monsignor Kruug called yesterday. I couldn't give him the telephone number where he could reach you because you didn't leave one with me. Would you let me know where you'll be from now on so he can reach you if he calls again?"

"If possible I will," Tom answered plainly.

"Thank you, Father." She closed her door softly, leaving him in the dark hallway.

In minutes, Tom was handing the license plates to Miss Jane and following the large black woman into her office. She took the papers from Tom and stamped Katelyn's signed registration.

"Grease did a helluva job on that engine. You can change that two-hundred-dollar sign to nine hundred now."

"Did *you* paint the two hundred dollars on it?" Tom asked.

"No," she said with seriousness. "I'd never do that. Some kids drove in here and begged me to buy it with the sign painted on. I gave them one and a quarter, and to tell the truth, I never even looked at the engine. But Grease tells me you got a terrific deal."

Tom shook her hand and went outside. Grease had screwed on the plates. Tom handed the mechanic a five-dollar bill and jumped into the driver's seat.

"She needs *gas*," Grease warned as Tom pulled away.

"Thanks." Tom waved.

He pulled into the first gas station he came to on the highway, filled the gas tank, then moved out, flooring the engine all the way to Napeague, past the radio towers, not slowing down until the sunlit villages of Amagansett and then East Hampton.

When he reached Wainscott, he made a left turn toward the ocean and jumped out. He took off his jacket and collar and jumped back in.

Wind lashed the fields of late corn that stretched like green oceans on either side of the car. The farms, rimmed with plump maples, resembled the Chilean countryside.

Air blew into the van as it sped toward the ocean, springlike, flavored with the new green of rest crops after the devastation of summer, soil turned inside out, its wetness evaporating in the hard sun. The wind blustered into the van, filling up his shirt until he felt he would rise like a balloon. White clouds beckoned over the ocean, and through the rear-view mirror he could see his wake, a tornado of dust lifting behind him.

He parked the van on the grass before Katelyn's shack, jumped out, and walked around to the rear, stepping over her tubes of paint and washed-out brushes. Old, frayed white wicker chairs sat on the cedar deck. He stepped between them.

"Katelyn," he called softly. No answer. He peeked into the window and knocked gently on the glass. The interior was small. One room. No one was there. He pushed the screen door and stepped onto the freshly swept wooden floor. A curtain painted with large palm leaves and pink hibiscus covered her bathroom area. The kitchen tabletop was of white porcelainized metal with a black diamond design in the middle and a checkerboard black-and-white trim around the edge. A black Chinese teapot, boxes of teas, and a bamboo strainer sat on the table next to an old-style wind-up clock, which ticked loudly. The walls of the shack weren't insulated, but black tar paper had been neatly layered between the cedar studs, leaving the studs floating like the posts of a porch that looked out to endless night. The woodburning stove would not be enough when the cold came. He might offer to insulate the place for her.

Everywhere wild flowers were hanging to dry—thistles, asters, grasses, and reeds. Those too tall to hang stood facedown on linen cloths in the corners—phragmites and joe pie weed. She had apparently pushed two single beds together to make one large field, too large to be covered by a single spread or a blanket, so a tan-and-peach chenille spread was combined with a khaki blanket and an Indian rug to cover the area. A bed lamp of chrome, Saturn-like, with its tilted ring, stood on a trunk near the bed, with a translucent red plastic shade laced to its frame with plastic thread. A rusty refrigerator stood against the wall as did an old white sink with brass fixtures. Gray curtains on a string hung under the sink, printed with white orchids and bromeliads; and an old browned lace window curtain, stretched between thin rods over the sink window, was pulled apart to reveal the mysterious interior of a cedar. Shelves were squeezed between posts next to the sink, full of jars and tubes, brushes, clipboards, rolls of paper, pans and dishes—all mixed together over a plywood work counter that ran to the corner of the room. It supported a portable electric range with a black frying pan on top.

He walked cautiously to the long, palm-printed curtains, pulled aside one panel, and peeked inside. It *was* a bathroom. No sink, no shower, just a john with a window behind it at eye level. One of the glass frames of the window had been replaced by a mirror. He brought his chin forward, catching his eyes in the mirror. At first it appeared to be some other man's face peeking in from the outside, a passing stranger or a farmer with dark hair and a light sunburn. He ran his hand through his hair and fixed his part; the man in the mirror still remained the stranger. He moved closer, but the eyes were not familiar. Living under all that sky near the mirror of ocean had bleached out the gray, enlarging the iris. As he turned to leave, he could not shake the feeling that the stranger was following him.

He went to the kitchen sink and turned on the water, looking out into the dark center of the cedar that hugged the house. Its spongy dark-green foliage and its tiny pale-blue fruit played tricks with his eyes. From that window the shack literally stood inside the tree. Its white trunk, its peeling bark of soft, reddish tissue, trembled in the wind.

Suddenly, hundreds of white daisies splashed upon the window, brushing along the glass, carried by someone he couldn't make out. He quickly threw water on his face, dried it on a towel, and looked to the doorway as Katelyn stepped onto the high wooden floor, arms full, her voice calling out: "My, my."

"Welcome," he shouted to warn her of his presence.

"Welcome to *you*." She laughed, happy to find him standing there. "You're early." Her hair was swept up again, making her neck longer. The tall bouquet of camomile daisies and the cloud-like violet asters made her arms so full that she could have been a schooner with full-blown sails coming toward him. She dumped her bouquets on the kitchen table, brushing debris from her arms and reaching for a ball of twine.

"I was at the ocean," she said breathlessly, bending to sit at the table but springing up before her bottom could touch the chair.

"Did you see your van out front?"

"Who could miss a two-hundred-dollar, four-foot-tall red sign? Let's have a cup of tea before we deal with it." She clicked on the burner, juggled the whistle-kettle to estimate the water, and put it down. She stretched toward cups and saucers behind him. Suddenly, as if the asters flew off the table, the illusion of tiny violet blossoms hovered around her face. He blinked, and they metamorphosed into her eyes.

She began to wind the string around the stems of the daisies. He watched her silently, feeling the slightest anxiety about committing himself to spend a block of time with her.

"What are you doing with those flowers?" he asked.

"Drying them, for the seeds, which I'm going to seal in these plastic bags."

"What for?"

"I can't afford even a tiny chunk of this world, so I'm taking some of it away with me."

"Where to?"

"I don't know. Maybe next spring I'll take a trip up to my Aunt Ency in Halifax and look around."

The smell of her body was in the room, sweet and subtle, more like a fine radiation.

"Put the tea in the pot," she ordered with please in her voice.

His body unlocked and he obeyed, relishing the odd feeling of
honoring a woman's command. He imagined her sewing buttons
on his shirt. She pushed her asters aside and looked up. "Like
cookies?" she asked.

"Sure," he answered. She tilted her head in an expression of
curiosity. "What are you looking at me that way for?" he asked,
smiling. "Do I have a fly on my nose?"

"No," she said. "You just look different today."

"Oh?"

"I think it's your eyes."

"My eyes?"

"Are you in the middle of a meditation right now . . . or
something?"

"No," he said simply.

"How would you like to see Potato Beach?" she asked, handing him his tea.

"It's a must," he answered.

"We can go for a swim."

"I have no bathing suit."

"Oh." She paused, wondering why that should matter.

He blew on his tea, then slowly met the cup with his lips. They
sat, sipping and blowing, as the ocean quietly rumbled. She put
her cup down, folded her hands, and closed her eyes. A morning
dove cooed in the cedars. It might have been cooing all along,
but the silence seemed new. She was tempted to speak, unnatu-
rally, to fill the quiet space. *An owl spent the night in the cedar.
It infuriated the crows. There was a dead bird in the woodburning stove.*
. . . But she held back her words, letting the ocean fill the room.
Why were they so quiet when yesterday they had been so free
and chatty? She lifted her cup again, sipping, looking out the
window a trifle self-consciously. In that light his eyes were
raindrops on a windshield. "Should we test-drive the van before
lunch?" she asked.

The van drove like a top. They drove it to the hardware store
and bought two gallons of flat white latex paint and brushes.

They put the van through the car wash in Southampton and returned to the shack, where Katelyn cut a hole in a sheet and threw it over Tom's head to keep the paint off his black trousers. In an hour the van had its first covering, and the two-hundred-dollar sign was reduced to a vague pink. Tom had splattered paint on his shoes, so they took a break in the wicker chairs in the sun while she cleaned his shoes. He felt like Christ having his feet bathed in oil. After the next coat, they washed their hands at the pump, and she handed him an apple corer. "Here, peel these apples." He obeyed, and that awful, lovely silence descended upon the shack again, broken occasionally by cooking noises. She was steaming zucchini with fresh tomatoes in a skillet and boiling potatoes to be served with butter and chopped onion grass. She sliced cherry tomatoes in half and dressed them with lemon and fresh basil. She opened a bottle of white wine. When he was done peeling the apples, she put them out with cheese on a linen cloth embroidered with sombreros and cacti; then she set up the coffee in the percolator pot, using the bottled spring water. She set out the food with quickness and grace, inviting him to sit next to her at the table. When she picked up her napkin and laid it across her thighs, his hand flew up to his forehead. He looked at her, embarrassed by the impulse to bless himself.

"Something wrong?" she asked innocently.

"No." He picked up his fork and pierced a tomato slice, sticking it into his mouth. "Delicious," he murmured, chewing, pink-faced.

"Thank you." She smiled, offering him bread.

Halfway through the meal, he took in a long deep breath, letting it out slowly with a smile. He was surprised to find himself relaxing. When he was a boy, his mother was often harried at mealtimes, sometimes even resentful. And meals in the seminary and Head House were loud with the clatter of dishes and serving trays, but in Katelyn's shack he sensed what wasn't even present in a rectory. He sensed home. He sensed inviolate solitude and privacy. They finished the meal peacefully, matter-of-factly. They had made a constellation of three with the table.

She took him to Potato Beach and showed him the collapsed water tower that her father used to paint. They returned and finished the wine. He fell asleep on her sleeping bag. She woke him at sunset and handed him a glass of wine. It was growing dark rapidly.

"Wish I could stay." He leaned back in his chair, stretching.

"Do. I'll make an omelet for dinner."

"No, no. I simply meant that it feels so good to be somewhere in the world where nobody knows where I am, no bishop, no superior of any kind. No one. You don't know how exotic that feels."

"Good." She lifted her glass and crossed her legs.

"I'd like to visit again. Without interfering in your work, of course, just . . ."

"Don't you have a lot of duties at Stella Maris?"

"I have very few duties, actually. I'm really a missionary priest. I've spent ten years in Peru. I'm a Jesuit; that's generally different from the parish priests."

"Why are you working as one?"

"I like working with people. Actually, I'm on kind of a sabbatical, and I'm not fond of teaching."

"So this is temporary?" Katelyn asked.

His expression grew pained. "I guess I'm going to have to take the bull by the horns soon, as soon as I get a few things straight."

"I see." She dropped her gaze to give his discomfort privacy. He had hesitated, looking blankly ahead as if the words were stolen from his mouth.

"I'm really floundering; why deny it?" It was the first indication of his confusion that he had been willing to make.

"Floundering from what to what?" she asked gently.

"I don't think I could tell you, Katelyn."

"It doesn't matter."

"Oh, it's no secret. It's just that, frankly, I don't know."

"I see." She tried to keep a matter-of-fact expression.

"And Stella Maris is just another strange situation for me. Monsignor Kruug is far too gung-ho for his simple job. He's the pastor. He offered me this appointment out of kindness, really, but frankly, there isn't enough work here to keep me happy."

"What about those children I saw you with?"

"They were from another parish. I was just helping out."

"Kruug is not the one you call Gene?"

"No. Gene's like me, stationed there. Kruug's on vacation."

"Does he worry you, this Gene?"

"What a strange question. I mean, how could you know to ask?"

"He looked troubled."

"He did?"

"Definitely."

"That makes me feel worse."

"Why?"

"Nothing."

She sensed that it was wrong to press him. His brow gnarled with worry. "What time did the sun go down tonight?" she asked, changing the subject.

"Was it seven?"

"The days are getting shorter. It's sorta spooky."

"I suppose."

"I've got to start painting sunsets. Have you ever painted?"

"You mean on canvas? No."

"Would you like to try?"

"Sure. I'd give it a try."

"How about Monday around six?" she asked.

"Fine."

She followed him inside, where he put on his collar and his jacket in the dark. He took her hand. She knew that it was going to be hard to put his eyes out of her mind. On his way to the screen door, she clicked on her little chrome Saturn lamp with its red plastic shade. It suddenly lifted the cabin off the ground. As he opened the door, he felt he could easily stay, living there on the edge of the world with her, never returning to his former life. The moment he realized what he was thinking, he looked down at his feet and stepped out onto the deck. He softly spoke his last word: "Goodnight." He jumped off the deck into the grass and walked slowly around the shack, leaving her standing in a red glow behind the screen door. When he reached the front of the shack, he realized that he had brought her the van. He had no car to return with. He rushed back, and when he turned the corner of the shack, his head crashed into hers with a blinding crack. She fell back with a hand over her eye.

"Oh, no. God! I'm sorry."

"No, it's all right." Katelyn leaned against the shack.

"The car . . . " he attempted to explain.

"I know. I'll drive you back."

He peeled her hand off her eye. "Are you all right?"

"I think so. Are you?" She blinked up at him.

"I'm fine; I'm fine."

She jumped with embarrassment into the van. She drove off the grass and opened the door for him. He got in and she headed solemnly toward the highway. After a mile or so, she started giggling.

"What's so funny?" he asked.

"I don't know." She let loose, suddenly laughing uncontrollably. She had to pull the van over. She clamped both hands over her mouth, but it didn't help. Tom took over the driving with a confused smile.

She had grown silent when they entered the village of East Hampton. But then, out of the blue, Tom started chuckling. That started her off again worse than before. She had to open the window to catch her breath.

"*Your face,*" she screamed, pointing at him.

"What do you mean?"

"Your face was so . . . "

"*What* was it?"

"*Surprised.*" Her answer was a squeal. "*Shocked.*" He laughed, again not knowing why.

They never quite composed themselves. When Tom stopped the van on the cliff road near the gates of Stella Maris, Katelyn's face turned serious.

"Forgive me."

"Nonsense. See you Monday." He shook her hand.

At ten that night, as Tom watched television, there was a phone call for Gene. A man's voice.

"I wanna talk with Father Buoncuore."

"He's not here just now. Can I help?"

"Just you leave the message that Zimmie called. And tell him it's not okay with me."

"It's *not* okay?"

"Tell 'im."

"Can't *I* help? Hello? Zimmie?" The man had hung up.

By eleven Tom decided to leave a note for Gene and to go to sleep.

> *Gene,*
>
> *Hope I see you at my mass tomorrow (Sunday). You okay?*
> *P.S. Zimmie called 10 p.m.* He's not okay. *Try to reach him.*
> *Tom*

Gene's arrival woke Tom up around one. Tom jumped out of bed and pulled open his door. Gene turned, startled by the light.

"Tom!" The hurdle jumper's eyes were still quick but very tired.

"Where are you?" Gene shaded his eyes.

"Here." Tom gave him his hand and pulled him into the room. "I left a note in your room."

"Okay. I'll read it in my room." Gene saluted and turned.

"Wait. Are you okay?"

"I'm fine. Sorry about hoggin' the car all day."

"No. Not at all."

"I want to get my licks in before Kruug gets back."

"Sure. I understand."

"Goodnight, Tom." His voice was hoarse.

"Gene, wait."

"Huh?" Gene opened the door, letting the dark hallway show itself.

"Is everything all right between you and me?"

"Why not?"

"I don't know. Can we talk tomorrow?" Tom followed him into the hallway.

"I'll try. Okay? Go to sleep for now. Everything's beautiful with you and me. Don't worry." He closed his door, leaving Tom alone in the dark.

"Goodnight," Tom said to the door.

As he lay in bed later, looking at his ceiling, he worried that Gene had lied, and that he had lost the trust of Gene Buoncuore as quickly as he had earned it.

One person attended Tom's mass: Muriel, wearing a black pill-box hat with black veiling, black gloves, black dress—so dressed up it struck Tom as bizarre. Her only colors were the multicolored ribbons of her Sunday prayer book. She wore no makeup, but her forehead was shining, as though she had used cold cream to soothe her raw eyebrows. Gene came in late, through the sacristy door, in his cassock. He genuflected and went to the rear of the church, where he knelt in attendance behind Muriel. At the communion, Tom noticed Gene entering the sacristy, leaning against the heavy oak door, and disappearing into the morning light. The car engine started. Tom heard it skidding on the pebbles up the grade, then fading out down the highway.

Gene returned that evening at six-thirty, just as Tom was finishing dinner. He threw the car keys into the dining room. "Catch."

Tom caught them as Gene moved on. "Wait, Gene." He threw down his napkin and jumped up.

He moved in close to Gene and whispered: "Why don't we take a ride together tonight, go see the lighthouse?"

"I couldn't." Gene turned away, refusing to connect with Tom's eyes. "My ass is flattened out from that car seat as it is." He opened his door, then closed it gently, shutting out Tom. All at once it dawned on Tom that Gene was driving into Brooklyn to look after Zimmie. It made him feel better.

When he returned to the dining room, the kitchen door was gently swinging as if someone had just passed through it. Tom bounced the keys to the parish car in his hand. Muriel burst through the already swinging door. She lifted Tom's dish from the table.

"Father, may I ask a favor?" She surprised him.

"What is it?"

"Please close your door when you watch television tonight?"

"I won't be watching television tonight, Muriel."

"I see. And if Monsignor Kruug calls and asks for you?"

"Tell him I didn't feel like watching television tonight."

It was ten minutes after seven when Tom pulled up to Katelyn's shack. The setting sun was drawing everything to itself, every tree and blade of grass, into the glowing furnace of sky.

"I'm leaving to paint," she announced the moment he walked in.

"I'm sorry, just gambled."

"Well . . . come and paint with me. I'm packing some food. We've got to hurry, though. It's sinking fast."

"Are you sure I won't be in the way?"

"Just help me pack the van. Here." Katelyn placed a folded sheet at the bottom of a cardboard carton, threw in plastic containers, string-bean salad, couscous, tomato slices dressed with olive oil, bread, and a half bottle of red wine. Tom obeyed her orders, carrying paints and pad and rags to the van. He didn't mention that he had had his dinner.

Katelyn drove toward the little bridge, then along Ocean Road, coming out at the Eagle Monument at Melon Restaurant. As they crossed the highway into dark maple shade, a group of black men appeared in dusty work clothes, coming home past their neighbors, who were sitting quietly in groups near run-down shacks. A young bandannaed woman was holding a child to her breasts. An old man smoked his pipe on a sagging porch, and near the railroad tracks a dark circle of bony, bent-over black men in oversized pants, held up with suspenders, smiled aimlessly at the passing van.

"How did we get here so suddenly?" Tom asked. His face had deflated into an expression of shock. "Where are we?"

"Bridgehampton," she answered, worried about his discomfort. His expression didn't change even when they entered the pleasant village of Sag Harbor. The place reminded him of home. They drove over its lovely bridge, toward Great Peconic Bay, and stopped at a beach that stretched a long way before the setting sun. "We have to work fast," Katelyn called out, jumping from the van. She acted nonchalant, hiding the fact that his face was worrying her. Maybe the poverty of the blacks had started him thinking about his work. She pretended to be completely unaware. "Here's five colors. You dab some of each on this palate and you mix. Like this. Red and green'll give you gray; you use white to lighten. Play around on the paper if you like. Make mistakes."

"What do I use to mix them?"

"Your brushes. Here."

"Thanks."

"Now watch. You use this to thin."

"Okay."

"Then you look ahead there, and you try to make the color you see happen on this paper. You don't have to reproduce what's there. Just let it inspire you. Look at that sun, for example. Or paint something in your mind. Water, those trees, anything."

"I see." She noticed how his forehead was gnarled. His hand was very tight as if he were holding an ax.

He slowly squeezed more paint onto his tin, watching her working out of the corner of his eye. Her face had grown tight and saintly, he thought, as the color yellow seemed to pour out of her brush onto the white paper. Then quickly, from a smaller brush, she laid down a streak of blue, then green. A scene was materializing on her paper, but in a different way than its reality. Bold greens, violets, and oranges gathered on the paper as he watched, until a more complex vision appeared there—more violent, more energetic, though it was definitely related to the scene before them. She had given the horizon more danger and more beauty than the sun was giving it. Her virtuosity intimidated him. He wanted to turn his back on the sky. He wanted nature to continue to exist as it always had, outside his head. He wanted to keep it there. Nevertheless everything his eyes beheld challenged them—the green-and-gray dunes, the movement of the reeds, the water, trees—everything. But he had no technique, no powers in this game.

"I'm not getting anywhere, Katelyn. Do you mind if . . . "

"Why don't you just dab some paint onto the white paper?" she suggested, not looking at him. "Paint is expensive. Don't let it go to waste. Stick your brush into it."

He felt a little angry at her for not letting him off the hook. He sheepishly dipped his brush into his green and ran it across the hard paper. He stared at that, then, selecting a fatter brush, which he dipped into turpentine and then into the white, he ran a thicker line above the dark-green one. That line swelled and dripped. "What in heaven's name am I doing?" he mumbled to himself. He had merely wanted an excuse to be with her. Why hadn't he admitted that? Now he was feeling *anger* at the horizon, *anger* at the trees. He attacked the paper with his fattest brush, splashing a sun of yellow oil onto the paper; then the trees, impatiently, carelessly, blobs of greens, light and dark. Vaguely, there formed a harmony. "Yes, trees," he mumbled to himself. So this time he took care. Using a thin brush, he outlined his trees, in yellow, the way he'd seen in a Van Gogh. Accidentally, he mixed a putty color, which he used for his dunes, resolving to outline all his blobs. Then, softly, mixing the putty with some white, he printed the beach onto the paper with his thumb.

"My," she called out, watching him, "you've got your own technique already." She was relieved to see him smiling.

"It's awful, but it's mine." He held it up.

He shared a little of her dinner on the sand as the sizzling red sun blended with the bay, sending up steam and smoke of dusty rose. Their paintings lay nearby, face up to the sky.

When the water began to turn black and streaks of orange

reflected the final glowing of sky, she stood up, brushing off her skirt. "I'll make us some hot tea at home."

She avoided the black section driving back, taking the farm roads toward Bridgehampton's twilight. His eyelids were heavy, but his eyes moved nervously the way her father's did after work.

"Can I guess what you're thinking?" she asked.

He sat up. "Go ahead."

"You're feeling a sense of power."

"Hmmmm. I wouldn't call it that."

"Every bit of color you see means something else now. It's the object of a skill. You can *paint* it."

"I can try, you mean."

"True. But you're experiencing your first taste of being a creator in your own right."

"On the contrary. I feel helpless."

"Yes. But still, you *surmise* that power. You can guess at it now."

"True." He smiled, his face lighting up with satisfaction. "I think I can guess at it."

"Isn't it ironic, your being a priest and never having felt that before?"

"I'll have to think about that one," he said with the slightest distrust.

She braked at the stop sign at Scuttlehole Road. Bridgehampton and the ocean were ahead in moonlight. "Is becoming a priest like getting married?" she asked, looking both ways.

"You wear white." He laughed.

"Really?"

"Sure. Ordination day."

"Tell me about it." She moved the van out.

"The things I remember are the corsages pinned to the mothers and sisters."

"Do you have sisters?"

"No sisters, no brothers. My parents were dead before I was ordained."

"Oh."

"But those white roses, those white carnations. How they

smelled! Gardenias with silver ribbons. A thousand men and women in the pews of the cathedral, sweating off their deodorants and aftershave on a hot June day." His eyes were fixed ahead. "Those big old-fashioned General Electric floor fans were spinning behind us like airplane propellers. All of us new priests, like white lambs in our albs, with the sun coming through those ruby windows, making us look like we were drowning in cherry soda. And we were all floating around, blessing one another. New priests blessing new priests."

"Sounds beautiful."

"It was very beautiful," he said, his eyes twinkling more happily than she had ever seen them.

She brought the tea and cups out on the cedar deck. They sat in the old wicker chairs under the stars. The moon illuminated the dampness. Crickets were loud as she poured. He took note of the small ring on her small finger.

"Pretty ring. Is it old?"

"It's a child's ring. It belonged to my mother. Lizzie won't wear it."

"What's the color?"

She laughed at the question. "I often ask myself the same thing. Pink, I call it sometimes; sometimes blue. It changes, like those sweet peas at the ocean. You can't decide if they're blue, purple, or red." She touched the tiny stone. "It's like a chip of rock candy soaked in blue lemonade." He looked at her as if she'd gone crazy. "Why not?" She laughed.

"I have nothing whatever of my mother's."

"How sad."

"Not a button or . . . or a spoon, or a book. She died while I was away in the seminary."

"Didn't they let you come home?" she asked, blowing into her cup.

"Oh, yes, they did. But after the burial, my parish pastor warned me that I should go back to the apartment to sort out her things and decide what was to be done. . . . "

"Where was your father?"

"Oh, he had died a couple years before that."

"Oh."

"Well, in the seminary you can't keep things, I mean possessions. It used to be sort of monastic in that sense, and I hated the idea of going back to our apartment."

"How old were you?"

"Nineteen. Old enough, but I just couldn't imagine what I'd do with all the stuff." She looked away as if something were causing her discomfort. "Then I thought of the scripture about the lilies of the field, how they neither toil nor spin, and yet they are beautifully adorned, and I used it as an excuse to grab a taxi right from the cemetery to the airport. I never saw the apartment again."

"Are you . . . anything like them, your parents?"

"Well, I'm certainly not like my father."

"Oh?"

"And . . . well, I probably do take after my mom, in a way." He looked away toward the cricket noise.

"My folks are gone, too," Katelyn said softly.

"Really?"

"You're surprised?"

"I don't know. You seem so young." He lifted a foot up to the chair and embraced his knee.

"I'm thirty-one." She took a deep breath and listened to the air. Then she lifted the teapot, stood up, and carried it inside.

Tom sat at the edge of the deck and removed his shoes. He lay back upon the cedar planks, sticking the pad of the wicker chair under his head, letting his feet hang into the cool grass. He fingered the splintering edges of the deck as he watched the sky. A plane moved mutely, like a drifting star, overhead. He followed it faithfully until it disappeared in the south under the moon.

The screen door slammed, and she returned with fresh tea. He could hear the pouring near his ear. He could feel the warmth of the pot near his face. He was unaware that he was pulling a large splinter out of her deck. He spoke up softly. "Sometimes I feel aspects of my father in me, vaguely, but I never knew him really. My father and I, we got together for two minutes every night, and there was never much more than that between us."

"How do you mean?"

"We used to have to take care of Mrs. Sharskey's furnace. She was an old widow, the landlady. It made our rent cheaper. He'd say four words to me down in the cellar: 'Open. Shovel. Close. Upstairs.' One-word sentences. Orders. God, I remember falling asleep to the noise of that furnace, feeling the vibrations through the bedsprings all the way up to the second floor. The radiators knocked, shooshing all night, and I just lay there remembering those hot glowing coals downstairs, saying to myself: Hell is that."

"Hell is what?" she asked softly.

"Those glowing coal fires, and somebody not talking to you that way."

"Your father?"

"Yes. Or anyone."

She noticed how he was pulling splinter after splinter out of the edge of the deck.

"I smell pain," she said sympathetically.

He turned his head and looked up at her sitting in her chair. "What do you mean, 'pain'?" he asked almost indignantly.

"It's hard to talk about one's folks."

"I'm not afraid to talk about them."

"I didn't say *afraid.*"

"Oh." Tom caught himself. "Although I must admit, I was there the other day, in Waterford, and I didn't want to see their graves. The memories ... they're all fractured by my being young when they died. They exist in my mind like some house that never got built, a half-finished structure with no shape." His eyes drifted. "Sometimes I want to nail the house together, to finish it somehow."

"Don't go into it now if you'd rather not." It was as if he hadn't heard. He went on speaking as if his mouth were projecting the words before his own eyes.

"She made me read *The Yearling,* by Marjorie Kinnan Rawlings, when I was in eighth grade. She quit high school in third year and kept *Tender Is the Night* on her dresser next to her missal because she liked the title. She only read the first chapter. She made me promise that before she got old, I'd take her to a rose-colored hotel like the one in the book."

"Really?"

"She also had this thing for Mardi Gras. She never saw one, but she always said she was going to take me to New Orleans someday."

"She sounds very romantic."

"But she wasn't happy. I mean, once or twice she'd drop her guard with my father and have a real laugh, but other than that, I rarely saw her laugh, except at the five-and-ten. She loved that job. If the people she worked with could ever see our upstairs apartment in Mrs. Sharskey's two-family house on Elm, they'd never believe it, because she went dressed like she lived in a big stucco palace, like she owned a whole shopping center, in ironed dresses, hair all fixed up. She wanted people to notice how her favorite color was blue. I'd wait for her to get off work, and I'd watch the people's faces when she spoke to them in the store, how everyone listened, how she smiled to each of them, making their faces go soft as if they had finally found the one person totally responsible for their happiness. But at home, she'd always have her headache, and my only thought was: How can I make her feel better; how can I save up and get her to that rose hotel, or just make her smile. Alice is a tough name to live up to, she used to say. Her maiden name was Driscoll. But I couldn't please her. Not with marks, not with anything. My father's drinking, or some failing in their relationship, just killed something in her way back. He was a cabinetmaker. He often had to be a spackler or a house painter in order to work. Maybe that disappointed her. I'll never know what crime he committed in her book. 'You're half drunk,' she used to say to him whenever he'd try to talk to her." Tom went on, "She reduced him to a problem, like a dog that's wet on the rug, and I . . . I didn't have the strength to stand up for him. Sometimes I used to wonder how come he was living in our apartment, as if he were a boarder that paid rent. I actually thought he *wasn't* my father until I got to be five or six. I grew up wanting to disown him, to go out and find another man to be my father. That's how merciless a child is."

Katelyn dared not turn away from Tom's eyes. His face had become a shell as he spoke, as if his insides were turning to smoke. He had wandered too far out. She wanted to call him back, but his words kept coming, like a python escaping his mouth, a snake curling in her lap.

"I used to love to wait for her to get off work. The store smelled of oilcloth and caramel popcorn. She sold nail polish, cold cream, hair nets. It didn't close till after dark in the wintertime, and she went to the movies afterward a lot. She'd send me home with instructions not to talk to him. So, instead, I practically lived at the church all winter. I'd go have chow mein sandwiches with her for lunch, then go back to school and spend the whole afternoon and evening inside church. The cathedral was warm in the winter—hot, in fact—before the oil crisis. I'd learned to pray while the pipes banged. It was so beautiful. I volunteered for evening altar boys, novenas, benedictions. I dusted the sacristy every night, swept, and laid out the vestments for the next day's services. The nuns gave me milk and cookies. Sometimes I even ate supper in the convent kitchen. It was the hub of life in those days, the parish. I did my homework in the sacristy, standing up near a lamp.

"On Sundays she'd always try to act like a mother, cooking a meal. He'd take a bath and go to mass with her. They'd see me up on the altar wearing the very surplice she'd ironed the night before. Then she'd rush home to bake her chicken. She'd break up Uneeda biscuits with parsley and butter and eggs. Yellow stuffing, she called it, or cracker stuffing. She'd make red cabbage and potatoes and onions alongside the chicken. I'd love to scrape the pan. She had gray hairs in her eyebrows, and no matter if she plucked them, they'd grow back. She told me I had my grandfather's head of hair. 'You're your grandfather Thomas,' she'd say, and I felt sometimes that's who I was, her father. And his too."

He turned and caught Katelyn's eyes, surprising her. "When I went into the seminary, my priesthood became the one thing we all shared together." He sat up. "It was like a new refrigerator, or a diamond ring in the family, or a car. It required sacrifice, but it was the major investment, the major blessing. And I was driving it around, like a shiny new Chevy, scared I'd get it scratched. He died while I was in Canada. I didn't go home for the funeral. I went home that following Christmas instead and she was laughing and wearing a new hat and chattering away. But by the next Christmas she had those headachy eyes again, and the Christmas after that I had to get the Nursing Sisters of the Sick Poor to come take care of her because she had breast cancer and had let it go too far."

Katelyn wanted to close her ears against his words. "Forgive me, Tom, but every time I hear this kind of story I feel so helpless. Each morning I see shells and dried-out crab legs washed up on the beach, and I say: Nobody's complaining here. The ocean gives and takes and there's no whining about it. It turns its waste into sand and we sit on it in the sunlight. Why can't we feel the same about ourselves?"

"That's exactly what I'm trying to do by talking to you," he said. "Washing it all up into the sun to dry."

She looked back at him quizzically, seeing his strength and his indignation. "All right. I'll buy that." She smiled with some relief. "I'm glad you trusted me." She paused. "Should we go for a walk? C'mon. I'll show you some beach flowers, if there's enough moonlight." She took his hand.

"Wait a minute." He thought of Gene at that restaurant in Waterford, how he had wanted to leave and how Gene had made him sit still. "Can we stay put a minute longer?"

"Why?"

"You said you were brought up out here?"

"One life story is enough for a night."

"Nearby?" he asked stubbornly. "Have you gone to the place yet?"

She rose without a word, threw the Irish knit afghan over her shoulders, and jumped off the deck, walking briskly toward the road. He followed her down the moonlit road, a half mile. She refused to talk the whole while. She walked somewhat angrily, until they reached a cluster of chestnut trees that seemed to move when they passed under them, their thick arms creaking in the dark.

"I'm sorry, Katelyn."

"Shhh." She took Tom's hand. The noise of the leaves was so loud it seemed they were standing under a waterfall. Two gray barns emerged indistinct, and a wind tower far off, spinning, caught the moonlight.

"Right here," Katelyn said, squeezing Tom's hand, "there was a smell in the morning like a vapor, the soil, the sweat of the horses, the grass, everything turning itself into mud thick as pudding; the rot of wood and manure on the barn floor. You get a sense of it?"

"No."

"It's because it's all dead here now, although these trees are still constantly moving. On the stillest days there was a murmuring in the leaves here. It's odd that the trees should still be moving and the house and barns be dark and still." She spun around with eyes toward the ocean, then again to the north, to the low moonlit clouds. "This morning smell would get into the house somehow, into the bedding, into your mother's apron, into your skirts and sweaters."

"Are you sure it's gone?" He sniffed a little, embarrassed.

"Oh, yes. It's gone."

"But isn't that to be expected?" he asked.

"Sure," she said, frowning. "Look. I'm sorry that I felt uncomfortable when you were talking about your folks. I'm a coward about memories. They're packed in frail crates somewhere in my chest. When they escape, I cave in, like I've been run over by a truck. I know we have to visit the past to learn, to understand. I'm doing it right now, standing here. Okay? Maybe the past teaches us what we should try to make happen again, but it's also like opening a grave, which is maybe why I dragged you here."

"Huh?"

"This is it. My past." Tom looked at the dark house and the barn.

"I figured."

"You need someone to go along with you so you don't fall in."

"Maybe you'll come with me to Waterford sometime."

"Don't count on it. I'm a coward."

"A coward wouldn't have brought me here tonight."

"You mean I get your citation for bravery?" she smiled.

"Yep." He squeezed her hand. "You get my highest honor."

They walked for a couple of hours through the warm, dampish back roads as the stars changed their positions in the sky. In the light of the moon, she pointed out the place where her father had showed her the green sky. Beach roses were reblooming.

"You remind me of my father in a way," she said, leading Tom up a dune. The ocean stretched below them. "He was born here. His sister left these farms when I was ten, to run away to Halifax with a married postal clerk. She originated adultery, as far as I'm concerned, my Aunt Ency. He died two years later. She writes to me now. The Snows had that Yankee strength. But my mother's side was troubled." She looked behind her to the floating island of chestnut trees they had come from. "Mother remarried, a man with money, finally getting her life's wish. He took us to Florida. I went to high school there, then to Smith. She died. I met a graduate student"—she laughed ironically—"from the Harvard Business School. A passionate southerner who sprang the question and I said yes just as fast as he sprang it. My friends couldn't believe I could've picked such a man."

"What kind of man?"

"He was sweet in his way, balding and potbellied at thirty. Pale and nervous. Opinionated. Scared. Isn't it funny? I don't know why I married Lou. I go back to the time, reexamining it, asking myself: What did you both *feel?* What did you *want,* what *promise* was there? And frankly, it's as if some other two people made the choices. I look at him now and feel, Who sent you? Who assigned us to one another? Were we born together, like brother and sister? Anything seemed possible but the fact that we picked one another. Then Lizzie came, like a third stranger; she came like my graduation from high school, like my first period. My poor darling, she came like a bedwetting doll for

Christmas, and I smiled. I look at photographs of us, smiling. I take a magnifying glass sometimes and look at my eyes in those old pictures—I can't stand the way I wore my hair. What were you thinking then? I ask myself. What were you so stupidly smiling about? And I can't remember what the emotion was. I can't remember one moment of *knowing* what was going on. I was too scared to ask. When I finally tried to tell Lou something was wrong, he suspected *everything*—that I was lying, that there was another man—everything but what was really going on. And it was frustrating because I needed Lou to help me out. I needed help with Lizzie. He was her father, but he couldn't see what our confusion was doing to Lizzie. Funny . . . " She stopped speaking and looked out over the ocean where the moon twinkled on the water. "He married less than a month after our divorce, after all his protest. I wonder about that so often. I wasted so much time protecting his feelings, and he never needed it."

"Do you really think that's true?"

"People are surprises. I could have lived with him sixty years and never have known that I didn't know him."

"You sound like you miss him. Do you?"

"Do I *miss* him? God, what a question!" She looked at him. Her eyelids shuddered. She looked down and moved the sand with her feet. "I miss having the illusion that somebody is thinking about me, somewhere, at least part of the day."

"He probably loved you."

"Oh!" She let Tom see her moist eyes. "Then why was I feeling so rotten?"

"Because you didn't love him."

Tom's words stopped her. She stared as if waiting for a rebuttal to come to mind, but nothing came. "I can't believe that I didn't love him at some point."

"But you said it yourself, just now."

"When?"

"Describing how you examined your photographs with the magnifying glass trying to decipher the emotions you were feeling."

"Yes, and what did I say?"

"That you weren't feeling *anything*. An important piece of the puzzle was missing. Your reason for being there was missing; the thing that got you there was missing. People who marry because of infatuations know what got them there, and after it all cools down and it isn't working, they smile and say *c'est la vie*. But you, you never knew what *got* you there. You said it yourself. Your feelings didn't do it. Something else did." She grabbed his arm tightly and stepped into a dune bowl. "You're an artist," he went on, gambling that he knew her well enough. "You get bored with the mundane. Ordinary things don't satisfy you. You're always on some kind of threshold in your work, and for some unknown reason, you married a man who didn't excite you."

"I cared about Lou."

"I don't think you could not care. But did you love him? Was that primal thing there?"

"How do you know so much?"

"Was it *there?*"

"No," she said securely.

"Then give yourself a break," he said. "You made a mistake. Paint yourself a sign over your kitchen sink, and move on."

"What sign?"

" 'I, Katelyn Snow, made a mistake,' " he said, depicting a sign with his finger. " 'I, a stubborn Yankee, got foiled at trying to act like a well-behaved housewife,' " he ridiculed her gently.

"Stop!" She laughed. "What about you?" She poked his ribs. "You . . . you fairy-tale virgin."

"Okay. Quit it." He reached to tap her cheek, playfully, though his face pinkened.

" 'I, monk and lover of God . . . ' " she went on, escaping his grasp.

"Stop it, Katelyn."

" ' . . . make love in my *dreams*.' " She laughed.

Tom froze as though he had been shot. "Huh?" He stepped back, his heels in the sand. He tried to recover from the embarrassment, to smile, but he had no power over his expression.

Katelyn's smile broke. "Oh, Tom, I'm sorry. I was kidding."

His hands came to his forehead, pressing. He turned away from her.

"How stupid. How cruel of me." She touched his shoulder.

"No." He reached back for her hand to reassure her. His collapsing defenses surprised even him.

"Do you feel okay?"

He answered by nodding yes.

"What just happened?"

"Don't make fun of me that way," he said. "Please . . . "

She moved around, facing him, taking his head in her hands. "I promise I never, never shall. I was teasing. I'm very, very sorry. Do you believe me?" He gradually embraced her, and he felt her hair on his cheek, her hands pressing his back. Now something else began collapsing in him, something structural. But this time it was a relief. He let the pieces fall into her arms.

"Hold me," he asked.

She squeezed her thin arms around him as tightly as she could, till they trembled. The scent rising from her breasts was a pillow for his face. Something released at his groin, like linen ribbons coming loose, floating up, unbinding, freeing emotions which he couldn't name, like doves, flying out of his mouth, in sobs, leaving him hollow. He broke away gently, giving her hands back to her body. He walked ahead of her, out of the dune toward the road.

"Are we going back?" she asked.

"Yes."

"Would you rather I walked ahead and left you alone for a while?"

"No. Let's just go back." He started walking faster.

She half ran all the way back to the shack to keep up with him. Then he wasted no time getting into the parish car.

"Will you come back?" she asked fearfully.

"I will." He turned on the engine.

"You will?"

"Yes," he said simply. "I will."

"Please do," she said, stepping away as the car took off.

The next morning after mass Tom noticed that the parish car was gone, so after breakfast he knocked on Gene's door and pushed it open. Gene was gone too. His suit jacket was missing from the back of the chair.

In his own room, he found a note on the pillow.

Tom,
Sorry I had to take the car one more time. Be back late tonight. Next week it's all yours.

Gene

That afternoon at a garage sale Katelyn picked up two mixing bowls for fifty cents, four wineglasses for a dollar, and a mouton lamb coat with puff sleeves for ten dollars. She held the coat tightly in her arm as she looked around, satisfied to possess something warm at summer's end. She saw nothing resembling a man's bathing suit. From a huge Whirlpool washing machine carton, she fished out three pairs of men's twill cotton tans. Tom was too tall for any of them, but the waists seemed right, and she could cut them into shorts for swimming. She bought the three pair for fifty cents. A very large woman in a muumuu of turquoise took her money with fingers stacked with jeweled rings. She threw the three pairs of trousers and the rest into a brown paper bag.

She knew, as she jumped out of the van with her treasures, that when the time came to cut his shorts, she would have to approximate. He'd surely misunderstand if she asked him to try the trousers on.

When she turned the corner where they had cracked skulls, she found Tom sitting in the unraveling wicker chair, dressed in duck pants and a white long-sleeved shirt. His black socks and shoes jumped out, along with his hair, which was groomed so carefully that his part seemed like a ruled line. He was lightly sunburned, and with his sleeves rolled up, he looked extraordinarily handsome.

"I helped myself to your shower," he said a bit cautiously.

"Please open the screen door for me?" she asked. He pulled the door, and she walked inside to the table and dumped everything.

"How did you get here?" she asked, peeling hairs away from her damp forehead.

"I thumbed."

"You hitchhiked?" she asked incredulously.

"What else?"

"Where'd you leave your black clothes, under a bush?"

"One doesn't hitchhike in a clerical collar," he said with a little embarrassment.

"It'd be much easier to get a ride," She smiled.

"I had no trouble."

"Yeah. I can imagine." She turned away. "Can you stay for cornbread?"

"No. And neither can you."

"I can't?"

"I'm taking us out for dinner."

"Aren't we both too poor for that?"

"You provide ze transportation, and I ze deenair." He bowed.

He was trying to be funny and gallant, though his eyes told her he was taking big risks with that kind of behavior. "Charmed by your invitation, monsieur." She curtsied, giving him her hand.

They had a satisfying dinner at Bobby Van's Restaurant. Katelyn usually never drank more than a glass of wine, but she had two, and a brandy, so she wasn't surprised when she needed Tom's hand to pull her up onto the deck when they got back to the shack. The screen door flew out of her hand when she opened it and smacked the side of the shack with a loud whack. She laughed and walked straight to the brown paper bag on the kitchen table. She pulled out the wineglasses, the bowls, and then the trousers.

"Put these on so I can cut the legs," she said matter-of-factly, throwing the three pair over her shoulder.

"What for?" He blinked, catching a pair.

"I'm making you swim shorts. Go. Behind the curtains there, and no more of this dumbfoundedness." She was dizzy.

He went self-consciously behind the palm-printed curtains. In a moment he came out laughing, looking like a clown in his black socks and black shoes, with the cuffs of the trousers up around his calves. Katelyn laughed hysterically.

When they both calmed, she cut through the left cuff, upward, past his knee to his thigh, then around, careful not to touch him with the scissor, causing the hairs of his leg to stand erect. There was absolute silence as she placed the pins. The ocean purred and rumbled far off. He looked down at her hair as she knelt before him. She was careful not to let her fingers up inside the trousers. In spite of that, he imagined her touch. He looked away to the cedar roof, relaxing his body, giving in to the attention she was giving. He felt the urge to fall asleep, as if suddenly it was all he ever needed in his life. He could almost let his spirit fly up out of her hands to some dark place to rest forever.

"Are they short enough?" She looked up.

"I guess so," he said, peeking down, not really knowing.

"Now I could cut the others according to these, but I'd rather you tried them all on."

"Okay." She stood up and he went once again behind the palm-printed curtains.

He carefully removed the shorts so as not to disturb her pins. But looking down, he noticed that his penis was twice its normal size. Though it was still pendulant, it was close to becoming erect. He quickly grabbed his white trousers off the hook and put them on instead of the tan shorts, hoping he would have a good explanation for her when he came out. It wouldn't be fair to become sexually aroused without letting her know she was having that kind of effect on him. If it went any further, he would have to end the relationship. The laws of the Church required it. She would become an occasion of sin, and he didn't want any confusion over her. He wanted a clear conscience in order to keep her friendship.

"What's wrong?" she asked when he stepped out in the long white pants.

"I appreciate the shorts, but I've got to go."

Suddenly she felt guilty, wondering if he thought her mischievous, seductive. "I only wanted you to be able to go for a swim," she said. She picked up the cut shorts. "These never dry when salt water wets them, so I thought it would be smart to have a few pairs," she said, growing pale. "Was I *disrespectful?*" she asked, trying to leap out of her embarrassment, then immediately hating herself for using the word.

"Disrespectful?" he asked. "Not at all. It's simply that I have a special problem, relating to women, that, unless there's an understanding between us, things can be spoiled."

"What's the special problem?"

"I can be tempted, like any man, but with me it can make a situation *dangerous,* because I have these vows, not to . . . "

"Not to associate with women?"

"I can *associate* with women. I just can't . . . I . . . "

"You can't have sex?"

"Right. Not with anyone, ever."

She tried to resist the angry feeling pressing in on her. She tried to remind herself of his eyes, his hair, telling herself that they made him very special to her. But his good looks for the first time made her resent him more. She forced a laugh. "Actually, I was about to say *I* was getting tired. I'm exhausted, actually." She turned away.

"I'll leave."

"I certainly hope you don't think I was pursuing you."

"I never thought that once." His face reddened. "The problem is my consent, not yours, not your consent or your lack of consent or desire."

"I assure you I have no desire whatever."

"Good." He smiled.

She looked at him, dumbfounded. He meant it. He was glad to hear she was not interested in him, though she had lied.

"Have you ever been with a woman?" she asked boldly.

"Never with a woman."

She paused, examining his translucent eyes. "A man?" She hurled the question gently.

"No." He laughed. "Of course not."

She sat down slowly at the kitchen table. The anger started to drain out of her. She rested her head in her hand. "How old are you, do you mind?" she asked.

"Forty-one."

"Forty-one." She repeated the words almost disparaging. "You have been jumping up like this for forty-one years, leaving places?" She was trying to be funny, but he sensed beyond that she was also a little frightened.

"Katelyn," he said, looking down at her with a sort of question in his tone, "I'm having a tough time holding on to the things I'm supposed to believe in, and for me, what I believe in actually makes my day every day. I mean for you, God can exist or not, and it wouldn't change your Tuesday or your Wednesday. But for me, it would blow my life to pieces. I've put myself out on a limb for my beliefs. My whole life is out there. The older I get, the further out I go because of the tremendous waste it all will have been if . . . if . . . "

"If what?"

"If there's no *reason* for the sacrifice. It's my vows too. A woman could only be an occasion of sin if I *did* something with her, I mean sexually. Then I wouldn't be allowed to come back, because as far as my conscience was concerned, you'd be morally wrong to be with again, and I couldn't do the most innocuous things with you anymore, like talk, or paint, or pick wood on the beach, or have a glass of wine. All these simple things would become infected."

"I feel like a character in a Bible movie," she mumbled, "or a cripple on a TV salvation show." She waited for him to smile, but he didn't.

"I never wanted any more than to be your friend," he said simply.

She almost laughed at the cliché. *What a lie,* she longed to shout, but held back, forgiving him only because of the hound-dog expression in his eyes. Not that he hadn't disenchanted her with his explanation, because he had. But in a way, he was offering her more than other men had. They all demanded sex. He wanted none at all. She should be fascinated, she thought, but she didn't like being told how it had to be. After all, you can get friendship from another woman, or even a puppy. Who wants just friendship from a forty-one-year-old man with eyes and hair like *his?*

She did feel sorry for him, though. There was such stubbornness in his delusions, sincerity even. Well, that was his flaw. They all had one. He was blind to himself, like all the rest. She should have known. How could a straight, good-looking guy go through life as a Catholic priest and not be blind as a bat? she asked herself. He watched her pull in a breath, then relax in a sort of defeated acceptance.

"You need a ride home, don't you?"

"Yes. Please."

Tom drove the van, letting Katelyn catch air on the passenger side. She closed her eyes, almost pretending sleep. He wasn't satisfied with what had happened, not happy at all. In the silence his mind raced. If he had owned the road, he would have pressed the accelerator to the floor.

She said goodnight at the Stella Maris gate, groggily moving over to the driver's seat. It was late but Tom could tell that her sleepiness was false.

"You've got my flashlight," she muttered as he stepped out.

"I'll get it back to you," he said, slamming the door.

"Goodnight." She threw the van into gear, turned around, and was gone.

Tom walked down the pebbled drive toward the parish car. He searched the backseat, the floor, and the trunk for Katelyn's flashlight, but it wasn't there.

During the next few days he felt vaguely like a hypocrite. His sexual purity had always been something he was proud of in his priesthood. His explanation to Katelyn about the occasions of sin, the pedantic intellectualism of it, embarrassed him. But more than that, his pursuit of the woman, telling himself it was for the experience of friendship, when on some level he knew he wished for more—these realizations turned him against himself.

He thought of Katelyn constantly. She seemed to be inside him, mocking everything he stood for, and he came to see Stella Maris in her harsh light. He hated the mausoleumlike chapel with its stained-glass windows, expensive enough to feed all the poor of the Río Rimac for the next ten years, the dreary rectory with its dark-paneled hallway and its absurd glass door, its overcleaned kitchen, and Muriel, like a dumbstruck old bird sitting on eggs that weren't her own, guarding the nest against enemies who did not exist—it all depressed him. He walked to town along the ocean each day, literally looking for work. The village of Montauk was beautiful and friendly. The ocean was a stone's throw from garden nurseries, pizza parlors, and laundromats. The place was clean and alive. But it needed no help from him. Now Tom felt angry at Kruug for trapping him out there. He also felt he had betrayed himself by leaving Peru. And yet, he pitied himself too, just a little, because it was all, obviously, far more complicated than that. He had been very unhappy for a long time, and the mystery of that unhappiness went far back.

Gene came in late each night and drove off each morning while Tom was praying mass. Granted, Gene seemed nervous, but in the light of the past few days, Tom was appreciating him more. He only wished the man would hold still for a day so he could pin him down and talk.

The next morning at breakfast Tom felt the dining-room floor vibrate under his feet and wondered if it could be the thud of Gene's barbells. He went into the hall and knocked on Gene's door. It opened a few inches.

"It's Tom."

Gene eyeballed the hallway. "You alone?"

"Of course."

Gene opened all the way, revealing himself in bare feet, wearing nothing but a cotton bathrobe. He was sweating, puffing. The overhead light was on; the shades were down, closing out the morning. He shut the door.

"I was workin' out," Gene explained, moving aside the barbell and rolling the hand weights away. He wiped his sweat on a towel.

"Does Kruug allow muscles?"

"Only above the waist," Gene muttered.

"You seemed nervous when I knocked."

"The room's sloppy, and I don't want Muriel sneaking in to clean before Kruug comes home today."

"Oh, I'd almost forgotten he was ever going to show up."

"I assure you, *he* hasn't forgotten. If you think Muriel is a trip all by herself, wait till you see her teamed up with Captain Kruug."

"May you be exaggerating, just a little?" Tom asked with mock hopefulness.

Gene straightened and looked Tom in the eye. "My paranoia does not originate in a vacuum. You're going to find that out. Now, what can I do for you?"

"Did you find a marine flashlight, a black rubber one, in the car?"

"I used it as a running light on my boat the other night."

"Well, it isn't mine and . . . "

"No need to explain. I'll get it back to you."

"No rush." Tom looked about the room. Shoes and sneakers were scattered as before. The blue-and-gold cardigan team sweater hung limply next to a cassock in the closet. "I need some advice," Tom said bluntly. Gene came out of the bathroom, not looking at him. "Did you hear me?" Tom asked.

"I heard you. You need some advice."

"You're still angry with me. Why don't we talk about that first?"

"Talk all you like; I'm not angry with you."

"I know you've put me in Kruug's camp when it comes to you, and I don't know how to make you see it differently. From where I stand you're a good priest, and I trust you as much as I've ever trusted anyone, or else I wouldn't be in this room right now."

"What are you prepping me for?" Gene asked, grabbing his jeans off the bed.

"I'm not prepping you."

"You have a problem?"

"Well, yes I do."

Gene turned his back to Tom and slipped on his jeans. He pulled on a sweatshirt, grabbed his cigarettes, and jumped on the bed, sitting with bare feet up. He lit the cigarette, threw down the matches, and hugged his knees. His nose was stuffed; he tapped the side of it. "Okay, talk. What's your problem?"

Tom looked down at his hands, deciding not to mince words. "I'm on the brink of . . ."

"Yeah?"

"Falling into hot water."

"How?" Gene blew smoke out over Tom's head.

"By breaking my vow of chastity."

"So? What else is new?"

"Well, up to now, I've managed to keep it. I don't want to lose that."

"Well, what do you mean, 'keep it'? You've acted out solitary sex, haven't you?"

"Not since I went into the seminary."

"You're putting me on." Gene flicked his cigarette and smiled for the first time. "I always wondered if there was any one of us who could really do it."

"I never argue with anyone else's way of being a priest. I do what my conscience tells me. Only lately I'm afraid I'm going to wash out. I've been tempted, almost to the point of . . ."

"Tell me about it."

"But not to do something solitary."

Gene's eyes narrowed. "Oh?"

"I've been tempted with a woman."

"I see."

"Much different?"

"Yes. The one you were with the other day?"

"Yes."

"I wondered about her."

"It's her flashlight. She left it in the car. She's a good person. Terrific, in fact, and I thought: Why shouldn't I be allowed to . . . to interrelate purely socially with someone like her. She's a window on a world people like us never get near."

"So it started out platonic, right?" Gene said. "You figured: What's wrong if a friend happens to be the opposite sex? Right?"

Tom resented Gene's presumption. But he couldn't refute him. He detected alarm in Gene's eyes. "Is this upsetting you?" Tom asked hesitantly.

"I'm getting a cold."

Tom looked down at his hands. "I've managed to keep clean with her. Don't misunderstand. But the past couple of days away from her. I don't know. Walking around this place, thoughts press in on me, about this whole setup here, about celibacy and chastity, and what you said on the ferry, that we have to know about sexual love before we can validly take vows."

"Is that what I said?" A warmth pushed through Gene's eyes. He smiled sadly at the tall Irish priest sitting awkwardly in front of him. "I don't know, Sheehan. You can't be this naive. You better talk to another jebbie, someone you can't manipulate. You shouldn't talk to a dumb parish priest about big stuff like this."

"Did they ever bring up this question of priests and sexuality at one of your clergy conferences? Could you refer me to a specific text or something?"

"Specific text? Wait a minute." Gene turned his face, almost laughing, and squashed his cigarette in the ashtray. "Well, I know for sure that in the past ten years the books say masturbation is okay, depending on the theologian, and that's your out, if you want my opinion. Just relate to yourself."

"What do you mean?" Gene made a gesture with his hand. "I don't want to do that." Tom rose.

"What's this obsession with being so rigidly chaste? Grow up."

"You're *kidding*, Gene."

"Listen, shrinks are coming down on us left and right. They say sexual repression reinforces compulsive behavior; it leads to drinking in the priesthood. And you know about drinking."

"How do you mean?"

"I mean it's common knowledge how they say we *drink* a lot."

"Oh."

"I wasn't getting personal."

"That's okay. I'm . . . I'm quitting the Scotch anyway." Tom started pacing in a slight panic.

"Now don't get hysterical."

"I'm not going to let this happen to me." He wiped sweat from his brow.

"You oughta try the other."

"What other?"

"Masturbation. Or do you want some doctor shoving his finger up your ass once a month to squeeze the juice out?"

"My dreams do it," Tom said with seriousness. Gene just looked at him, then spoke softly.

"Oh, God, Tom, when are you gonna realize? Time played one of its famous tricks on us. They're laughing at us already. We're just a bunch of faked-out heroes like those Vietnam vets." The sorrow of Gene's eyes, Gene's smile, his melancholy, the disheveled room, the two of them sitting there so frail, so confused and uncentered—all had such sadness in it. Tom longed for the conviction of the years before his priesthood, when he was a young man coming home from school in brown corduroys and moccasins, talking to God as he passed under those giant elms, solid, in the state of grace after confession, willing to die at any moment, hoping to, so he could walk right into heaven. But what he had turned into was a small and blind middle-aged man whom life never really touched. This time Tom couldn't force the beast back down. It rose to his throat with total force and authority of its own. It touched the backs of his eyes, escaping through water, through tears. He leaned forward and placed his knuckles into his eye sockets.

"Holy geez!" Gene jumped up. "Tom . . . "

"Gene, I swear to you, I don't know why I'm doing this." Tom wiped his eyes.

"When did you start *thinking* about all this stuff?"

"Oh, God, I don't know. Yesterday? The past couple of years? Whatever this woman means, it's all adding up to: I'm not who

I thought I was. This is all a posture, an enforced life. She's free as air. I envy her. I want to be with her. I want to be *like* her. And this morning, even while I was praying mass, something inside me was saying: Put down everything and just walk out of this church and go after it. Let it be over fast. Stop thinking. Just let it all go. Pack up your chalice and a few clothes. Make a clean break before it gets complicated. Be a carpenter; get a job. Go back. Marry her. Make love to her."

"Shhhh." Gene's hand flew up, and his eyes shot to the door. Tom remained open-mouthed. Gene sprang off the bed gracefully and tiptoed as Tom watched, eyes still wet, amazed, confused. Gene put his ear to the door, then jerked it open. The hallway was empty. He stuck his head out, then came back inside, snapping the door lock shut. "She just closed her door down the hall. She was out there."

"Listening?"

"Of course she was listening. We have to be careful."

"Holy God in heaven! Gene," Tom whispered, "what is *happening* to me? I'm scared. What is wrong suddenly?"

"You tell me. Go ahead. Try."

"The *lack* of her is wrong. She is what is missing. Is that possible?"

"You sound like some teenager."

"C'mon, Gene."

"Listen to the songs on the radio." Tom was stunned.

"Songs on the radio? What the hell are you talking about?"

"You've got a crush on this woman. You're hung up." Gene lit another cigarette.

"A crush?"

"Tom, why do you think I embarrassed myself on the ferry? Remember?" Gene's face reddened. "What do you think I was asking you for? All of a sudden you come in here and tell me you don't want to be alone anymore. Are you *kidding?* What a joke. What the hell do you think we've all been living with all these years?"

"But you wanted me to make some kind of pact. Friends don't

make deals. There's something wrong if people need a guarantee."

"Oh, no," Gene snapped. "*I* need a guarantee, and there *is* something wrong."

"But we're in the same rectory. I'm not going to run away."

"The same rectory? What the hell difference has that ever made to any one of us? Here you are spilling out your brains about running away, in love with some woman. During mass you're thinking of throwing the priesthood out the window. All in a couple of days you decided this, out of the blue, and you wonder why *I* want guarantees from people?" Tom watched him, as Gene angrily smashed his unsmoked cigarette and started pacing in his bare feet. "I've had women after me too, you know. I'm not made of wood. But they're *exactly* what we all gave up, dammit to hell. Didn't you know? *Women.* That's what *you* gave up, jebbie. That's what I gave up. That's why the priesthood is so bizarre and so hard. Never mind Kruug forcing us to wear black, that's peanuts compared to this. You think I haven't been tempted to go off and be a carpenter or a plumber or a bartender, for cryin' out loud, and get laid every night? Why don't I do it?"

"Why don't you?" Tom wasn't being sarcastic, but the question enraged Gene. He pointed into Tom's face.

"Don't come in here to check *me* out, jebbie. Worry about your own hormones."

"Huh?" Tom was sincerely confused. "You misunderstood."

Gene's hand went to his forehead. He turned. "I'm sorry. Look, I have no luck communicating with priests lately."

"I only wanted to know what works for you, what helps you, what is holding you here?"

"What's holding me? I'm *stuck* here. I don't know. I made a commitment, like you. I followed a dream. Jesus!"

"But you hate it. And this room."

"I do hate it here, but I'll never jump the league. Okay? Never. I'm in trouble right now. Okay? If I crack, I crack. But these lousy monsignors will have to bury me. That's what's keeping me here: stubbornness. Okay. But why am *I* on trial? You're the one with the girlfriend."

"She doesn't matter, I don't think. It's me, my thoughts about her, that worry me."

"It really pisses me off," Gene went on. "You're the one gets the flash to run away, and instead of questioning yourself, you come in here to interrogate me."

"No, Gene."

"What the hell right do I have to be secure if someone pure like you has doubts? Right?"

"You're totally misunderstanding why I came in . . . "

"Dirty your hands a little bit, Father. Start jerking off your dick, start feeling things. Get confused like the rest of us. Sure, you'd love to cut out, end it with one neat chop. No indecisiveness, no hovering on the fence for a jebbie. You gotta get out from under that avalanche of guilt. No anxiety attacks, no depression, no feelings, no shame. You go from sainthood to leaving the priesthood in one shot with no struggle in between. You'll never have to stoop to sounding like a creep, like I did by asking another man for something."

"I really hurt you on that ferry last week, didn't I? And I don't understand my shortcoming, my ignorance. I'm in too much pain myself, Gene, on top of it. I didn't say no to you. Did I? *Did I?* I'm your friend."

"Yeah. And you just walked in here to tell me you're running away with some woman."

Tom's eyes fell to the rug. "No. That's not true."

"You're way behind me, man." Gene turned his back to Tom. "I've been where you are. You may be ordained a little longer, but you're way behind me." Gene lit a fresh cigarette.

"What the hell did you expect from me on that ferry?" Tom almost shouted. "We're still too young to be so needy, to grab onto one another that way. That's sad. There's too much life left."

"Well, what the hell *else* am I supposed to do?" Gene shouted back. "I can't work. My life might as well be over. I'm dead here." Silence came back slowly to the room.

"Maybe you're what we should be talking about," Tom said softly.

"No. Because you had to come here to tell me you're about to fuck somebody."

"Huh?"

"You need permission."

"No, I . . . " A noise in the hall again, but Gene didn't seem to notice this time.

"You rule-keepers are the worst, you know it? Ice palaces that melt in a half hour. All intellectual, until bingo. It's like you never developed the right immunities. The first time you smell a woman up close, you're lost to nature."

"I don't think that's true," Tom said softly.

"You and Kruug are exactly alike. You're legalists. You think the law will save you if you stay on its side. Well, you have stayed on its side, Tom, and you aren't saved, are you? I'm glad you're finding that out, Sheehan. Holy Jesus! You make celibacy into some kind of physical feat, like holding it in. Celibacy is giving your damned life to the people."

"Like a salmon shooting all over?" Tom asked sarcastically.

"Well, yes, at times it's like that. But if you're stupid enough to ignore the part of life that makes two people get closer to each other than they are to all the rest, then you deserve what you get."

"I've given myself to the people, don't worry, Gene. I also have a vow of chastity to keep. So do you. It's a fact you seem to overlook."

"I don't overlook it. You took the easy way out, Tom. You kept clean. Okay? There's a price with that, and now you're paying it." The two men stared at one another. "Look, I'm really tired," Gene said sincerely, "and I've got to clean up this mess." Tom rose awkwardly as Gene bent over, grabbing up his scattered shoes.

"Can I help?" Tom asked.

"No thanks." He hesitated and looked up. "You caught me off guard."

"Gene, I'm sorry if I . . . " Tom offered his eyes, but Gene wouldn't look, grabbing things up in a rush. He didn't seem to know what to do with whatever he picked up. He just stalled and turned, dropping it again. Tom backed toward the door, turned, and opened it. No one was in the hall.

Gene still didn't look up. "Don't mind me," Gene said to the floor, wild-eyed. "I'm not fit to talk to when I have a cold. I'll get back to you."

"Sure," Tom said.

"Yeah," Gene said, picking up the towel in the corner. Gene straightened up, his eyes open wide. He sucked in his runny nose, and he called out to Tom. "Wait. Get back inside. Please, for a minute." Tom obeyed, closing the door behind him. "Could you tell a lie to Kruug? Do you have the nerve?"

"I've lied before. Why?"

"Tell Kruug you're going home for a week or so on that vacation he promised. Okay? Instead, you go spend some time with her. Find out what's really going on between the two of you."

"Are you serious?"

"What other choices have you? Stay here and hate yourself and all of us?"

"It's probable that she and I would . . . "

"So maybe you'll spoil your perfect record, or would you rather go be a carpenter and throw in your cards because you're afraid of losing a hand?"

"I'll think about this. But thanks for being so strong with me." Tom opened the door.

"Strong?" Gene laughed.

Tom stepped dejectedly into the hall.

"See you at lunch," Gene said.

"I don't think so."

"Well, you'd better tell Muriel. She's cooking up a storm to welcome home her black prince."

Tom went through the dining room to knock on the swinging door to the kitchen. No answer. He pressed it open, and Muriel entered from the hallway without giving him so much as a glance. She slammed closed a cabinet door, then opened the refrigerator and started loudly pulling out one of the shelves. A white turkey was defrosting on the countertop in a pool of pink water.

"Muriel, I'm sorry, but I'll be missing lunch."

Her eyebrows were sore and freshly plucked. "You don't have to apologize to me," she said without looking up. "What time will you be back?"

"I'm not going anywhere." She straightened and looked at him. "I'll be missing lunch in my room," Tom said simply. She was about to speak again when outside the kitchen window there was a noise that distracted her, like popcorn exploding, or pebbles popping under car tires. Muriel's fingers touched the table tentatively, then she stared at the wall, as if the noise might have been a rumbling of the very earth. Tom saw the chrome rack of a station wagon going by under the window.

"He's home," Muriel said, trying to yank off her hair net. It snagged. She pushed through Tom and ran to the image waiting for her in the dining-room mirror. Frantically, she pulled at her curlers, which were hopelessly caught in her hair net. When Tom passed behind her, he paused. Muriel froze when she saw him watching her in the reflection. Tom's eyes immediately released hers. He turned toward the hallway and disappeared into its darkness.

Tom was grateful for his room's dark coolness. He longed for a shower and the sweetness of rest on his hard bed. The room was dark even in daytime. He was glad for that. He needed the darkness to rest, to pray, maybe even passively, to think for a few hours alone, behind locked doors.

Gene's words were burning in his mind. Gene made more and more sense. He was actually ahead of Tom in his struggle to keep his priesthood. Gene had long ago bargained with the devil. He had given in to his body, given up his pride. Sensuality only wounds a priest, it is his pride that destroys him. Maybe that's what Granger, in spite of his ugliness, was trying to say that night of his roast-beef dinner, Tom thought.

He undressed, shivering when he stepped nude onto the floor of the white tile room. The light was weak and gray. He turned on the shower water, then flipped the overhead light switch. The bulb blew out in a blinding flash, revealing a nude body in the wall mirror, then plunging the room into semidarkness. The momentary image in the mirror glowed in his mind. A thin man, standing tall and nude, white skin, black chest hair, black line down his stomach, soft white penis alone in its black bush of hair. When his eyes adjusted to the low gray light, the nude man materialized once again like a ghost in the giant mirror. The only light came from behind him, through the rippled glass shower door which broke the light into hundreds of tiny soft moons. The mirror reflected them all, except where the figure blocked them. The face of the man was unrecognizable. It seemed to Tom that the figure could, at any moment, step into the room and stand next to him, so he moved back, distancing the reflection. He realized the figure was he; still he reacted to its rude presence as if it were an impostor, a voyeur, a passing stranger, like the man who had looked at him through the window of Katelyn's bathroom. Only this time the stranger was nude.

Tom placed his palms on the mirror, palm to palm with the figure, accepting the man as himself, and suddenly Gene's words came back to him: *Dirty your hands a little bit, Father. Start jerking off your dick, start feeling things. Get confused like the rest of us.*

Tom peered deeply into the eyes of the man in the mirror. The eyes looked steadily back until his breath fogged up the face. He dared to let his hand drop to his chest, passing over his nipple, gently. He closed his eyes for this, imagining that it was not his hand, but a hand coming out from the mirror to finger the hair of his chest, then to move down, through the black silken line to his navel, down to where the hair puffed coarser, thicker, where his fingers found the stump of a swollen penis. He kept his eyes strictly closed. The prospect of opening them and seeing his penis erect scared him. He had never really looked at it that way, in a mirror, with an erection. If he were to "soil" himself, as Gene put it, if he were to reach that point of no return, of consent to the mortal sin, there in the gray-white tiled room, he would open his eyes. He stood, indecisively, for several minutes until, finally, he did open his eyes, looking down at the totally engorged, streamlined penis. Tom felt its throbbing in his hand. It waited for him to do something, whatever would advance its pleasure. To be at the controls like this, directing his sensations toward a specific end—this he had forgotten about. This he wished deeply, deeply, to experience again, and that wish had turned into consent. He swallowed with a dry mouth when he felt that consent click inside him, the finality of it fall into place, and he was going to masturbate. The intention was solid. The sin had already taken effect.

That fact was dizzying. He had rationally put himself across the line, outside of the state of grace, according to some. Yes, he dared the risk. "Yes," he whispered, "I consent." And an unfamiliar sensation began rising up from his thighs.

Mentally he invited Ruthie and her ice cream cone to come on the scene, but she refused to appear, so he gave his full attention to the nude in the mirror, the impostor, standing unabashedly with his penis in hand, staring brazenly, waiting for him to make a move. Tom started sliding the skin of his penis back along its hard bone. Then both Tom and his image bent their legs, touching knees, four knees touching, four thighs filling, muscles bulging, two penises in hand, two sets of balls swinging toward one another as he jerked off, faster, sliding the skin back and forth over the hardness, rapidly, smoothly, over the glowing bone with its tiny gaping mouth. It felt as if rays of light were leaking out of his chest, something magical happening near his testicles. Weakness mixed with pleasure, increasing, promising more. More light into his chest, more joy. He wanted that avalanche, that joy, to explode in him. His hand was working so fast it had become a blur in the mirror. His thighs were full and hard, shining with sweat. His forearm began to bulge and to ache. He bit his lip, but he wouldn't stop until it came out of him, until he was ready to . . . "Oh!" He groaned, feeling something break loose inside him—a burning liquor, shooting up inside. He groaned, as if he was about to overflow, to spill out, any moment . . . and he did, shooting out. "Uh. Ohhhh!" he cried softly. The come hit the mirror. A white flower appeared there. Another. Then several, as if the blooms shot out of him, open, onto the glass that way. His knees touching, knees to knees, as he leaned against the mirror. And even more came out of him, smaller white flowers, dripping down like the spidery petals of a rare orchid. His legs trembled. His body suddenly felt light as air, about to rise. He saw his face in the mirror, pained, ecstatic, like the face of Christ on the cross, and dripping longer and longer, the spidery petals of an almost transparent white bloom, dripping down, huge, delicate orchids, all over the mirror, hanging from his hand.

After his shower, he felt leaden, exhausted. Hair wet and flattened; dark shadows in the mirror, around his eyes. They were not as sharp as the man's eyes in Katelyn's bathroom mirror. These eyes seemed tired, older. He pressed wrinkles out of his forehead with his thumbs, but, of course, that didn't make them disappear. He had looked young during the orgasm, ghostly, angelic. Now his face was older than ever. He held his wet hair back off his face. "Too late, Tom," he whispered into the mirror, without fully understanding what he was trying to tell himself.

Then the sadness came, the same sadness that had made him weep in Gene's room. But this time the emotion was attached to an image, the cause of his tears: Katelyn. It was Katelyn he wanted, not the man in the mirror. He fell on the bed and tried to blot out thought. He lay there for more than an hour until he fell asleep.

Chapter Nine

IT WAS THREE IN THE AFTERNOON when Tom called the jitney from the hallway phone at Stella Maris to learn when a bus was leaving Montauk. He put on his black suit and clerical collar. He threw a razor and a toothbrush into his suitcase and knocked on Kruug's door.

"Come in. Come in. Looks like you and Montauk got to know one another." Kruug's face was bright and rested, his gray crew-cut freshly trimmed.

"Welcome home."

"Thanks. At lunch I heard that you're getting along with Gene."

"Yes, thanks."

"Tom, I want you to do me a favor and find an architect to take out that altar rail and to make the right changes in the church. Also, just drive around this town with me in the next couple of days so we can sniff out some work to keep us busy."

"Well, yes. But I came to ask *you* a favor first."

"What is it?" Kruug's eyes went to the suitcase.

"I'd like to take some of those vacation days to visit Waterford, say, till Saturday."

Kruug reacted as though Tom had asked a complicated question. The monsignor remained open-mouthed, then became animated, flipping through the large stack of mail on his desk. "Would it matter terribly, Tom, if we held off a tiny bit on those vacation days?"

"Yes, it would." Tom frowned. "To tell you the truth, I wouldn't like holding off if it doesn't cause any grave inconvenience here."

"But I just got back." Kruug offered a weak smile. "There's so much I want to go over with you." Tom's obvious discomfort stopped Kruug short; he shrugged his shoulders and stepped behind his desk. "Forget it. Go, if you like. I promised you."

"Thank you." Tom managed a smile.

"What's this," Kruug said slowly, pretending more interest in the mail than in what he was saying, "that I'm told about this woman? Is her name Katelyn?" Kruug looked up suddenly, catching Tom's surprise. Katelyn's name on Kruug's lips was such an improbability. Her name filled the room, a block of marble hovering in midair.

Tom jumped ahead of the question. "Monsignor, I appreciate what you're trying to do for me, and I don't want to sound impertinent, but Muriel has got to keep her place around here if I'm to stay."

"Oh? What has Muriel to do with this?"

"She obviously spies and reports to you."

"You've been talking to Buoncuore." Kruug smiled.

"Then how did you find out the woman's name?"

"All right. Muriel told me you had a visitor."

"Uh huh."

"But Miss Jane's Auto Body called me about her check, which bounced, by the way."

"I'll stop at Miss Jane's and make good for it," Tom said, embarrassed.

"No need. I told Miss Jane to redeposit it and to let me know if there's any problem."

"Thank you." Tom looked down in embarrassment. "I still think you should talk to Muriel."

"Muriel, Muriel." Kruug shook his head to the sky in comic supplication. "Muriel's a true tragedy. She's full of flaws, but I'd give the shirt off my back to her sooner than to the holiest nun. She's had more heartaches than ten of us. Husband set the house on fire; he died in it; only child, a daughter, died in it. She's a finished lady, Tom." Tom felt guilty as Kruug spoke so matter-of-factly of Muriel's terrible fate. "I started counseling her and got her to want to live. Me and this place are all she's got. I'll never pull the rug out from under Muriel. Maybe she snoops. Who cares?"

"You're paying a high price for her."

"Don't worry, Tom. When you get a little older, you'll see more and more how priests have to *make* solutions for people or they just refuse to occur." Kruug seemed solid in his defense. He had fully played out the subject of Muriel. Tom anticipated the danger of his next question. "Have you really known this Katelyn Snow over a year?"

"Monsignor, I don't understand the importance you have placed upon this woman. I met her on the bus that you suggested I take out here. I never saw her before that in my life. She's not even Catholic. Yes, I lied about knowing her a year to help the woman get a car. That's all. I *made* a solution, as you say." Tom hated how he sounded. He should have answered more calmly, more simply.

"I didn't ask for a detailed explanation."

"I merely *tried* to help someone *out,*" Tom said with unnecessary finality, "as a *priest.*"

"Good. That's what we're here for. Did you help her?"

"Yes, I certainly did."

"So there's no need for you to see her again, is there?"

"Huh? I beg your pardon?"

"Did I say something wrong?" Kruug smiled.

"Why make anything out of my seeing or not seeing this woman again?" Tom asked quickly.

"I thought you said she was all right now."

"Well, she is."

"Then why would you have to see her?"

"What if she's become a . . . a friend of mine?"

"Ohhhh. I seeee."

"Well, why not?"

"No reason, but . . . " Kruug stood, not looking at Tom. "I hope you won't mind it if I say I don't favor your seeing this woman anymore." Kruug said it as though he were breaking very bad news.

"I certainly *would* mind." Tom's face turned so red that Kruug turned away. "I mind that you presume to forbid me such a thing. I didn't come all the way to Montauk to repeat my situation with Granger."

Kruug held motionless, looking out the window.

"You diocesan priests have got the whole thing wrong." Tom's voice dropped.

"What thing?" Kruug asked, frowning and turning back to Tom.

"The priesthood. You've made it a kind of fraternity, a big-brother commune."

"Okay, then. Tell me what I'm doing wrong here and I'll change it."

"I'd like you to focus in here, okay? I'd like you to get off Gene and give him back his work and drop this black-dress rule, drop this quarantine, and after that, you and *I* have to agree on a few other things, like the fact that you have no authority to forbid me to see people because they're a certain gender. That's out. I would question anybody's right to do such a thing. Okay?" Tom was talking strong but wild now. "I can't let you pull a stunt like that, Monsignor."

"Did I *forbid* you to see her? What did I say? I said I don't *favor* your seeing her; she's not a parishioner. She's not even Catholic."

"Monsignor, don't pull that parochial stuff. We're here for humanity."

"I didn't *forbid* you anything," Kruug repeated strongly. "Let's get that out of the way first. And when it comes to Gene Buoncuore, again, I emphasize, I do not *favor* your interference. He's an extremely complicated guy, and I obviously don't have your sympathy with him."

"In other words, mind my own business."

"Precisely."

"What if I tell you I'm gravely worried that you are going to destroy his priesthood?" Tom asked.

"Do you really think I would let such a thing happen?"

"You may not intend it, but you will be the instrument of it."

"Now *that* is presumptuous." Kruug pointed a finger at Tom's face. "And a little ironic that you should be worried about Gene's priesthood when yours is in trouble enough."

"What trouble is my priesthood in?"

"Oh, come on. Look at you. You walk in here to tell me that you're leaving before I've even had a chance to say hello to you, before we can talk about your work. You're a Jesuit of sorts, who bounces around, who doesn't want the missions, doesn't want to teach. What the hell *do* you want?"

"I came out here to work, but I don't see much work around. What did *you* want to do with me?"

"You're in Montauk because you couldn't handle Granger," Kruug jumped in. "That's the number-one reason. Face that first."

"That's not accurate and you know it. I lasted longer with Granger than any diocesan curate, didn't I? And we're talking about Gene here, if you don't mind."

"You haven't a clue to the trouble Gene is in." Kruug turned with a look of disturbance clouding his face.

"So he socked one of your monsignors. From what I've seen of the monsignors up here I find that quite natural."

"I don't find that amusing."

"I don't mean you. I'm trying to wake you up to something."

"Oh, are you?"

"Gene's in more trouble than you realize."

"No," Kruug shouted. "He's in more trouble than *you* realize, and if you weren't so damn thick-headed, you wouldn't believe him so totally. You'd shut up and listen to what the hell I'm trying to tell you." Kruug was yelling. He cleared his throat and turned, knowing he couldn't talk reasonably at that pitch. He swallowed painfully. "I won't go into his narcissism; I won't go into his adolescent, stubborn authority problem, or the other problems of Gene's personality. DeGroot alone is enough for now. DeGroot has turned this assault thing into a grand opera. He's playing cat and mouse with the bishop over it. He's got us all by the short hairs. *He* calls the shots. He's the one insisted on Gene's faculties being suspended, all of Gene's functions terminated, not me. He got himself a non-Catholic lawyer, and every time he wakes up on the wrong side of the bed, he threatens the bishop with a civil lawsuit. DeGroot's got a portfolio of jaw X-rays, doctors', dentists' statements, and you wonder why I have to keep the lid on Gene?"

"Why doesn't the bishop let DeGroot sue and get it over with?"

"How would Gene like being on the cover of the *National Enquirer?*"

"Gene's so bored he'd love it."

"The bishop is not that bored."

"Then why do you make it harder for Gene by imposing this black-suit law and this ridiculous quarantine?"

"I believe in the black suit and white collar. Okay? I'm a nut."

"Oh, come on, Monsignor."

"I have a plaid shirt in that closet"—Kruug pointed, moving out from behind the desk—"but you'll never see me outside this room wearing the damned thing. Out of *principle.*" He slammed his palm on his desk. "I wear a cassock or black suit and collar and nothing else, except my skivvies in bed, and not because I love a uniform, but to do my part in keeping this priesthood of ours from going down the drain."

"But why force Gene?"

"Didn't you entertain the possibility that Gene Buoncuore had some problems of his own, before DeGroot? I'm sure Buoncuore didn't tell you everything." Kruug paused, a little out of breath. "Don't be so cocksure, Tom. People in this diocese know a lot more about Gene than you, and everybody agrees his spirit has to be broken."

"Monsignor, people don't hold still to have their spirits broken."

"Gene will. He'll have to, dammit." Kruug shoved a drawer closed with his knee. He had a temper of his own. "Maybe the

word *spirit* is wrong here. Maybe I mean his thick-headedness.
I don't know."

"Well, get yourself clear on it, because there's a big difference."

"Don't be a moral prig, Tom." He held Tom with a clear
warning and steady eye. He moved to his four windows, then
shifted uneasily back around, facing Tom. "I appreciate your
defending him. A lot more could be said that I can't say, I won't
say. But Gene has one major social defect. He assumes authority
over everyone in order to get along with them, authority that
was never dispensed to him, authority that others won't *allow*
him to exercise. He's even a bully with me. If a child wants to
drive a truck off a cliff, do you give him the keys? He'll destroy
himself and me with him. Oh, he's fooled you. It's a power
struggle with him, a death struggle with the child in him. He's
begging for what I'm giving him, and don't make the unclever
mistake of thinking otherwise. He loves the game."

"Do you?" Tom's question was a surprise.

"Do *I*? Yes, maybe I do, deep down. But I also believe Gene
is very scared of his power. He's dying to be saddled, longing for
someone to beat him at his game, because he *wants* to be let off
the hook. He *wants* to be broken. He wants someone stronger
than him to protect him, to control him."

"You talk as if he were a horse."

"He is. A very wild one."

"He'll kick your walls down, Monsignor," Tom said with
calm authority. "He'll escape you. Don't play win-or-lose with
Gene."

"The man isn't worth a dime to me. There's a million Genes
out there. It's the priest I'm out to save. If Gene breaks the stall
down, let him run, let him join the billions out there like him.
If he doesn't, then the Church gains a priest."

"And loses a man," Tom said, embarrassed by the cliché.

"One man less in the Church won't matter. It's priests we
need."

"To swing their capes in the people's faces?" Tom said boldly.
"How many women and children are beaten by their husbands

in this parish? Do you know the figure, Monsignor?"

"Oh, why this now?"

"How many migrant workers out here? How much do they get paid? How many people are psychologically depressed around here? How many suicides? How much vandalism? How much unemployment? How much delinquency, drug abuse? How many murders? Why aren't you working in the city where one apartment house has more problems than ten parishes out here? Why aren't we all there?"

"Because you needed a bloody rest," Kruug slipped in, "and because Gene Buoncuore broke somebody's face in half."

Tom turned. "Then give me the rest I'm asking for. Let me go for a few days. And as for Gene, let me assure you he'd be better off passing out food vouchers in Brooklyn instead of sitting here in a black suit and collar like a Carthusian monk in solitary confinement. He lifts weights in a box of a room all day when he could be climbing stairs to find out why people are crying behind their doors. Those tragedies out there—multiply your Muriel a million times over. Punish a priest with work, Monsignor, don't try to break his spirit."

"A priest's work isn't worth crap unless he has humility, Tom. He can tap-dance till doomsday." Kruug turned, voiceless in the aftermath of his own words. His eyes strained out the window, to a spot in the sky above the ocean. "Will you be staying with your folks in Waterford?" The monsignor asked softly, though his head was throbbing from the power of his heartbeat.

"My folks are dead," Tom answered.

"Relatives then?"

"I'll be in a motel." Tom cleared his throat. "I have no relatives."

"What motel?" Kruug's voice struggled to avoid a manipulative tone.

"I have no idea what motel, Monsignor." Tom was sorry he lied.

"You'll call and let me know what motel, when you're settled?"

Tom did not look away from Kruug's poker face. "Why must I call you? I don't understand."

"No *must* intended, just simply call, the way you would call your family of your whereabouts in case anything happens."

"I don't want to have a family at this point in my life."

It hurt him to say it, but he didn't trust Kruug. Muriel might have heard at the door when he and Gene planned the lie. She might have forewarned him. In fact, now it seemed to Tom to be exactly the case.

"I understand," Kruug said with a suddenly relaxed throat and closed eyes, "that you already visited home, the other day, with Gene, by ferry." His eyes blinked open.

"That's correct." Tom swallowed. "May I ask how you know that?"

"Oh." Kruug turned. "Gene mentioned it at lunch."

"I see," Tom said, blinking, but not avoiding Kruug.

"I just wondered if it's best for you to spend more time there, with no relatives. To what end?"

"Nostalgia," Tom said simply.

"*Nostalgia,*" Kruug repeated mockingly.

"My parents' grave. To visit it." Tom hated himself. The guilty feeling was sucking him in deeper.

"I see," Kruug said with humility.

"It was foggy the other day, and the cemetery seemed pointless."

"Yes, Gene said it was foggy."

"Oh. Did he?" Tom was dizzy, confused. He couldn't tell the difference between what Kruug knew through Muriel's eavesdropping and what he knew from talking to Gene. The possibility that Kruug knew he was going to Katelyn made standing before him extremely difficult. Tom's lie obliterated all the logic of the conversation.

"Well." Kruug straightened up and put a hand to his back. "I suppose I should say good-bye, for the next few days. I had thought we'd talk about things, the work. There could be a solid parish here, with effort."

"I'd love to talk about it," Tom said softly, "when I come back."

"Yes. When you come back," Kruug said calmly. "Who is going to drive you to the ferry?"

"Huh?" Tom hadn't anticipated this question. "I don't know what you mean."

"How are you going to get to the New London ferry?"

"Jitney, I suppose." Another lie.

"The jitney doesn't go to the ferry from here. Take the parish car." Kruug's offer seemed sincere.

"I thought I'd leave the car for Gene."

"Take mine then." Kruug fished in his cassock for his keys.

"I couldn't. I'd rather get there some other way."

"There's no way to Orient Point except by car." Kruug threw the keys onto the desk. Tom hesitated, then reached for them.

"Thank you very much, Monsignor. Good-bye, then. I'll be back soon."

"Have fun," Kruug said lifelessly, turning toward his window. As Tom closed the door he could see Kruug still standing there, arms folded, looking out to the ocean.

That first night that Kruug was back an intense silence pervaded the rectory. Only a thin yellow light showed under his door. Muriel's room was mute, except for the tinny sounds of her miniature TV. Gene walked aimlessly down to the water in his cassock. A month ago, at that same hour, the sun was hovering on the western horizon. Now it was long gone. By December it would get dark at four-thirty. Gene looked longingly south, toward those islands of hibiscus blossoms and palm trees that floated in transparent waters near the equator. When he got back to his room, he took two aspirins and read till three.

In the morning the bedside lamp was knocked over and his ashtray was on the floor. He cleaned up, vaguely remembering extraordinary dreams. His cigarette ashes left a ring in his toilet bowl. As he flushed it over and over, one dream came back to him, of white dunes, a black ocean, a violet sky and sea grass growing, and a real estate man walking through sand, wearing dress shoes and black silk socks, leading him to a mountainous dune, behind which sat the sun, itself constructed of thousands of cedar planks, each wider than a billboard, huge nails rusted, weathered planks fallen, entangled in one another, a vision of a great corroding wooden sun, a giant lens of ancient cedar, the skeleton of light.

Gene lifted weights that morning, trying to chase those dream images back into his unconscious. He watched himself puffing in the bathroom mirror. His eyesockets were darker. It was time to get Kruug on his side. He felt his ego crumbling. He considered offering his transformation up to God the way they suggested in the meditation books, but he held back with distrust, fearing it would make him anemic and vague. He feared sanctity.

All day he flipped through magazines, and by the time Muriel's supper buzzer rang, he had worked out a plan to engage Kruug in a man-to-man confrontation about the quarantine.

He entered the dining room in his cassock, blessed himself, and sat down with the monsignor. He uncovered the silver dish of sliced white bread and offered some to Kruug. Kruug shook his head in refusal. Gene took a slice for himself and attempted to spread the hard butter on it. It tore the bread. He folded the slice into a square and bit into it.

"Tom out?" He kept his mouth closed as he chewed.

"He's visiting home." Kruug's voice was flat.

Muriel brought in their lobsters, and the monsignor passed his hand over the dead red creatures, blessing them in the sign of the cross. Then he went at his dinner with the finesse of a surgeon, so engrossed that he could respond only minimally to Gene's talk.

When the lobster shells were taken away, Kruug wiped his hands on a linen napkin. "There's a priest saying mass in church right now. He'll be doing so every evening at six for the next two weeks."

"Okay."

"His name is Foley, and he's vacationing at his parents' house here in Montauk. You might want to pay a visit to the Blessed

Sacrament and pray with him," Kruug said, standing. "Excuse me." Kruug threw down his napkin and blessed himself loudly, saying his thanksgiving after meals. He tucked his head inside the swinging door to the kitchen. "Muriel," he said with boyish intimacy, "Father Blake is picking me up in a few seconds. Will you hold my dessert and slip my phone messages under my door, please?"

"Yes, Monsignor."

"Thank you, Muriel." Kruug let the door close and made for the hallway.

"Why don't you speak to me in that tone?" Gene asked softly. Kruug stopped in his tracks.

"Don't get ugly, Gene."

"I'm not being ugly. I'm asking an honest question."

Kruug examined Gene's face. "All right, forgive me, then."

"Are you afraid to talk to me or something?" Gene asked.

Kruug's eyes narrowed with suspicion.

"Loosen up, for crying out loud. I'm not your enemy. I would like to be able to talk to you."

"All right. I'll *loosen* up. Talk." Kruug pulled out his chair, sat, folded his arms, and crossed his legs.

"Okay." Gene stood. "I want you to know . . . " He hesitated.

"I'm listening." Kruug swung his foot.

" . . . that I'm willing to meet you halfway."

"No halfway, Gene." Kruug shook his head with a knowing smile.

"Wait a minute."

"No halfway."

"Gimme a chance to finish."

"Okay, finish."

"I'm beginning to realize that I've got to be more civil around here, to get on the good side of you, frankly."

"How do you propose to get on the good side of me?"

"By talking, the way I'm doing right now. Obviously, I'm trying to communicate, to be friendly."

"Are you worried that *I* need the friendship?"

"C'mon. Have a heart, Monsignor. You know what I'm saying."

"You like shortcuts, Buoncuore, but they don't work with me. Your actions are the things that either reduce or expand the distance between you and me."

"I'm not allowed actions in this place. There's nothing I can act on, nothing I can do."

"Why don't you go into church and sit in on Father Foley's mass?"

"Huh? I don't want to sit in on mass. I want to pray my own mass."

"Have you kept your quarantine?"

"Monsignor, it's ridiculous."

"But have you kept it?"

"Of course I haven't."

"Thanks for not lying to me."

"I won't lie to you, Monsignor."

"All I'm asking, Gene, is for a sign you're keeping the rules here, signs that you're praying. Show me you respect what I'm trying to achieve with you. Let me know I'm the boss and that you're not the one in control here leading us all around by the nose, and I'll take you very seriously. But until then, neither your sweet talk nor your tough talk is going to sway me."

Gene took a deep breath. "I'm suffering, Kruug. I am."

"I know."

"But you may not know how bad. I hate this place."

"You're no softie, Gene."

"Kruug, if you appeared at the throne of God tomorrow, and God told you to look into your heart and lay out in front of Him the total truth about how and why you treat me as you do, what would you have to tell Him? The truth, now."

"I'd say: 'Lord, this Buoncuore may look tough, but he's a seducer, a charmer, a spoiled child, and You must grant me the power to resist his stubborn will, steel my heart to his cunning for his own good, so I can help make him a humble son and servant of Yours, in whom You can take pride, for there is no other way for a priest.' " Kruug's eyes appeared to be glassing over. "This is the kind of battle a priest must lose in order to enter the kingdom of heaven. Let yourself break, Gene. Don't be a coward. Let yourself lose."

"Oh, my God!" Gene whispered, turning away.

"You asked," Kruug stated firmly.

"I don't trust you. I don't believe you. I don't believe you believe yourself."

Kruug stood with a hurt expression. "It's obvious who has to give in to make you happy. Will you excuse me now?" Kruug went into the doorway and stopped. He turned, looking back. "As you know, Gene," he said with gentleness, "the Church is a monarchial organization. We have a hierarchy. I am your superior. To obey me brings a grace that God bestows upon people like you. If you cannot trust me as a person, at least you can trust in God. He wouldn't cheat you." Gene didn't respond. Kruug disappeared down the hall and into his room.

Muriel cleaned away the dinner table as Gene let go a mental prayer, up through the roof, through the clouds, and beyond. *If you exist at all, then rescue me.*

Muriel returned, backside first through the swinging door, balancing a tall slice of watermelon on a white dish. Gene pretended not to notice the smile that twisted her mouth. She put the watermelon before him.

"May I get you some coffee?" she asked with sweetness.

"No."

When he was alone again, Gene looked down at the bright fruit that radiated coolness under his face. He loved the frosty pink of fresh-cut watermelon, that red-pink, sweet and vibrating, like fire under ice. When he was a boy, he would break off the peak, the heart of the melon, and eat it when his mother wasn't watching.

A sudden wish to water-ski made Gene's legs fill with blood. In an hour the Atlantic would turn to fire as it swallowed the sun. He craved the excitement of skiing on red water. He would ski dangerously, touching his ear to the mirror surface, leaving twenty-foot orange fans in his wake. He would pretend he was flying toward the edge of the world, dissolving into the molten sun. He pushed out his chair and left Muriel's watermelon untouched.

He immediately started undressing in his room. A hot shower might calm him, he thought.

Gene pulled open the shower door and stepped under the steaming torrent. The water was extremely hot, but he didn't alter the temperature. He leaned against the white tiles, letting the water drench him with its heat. His sinuses opened with a click. He sucked the steam into his lungs. Then he stood up straight and soaped up with shampoo. He rinsed, watching the foam glide down his dark legs to his feet. He advanced the handle to cold, but he didn't feel the unpleasant shock he expected. His body tightened up, meeting the icy downpour with hard strength of its own.

He half-dried himself with a big white towel. Tying it around his waist, he stepped into the hall. He quietly dialed the marina and told the dock boy he'd be there in fifteen minutes. He impatiently ran back inside, grabbing one of the cartons near his bed. When he pulled open the cardboard flaps, he smelled his old rectory in Brooklyn. He peeled off a pair of cool, damp white cotton trousers, then a white dress shirt, thin white summer dress socks. He would be all in white, all clothes of his that had been washed in Brooklyn, all folded by Natalie, the Italian housekeeper with the beautiful face, whom the pastor had hired her first week in America. Everything fresh from Natalie's wash —everything white—smelling like apples, like straw, like a woman's hair.

From his window he watched Father Blake's black station wagon pull out with Kruug in the passenger seat. He plunged himself into darkness by pulling the light chain, and turned, checking for his wallet, keys. He hesitated before twisting the knob of the hallway door, giving thought to what he would say if he bumped into Muriel. His watch said six thirty-five. The visiting priest was now kneeling in the sacristy, facing the wall crucifix, making his meditation after mass. Muriel would be in her room unless the phone rang.

Slowly, Gene pulled open the door and peeked down the corridor. Quiet. Empty. He slipped into the hallway, closed the door softly behind him, and started walking down the carpeted aisle. No sign of her.

The floor under the rug squeaked.

Suddenly Muriel's door opened, causing all the doors to bang gently against their locks. Still, he didn't see her until he proceeded farther. She was in her doorway like a statue, arms folded, a lit cigarette streaming smoke at her elbow. She never smoked in the presence of the other priests. He often wondered if she wasn't inviting his contempt. It was all in the way she deliberately dragged on the cigarette, distorting her mouth in a half smile, suspending her usual nervousness, lifting her sore eyebrows as she blew smoke toward him with the expression of a servant turned master.

"Can we speak privately?" she asked bluntly.

Gene hesitated but stepped inside. She closed the door behind him and went to her dresser. She obviously ate meals in the tiny room. The drum table was set with a small round tablecloth, pepper and salt, teapot and cup. A tall sparkling glass held one spoon. The oversized dresser mirror was tilted inward, giving back to the room its own reflection. The dresser was black oak with comical squatty Queen Anne legs on wooden wheels. One wheel was split in half. The dresser and her metal wood-grained bed left little room for anything except a tall wing chair of peach satin brocade which had a flattened and soiled cushion. He smelled geraniums.

Standing before the mirror, Muriel appeared twice. Two hands rose, bringing two cigarettes to her two mouths, two mushrooms of smoke flew to the ceiling, her back was to another woman in another room, addressing another dark-haired man. A gold lipstick tube and a bottle of dark-red nail polish stood on the dresser. Gene's eyes were drawn to them. Her expression reprimanded his straying eyes.

"I want to get along with you, but I can live without it," she said, flicking her ash. "You might as well know I'm not about to do you favors."

"What else is new?"

"Don't be sarcastic." She took another drag, with complete confidence. She was enjoying herself. Gene assumed she desperately needed the therapy of acting out her cruelty on him. She was so swollen with hard luck. "I'd appreciate it if you'd tell your old parishioners not to call here. You're not supposed to be working, and we get more phone calls from Brooklyn than from Montauk. I'm too busy to answer your phone calls. I'm a housekeeper, not a secretary."

"I was working with a lot of people before I came here."

"Well, it keeps the phone tied up."

"If the phone is tied up, it won't ring, and you won't have to answer it."

She smiled like a bad little girl, turning away to take another drag as she spoke. "Monsignor doesn't want you holding up the phone, and that's it in a nutshell." She blew the smoke out.

"Let Monsignor tell me then."

"He *will,*" she said, widening her eyes. She paused, almost coquettishly.

"Is this all you wanted, Muriel?"

"You're not supposed to leave this rectory dressed that way."

"Oh?"

"He told me to let him know if you do."

"So let him know." Gene shrugged.

She hesitated, flicked an ash. "Okay," she sang, facing herself in the mirror. She opened the drawer and threw the lipstick and nail polish in, then slammed it closed. "That's all I wanted to say."

Gene hesitated, realizing he had lost some kind of contest with her. "Muriel, am I leaving the rectory? Look at me, please."

"What are you dressed in white for?"

"I'm headed down to the water, to roll up my pants and cool off my feet."

"With car keys in your hand?"

"Why not?"

"C'mon, Buoncuore. You're on your way out in lay clothes and he's only five minutes away. He left the telephone number." She smiled in an almost intimate way. "Why don't you do yourself a favor and go back to your room?"

"Muriel, I'm suddenly allergic to your cigarette." He started coughing.

"This is my room," she drawled.

"Yes, but you invited me in here, so would you please be polite enough to put it out." She took another drag, trembling warily. Then she crushed the cigarette in a glass ashtray, blowing the smoke over his head as she looked at him. He pointed a finger at her. "Good. Now you call me *Father,* Muriel, not Buoncuore." His eyes pinned hers with solemn authority. She wasn't strong enough for them. *"Father* Buoncuore," Gene repeated. "Did you hear? Don't *dare* call me anything else." He tried to filter the trembling out of his voice, but it overtook his throat, and he gagged momentarily, putting his fist to his mouth to clear it.

She grew a bit stronger in these few seconds. "Aren't *you* the respectable priest, *Father."* She drawled the word out in mock servility.

"Muriel, as a personal favor, you know what I'd like you to do?"

"No favors."

"I'd like you to go fuck yourself." The word surprised her. She threw her hands to her ears. "Didn't hear it."

Gene opened her door and stepped into the hall. "You heard it, you bimbo." He slammed her inside and walked toward the water, through the beach roses, to elude her eyes. But it wasn't Muriel who caused his blood to boil those few minutes as much as it was Kruug, for keeping her as a gargoyle to express his own hostility. He jumped down behind the pines to the dunes out of her sight, then he climbed back up the sharp side of the cliff where her eyes couldn't follow.

He entered the church through the west-side cellar door, crossing downstairs, and taking the inside stairs up to the sacristy. The visiting priest was kneeling at the prie-dieu, facing the crucifix on the wall. Gene realized he would have to tiptoe behind him to get into the sanctuary where the ski was hidden. When Gene stepped onto the white marble floor, into the huge sun-filled space, his eyes were drawn immediately upward. The church seemed roofless. Dust particles whirlpooled inside beams of light slowly, like stars crossing the night sky, little universes in the bands of late sun that were shooting down from tilted panels of stained glass. Deeply colored hues were flooding the upper church beyond the dust-filled sunlight. The effect was dizzying. He quietly lifted the sedilia top and took the ski from it, but when he turned to leave, and his soft-soled sneakers touched upon the Persian rug, he felt disoriented, as if he had stepped upon a moving cloud. He wished for heavy vestments to anchor him down in the immense space. When he genuflected, touching his knee to the rug, the spears of white gladiolas seemed to shoot out of their silver vases. He stood quickly, to dispel the illusion, walking away from the altar, off the rug, onto the marble. He looked down at his feet as they flew off the marble steps toward the church floor. His white sneakers flickering on the white stairs gave him the feeling he was not touching them. He tried to grip the stairs with his toes, to prevent his floating up bodily, beyond the bands of sunlight, into the deeply colored hues near the roof where Christ hung almost life-sized and crucified. He unlatched the golden altar gates quickly and jumped off the marble onto the dark church floor. Suddenly his sneakers squealed out on the rubber tiles, as though they deliberately intended to betray him. He stopped in his tracks, turning to see if the visiting priest would come into the sanctuary to investigate. No one appeared, so he resumed walking on tiptoe, holding the ski before his body, hidden from view.

He heard a far-off click, as if the sacristy door had opened. He had to run now. His sneakers screamed. Then a voice sang out, rising up to the dome where Mary was trying to escape through the center of the tornado of water.

"*Gene.*" The voice echoed like a gong, then melted. Gene didn't turn. The gong rang again: "*Father Buoncuore.*" Kruug's voice seemed to have no coloration of anger. But when Gene turned, he could see that Kruug was furious. The monsignor's face was pink and puffy. "Stay where you are." Kruug pointed, then genuflected. He marched down the steps, kicked open the gates with a clang, and stepped onto the dark church floor. "I want the car keys." Kruug held out a hand impatiently. Muriel's head peeked out the sacristy door, followed by the head of Father Foley, as Kruug in his cassock flew down the middle aisle toward Gene. Gene could hear only the shrieking gabardine Roman cassock swishing toward him. Kruug's black shoes kicked the cassock with each step, flapping and flashing its purple piping like rods of fire. As Kruug marched, his hair-covered fingers curled impatiently inward, as if luring the keys out of Gene's hand. "Gimme," he mumbled. "Gimme my keys, and get back into that rectory, and take off those clothes."

"I'm not in the mood for your bullcrap anymore, Kruug," Gene said quietly, but with a grim anger of his own.

Kruug kept coming. "C'mon. My keys. Throw them." He stopped about ten feet before Gene, suddenly noticing the ski. "What in the name of God is *that* thing?"

"It's a water ski."

"Is that your excuse for getting all decked out like an ice cream vendor?"

Gene tossed the keys so that they hit Kruug's chest and fell to the floor. The monsignor squatted into his cassock and came up, bouncing the keys in his hand. His face was redder. "Go into the rectory, you . . . " His head was shaking involuntarily.

"What for?" Gene said calmly, pretending a laugh.

"I beg your pardon?"

"What if I refuse to do what you tell me?"

"Huh?" Kruug stared open-mouthed.

"What if I tell you go blow it out your nose?" Gene yelled. "What're you gonna do to me?"

The visiting priest stepped forward into the sanctuary, gently calling: "Monsignor. Monsignor, do you need help? Monsignor?"

Kruug turned and shouted, *"Go back to your meditation, Father. I can handle this quite well alone."* Kruug's sentences blended together in huge echoes.

The visiting priest kept inching down the stairs to the golden gates. "Monsignor, may I suggest that you . . . "

Kruug pointed dramatically at the visiting priest. *"Stay there,*

Father, and don't take another step." Kruug whipped his head back
to Gene. "Go back into that rectory, Gene," Kruug ordered,
"before we have a mess here. All will be forgiven, provided you
bow to this."

"No bows. No more bows," Gene screamed. *"Fuck you, Kruug.
Fuck Muriel."* Gene's words rang like parrot shrieks off the walls.

"I can scream too," Kruug said weakly. "Do you want to *hear
me scream?"* The last three words harmonized, three shrill notes
rising fast as lightning up through the tornado, up past the soles
of Mary's bare feet, past clouds, to the eye of God, in heaven.

The two men stood facing one another, waiting for silence.
Kruug had brought out the total wildness in Gene. He wondered
at his easy power to do that.

"You . . . kill . . . my hope. You shouldn't be allowed," Gene
stammered.

"I will not argue in the presence of the Blessed Sacrament."
Kruug blinked nervously, reaching for the water ski. "Give me
that thing."

Gene jumped back like an ape, holding the ski like a baseball
bat. "Get away from me." Kruug's eyes widened with alarm. "Or
I'll . . . I'll . . . "

"You'll what?" Kruug pressed in mock calm. "You'll *what?"*
he repeated.

The visiting priest came forward. "Monsignor . . . "

"I'm calling the police," Muriel shouted into the sanctuary and
disappeared.

"Stop her," Kruug commanded the visiting priest.

Gene blinked away tears. "You . . . you are deliberately
killing . . . "

"I'm killing what? Speak up." Kruug was smiling stiffly.

"Me. *Me."*

"That may be true. Do you want to live?" He pointed a
shaking finger at Gene. "Then leave here on your own. You are
not going to break me. You are not going to win. Find yourself
another protector. Deal with DeGroot's lawyers yourself. You're
violent; you just confirmed that." Kruug's white hair made his
face the redder. "You probably don't belong in the priesthood

anyway." He turned and began walking up the aisle. "So go ahead. Leave, but don't come back."

Gene felt dizzy as he watched Kruug walk off, shocked by the clarity of Kruug's ultimatum, as if the whole scene had been rehearsed by Kruug to effect a sudden expulsion of Gene from the priesthood. "Hold it, Monsignor," Gene called, trying to force conciliation into his voice. Kruug kept walking. "Monsignor, *please,*" Gene called louder. Kruug sped, without turning, toward the marble stairs and the sanctuary. Gene called out, *"I beg you to turn around, Monsignor. Monsignoooooor,"* Gene screamed.

But Kruug neatly stepped inside the gates, locking them together with purposeful gentleness. Then, in a rage, Gene let go of the ski, sending it up over the hanging crucifix in an arch, so that it would fly over Kruug's head and fall in his path, stopping him. Like a javelin, it sailed over the hanging wooden cross, but it didn't arch. It kept going toward the stained-glass window behind the altar.

"Look out," the visiting priest cried. But Kruug couldn't understand what he meant, until the ski was stopped by the marble spire and came crashing down awkwardly, knocking over altar candles and silver vases, spilling water, dumping gladiolas onto the linens. Kruug didn't fully believe what he was seeing. When the ski tumbled from the altar table to the rug, he simply stared down at it, wondering how it had materialized at his feet. Only when he turned around and saw the ski no longer in Gene's hands did he comprehend what Gene had done.

Gene was becoming aware, with slow, growing panic, that he had just committed another irrational act exactly like the one that had gotten him into trouble with DeGroot. His face glowed hot; his whole body felt feverish, burning, as if his anger had set him on fire, as if flames were licking out from under his shirt sleeves, from under the cuffs of his trousers. It seemed impossible that the ski was no longer in his hands. He fell into a pew, half kneeling, suddenly sweating. A whisper flew out of him. "Kruug, I'm sorry. Please. Wait. Kruug, don't leave it this way."

Kruug came forward and looked down at the priest slumped in a pew of his empty church. Gene looked up.

"Why?" Gene asked gently. "Why did I give you something else to point to? Kruug, help me."

"I do have something else to point to now, don't I?" There was complete control in Kruug's voice.

"*You* started it, really. You," Gene pleaded.

"This is exactly what you wanted, Gene. You made it happen all over again. The moth just had to touch the flame again."

The visiting priest left the sanctuary. Kruug was about to follow when Gene narrowed his eyes and pointed a finger to hold Kruug for one more word. "*You're jealous of me, Kruug.*"

Kruug smiled sadly. "Who would be jealous of the trouble you're in? I'm going to have to contact the police." Kruug turned his back to Gene as he glided into the sacristy, where the visiting priest waited in the shadows.

The sacristy light went on. Magnified, unintelligible hisses filled the body of the church where Gene sat, as the visiting priest and Kruug whispered in the sacristy. The sacristy door slammed, locking total silence into the church. Gene remained half kneeling. He let his head hang down. "Jesus," he whispered to himself. "Jesus . . . Jesus . . . " He looked at both his hands, knuckles down, on the seat in front of him. He wanted to ask God for help, for a favor, but he couldn't. He tried to force some words out, but it was as though a hand were over his mouth. He had to blow the words through a vise. "Please. Please." But his voice didn't rise. The words dropped like dry crackers out of his mouth, littering the floor around him.

He could hear footsteps coming and going from the sacristy, the outer door opening and closing. He heard the safe door clang open, and when he lifted his head, Muriel was carrying Gene's chalice in its black case and several hangers of clothes, which she laid over the altar rail. Gene watched in shock as Muriel made several trips, obviously under Kruug's orders, to place all of Gene's things on the altar rail. Gene couldn't react. He sat back and watched, the way old ladies do after mass, lingering in the pews. He watched, under the tornado, as Muriel slowly brought out, respectfully, most of the things he owned: his boxes from Brooklyn, his shoes, his cassock, his books—everything appeared at the small marble altar rail.

Then the visiting priest appeared, snapping his fingers from the sacristy, signaling Muriel to come back. "What the heck are you doing?" Gene heard the visiting priest asking Muriel.

"The monsignor ordered it."

"Do me a favor, please?" the visiting priest asked, closing the door. His remaining words were muffled. Muriel raised her voice.

"I don't take orders from you, Father, and I . . . I have to clean up that mess on the altar."

"I'll clean it up," the priest insisted. "You go tell him what I said."

The oak drawers in the sacristy banged. Muriel obviously left, slamming the large oak door. The visiting priest entered the spacious sanctuary, carrying rolls of white linen across his arms. He climbed the altar steps, and laying the rolls of linen on the rug, he began to strip the altar with the vigor of a housewife changing bedsheets. Kicking off his shoes, he jumped up onto the bare altar with dexterity, righted the vases and candelabra, and gathered the fallen gladiolas. He dropped them neatly to the side. Then he jumped down and started drying the altar with his handkerchief. He picked up the fresh linens and, like a fisherman throwing a net, he let the roll fly above the altar, snapping it like a sail in the wind, until it fell exactly into place. In minutes, the altar was cleared, its symmetry restored even more precisely than before. The priest genuflected, then faced Gene. He was so young, light, curly hair, big hands, small waist. His eyes were close together, but beautifully soft, light brown.

"Gene," he called gently, coming through the altar gates. "My name's Vinnie Foley." He touched Gene's shoulder. "You've got to talk with Kruug."

"Didn't you hear me? I just tried to."

Foley's eyes were wide with confusion. "If you approach him, he has to talk, doesn't he? I mean, this is awful what just happened here."

"Did he call the cops?"

"He's told the woman to bring all your stuff down here, as you can see."

"Good," Gene said, trying to hide his uncertainty.

"But I think he *is* going to call the police."

"What the hell is he doing that for?"

"I guess you scared him. You did throw that thing."

"I didn't throw it *at* him. I threw it in his path because he was walking away while I was pleading with him."

"Hurry in and explain that to him in just those words."

"No. No!" Gene stood up with red eyes. "You don't understand." Gene opened the buttons of his white shirt and pulled its tail out of his trousers, revealing a bare chest and arms. "He *wants* it this way. He *loves* it this way." He tossed the shirt to the pews, unbuckled his belt, and unzipped his trousers.

"What are you doing?" Foley asked in alarm.

"I'm going to go," Gene said, letting his trousers down and stepping out of them. Gene was standing there in the middle aisle of the church, totally nude. Foley stepped back in shock as Gene went to the clothes that Muriel had piled on the altar rail. He found his black suit, pulled it off the hanger with his bib and white collar. He first fastened the collar at the back of his neck and tied the rabat around his waist. He threw on his black jacket over his bare skin, jumped into the black pants. Except for the sneakers, he seemed fully dressed as a priest.

"Killers," Gene muttered, beyond embarrassment.

"Who?" Foley asked quietly.

"All of you."

Foley tried to put an arm clumsily around Gene's shoulder. "Please come inside."

"No." Gene protested verbally, but he didn't slip out from under the priest's arm.

"What is it we kill?" the visiting priest asked, obviously stalling.

"Dreams," Gene said bitterly. "People's minds." Gene turned, walking toward the golden gates of the sanctuary.

"What are you going to do?" the visiting priest asked.

"Going to the overlook," Gene mumbled, "to see."

"To see what?" Gene did not answer. "Uh . . . are you walking there?"

"I'm walking. Yeah."

"Well, I'm going that way. I've got a car."

"Good for you."

"Would you like a ride?"

Gene stopped in his tracks. "Yes."

"Let's tell Kruug where we're going." The young priest's face was pasty and scared.

"Forget it." Gene turned in distrust.

"Wait. Just let me unlatch this gate, help you up these steps," the priest whispered. "Where, did you say? Which overlook? You direct me, okay?"

When the two men stepped outside, through the sacristy exit, Gene saw Muriel watching from the kitchen window. She was a fairy-tale Queen watching from her tower, like the witch in Snow White. He had not eaten her poisoned apple; still, he hadn't eluded her ire.

As they walked toward Foley's small blue Fiat, Gene sensed the priest waving an assurance to Muriel behind his back. Her mouth was going behind the glass, silently, reporting everything to someone behind her.

As the Fiat drove off, Gene couldn't erase Muriel's eyes from his mind. The entire world was her enemy, all except Kruug. Not even when Foley threw the Fiat into fourth gear, flying up over the asphalt hump onto Old Montauk Highway, could Gene erase the witch in Snow White from his mind and Muriel's blabbering, wrinkled mouth, soundless behind the kitchen window glass.

"Brakes," Gene ordered at the overlook. Foley pulled over. Gene jumped out. "Thanks." He reached back and shook Foley's hand through the window.

Foley looked back at Gene's serious face. "Now wait. Where you goin'?" Gene ignored him and jumped into the woods. Foley's eyes tracked him climbing up the small hill onto the asphalt overlook. Foley jumped out of the car and called out: "How's about just telling *me* where you're going? I'll keep it to myself, honestly." Not getting a response, Foley jumped into the Fiat and backed it up. Then he made a fast turn, speeding downhill, toward town.

When Foley was gone, Gene simply walked out of the woods and onto the road, putting up his thumb. A pickup truck stopped for him and took him to the crossroads from which it was a short walk to Westlake Marina.

The sun had set and the dock boy had given up on him. But there was still some light in the sky. The horizon was full of fine streaks of yellow and purple when Gene jumped into his little boat. The waters of the marina had turned to molten gold. Katelyn's flashlight was still fixed to the stern. He switched it on, so he wouldn't be stopped by the Coast Guard for not having a running light.

He detached the empty gas tank from the engine and set the new one in place. The engine burst into life with one pull of the cord. In minutes, Gene and his boat were calmly rounding the marina buoy, passing through the golden waters, out into the green choppy sea of the Atlantic.

He used up nearly half the tank of fuel just to get through the rip at Montauk Point. Then he slowly turned the tiny boat into the changing tide, rounding the lighthouse, as rod-and-reel fishermen watched from the rocks. Gene stood up in the boat, with one hand on the tiller, sniffing the wind. All he cared about now was speed. He'd have to go in the direction of the wind and it was out of the north, a land breeze they'd call it on the south side, and the water was rolling southwest, so he threw the throttle into high and went with the wind, in the direction of oncoming darkness. He remained standing, exploiting the strength in his legs, the muscles of his thighs and buttocks enjoying each skip of the boat. Now the wind was hitting his face, flattening his hair, filling him. It was a free-falling feeling, the kind he had had when he jumped off the Cross Bay Bridge at its highest point when he was twelve, grabbing first at the sky, then descending, like a spear, faster and faster toward the dark water.

The boat bucked monstrous swells, and he felt the boy inside coming to life, the same boy who would steal from his mother's purse to ride the Coney Island Cyclone in the front seat, over and over and over. That love of falling was his again, that fearless love of hurling downward, of staring gravity rudely in the eye. He roared a scream into the air above the noise of wind and his outboard. *"I'm coming back. I'm coming back, you sonofabitches."* He was warmed by the inner laughter of that boy who had become free at last, free to be once again on the side of danger, of recklessness and risk, and ironically, to be safe there, because it was so familiar. The boy screamed a squeal of joy, and the man a roar of triumph, both finally blending into one voice, one victory, a strange victory, of one over the other. Both now flew toward the darkest part of the horizon. Gene's black suit, all wet with spray, was sticking to his body like seaweed, while the ocean hissed and screamed at his face, to prove that it could be more out of control than he, or any man. The gauge of the fuel tank read far less than half full now. He could never get back to the marina against the wind and water. He couldn't even get back to the lighthouse, and after turning to glance back at the shore, he realized with wild excitement that he couldn't even get back to the beach. He was at the top of his leap now, reaching for the sky, in that rare moment of inertia, when there is no returning to the platform, no choice but to drop, into the dark, into the unpredictable, hollow unknown.

Chapter Ten

I'D LIKE TO STAY FOR A FEW DAYS," Tom said
bluntly, putting his black leather suitcase down on the cedar
deck. It took her a moment to react. He was so stiff, so very
nervous. Strain showed in his eyes. She knew to be very careful.
It was no time to say no. So she said yes with a little hesitation,
and it felt all right.

"Those shorts ready, by any chance?" He sniffled and tried a
smile.

"The one pair, yes."

"Good. Will you come swimming?"

"Do you mind if I continue working?"

"Not at all."

"Then I'll hang behind."

He went behind the palm-printed curtains and came out wearing the shorts.

"Perfect," she said with a deliberate smile.

While he was gone, she threw herself into her painting, even
though she was no longer in the mood. When he returned, she
didn't feel much like talking, but she was careful not to let it seem
like anger. She had prepared a snack of egg salad on brown bread
with apple juice, leaving it for him on the table inside. He

changed into his street clothes, laying the wet shorts on the wicker chair to dry.

Around eight he took a ride and returned with Chinese food. The light was gone by then and the wind had died down; still, there were no mosquitoes, so they ate outdoors.

She kept on the subject of painting, hoping that he would interpret her hyperactivity as creative overstimulation. But deep down, she was asking herself why she was so nervous. She knew it had to do with him, most assuredly, but whether it was anger at his being there, or excitement, she couldn't decide. At coffee, he looked from the deck toward the enormous rising moon and invited her once again to go for a swim. She declined, saying she had to clean up. He grabbed up the damp shorts and went inside. When he came out wearing them, she didn't look at him, though she warned him casually to be careful because the ocean could be nasty so late in the season, especially at night. He thanked her, saying that he'd noticed the ocean was behaving a bit crazily, and he left, wearing only the still-damp shorts. She watched him from the cedars, walking down Daniels Lane in the vague moonlight as if he were something wild in the road, no shirt, no towel, as if he were going to join the foxes and the hawks.

This time when he returned, she had a pot of tea waiting in the light of the red lampshade. He jumped onto the big bed and she brought cookies on a tray, propped herself up on pillows, and served him, squeezing a lemon wedge before dropping it into his cup. She tried not to notice the hair on his legs.

He seemed quite unlike a priest to her in the tan shorts she had made for him. They were wet, but she didn't suggest he change them. He propped himself up on his elbows. The soles of his feet faced her. His hair was drying curly from the water. Salt frosted the hairless parts of his body, his shoulders and arm muscles.

"Was the ocean crazy?" she asked.

"Yes. But beautiful."

"Like what?"

"Like a theophany."

"How?"

"Like a chorus of millions of angels."

"What were they singing?"

"I couldn't tell you in words." He laughed. "But it was something big."

"Oh? Then maybe it was a theophany I saw today."

"You *saw* one?"

"The monarch butterflies. But it was quiet."

"A quiet theophany?" He laughed.

"I think this is one of the places they come to die."

"They seemed to be throwing themselves into the ocean just now."

"Really?"

"It's pitiful to see them dead all over the beach."

"They're just going to sleep."

"Are they?" he asked with a child's eyes.

"Sure," she answered, not sure.

He *was* an extraordinary man, she thought as she watched him. The priesthood had preserved him, put him outside of life, set him apart from women, from cares of money and competitive work. But that hadn't stopped him from developing. On the contrary, it might have preserved him, or else how could it be that a man could grow to the age of forty-one, unfettered by a wife and children, and be lying there on her bed in such innocence, such intelligence, looking up at her with rain-colored eyes? She drew a breath and toughened herself, or else she'd spoil the moment, crack it by looking too closely at it. She forced a laugh to put her inferiority to flight.

"What's funny?"

"Oh, just that when I first saw you, I thought: Who's this hunk of a man?"

"Oh?" He smiled.

"But up close I see you're Huckleberry Finn."

"Grown-up, I hope," he corrected.

"Very much so." She smiled.

"Well, I would like to say I thought you were pretty ramshackle when I sat next to you on that bus, Katelyn."

"Oh, please don't."

"But wait . . . " He turned his body around like a propeller, putting his face where his feet had been, close to her knees. He was having difficulty acting natural, but so was she. Her legs were apart. She was about to bring her feet together when his elbow skipped over her knee, resting between them. She stared down at him. Another wordless moment. He smiled. She smiled back, watching his eyes fill with the light of the lamp.

"When I saw you again in Montauk, I could see that you were really a pretty darn good-looking girl."

"Nobody says 'girl' anymore." She looked down at her fingers and he moved up, closer to her face. *Do you want him for the long term or the short term?* she asked herself.

"Lemme see your hands." He took her hand in both of his. She held it limply, passively, as his ten very large fingers played with her five.

"They're getting old." She tried to smile as she said it, trying hard to keep her hand relaxed, not to pull it back.

"No. They're fine. Just like a woman's hands should be." He played, lost in amazement, with her hand. Suddenly she caught the fact that his penis was hard and showing a few inches out of the damp shorts. He was obviously unaware of it. Her heart quickened. She took in a deep breath.

"You okay?" He looked into her eyes.

"Fi . . . " She cleared her throat. "Fine." She got out the word, trying not to let him see that her body was stiffening. It was almost impossible to keep her hand relaxed in his. He could feel her tensing up, so he let go, turning on his stomach and resting his hand on her thigh, while his other elbow supported him on the mattress between her legs at the knees. *Could it be that this is what he imagined platonic, affectionate people do?* she thought.

He did sigh when he rolled over, greatly relieved and exhausted, not the sigh of a seducer. Quite the contrary. Yet, his penis *was* hard. She could see that. *A man's mind is not in his cock,* she reminded herself. *They don't always have control over what happens down there. Close your legs,* she commanded herself mentally. *If you're interested in keeping him for the long term, close them, because he could be testing. He may be needing to burn up his caring about you in the fires of sex. Oh, he'll come across. Then he'll recoil from you afterward, condemn you as dirty . . . close those legs . . . if you want to keep him, because . . .* "It's the long term I want." Her voice slipped out.

"What do you mean, 'the long term'?" He lifted his head with a mildly alarmed expression. She couldn't mask her horror at what she'd said aloud. A raw moment followed between them. He had to fight shyness to look hard and steadily at her. It was as if he were leaping off a cliff, into her arms, without knowing if she would catch him. Though subtly, at the same time, he let the palm of his hand rub her thigh, flat and caressingly, the way she had touched herself when they were driving through Napeague.

"Please," he said simply, holding on to her eyes. She couldn't understand his use of the word *please* or the reason for the wetness in his eyes. Were they tears? Why tears? How did sadness mingle with passion? As if he were saying good-bye to a friend?

Then, without a smile, without a word, but with great seriousness, he proceeded to lift her skirt, to let his hand inside, onto the skin of her thigh, and as he did, she caught his wrist and tried gently to remove his hand. He resisted, obviously frightened by his own daring.

"Please?" he asked again. She didn't answer. She sat stiff as stone, holding his wrist still, in spite of the fact that his fingers had reached her vagina. She wished he hadn't used that awful word *please*.

"Without a kiss?" she asked with disillusion.

"Huh? I'm sorry," he said with a change of expression. "I *have* been kissing you . . . in my mind."

"Oh? I didn't feel it."

"I'm sorry. I . . . "

"Don't force me to . . . to push you away, Tom." Her words shocked him. He pulled back to look into her eyes. His face was flushing as red as the Saturn lampshade.

His eyes never gave up contact with hers. He merely repeated that word *please*. He said it softly as his two fingers trembling, gently, continued searching in her genital hair.

She looked down and wondered if he possibly could be unaware that his penis was now sticking all the way out, ungracefully, swollen, out of the leg of the shorts. A cold sadness touched her. She turned her eyes away, but the next sensation surprised her, something going on inside her breasts. Her nipples seemed to be burning, growing rapidly tight and hot, as if something were melting inside them, like capsules of warm liquid, which started flowing downward, toward where his hand was. Like a school of tiny fish swimming inside her body, downward, blindly, in semicircles in search of him. And when his finger entered her vagina, they rushed to it, millions of hungry tiny fish, nibbling at his finger inside her. She arched her back, stretching her body, offering it more openly to him, almost expecting what her husband would do, to plug her with his thumb as if her vagina needed to be stretched and widened before he entered her. But this man was so very different. His touch was so light that she felt her body come loose from its moorings for him, as if it were floating up in the dark, with him attached to it, weightlessly, as if she were a runaway dirigible on her way to the moon.

Only until his other hand came around her back was she grounded, like a tree, suddenly planted, branching out with leaves which grew and multiplied from her fingers and toes. Somewhere a large winged creature fluttered clumsily among her leaves. She lifted her foot, grabbing the waistband of his shorts with her toes. She pushed until he opened the top button and his shorts flew downward over his buttocks and his penis bounced out. He kicked them off. She saw them fly through the beam of moonlight onto the floor. His buttocks rose, smooth and round, soft, with a down of dark-brown hair, and he crawled up to her. She reached for the chestnut fur of his curly head, pulling his face up to hers with her hands. She strained to meet his lips. His fingers still fished for the entrance to her body. She didn't want his fingers. She reached down and pulled both his wrists upward toward her, placing his hands on her breasts. He fell between her legs. Her knees caught him around his ribs. But his penis couldn't find the place on its own until she lifted her buttocks high and reached her hand down, guiding it into her. He pressed forward, but instead of entering her, he slid upward along her clitoris.

Suddenly he was coming, pumping, squirting up onto her belly and between her breasts.

She felt the heat of his come. She felt it hosing out of him as he squirmed and jerked, missing every attempt. Finally, she reached down once again and pointed it into her. She eased down upon it, surrounding it with the warmth of her whole body, deeply to the hilt, kissing him, holding his trembling body sweetly with her knees and her arms. He lay there, sweating, breathing heavily, shocked to be so deeply inside her, his heart drumming into her chest box. "God!" he said. The coolness of being inside her, the completeness, the comfort of it all surprised him.

His mother flashed into his mind. He blinked her away. Katelyn kissed the salt from his shoulders and combed his curls out with her fingers. He closed his eyes, letting his weight down on her, and huge steel doors in his imagination slid away, opening up to a large green field where a young man walked. He held the doors apart with his mind until the boy came toward the darkness of his doors, entering slowly. Then he let the doors slide shut. He felt the boy walking inside his chest. He touched Katelyn's cheek with his forehead, confident that she wouldn't be repulsed by his sweat, knowing it was all right. Everything they had done was right: the juices, the smells, all emanating from places inside them both that were designed without their help for exactly what they were doing, organs that had their own knowledge, their own morality.

"I goofed," he said with a small laugh.

"No, no."

"It was too fast. I couldn't control it," he said, blinking sweat out of his eyes. She loved the heat of his face on her chest. "Am I squashing you?" He pulled his head away to look at her politely. He still was breathing heavily.

"You're not squashing me in the least," she said, holding him tighter.

"You probably didn't know what was happening till it was all over," he fumbled.

"Shhh. I'm okay."

"Do you need me to do anything?" His eyelashes trembled, wet.

"I'm happy this way," she cooed. "Just relax." She let her mind go up to the rafters. She was breathing so easily, so pleasurably, contentedly, thinking of how he had sprayed all over her. Smelling his come, hoping some of it caught her vagina, enjoying its presence, trying actually to feel its stickiness, gluing their bodies together. Her thoughts were surprising her. She felt absolutely no repulsion of pregnancy by him. She felt that way about him, romantically, the way she used to dream she'd feel about a man, when she was thirteen.

"Am I hurting you," he asked, "staying inside you this way?"

"Don't be silly. It feels terrific."

"Thank you," he said, "for being so . . . "

"Shhhh." She pressed his head down between her breasts, lightly fingering his hair, making slow tight little curls around her index finger, then releasing them. "Sometimes it can be sweet . . . and sometimes it gets stormy, but it's all good. You can't be afraid. You have to let it carry you. It'll lead you right."

"Good." His smile scratched her chest. "That's what I needed to hear."

"You can be calm, or a little bit crazy. It's all the same. Sometimes it gets a little combative, in a civilized sort of way." She brushed his hair back with a strong hand, stretching the skin of his forehead. His eyes shone, isolated that way; dizzily looking backward for hers, and not finding them, he lifted his head until their chins touched. Then he kissed her, gently, softly, over and over, touching her lips with his. She held poised for these little kisses till she felt him quicken inside her. She pressed her palms to his ears, allowing his many kisses to blend into one, and his knees came up, pushing open her thighs, giving him leverage. He pressed into her again deeply, deeply as he could, pulling back slowly, looking down, then thrusting gently forward, finding the deepest parts of her, pulling out and pushing in again, over and over, with control, with strength to spare, lovingly, generously.

They made love that way through the whole night, falling asleep several times over in each other's arms. Each time he exercised more power, more authority, and each time he came, he felt more and more as if he were turning into light. The feeling didn't leave him as he slept. Each time he awoke and kissed her, he felt he had lost more density. He felt, at one point, close to having no body at all, as if he were turning into pure thought. He was a being of light, almost an angel floating next to her, as she fell to sleep in the last hour before dawn.

He kept himself awake, looking up to the rafters of the shack. The cedar crossbeams and shingles mesmerized him, suggesting the insides of a giant canoe. Once again, Noah's Ark came to mind. He was tired, but resolved to stay awake through dawn. It was the hour of the wolf. He didn't wish to confront the phantoms of his dreams. He decided, for once, to deprive them of himself, and to stay awake, imagining the stars beyond the roof slowly becoming extinguished by the sun, as the ocean crept softly upon the land.

The next day she drove him through the tall dried-out cornfields along the dirt roads coming out onto the asphalt farm roads that ran right through the middle of oceans of purple cabbage and waving seas of new corn, calling out colors, pointing to light. Tom leaned back smiling as the wind inflated his shirt. He was looking infinitely better than that first day they had met— browner, healthier. She sensed he was getting caught up in a new idea of himself. She could feel it happening as he sat next to her in the van, as if a new man were entering him. She saw it in his relaxation, in his generous talk and laughter. A casual new being was present, a handsome, middle-aged man of surprising intelligence and grace.

That night they made love, after dessert, and she drifted off half asleep, sprawled with him all over the bed. His head was between her legs and he had wrapped himself in a fetal position, hugging her thigh. His ear was to the mattress, and his rich brown hair mingled with the blondish hair of her crotch. She was dreamily wondering if people from outer space could possibly come to steal him away as she slept and carry him off as a rare new sample of man on earth. But suddenly she worried, realistically, that he would become wise to his rarity, that he would discover himself as she saw him and decide that she was too ordinary for him. Her mind often had gone sailing off that way in the few days they were together, and only his arms pressing around her, or his knee touching her in bed, or his kiss, would bring her back to earth.

As he lay there with his head between her sprawled, open legs and his ear to her mattress, his mind roamed too. His eyes were tiny horses galloping on her thigh, as if her belly were a smooth desert seen from the air, as if his head were a dark forest between her thighs; and to the north, above it, she was a continent of mountains and lakes. Actually, his longish silky hair touching her crotch made her ashamed of the stiff hairs down there.

She had no idea he was basking in her odor, an odor he recognized faintly on his fingers from time to time after he had touched himself, though his odor was delicate in comparison to hers, not nearly as strong. He considered that her salty, fishy smell was a primary source, the source of his. And with that, his penis hardened. He felt his freedom with her body, really completely, for the first time, and almost uncontrollably he turned his face to that continent to the north, placing his palms gently under her buttocks, lifting her, as if to look deep inside, and compulsively placing flat his tongue upon her opening, he licked upward slowly toward her clitoris, somehow forgetting who he was, who they were, where they were, diving face forward into her, licking, obsessively nibbling, falling into this new dark region, closing his eyes as he ate her, holding her legs open against her protests.

His heart ran away, beating faster and faster as he went at it, not allowing her thighs to squirm out of his strong hands. Suddenly he lifted her, to enter her, putting his penis in place, but not injecting it, holding back, wanting first her kiss. She turned away from his mouth in surprise. His hands came up to her head, holding it as in a vise. He forced the kiss, insisting she accept the taste of herself upon his lips. She gave up her struggle, yielding to his lips, kissing him deeply, until his mouth began to produce the sweet taste of himself again. Then he pressed forward into her, with a slow thrust up into her body, filling both her mouth and her vagina at the same moment. Her kisses turned to gasps, which he picked off her lips with his teeth. Her surprise evolved quickly into the joyful discovery that he was acting on his own now, assuming responsibility for his own pleasure, taking authority, and she abandoned herself to his new primitive strength, letting go all her caution, trusting him completely. She closed her eyes and threw back her head as one who is diving backward off a cliff, into clouds, softly, dizzyingly, letting the bottom half of her body rise over the top, giving him all her insides.

Once again Tom fell asleep looking into the rafters of Katelyn's shack. But this time, in that hour before dawn, he was startled awake. He lay there confused, and no matter how he tried, he couldn't remember where he was.

At first he thought he was looking up at a barn wall. More than a dozen wooden crosses appeared in the horizontal planks and vertical beams before his eyes. He tried to blink the vision away, wondering why his mind isolated the crosses in the framework and not the other shapes. It took him a while to realize that he was still on his back, on Katelyn's bed. He turned and to his right he saw the quilt-covered lump that was Katelyn. Her body seemed so much larger than it should have been, as if pillows were stuffed under the covers, not her. He sat up alongside the lump, peering into the cavelike opening where Katelyn's head should be, to catch sight of her yellow hair. He leaned over to peer deeper, but Katelyn was not there—only the cavernous dark. He sprang away in sudden terror. His eyes scanned the room.

"Katelyn?" he whispered with a half smile. *"Katelyn."* There was no answer. *"Katelyyyn,"* he called louder, with annoyance. The room echoed his voice. He threw away his covers and jumped into his trousers, then his shoes without socks. He grabbed his shirt and threw himself toward the screen door, pushed out and flung himself onto the silver-blue grass that reflected the white night sky. The moon was small and sharp. Kruug's black station wagon and the van were where they had left them. The wind was strong in the trees, soothing and cool on his face. He jumped into Kruug's car to check if the key was in the ignition. It was. He twisted it. The engine burst on. He pulled the headlight knob, and light shot into the big cedar, flushing out crows. He pressed the electric button, lowering the window.

"Katelyn," he yelled out one last time. The stretch in his voice, the alarm, magnified his panic. *What the hell is going on?* Was it only a lump in bed next to him? Where was Katelyn? Would she play a tasteless trick? No. There had been something weird going on inside that shack; those crosses in the framework. He backed the station wagon into the road, then put it into first and moved forward, away from the shack, vaguely toward the highway. He drove blindly for a half mile, hesitating only at a blinking light, then crossing into a pine-wooded area that stretched for miles between Sag Harbor and the blinking light. He panicked when he realized he was headed in the wrong direction. He turned the car around, but he had to urinate. He stopped the car, put on the emergency blinker, and jumped out into the dark at the side of the car, between the long yellow stretch of headlight and the red, burning glow of the rear lights. He urinated, long and slow, as the red, strobing rear lights blinked into the oaks and pines which appeared and disappeared with each blink, drenched in redness—there, then gone, there again, gone. But it appeared, in the dark at moments, that something was shining in the woods, silvery. He heard leaves, but he couldn't see them, swirling in the air, unless it was something else causing the rustling noise. Feet plodding through the oak piles. Then he heard—though he didn't want to—men's voices, mingling with the sound of crunching leaves, men's voices chanting low, like monks in choir: *Deee yaze. Eeeeray. Deeee yaze. Eeeeraah*—from the Mass of the Dead, all flat notes, the black keys, the in-between notes, sour, off, slipping through the spaces between the white keys, not a solid note, not a note of clear unmistakable resolution was among them, and the crunching noises of the leaves were coming closer, more widespread. His groin tingled. He suspended ultimate panic, in hopes everything would suddenly converge into a single natural occurrence that would be understandable.

Maybe several deer approaching—that could be. . . . But the deep male voices rang out unmistakably.

Ddeeeee yaze eeee errrr aaaaaaay, deee yaze eeerraaaaaaah. Solvet saay cloooo oooom eeeen, fahvee e e laaaah!

An act of contrition. He tried to utter one, but his jaws were locked. He pushed the words through clenched teeth like groans: *Oh, my God, I am . . . heartily sorry for having offended Thee . . . and I detest all my sins, because I dread . . . the loss . . . of heaven and . . . the pains . . . of hell.*

"Tom?" It was Katelyn's voice.

"I . . . I firmly resolve . . . I . . . firmly . . . "

"Tom?" Someone was grabbing his shoulder, pushing him.

He blinked open his eyes. "Katelyn." She was lying next to him where she was supposed to be, and he was drenched in sweat.

"You're having a nightmare," Katelyn said, holding her hair off her face.

"Oh." He saw Katelyn's frightened expression in the light of the red lampshade.

The room smelled sweet, of cedar and her drying flowers. He was safe, back in the place where horrors do happen, but not so often as in our dreams, back in real life, which was still full of small islands of peace. He squeezed her hand and sat up out of his gnarled, damp sheets, then threw the covers off his legs and stood up. He turned, looking back at the twisted bedding. Katelyn, lying there, was a cold image.

"Come back to bed till you're fully awake," Katelyn said.

"No. I think I'd better go outside." Tom threw on a T-shirt.

"But you're sweating."

"It's all right. Maybe I'd better go back to the rectory."

"But why? It's two in the morning."

"I need the ride. I need the air. I feel closed in. I need the wind, to breathe."

"Please wait." She knelt up on the mattress and grabbed his wrist as he stooped to pick his watch off the night table. He pulled his wrist away from her, violently, trying to slip on his watch.

"Please let go. Dammit. Stop clawing at me."

"I'm sorry."

"You scratched me."

"I'm *sorry.*"

The sour black notes still rang in his head as he buttoned his shirt. He tried to force new music into his mind: *Te lucis ante terminum,* the hymn of Compline. *Oh, Lord, keep me as the apple of Your eye, hide me in the shadow of Your wing.* He hesitated, feeling he should kiss her, but he was afraid of reentangling himself. She stood next to him like a child in her nightgown. He turned and pulled the screen door toward him, jumping away from her, out onto the silver-blue grass. The moon was small and sharp overhead, Kruug's black-and-silver station wagon where he had left it. The wind was blowing strong in the trees, soothing and cool on his face. The black interior of Kruug's station wagon smelled sweetly of leather and nicotine. He twisted the ignition key and pulled out the headlight knob; the beams caught the big cedar. No crows this time. Only Katelyn coming toward him. He pressed down the electric window button.

"Good-bye," he yelled out to her through the wind.

"Good-bye," she whispered.

She ran back inside the shack, pulling the screen door tight and engaging the hook-in-eye. She closed the inside door, locking it with the skeleton key. A chill numbness ran down her back, as if a great scythe had grazed her. She embraced herself, walking to the bed, then sitting down.

She turned out the red-shaded Saturn lamp and the moon flew in through the window. She sat as if in a trance, too shocked to cry. Then gradually she slid under the covers into the very place where he had slept. His sheets were cold with his sweat, so she rolled to her own side, where the bedding was warm and dry. She grabbed at the covers, pulling them up to her chin, curling herself into a ball. How could she have scratched him? she asked herself. Her nails were shorter than ever. But it wasn't a scratch he'd pulled away from; he'd only imagined the scratch. It was her touch, her person, he was trying to escape. She squeezed her eyes shut hoping she'd fall asleep. She might wake to find it not so bad as she was making it, but even her tightly closed eyes couldn't blot out the memory of his face as he drove away, the face of a man struck with ruin, a man who had witnessed havoc in her house, havoc in her bed. Then the worst thought of all: *He may never return*, as she herself had predicted. The thought swooped down at her from above. She pulled up her shoulders, turned her face into the pillow, and covered her head. If she could fall asleep right away the thought might pass over her, like a hawk passing on to some other prey.

She slid down farther under the covers. Instantly she smelled a vague incense there, or was it some kind of tea? Then she realized it was only his sweat, evaporating there, rising up out of his sheets. She took comfort from his odor, using it to pretend he was still there in bed with her, that nothing had happened to worry about. She even let her hand gravitate toward his side, hoping to fall unconscious before the memory of his absence would return, before his sweat evaporated, before his odor rose toward the cedar shingles, disappearing forever through the tiny cracks in her roof.

Chapter Eleven

N OT A LIGHT WAS LIT in the rectory when he got there, not even the yellow bug light that usually threw a soft beam on the grass toward the cliffs. But the parish car was there, and that meant Gene was in.

Tom used his key to let himself in the front door, trying to be as quiet as possible. The pull of air as he opened the door caused all the doors in the hallway to click against their locks. Muriel's, the closest door, made the loudest noise. He tiptoed to the end of the hallway toward Gene's door. Under the rug, the wooden floors creaked.

For the first time, Stella Maris rectory with its plainness, its naive austerity, was a comfort. Everything from the crucifix on the wood-paneled wall to the smells of the rug and furniture wax made him feel safe. He wanted Gene to confess him. He wanted the Sacrament of Penance bestowed upon him, the sacrament that would forgive his sins and return him to the state of grace. He needed that familiar relief, the assurance that, whether devils existed or not, they had no business with him. He wanted a pure conscience again.

He knocked gently on Gene's door. No answer. But a faint line of light appeared under Kruug's door behind him. Tom quickly knocked again.

"Gene. It's me. *Gene,*" he whispered louder. There was a click as Kruug's door opened. The monsignor stood silhouetted in the light, dressed in his cassock.

"That you, Gene?" Kruug called softly, looking blindly down the hallway. "Or is it Tom?" Kruug's voice was forgiving and intimate.

"It's Tom, Monsignor."

"Is Gene in there?"

"I was just knocking."

"The door isn't locked."

"I didn't try it."

"Try it, Tom. Try it." Kruug's voice was gentle, worried.

Tom turned the knob, opening the door to darkness. He felt alongside the wall for a light switch and clicked it up. Under the light, Gene's room was cold. The bed was stripped. Folded sheets, a pillow case, and a fluffy blue bedspread waited on his chair. His possessions were piled before the dresser in painful symmetry. Gene wouldn't have stacked things that way. Tom clicked the switch down, throwing himself back into the vague light of the hallway. Muriel's door opened.

"Monsignor?" she called out. Her hair was in curlers under a net, and her face was greased up and puffy.

"Shhh. I'm here, Muriel." Kruug created a special voice for Muriel.

"What in God's name is happening now?" She clutched her nightgown to her throat. "Is he back?"

"Which one, Muriel?" Kruug asked in that same special voice.

"Buoncuore."

"Father Buoncuore's not back. It's Father Sheehan. Go back to sleep. I'm sorry we disturbed you."

She paused, reluctantly closing her door with a "Yes, Monsignor."

"Let's step into your room for a minute, Tom," Kruug said with authority. Tom walked in and turned on the lamp. Kruug had no collar on and his cassock was open at the neck, showing gray balls of hair. He sat down on Tom's folding chair. "I was a little tough with Gene after you left. We . . . we had it out, you could say." Kruug raised both black eyebrows and grabbed both his knees. "He didn't like what I told him, so he took off, Tom."

"I wouldn't worry about Gene," Tom said with genuine assurance.

"I have no idea where he is at the moment." Tom stared into a corner where the floor met the walls, stalling, trying to form an idea out of Kruug's strange discomfort. "I may be wrong, but I think I'm on the verge of getting somewhere with Gene, and I don't want your interference. Now, he's closer in age to you, and I expect him to confide in you and not in me, and I want you to be tender and give him support, as I know you do. But I also need you to understand what my strategy is so that you don't misunderstand me as being just cruel."

"Just tell me what happened."

"Gene'll tell you. I'd rather you heard it from Gene, even though he'll put me in the wrong." Kruug's voice was back to that mysterious softness. "He'll need your understanding when he comes back, but he will not get a smile out of me for a long, long time, and I don't want you on my back for it. If you want to baby him, do it, but I can't be soft, or he'll be lost to both of us. Do we understand one another?"

Tom wanted to say yes, but he held back because he honestly didn't trust what Kruug was up to. Kruug's words hinted at something's having happened, yet he wasn't supplying facts. He seemed to want Tom's approval for whatever he had done, without telling him what it was.

"How was Connecticut?" Kruug asked.

"Connecticut?" Tom asked, looking into the monsignor's eyes. "I didn't go to Connecticut."

"Thank God you told the truth." Kruug smiled sadly. He heaved a sigh, then with a clear, confident voice he spoke directly at Tom. "It's a horror to be left out of the lives of the people you work with in the church, because they're all you've got. That's what hurts me with Gene, every time. I've finally understood it. He *forces* me to be the authoritarian, the disciplinarian, and that's his way of distancing me."

"Monsignor, you're not forced."

"You don't have all the background on this, so I won't argue with you, but it hurts. Even you. I get you free of Granger and when I came back from vacation, you didn't even smile or sit and have a drink with me. God! But you're the one who's in trouble now, aren't you, Tom, aren't you?"

"Huh?"

Kruug's face was as open as Tom had ever seen it. The blue eyes offered themselves in a knowing way, inviting Tom to come clean. At first Tom resented the presumptuousness of it, but he had to admire Kruug's intuition and was too embarrassed and still too frightened to deny anything. "You're right." Tom grabbed the pack of stale cigarettes from the end table. Matches were still stuck in the cellophane. He pulled them out and tapped out a cigarette. He rolled it between his fingers, feeling its dry crunchiness. He put the pack down, breaking the cigarette in half as Kruug watched him intently. Tom walked to the wastepaper basket near the door, threw the matches, pack, and broken cigarette into it, and turned. "Can we confess, this way, my standing up?"

"Uh . . . yes." Kruug sat up straight with surprise.

"I wouldn't ask you if Gene were around."

"I understand."

"I feel the need."

"Don't explain." Kruug reached up to the bureau where Tom's purple stole was folded. He opened it, kissed the embroidered cross, and hung it around his neck.

"I woke up at her place, a little over an hour ago."

"The Katelyn woman?"

"Yes. She . . . she's very special, very unusual."

"I would expect that."

"But I think it was a mistake, to try to get close. My conscience gave out. I woke up from a nightmare on her bed. It's still going on in my head, in a way, as if the guilt weren't even rational. I can't explain. I'm assaulted by the guilt, not reasonably at all, not deductively, just emotionally terrified. It came up like a tornado on a sunny day, out of nowhere. I feel totally unbalanced."

"Could she have drugged you?"

"Oh, my God, Monsignor. No."

"You can't be sure."

"No, no, please, you don't understand."

"All right."

"No. I panicked is all, imagined all sorts of things. See, I had this nightmare, and it was as if . . . as if I hadn't woken up. Things were fine till then, between us I mean. I wouldn't have left her this way. And now I don't know if I'm really contrite, or just scared. I wish the sun would come up. In daylight I might feel different."

"Have some Scotch." Kruug's suggestion surprised Tom.

"No. No, I gave it up."

"All right then, you are confessing the sin of fornication. How many times?"

"Huh? Oh, God. Six or seven." Tom pushed hair back from his forehead. How could Tom himself reduce it to such vulgar numerics? Katelyn would hate hearing this. Then why was he doing it? Cowardice? Did he believe in God and in sin or didn't he? What did it matter? He'd made a vow, a solemn promise, and he'd broken it. As a priest Kruug was the appropriate person to confess it to. Tom believed in the tenderness of the sacrament, if nothing else. He wanted its warmth, its comfort.

"Are you resolved never to see this woman again?"

"Beg your pardon?"

"You know as well as I, Tom, that I can't give you absolution unless you agree never to see her under any circumstances ever again."

"Yes, although I should talk to her. I just ran out."

"Do you want to postpone this confession then?" After a silence Tom spoke.

"No. I agree never to see her, under any circumstances." His mouth formed the words, but they were dry and lifeless. There was no will in them. He reached conviction, but his heart was pulling him in another direction even as he pronounced the words. He felt so bad for betraying her, insulting her goodness. Perhaps it simply meant that he was a coward. Perhaps it meant he didn't have the mental strength to shake his values and enter a future world. He only knew he never wanted to reenter the agony of that terrifying predawn moment. He wanted the sacrament bestowed upon him with all its power, to cleanse and perfect him, and to assure him of his moral safety. And though this meant turning his back upon Katelyn, he had to do it, or else he would be turning his back upon his own, pained self.

Kruug closed his eyes and raised his hand. "With the power invested in me, I absolve you in the name of the Father, and of the Son, and of the Holy Spirit. Amen."

Kruug rose, took off the stole, and put it back on Tom's bureau. Tom remained facing the window, even though the curtain was drawn. He heard Kruug open the door.

"We're going to have a heck of a time here, Tom. We're going to make a joyous parish out of this place. We'll make that list bigger—get big shots interested, have retreats for troubled priests like Gene, for women too, local and from afar. We'll make Stella Maris a mission in the civilized world; we'll have weddings here.

"Tom, look at me, my boy." Tom couldn't. "You're not going to miss out on your share of living in your lifetime. I promise you that with all my strength. You've got plenty of years left. I wish you could've met my buddies Denny McCabe and Toots McCann. They died a couple years back. They weren't fancy Jesuits, just parish doughboys, and the dearest friends to me. They taught me what use a priest makes of his heart. You won't have to keep yours in the refrigerator, my dear Jesuit."

"I know," Tom whispered.

"Goodnight, Tom."

"Goodnight." When the door closed, Tom shut off the light, split the drapes apart, and lay down in his clothes on his bed. He saw the star of morning rising over the ocean. The ocean was just a couple of hundred yards away, closer than it had been at Katelyn's, yet the room he was lying down in could have been as far off as Kansas, with its oversized glass-topped dresser, its bureau and thick mahogany bed tables, its wall-to-wall rug and heavy drapes. At Katelyn's, the ocean seemed to have passed daily through the house, silvering its floors, leaving sand behind. Her shack was as free and unself-conscious as nature itself. Still, Tom wasn't sorry to be safe in Kansas. The rectory's clumsy hominess and mismatched fabrics were oddly comforting. There was no wildness in the room, none whatsoever, and the wallpaper was a different color behind the framed pictures. The closet smelled of mothballs and down bed pillows. And that star of morning over the ocean, that might be the very star of the sea.

Next morning in the sacristy Tom introduced himself to Vinnie Foley as Foley was removing his vestments after mass. Tom started to put on those very vestments. He liked Foley's face.

"Are you from St. Theresa's?" Tom asked.

"No. Visiting my folks' summer house in Montauk. I got two weeks."

"I see."

"I'm from the Brooklyn Diocese."

"Oh, really? I just came from working there."

"In a parish?"

"St. Barnabas'."

"Are you the Jesuit that got stuck with what's-his-name—Granger?"

Tom smiled. "Formerly stuck."

"How *was* that?" Foley smiled broadly.

"Not enthralling."

"So you're helping out Kruug for the time being?"

"Yes."

"What do you think about this Buoncuore situation?" Foley's face sagged. Tom was cautious.

"I don't really know very much about it."

"What a horrible afternoon." Foley shook his head.

"What afternoon?"

"I mean of the water ski."

"I haven't heard."

"I happened to be here in the sacristy when it all happened."

"What all happened?" Tom pressed.

Foley looked around, then whispered. "Kruug caught Buoncuore sneaking out with the ski and demanded that Buoncuore hand it over."

"No."

"Buoncuore refuses. All of a sudden Kruug turns around and starts walking away from Buoncuore. So Buoncuore flings the ski, I mean not at Kruug, but like over his head, and what does it do but hit the altar and knock over the vases. Kruug yells out that he's calling the police, and the next thing you know the housekeeper is marchin' in and outta the church dumpin' Buoncuore's clothes all over the altar rail as if he's kicked out. So Buoncuore starts this undressing in church. I thought I was dreamin'."

"Undressing in church?"

"In the middle aisle. He's nude in front of the Blessed Sacrament."

"No." Tom stepped back, falling into the sacristy chair. At that moment, the altar boy arrived, but Foley quickly shooed him out.

"Buoncuore starts putting on his black suit right there," Foley continued in a whisper, "his collar and rabat and all, and he says he's goin', confused like, so I offer him a ride. Really just to keep an eye on him, because his eyes were goin' real glassy. So he made me drive him to the overlook."

"What overlook?"

"Up over those marinas near Westlake? You know this area? Well, he runs into the woods on me. I'm only tryin' to stall the guy until everybody comes back to their senses, but he was too freaked to listen. I mean, he thought the cops were gonna show up here. I rush back here to tell Kruug what happened. He just sorta smiles and calmly says not to worry, that the guy was a bluffer and he had to call his card. But then the next morning Kruug's getting dressed for mass and he turns to me and asks do I think he should call the cops after all because now he's worried."

"Did anyone finally call them?"

"I don't know."

Tom looked up at the electric clock. Five of eight. The altar boy peeked in from the outside door. "Come in," Tom reassured the boy. He was a towheaded lad with a face brown as leather.

Tom sensed the boy's self-consciousness and was sorry he had to witness two priests nervously whispering in the sacristy.

Tom couldn't concentrate on the prayers of the mass. He wondered if Gene might have taken a motel room near the boat. The marina boy who drove the boat for him would know something. Or the marina owner. He couldn't wait to finish his mass.

At the consecration prayer, he lifted the large white unleavened wafer up to the Eternal Father. He genuflected, then, removing the cover from the chalice, he bowed, breathing upon the wine: "This is the cup of my blood, the blood of the new and everlasting covenant. It will be shed for you and for all men so that sins may be forgiven."

Then Muriel's voice: "Monsignor, *Monsignor.*" Through the open sacristy window, Tom could hear her strained shouts. "Monsignor Kruug." The urgency in her voice totally distracted Tom. He noticed that Foley was standing away from his priedieu, looking out the window. Foley turned, catching Tom's eye, and shrugged his shoulders. Suddenly Muriel's voice was inside the sacristy, reverberating loudly. "God in heaven, Father Foley, help me."

"What is it?"

"Father Buoncuore. The police say he's dead."

"They say what?"

"Drowned."

"Father Buoncuore?"

"Drowned. Yes. Father Buoncuore. Oh, the back of my head."

"Sit down." Foley stretched to see Tom, who stood at the altar merely staring back at Muriel, who was now sitting under the electric clock in the priest's armchair. Her eyes were burning out of her head. Her facial muscles were collapsed except around her mouth. Her lips made an effort to cling to her teeth.

"He's dead. He's dead," she kept repeating.

Foley, seemingly in terror, left her to come toward Tom. He genuflected next to him, then leaned to Tom's ear, and as if Tom hadn't heard Muriel, he said, "Remember Father Buoncuore in this mass. He's dead."

"Don't say that," Tom muttered. "We don't know that." Tom shocked the altar boy by walking away from the altar and following Foley through the sacristy door to face Muriel. As though her mouth had spoken fire and as if Tom had felt the fire must be stopped before it spread, he knelt to her and blew his words at her face. "Muriel, tell me where you got this."

"They pulled him up in nets with a load of fish. The haul-seiners. He's a mess on the beach right now with sand comin' out of his mouth."

"Who told you?"

"The cops. They called."

"Father Foley." It was Kruug's voice, calling from afar. Muriel sprang up and ran outside. A police siren wailed in the driveway. Silence. After a beat, Tom heard Kruug's voice rise: "Oh, no. No. Dear good God, no." Foley went out. "Jesus in heaven!" Kruug shouted. If there had been a tone of more color in his voice, and less tenor, Tom could have sustained his doubts for a few more seconds, but Kruug's white, flat, constricted shouts caught him like a whirlpool, lifting him up away from his disbelief, higher into the atmosphere of irreversibility.

"Gene . . . Gene . . . dead?" They were saying the unthinkable; it was unthinkable! But this was what was happening. Gene was dead and he was standing here in the sacristy before his mass was over; the altar boy was wandering in from the sanctuary in shock. It all simply meant that Gene was dead. Gene was dead.

Kruug insisted on going alone with the police to Ditch Plains to identify the body that the haul-seiners had pulled in.

When Kruug returned an hour later, he grimly asked Foley to go home, and ordered Tom to join him for a cup of tea in the dining room.

"It *was* Gene," he said simply over the table. "I recognized him immediately. His wallet was buttoned inside his back pocket, so there's no doubt. I've arranged for him to be embalmed, because they say he'd been in the water quite some time. He looked not so bad to me, but he's got a real nasty gash here on his left cheek. A chunk was taken out by a fisherman's gaff or something. Mahoney said he would do his best on the embalming. We've got to keep him laid out a couple of days. It's only Friday. We've got to contact his folks. Give them time. Better we close the casket for their sakes. Mahoney agreed with me we'd better keep the lid screwed down. I want him laid out in an alb and chasuble. I'll bring the vestments, some rosary beads, a pair of his pants to the undertaker. What do you say we bury him Monday?" Tom wanted to say shut up, but he only nodded. "I'll announce Monday. Now . . ." Kruug tapped all ten fingers on the mahogany. "Is there anything I'm leaving out?"

Tom's nausea prevented him from uttering a sound. He made a motion with his hand no. Kruug stood.

"I'm sorry on every level for this awful thing. I'm sick to my stomach, Tom. This isn't any fun for me. It stinks; I hope you realize that. I've got to call the bishop. We've got to call Gene's family, and then I must lie down. Any questions?"

"A lot of questions," Tom said in a low voice.

"About the immediate?"

Tom looked up. "No, about the preceding."

"Okay. Would it be appropriate to wait till he's buried?"

"If it has to be that way."

"And would it be appropriate for you to call his folks?" Kruug asked.

"No, it wouldn't," Tom said flatly, sitting back in his chair.

"Don't worry about it." Kruug turned and walked away. "I'll call his folks now."

The reddish waxed wood of the dining-room table seemed an inappropriate platform for Tom's stiff, helpless hands. He slowly rose. He slid his chair back under the table neatly and walked into the paneled hallway toward his room. News of death brings on a simple fear at first, the outrage that a friend can be shut off forever, like a radio that is dropped and broken. No life or sound will ever come through it again, no discussion, no song, no laughter or anger. The person is silenced as rudely as a child who is slapped for speaking out. There is cruelty in it, and such embarrassment, that it permanently affects those who are left behind.

Chapter Twelve

B Y THAT NIGHT, the little mission parish of Stella Maris
had reached its zenith of activity. The phone rang constantly. Kruug, in spite of weariness, handled everything
with the virtuosity of a corporation head. He seemed to exploit
even the smallest responsibility as if it were the long overdue
actualization of his dream, that Stella Maris was predestined to
become a center of vitality and movement. Kruug had decided
to wake Gene's body entirely in the church. He didn't want the
body brought into the rectory at all. He ordered the casket to
remain closed from the time it left Mahoney's right through
burial. He photocopied forms and thumbtacked them to the
sacristy bulletin board for priests to sign up for a round-the-clock
vigil with the body. He ordered the church doors unlocked for
the whole two days. It was to be an old-fashioned mass with a
deacon and subdeacon. Tom, Monsignors Tobin and Heneghan
and the rest would concelebrate. The choir of St. Theresa's offered itself for the mass, and he accepted, though he was hurt that
the bishop merely sent a hand-delivered letter of regrets.

About fourteen clerics arrived for the rosary on the eve of the
funeral, joking and laughing nervously, and among them, to
everyone's surprise, was the Monsignor Norbert DeGroot, a tall,

shoulderless man with a double chin. Kruug ordered ice, liquor, and a catered buffet of crêpes and shrimp scampi, so as not to lose sight of the triumphant aspect of death. Gene's foolishness in venturing out into a treacherous ocean at nightfall was put forth over drinks and hors d'oeuvres, but no mention was made of his argument with Kruug, nor of his troubles with Monsignor De-Groot, who shocked everyone by volunteering to lead the rosary over Gene's casket after dinner.

The Buoncuore family had requested the rosary, and they huddled in the open church as the words in unison rose up into the tornado over Gene's body. Gene's father was a short, slightly built man with dark skin and dark hair. He wore a gray business suit, a white shirt, and a black silk tie with a small, tight knot. He clung to a gray fedora. The man's face seemed wrung out by grief, his mouth turned down, but there was no anguish in his eyes, and no anger. He wore the resigned expression of a monk, a sort of proud, romantic acceptance of God's hard will, as if he were saying to himself: Yes, life is full of pain, and when it comes we must accept it. Gene's mother and sister stood obediently next to Mr. Buoncuore, holding back tears, standing straight as possible, as if a medal were about to be pinned to their black dresses.

Poor Gene, Tom thought, lying stiffly there, needing what no one was able to give him, needing someone to stand up and shout out in his name, needing a Christ to break into the church and kick over his casket and to point down to his sprawled-out body, demanding answers from everyone in the gallery, from Kruug, DeGroot, from every priest, including Tom himself. Gene needed someone to scream out those questions in his name, but all he was getting was bowed heads and the echoes of mumbling. *Holy Mary, Mother of God, pray for us sinners now and at the hour of our death. Amen.*

Monsignor Heneghan, the chancellor, arrived as everyone else was entering the rectory after the service. Tom wasn't introduced. Instead, Kruug asked him to drive Gene's family back to their motel.

In the car, Mr. Buoncuore asked Tom about the population

of Montauk. Mrs. Buoncuore asked about trains from Brooklyn, so that they could visit the cemetery. Tom was very tempted to speak to them about Gene's troubles, but he held back. He quietly wished them goodnight and drove back to Stella Maris.

When Tom passed his open door, Kruug called out from his chair for Tom to come in. The lamplight was low, and over Kruug's head Tom could make out the clear night out the top of the four windows, and the red blinking caution lights that surrounded Gene's freshly dug grave. Obviously, Kruug had been sitting there, looking out the windows. He swung his recliner around, facing Tom. "Would you mind sleeping in Gene's room tonight?" Kruug asked with a worn-out face. "I had Muriel make the bed fresh for you."

"Why in there?" Tom asked.

"Because the chancellor's staying overnight and he requested specifically not to sleep in Gene's room."

"Okay. I'll sleep there," Tom said with some annoyance.

"Take what you need before he gets into your room."

"Okay."

"How're you doin'?" Kruug asked with a sigh, unabashedly revealing his exhaustion.

"We can talk after the funeral," Tom said dryly. It didn't startle Kruug, who simply cleared his throat and looked out the window again as if the ocean had demanded his attention.

Just now the chancellor stuck his head in the door, and Kruug, catching the monsignor's reflection in the window, sprang up from the recliner.

"Where do I drop my duds?" Heneghan asked. He had a round, cherry-red face. He gave Tom a friendly wink.

Kruug flew immediately around his desk, once again not introducing Tom. He took the monsignor by the arm, deeper into the hall. "Wait here, Tom," he called over his shoulder, and closed the door.

Alone in Kruug's room, Tom let his shoulders sink into relaxation as he walked to the large windows. Standing next to Kruug's chair, high above the harsh lamplight, Tom could see out to the vast stretch of moonlit horizon. The same moon that lit the lawn pale blue was spraying the ocean with diamonds, while those battery-operated lights on Gene's grave blinked red—on and off, on-off—warning of the dug-out hole. Above it, an almost full moon was suspended. The ocean was a mass of twinkling blue-white sparkles stretching for miles. Only one remained constant, unblinking, about a mile and a half west. Could it be Katelyn's flashlight? Tom wondered. It glowed large and steadfast, like a man-made light, a flotation light bobbing in the water, with a yellow-pink constancy, and the tide detouring around it in long wrinkles made the light seem an eye. The ocean was a monstrously huge beast, a being of intentional passivity, relaxing casually below him, looking up, keeping a cautious watch on the world of men.

Tom felt a sadness at that moment, different from his original grief over Gene's death. It was a sort of calm remorse that transcended his fears of death. *We are only a small planet lost in the Milky Way,* the horizon seemed to be saying.

He was tired. His emotions were at the mercy of the moon, which seemed to be pulling the sadness out of him, like a tide, then spreading it back down upon everything in sight. Gene was lost among billions. He was now with the many who had died before him, so many men and women. Quite a very helpless few were ever left on the planet at once to carry on whatever it is they had all been trying to do. *And what have we been trying to do?* Tom asked himself.

"Monsignor Heneghan is delighted with your room," Kruug said, breaking in, still holding on to the overstretched voice he had used for the chancellor. "He demanded to see *his* room," Kruug whispered as he banged open his drawer for his car keys. "Now he wants to see the damned lighthouse. He says he's worn out, so I need another volunteer to wake Gene's body in his place, from six to seven. You're down from five to six. Could you take the two hours in a row? Tomorrow you can take the whole day off after the funeral. Take a couple."

"I'll take the two hours."

"Leave your alarm clock for Heneghan. You can use Gene's clock-radio."

"Sure."

Tom set the luminous dial of Gene's alarm clock for four-thirty, but he couldn't fall asleep in Gene's bed. He got up in the dark, made the bed, and paced up and down. He lifted Gene's shade, then the window, intending to watch the stars until dawn broke out, but after an hour he felt tired. He lay down on top of Gene's bedspread. He hadn't turned on the light in the room. He didn't want to see Gene's piled things: the clippings on the walls, the barbells, Gene's shoes.

When Gene's alarm woke him just before dawn, the early blue light of day illuminated the water-ski poster on the open closet door; his sweatshirts and sweaters had all been washed by Muriel. His cassock hung ominously in the closet, next to his blue-and-gold varsity sweater. His jogging shoes and sneakers were lined up neatly under them. His collar and rabat and black suit were missing.

Tom had forgotten to grab some underwear in his hurry to evacuate his room for Heneghan. He'd borrow a fresh change from Gene. He pulled open a drawer, but he felt guilty about touching any of Gene's cottons. In the bathroom Gene's presence was even stronger: Gene's soap and shampoo, his comb on the sink.

Tom put on one of Gene's T-shirts, a little squeamishly, remembering his words: *You know what my favorite vestment is . . . that a priest wears? . . . A T-shirt . . . .* Gene's T-shirt grabbed Tom's ribs and warmed his shoulders in the cool morning, and Gene's smile appeared so vividly in his mind that it dispelled, momentarily, the fact of his death.

"Gene," Tom called out softly, as if the priest were there to hear him. In the silence that followed, tears welled up. Tom ignored them, putting on his trousers. As he put on his socks, Katelyn came to mind. She'd be asleep, alone on the big bed, and the very same soft dawn light was coming through her small windows, the same ocean was whispering to her as she dreamed.

"*Katelyn.*" He whispered her name to the window, wishing he could follow the sound. He recalled those early mornings his alarm would wake him to catch Moonghost coming out of the blue hillsides of Lima in his white cassock and open jeep. Now, once again outside a rectory door, nothing but strangers existed.

Maybe he had tricked himself into becoming lost again, as though he couldn't bear to let things grow familiar, fearing the up-closeness of people again, not wanting to see the veins of their temples, the pores of their faces, the confusion in their eyes, their neediness, their claims. He had given himself too generously to the world, to the poor, to the dying, the lonely. He had made himself an object of their love to be used by them. He had given all his time without protest, time broken into moments, a few here, a few there, disallowing any congealment into anything large. He had emptied himself. His years were scattered.

In a sudden rage, he pulled Gene's drawer completely out of its sleeve and dumped all his T-shirts and shorts on the bed. He rolled up a T-shirt and stuffed it into his cassock pocket. He clipped his own cassock at his neck and tied the cincture, leaving for the church, where Gene's body lay in its sealed casket.

Father Blake of St. Theresa's was sitting alongside Gene's coffin, looking up and listening meditatively, as if God were talking down to him through the tornado. He was startled when Tom opened the big oak sacristy door. Tom signaled him with a nod, noticing that the church was deep in blackness, except for the dawn light pressing through blue stained-glass windows and the two spotlights that lit the russet chrysanthemums and yellow pompoms—flowers signaling autumn. Tom held out a hand to the smiling priest coming toward him. The man was bald; his eyes, dark and glassy. A medieval holiness shone in his face, a calm and a resignation.

"I'm Joe Blake," he whispered, "from St. Theresa's."

"Hello. I'm Tom Sheehan."

"Hi." The priest took Tom's hand warmly, then turned, lifting a long dark-blue cardigan sweater from the coat tree. "It was chilly sittin' out there a whole hour. Would you like to borrow my sweater?"

"No thanks, Father."

"See ya later then?"

"See you later."

Blake waved as he leaned his full weight against the thick oak sacristy door revealing the red blinking caution lights around Gene's grave.

As Tom stepped into the sanctuary, he heard the gentle chugging of Blake's car, up the pebbled path toward the highway, then fading softly on smooth asphalt downhill toward the village of Montauk. Silence once again. Except for the gassy whistling of church space and the distant sibilant sounds of ocean.

Tom felt the chilling aloneness of Gene inside the dark stone building. The metal casket was unavoidable to the eye, so imposing, spray-painted bronze, with a piano-hinged lid that had been screwed in place with butterfly tabs resembling thumbscrews of a violin. Tom stood looking down at the casket, imagining the awkwardness of Gene's body having to lie so flat, face up to the soles of Mary's feet, dressed in vestments Kruug had picked out and that Mahoney had forced onto his body in the cement-block cellar of the funeral parlor on Hickory Street. Was this what Gene wanted? Had he counted on this when he took out that silly boat of his? Tom asked himself, vaguely angry at Gene. Had he *wanted* to be dragged from the ocean in a fishing net, embalmed, and locked in a metal box, then rolled into a stone church to await burial under Kruug's window?

The T-shirt in Tom's cassock pocket—Tom had thought he could put it inside the casket somehow, so that Gene could be buried with it. He needed to earn some sort of forgiveness from Gene for that day on the ferry. Of course, real forgiveness was impossible now, but he wanted to do something courageous for Gene. When Tom had emptied the T-shirt drawer, he hadn't thought it would take nerve to actually open the casket and look in at Gene. He decided at first to turn only one of the screws, to test it, counterclockwise until it stopped. But then he turned one screw after the other. They all loosened quite easily. For a long while he looked down at the loose thumbscrews, trying to put his courage into place, trembling as much as any coward would, tight in the stomach, biting his lips.

He placed his fingernails under the lid to test its freedom from the rest of the casket. It rose half an inch. He let it drop again. Then, replacing his fingers with more security, he closed his eyes, and with a strong continuous motion, he brought the lid all the way up until it stopped on its own.

Tom opened his eyes and there was Gene before him, his face darkly glowing above his white vestments, his eyes closed. Rosary beads were wrapped in his stiff hands. The violet-toned, powdered face was in better condition than Tom expected, though the gash in Gene's left cheek was so large, the crater so clean, that the head seemed made of marble. The waxy mass that had filled the crater had obviously shrunken and fallen out, lying now near Gene's shoulder like a small egg-shaped rock. The other cheek was perfect. His hair and his eyebrows were dark and shiny in the low light, as if combed with Vaseline. His skin was darker than usual, grayish beneath the peachy powder. The undertaker had obviously been worried that Monsignor Kruug would change his mind about having Gene viewed.

Gene's mouth was not the same. The lips seemed held together from the inside.

Tom reached into his cassock pocket and pulled out the rolled-up T-shirt. He opened it, snapping it in the air over Gene's face; then, placing the collar at Gene's chin, he let the shirt fall over Gene's chest and hands. For a moment, Tom wouldn't have been surprised if the corpse had said, "Thanks, I was cold," or opened his eyes and smiled. Tom could not shake the expectation that Gene was about to say something, as though Gene had just heard a joke and his mouth was stifling a laugh.

"This is the best I can do for you. It's all I have courage for," Tom whispered, trying to ignore the immobility of Gene's face. He started closing the lid, then held up. He leaned down as if to kiss Gene's forehead. He did. His lips felt the hard, dry skin through its blanket of powder. "Good-bye, Gene," he whispered. The corpse's smile remained unaltered. The joke, unshared.

Tom let the lid down, then, one by one, he turned the thumb-screws clockwise until they could be no tighter. Only when the last screw was firm did Tom fully realize he had been sweating profusely, holding back breath as if to avoid taking in the powder from Gene's face.

With the suddenness of a shotgun blast, a wave of nausea hit Tom when he turned away from the casket. He skimmed the sweat from his forehead with a finger as he walked, on very shaky legs, through the sanctuary, not able even to genuflect. He needed *out,* needed the oak sacristy door open, needed to lean his weight upon it, to push it out—*Christ help me*—into the light, into the yellow cool morning.

But as his palms pressed the thick oak door, his trembling turned to collapse. No power in his legs. He couldn't *feel* his legs. Nothing existed between his scalp and the soles of his shoes. He felt blown through, like an inflated plastic doll exploded by shotgun fire. He fell against the great oak door, like a fetus dropped from womb, and he was suddenly drained of all belief, in life after death, in the resurrection of the body, in God. He couldn't believe in anything again from that raw, cruel moment on. He didn't want this to be so. It had all occurred in the half-moment between the sacristy stone step and the slate landing, in the vacuum of the swinging oak door, in the whoosh of its sucking action, in the draft. His faith had leaked out of him, his way of understanding, his understanding itself. He was losing it all in a matter of seconds. It was running out of him like blood from a grave wound, all in those few blind seconds that his mind and body had hurled against the oak door, into the early morning air.

The dawn sky was pink in the east as he stumbled down the steps, careening down the dirt path toward the ragusa roses, still sucking for air, under the pines, gasping, toward the dunes, beyond them to the sand, to the ocean, to its lip, his heart pounding too fast. He threw himself flat and scooped salt water to his lips, washing Gene's powder off them vigorously, even drinking a few drops. He stood. Beyond the breakers a pair of swans was moving regally westward. He closed his eyes to them. He needed oxygen. In a mirror, he would be dreadfully pale. He could tell from his hands, from their bloodlessness.

When he felt his heart begin to slow down, pounding harder, like a mute bell inside his chest, he was relieved. It meant his body was returning to his mind. He felt such gratitude simply for that. "Oh, yes."

He embraced himself, and he remembered Katelyn's words: *Each morning I see shells and dried-out crab legs washed up on the beach, and I say: Nobody's complaining here. The ocean gives and takes and there's no whining about it. It turns its waste into sand and we sit on it in the sunlight.*

How courageous, but how frail, were Katelyn's words compared to the tomes of theology and philosophy he had studied in his lifetime. The Greeks, Aquinas, Augustine—all had formed his mind. He recalled the excitement of those seminary years and his hopes for the Church, for the world, for every living thing. *Every stone, every pebble, had a finality of its own,* they used to say, *how wonderful a world God had made.* Every priest knew that, and like Christ, every priest might be called upon to save it all, to save all men, the planet, every pebble of it, all alone, singlehandedly if need be. Priests saved themselves by saving every man and woman, every wonderful one, saying no for those afraid to say no, saying yes for those afraid to be free; nursing, encouraging, inspiring—and yet, during this clearest moment, as Tom recalled his past hope, he had to recognize that new hopes were possible, hopes yet to be dreamed, hopes we are all too ignorant, too stubborn, to imagine.

There was a tingling in his hands and across his face, as though the cold, red morning air had touched him with alien promises. Even without the priesthood, he was quite a historical achievement as a man. At the same time, he was nothing. Time would roll on with or without him. Time was the key and the promise, everything advancing toward that omega point. He never doubted that. And in that moment, his mind clicked, adjusting him to who he really was—first an animal, an animal that precedes whomever any man eventually becomes, an animal with its own pure and selfish need, with the potential to wake up each morning with a fresh eye to an undiscovered world, not unlike the vision he had had from the surfboard in

Peru, riding toward the beach with Moonghost holding him up. He felt then an animal, though innocent and intelligent, as if he were returning from some pure and primitive place to the wonderful planet of this earth. It reminded him of how he had felt when he first decided to become a priest, that kind of lofty and honest intuition. And it reminded him of the powerful surge of adventure he felt with Katelyn. He loved her. He admitted that cleanly and firmly now, knowing how one loves. He loved the priesthood too, so lucky he had made that choice because of all the wondrous things it had given him. It was courageous to have become a priest, not at all a mistake for him to have chosen it. He was proud of the man he had turned out to be and proud of who he was to become, proud of the sudden newness he was feeling.

He walked along the ocean's quiet edge until his legs stopped shaking, mildly alarmed at the manic extremes of his thinking. He dared to lie flat on his back on the sand, cassock and all, stretched out and looking up at the sky. His back gave up its tightness. He imagined he could feel the curvature of the earth under him. There was a tingling in his hands and across his face, as though the sky had actually touched his skin with its promise. "Please, God, don't leave me. Never leave me." He waited, listening in the morning silence for God's answer—perhaps in the sound of a bird, or a sudden boom of the surf—but there was nothing, except the hum of his blood coursing through his veins.

His mind hungrily grabbed at the sky, at the undeniable, unchangeable truth that there would be future mornings—yes, millions of them—here and on other planets, with or without him; and his confusion, his wonderment, produced an ironic happiness.

Then, standing still, he brushed the sand from his cassock and started up the hill toward the rectory. Now he felt the tiredness, but a more reasonable form of it. What a waste of time it would be, to wait out his vigil with the powdered dead man in the spray-painted casket.

He quietly went back to Gene's room, washed his face, opened the closet, and took out the white shirt he had hung there the night before. He put it on, rolling up the sleeves. He threw razor, shaving soap, socks into Gene's canvas overnight bag. He lifted Gene's old blue-and-gold varsity sweater off its hanger, threw it over his shoulder, and sat down to write a note for Kruug.

Since I'm not scheduled for the funeral mass, I'm cutting out beforehand. I need some time to myself. I'll be gone for a few days.

Tom

He turned his left ankle as he stepped onto the asphalt Old Montauk Highway. A swarm of swallows crossed over him in a dark wave, as he limped slightly, working out the momentary pain, downhill, toward the ocean and the red phone booth in front of Miss Jane's Auto Body. He felt the thrill of guilt, an echo from boyhood, when Sister Mary Lawrence had sent him home with a fever, and he wandered the quiet streets of Waterford, among the big houses, like a ghost, during school hours.

He dialed a taxi number printed on a sticker in the phone booth.

"I'd like a cab to Orient Point, to the New London Ferry."

"When for?"

"Now, please."

"This minute?"

"Yes." He waited at the roadside, and eventually his cab appeared. He sat deeply in the wide backseat, hands in his pockets. The decision to go to Waterford had occurred to him as easily as if it were twenty-five years ago, and he had to be home for supper. If he were to find himself blinking awake on the high school bus, he could easily accept that his entire adult life had been something he dreamed between Pequot and Atlantic avenues. Out the taxi window the swallows seemed to be gathering for a migration.

The ferry ride seemed quicker. He rented a car at the railway station, and when he noticed that Southampton was on the drop-off chart, he decided on his return to drive the car back onto the ferry, drop it in Southampton, and hitchhike to Stella Maris.

In the noisy railway diner he ate poached eggs on toasted muffins and drank coffee, staring at laborers, men like his father, painters, carpenters, plumbers, loudly teasing one another.

He drove to the cemetery and stood, under that enormous sky, looking down at a regulation-size stone marked SHEEHAN. Not a tree in sight. The whole planet seemed bald. Polish, Irish, Italian names stretched in endless rows. It was as if a huge common grave had been dug for the Catholic immigrants.

He felt weak in the groin standing on their grave, knowing that the two who had made him were under his feet. It made him feel top-heavy, especially since nothing was taller than himself as far as the eye could see. But their faces and voices were as rich and clear in his memory as if he'd heard them yesterday.

He went on in his mind for several minutes, laying before them all they had missed, asking their forgiveness for his coldness to their memory, and forgiving them in turn for everything he could think of, that they had done to hurt him. He spoke casually, as if they were people his own age, people with uncertain instincts and unruly egos, who had tried as much as anyone to uncover the secret wonders of life.

When he was done, he walked away.

In an hour he had driven through all of Waterford's changeless streets. Autumn had not yet set the town's great trees afire, although the horse chestnuts had become quite singed. He drove along the bus route, all the way to its final stop at the five-and-dime. He parked the rented car and went inside. He circled the cosmetic station his mother used to work at. It was now a candy counter. The wooden floors were gone. He bought a candy bar, then started walking toward Elm and the newly aluminum-sided two-family house in which they used to live.

The place stood white, in stark light near an elm stump, vulnerable now, without the umbrella of the old tree pouring down from overhead. There was no motion behind the windows or around the house. New silver storm-and-screen windows gave the flat-roofed structure a hard, unfriendly look. No doubt more than one new family had inhabited those upstairs rooms since the Sheehans. What had happened to the thick dining-room set that was too big for the room? Her gold bracelet in the top drawer of her chifforobe? Her mother's lavaliere? Her dresses, his overalls, his one dark-blue suit in the closet, her reading glasses, his fat, shining, black wallet full of receipts and notes, his gray fedora, her good black leather pocketbook, her cut-glass perfume bottles, that rubberish rose-colored perfume atomizer she never used, the wallpaper? He imagined the bathroom mirror, his teenage, blemished face in it, practicing a grown man's voice.

Almost unconsciously, he was crossing the street toward the aluminum-screened front door with the monogram S soldered to the frame. The S had stood for Sharskey in the old days, the landlady's name, but by now it probably belonged to a nephew or some new owner whose name began with S. He stepped up onto the familiar brick steps flanked by the same two cement flowerpots containing tiny-blossomed red begonias. He pressed the bell, not sure of what he would say to whomever answered the door. He heard the chime ringing softly inside. It had replaced the old raspy buzzer. There was no response, but just as he turned to leave, a wrinkled hand slipped between the curtains and knocked weakly on the glass.

"What do you want?" a pebbly voice asked, the voice of an old woman.

"My name is Thomas Sheehan."

"Who?"

"Father Thomas *Sheehan*. I used to live upstairs."

"Just wait now." The lock on the front door made a loud crack. The door opened, revealing old, faded blue eyes, looking up. The old woman was more dwarfish, more gnarled, thinner than he remembered Mrs. Sharskey to be, but it was, nonetheless, incredibly she, in a clean blue flowered apron-dress that reached her slippers, smiling more pleasantly than he ever remembered. She reached a shaking, almost transparent hand up toward his face, fingers out of control. As she recognized him, her mouth collapsed, trembling. "Tommy. The priest? Where's your priest's collar?"

"I'm on vacation."

"Oh. You're on vacation from China?"

"Peru," he said loudly, but she didn't hear.

"Oh. Come in. Come in. Come in," she said, leading him back into the dark railroad rooms, shuffling in her oversized slippers on a dark, narrow path through thick plastic-covered furniture, under low, dirt-encrusted chandeliers, past her clocks which were all ticking, past her dusty collections of bells, music boxes, figurines, ladies in period dresses, French gentlemen, porcelain animals, glass grapes in a gold-rimmed bowl, her piano against ostrich feather wallpaper, and a china parakeet in a cage. Tiers of small oriental rugs covered the modern, large-flowered wall-to-wall rug. The kitchen hadn't changed much, though all the rooms seemed smaller than Tom remembered them. Mrs. Sharskey reached up into the cabinet and pulled down a small jar of instant coffee.

"Or would you like tea?" The old woman turned, searching for Tom through her thick glasses.

"Tea would be fine."

"I have no cookies." She laughed.

"Just tea, please."

"Sit. Sit. Oh, this is a terrible surprise." Tom sat and listened as the old woman apologized for her slowness. She recited a litany of physical problems that had beset her over the years. Finally she joined Tom at the table and poured water over the tea bags with great difficulty. "Two women live upstairs now. They work all day. One is a nurse. They're *too* quiet. I like a little noise." She laughed. "I remember you running down those hall stairs, three at a time. Milk or sugar?"

"Nothing, thanks."

"When do you go back to China?"

"I'm working on Long Island now."

"Oh, God has been good to you."

"Yes, He has." Tom pulled his tea bag out and dropped it in the saucer.

"No cookies. Did I say that?"

"Just tea is fine." Tom brought the steaming cup to his lips. "Terrific." He put the cup down and grinned at the old woman, who trembled and smiled back as she lifted her cup. He could almost see through her kitchen ceiling, up to the table where he sat as a boy, studying his catechism under the rose light of a gooseneck lamp. He longed to go upstairs, to introduce himself to the boy and to take him to the ice cream parlor or to the ball field on Gardiner Avenue where he could meet new friends. "I wonder, Mrs. Sharskey," he then said loudly, "would you know of any small thing that might have been my mother's that was left here? Something of my mother's?"

"There's your father's carpentry tools down the cellar," she said with an expression of alarm. "Don't forget them. Come, let's try to get them." The old woman stood up painfully.

"I was thinking of something of my mother's."

"You should've taken something when she died, Tommy. Nobody came back, and the St. Vincent de Paul Society cleaned out the upstairs down to a toothpick. But you know what I got?" She held up a brittle finger. The old woman turned and shuffled back into the other room. A long moment of silence passed, then she returned with a green glass fruit bowl, full of wax fruit. "She brought me this home from her five-and-ten one Easter. Take it with you." Tom guided the bowl to the table: a banana, a pear, an orange, and an apple—old and scratched wax fruit. He picked up the apple and held it in his hand. "Take the bowl and all," Mrs. Sharskey urged. "I'll put it in a bag."

"No. My mother would want you to keep it."

"Put that apple in your pocket. Do."

"No." Tom laughed. The woman wrested the apple playfully out of his hand and slipped it in his sweater pocket the very way she had forced money on him when he did her errands long ago. She took Tom's hand and urged him to stand. "Now come down to the cellar," she said, bravely switching on the cellar light. "Let me show you my new oil burner."

"Are you sure we should?"

"Yes. Yes."

Tom helped her through the kitchen door to the back vestibule near the cellar stairs.

Looking up at the back staircase, it was unreal to know he was with Mrs. Sharskey, standing before the very wooden stairs he and Frank Sheehan had come down each night to stoke and feed the furnace before bedtime. An hour ago, he had felt light-years away from those stairs. Now he looked up to the second story at the fancy white-frosted glass shade of the Sheehans' hall light and the worn knob on the door that had opened for years to the Sheehan household.

Step by step he helped the old lady down to the last cellar steps. When he looked up, he was surprised by a spare, rectangular space with a newly cemented floor. Red iron posts had replaced the wooden ones, and an oil burner stood neatly where the furnace had been. No coal bin, and yet the damp odor was the same. His father's workbench was still there, and on top of it, covered with dust, a long mahogany box, Frank Sheehan's brass-hinged mahogany toolbox with its thick leather handle.

"Turn on the light and open it," she encouraged him.

"No need. I'd rather not." He didn't want to touch it.

"Do you have a car?" Her blue eyes twinkled in the dark.

"Yes."

"Then it's settled. Turn on the light." He did, to please her. "Take the tools. Do! Lift the box." Tom lifted the heavy box. "You've got to help me back up now." She threw a foot on the first step. "Your father carried those tools every day, back and forth to work," she said as they made their slow way up the stairs. Tom helped her with his one free hand while he held the heavy toolbox around, resting it on his hip. "I remember him in the freezing winters," she went on, "walking down Elm Street from the bus stop with that thing on his shoulders, like a baby's casket, trying not to slip on the snow. You going to stay overnight?" She tried turning on the stairs.

"Uh. Maybe just tonight."

"I have a bed inside."

"No, thanks, Mrs. Sharskey. I have a place."

"You sure?"

"Yes."

She had grown even kinder, more open, in her extreme old age, Tom thought. He kissed her when he left, and she held his face to hers a very long time, not wanting him to get free too soon; her fingers holding his head felt like butterfly wings.

"Pray for me," she whispered in his ear. "I can't live much more."

It felt strange the next morning to wake up as a guest of the Lighthouse Inn. Tom ate breakfast in the large dining room, then left to catch the first ferry back. He drove the rented car right up into its hold, locking the car, leaving Frank Sheehan's carpentry tools on the backseat, then climbing the clean white iron stairs to the top deck, where there were rows of seats facing the sun.

He sat there up in the wind, waiting for the ferry to move, tightly wrapped in Gene's gold-and-blue team sweater, looking boldly into the faces of the other passengers. He was glad not to be wearing his black suit and white collar.

He remembered the private sermon Father Swain gave to his ordination class, when the old priest pulled his white starched collar off his neck and held it high above his head. *Now that you are priests, I can tell you that this little collar will mean less and less as you grow older. Every man and woman who loves this world is a priest. You'll learn that. Einstein called himself a priest. Musicians do. Poets do. But they are not priests by the same lovely sacrament as you. That is your own indelible mystery. You can never erase it from your soul. Not even the Pope can take it away from you. It is stamped upon you forever. But that is no guarantee that you will be a good priest. Priests have gone to hell. . . .*

Tom threw his head back on the windy top deck and rested his arms out on top of the bench back, looking straight into the sky. He was happy for the first time since Peru. The feeling was so rare and strange. It was as if Gene were smiling inside him.

There was a loud clang as the winch turned, lifting the huge iron flap of the back of the ferry. He imagined a lad in moccasins and brown corduroys leaping across the water, then disappearing among the cars in the hold.

Chapter Thirteen

THE MORNING AFTER TOM LEFT HER, Katelyn woke up, swept the shack before breakfast, then marched to the post office. She felt guilty asking for her mail at the window, guilty in the general store for peeking at the headlines of the New York City newspapers. She felt soiled, criminal. She thought that Tom would return that afternoon with apologies or explanations, and she dreaded it.

When he didn't show up after the second day, she began to worry. It crossed her mind briefly to call the rectory, but she decided that would only make things worse.

The third morning she woke up wanting to cry. She told herself it was because the days were getting shorter. She walked along the ocean's edge, speaking internally, as if the waves were oracles, creeping up to her feet to hear her words.

She started thinking about her future. Who would be the central person in her life? Lizzie's mind was already on boys. Her old husband had a new young wife; they'd have a child, Lizzie would have a brother or sister. Her breasts felt heavy, and she was feeling bloated. Her period was coming.

The next morning the sound of the waves made her think of the world before there were machines, before there was the human voice, when the thunder of the ocean was the only song rising from the planet. She ignored the splendid light, painting furiously inside the shack with big strokes. She worked through sunset and into the night, going back to the ocean at dawn and unleashing her eyes on the sky, asking the dunes to help her, talking to the sky, to the stones in the road, begging the swallows to stay behind, begging the north horizon to keep its distance.

The following day hammers started echoing down from a new house going up behind the hill near the shack. She covered her ears, telling herself that she hated Long Island. The rug was being pulled out from under her, and the worst part was that there was no promise, no warmth, in any other place she could think of.

The next morning after waking, she grabbed a shawl and left, slamming the screen door so hard she almost split it. She had bought note paper and a new calligraphic pen at the highway. She brought them to the violet light of premorning.

Swallows zoomed over her as she wrote, sitting on a driftwood tree trunk facing the water.

> *Dear Aunt Ency,*
>
> *I'm writing this in a kettle of red-winged blackbirds: Peters Pond. I've picked rosehips here and collected seeds, thinking I might plant them up near your ocean there in Halifax. I can't stay here.*
>
> *Bridgehampton's turned into a fancy little city that you wouldn't recognize. The Snows couldn't afford to live here today, I don't think.*
>
> *Aunt Ency, I was involved with a man. It's over, and I need a "curing rest" as you would call it. Tea and quiet. Can I come up to you? Lizzie did go to her grandma's for school. Now don't hesitate to say if it's not the right time, but would Lizzie and I be too much at the Christmas holidays? I just don't have the guts to be alone this year.*
>
> *Think of you often and lovingly.*
>
> > *Katelyn*

She stood up, catching the breeze. Four swallows banked over her head, but the hawk ignored her movements, hovering for a kill as she walked away. The damp sand was putty-colored, while the cottony waves turned orange, catching the rising sun.

She walked back to the shack, drank tea, and stared calmly out the window into the dark cedar. At eight-thirty she walked out under the burned-out horse chestnuts to the general store and post office.

As the stiff pink envelope slid out of her hands toward Halifax, she felt a physical love for her father. She recalled her mother's voice telling her he had died. She was sitting in the maroon-and-gray living room. She remembered a burst of white surrounding her mother's face as she spoke. And that numb feeling of amputation, of something having been cut out of her body.

She smiled at the nice postman. "Snow. General delivery, please?"

"Snow? Snow. Nothing today."

"Thank you."

She needed milk. She crossed the porch to the general store, and when she pulled open the screen door, the headlines leaped at her from a pile of local newspapers: FUNERAL FOR DROWNED PRIEST IN MONTAUK. She tore at the newspaper and read:

Funeral services held for the curate of the Stella Maris Chapel here in Montauk, victim of a boating accident.

She threw thirty cents on the counter and stumbled onto the porch in shock, reading as she drifted down the stairs to the middle of the road.

The body of the Reverend Eugene Buoncuore of the Brooklyn Diocese was discovered by haul-seiners off the south coast of Montauk Point.

The shock of thinking it was Tom had nearly stopped her heart, flooded her ears. Her body thumped, haltingly, brutally, without her. She drew a breath and started walking, confused at how she could feel so much for someone who considered himself a stranger now. She abandoned the road, cutting into the field of alfalfa behind the Foster farm, which had grown so high she had to leap, like a deer, to get through it. The dry growth scratched her legs, but she didn't turn back. She had to be home, thrown across her bed, safe, as soon as possible.

When she stepped up into the large room of her shack, she was panting. Tom was standing there at her sink, calmly, drinking water from her glass. His white shirt was sweated. A blue-and-gold team sweater was on her bed. His shirt sleeves were rolled up. Sweat beaded his brow. His face glistened, wet. He put down the glass and wiped his forehead with a paper towel.

"I had to walk a long way with that damned toolbox," he said simply. She couldn't speak. Couldn't find an entrance into his moment. She angrily brought her milk to the table. "Damn thing must weigh a hundred pounds." Her bottlenecked anger was beginning to spout.

"The paper says your friend was drowned." The words came out of her mouth like square blocks.

"Yes."

"Is that why you didn't come back?"

He turned to wash out the glass. "No. It wasn't the reason I stayed away," he said, almost inaudibly.

She glanced at the brown paper bag and the toolbox on the table. "What's in the paper bag?" She pointed.

"Corn. I thought you might like some. I . . . I've been to Connecticut."

Then she eyed the canvas bag. "Do you intend to stay overnight?"

"Is it all right?" He looked to her, testing. He really hadn't intended to stay.

She turned her back to him. An overwhelming physical reaction was taking place in her. She was shaking. He came up behind her, gently encircling her with his arms. She pushed out of them and walked to the screen door. "You can't walk in here anytime you feel like it and yank my chain this way." She turned.

He stared, speechless. His face started draining of color.

"What *happened* to you? Why are you back? What do you want from me now?" Her rapid-fire questions struck fear into herself, because if he floundered, groping for explanations, it would instantly ruin him for her.

"I had a great deal of confusion and guilt when I ran out of here," he offered hesitantly.

"Guilt over what?"

"Over what we did."

"What did we do? Sex?"

"For me, it was much more. It felt like my whole life was washing out, collapsing. My solution was to run. I admit it." She could see by his eyes the memory was fresh. "I was just scared, Katelyn."

"And you walk in here with an overnight bag? What's to prevent it from happening tonight?"

"I would just bite the bullet and get through it."

"Bite the *bullet?* Is that what you call sleeping with me?" She started pacing. She couldn't hold in her bitchiness, so she decided to let him have it. "My feelings were battered too." The words came trembling out of her. "I paid a high price, *too,* for that night, emotionally. What do you think I am? A battleship? Any person that invests *feelings* in a . . . a dog would deserve better than to suddenly be treated like some snake who crept into your bed, when it was *my* bed you crept into, *creep.*"

"Easy, Katelyn."

"Well, what did you think *I* was feeling when you ran out of here? Did it cross your mind?" She was too loud. She couldn't hear herself. " 'Stop *clawing* at me,' you said. Ugh." She embraced herself.

"I don't remember using that expression."

"Well, you did, goddammit. And I felt like shit for three days."

He waited for silence, and when a crow flew back into the cedar, he spoke up, softly. "Do you remember how it was in the tunnel?" he asked quietly. "When you begged them to let you off the bus? That's the way I felt that night." She paced, wanting to say something in rebuttal, but nothing came.

She stopped in the middle of the room, put a hand to her forehead, and threw a glance up at him. Sincerity was there in his eyes, but insincerity was never his problem. His problem was . . . was . . . Her train of thought was shattering. Water was filling her body, her chest, her throat. She could identify the emotion that flowed out with her tears. It was, simply, disappointment, so many years of it, that had characterized her history with men. She was weary of the same old story, exhausted, and newly frightened by it.

"You all right?" Tom knelt with her as she sank into a chair. She gripped his hand, though it felt very much a stranger's, extraordinarily a stranger's. "What's the matter?" Tom asked. "Why are you crying?"

"Oh, God." She tried to attach any available words to her feelings. "I'm just so goddam mad, and so goddam scared." She dammed back the flow. "I came out to this place because my life had completely disappeared, all but a few dishes."

"Huh? Dishes?"

"Yes." Her voice squeaked, though she kept back the tears. "Things broke that we owned, do you know what I mean, from one apartment to the other." She brushed her hair off her forehead. "And I got tired of saying good-bye to chairs, lamps, sideboards because they were too big to take along. Three generations of stuff dwindled down to a few shopping bags on that damned bus." Tom listened with care, but he wasn't fully understanding. "Then I came out here." She looked out the window. "Thinking, somehow, the place would give me something back, something it owed me, something I'd recognize, but it's turning into bulldozers, swimming pools, people who are strangers."

"I'm no stranger." Tom tucked her hair behind her ear. "Am I?"

"Oh, God, yes, you are," she said, squeezing his hand. "You're the biggest stranger of them all."

"A stranger couldn't have made you feel this bad, could he?"

She shrugged, as if he wasn't getting her point.

"Would you look straight at me?" he asked. "I'm sure I'm not saying this the right way, but, would you marry me?" He waited for her to speak.

She just stared at his lips. "Are you all right?"

"Yes. Yes."

He gripped both her hands as if her body had given him the message that it was losing equilibrium.

"You see, I've decided to leave the priesthood, Katelyn." She remained frozen for several seconds that way, as he picked the flyaway hairs off her face, combing them with his fingers back into the body of her hair while she sat there blinking. Then pulling her hands to herself, slowly rising. He rose. "Was I wrong to say this?"

"Not that."

"Are you sure?"

"Yes. Really." She was lying.Why did it seem cruel of him to bring up marriage at that moment? Why did it deface him, make him clumsy? She had just started feeling soft and safe, expressing her innermost feelings, when he dropped his bomb on her. Now she had to hide a new anxiety. Why this reaction to the word *marriage?* Where did *he* get it from? Her confusion seemed oblique, disconnected from its cause. She didn't dare let on. She hoped it would distill, become clearer, before she spoke. She went to the sink for a glass of water. She drank slowly, then turned back to him. He seemed a total stranger in her house. Though he wore a white shirt with the sleeves rolled up, he was still very much the Catholic priest in his black shoes and trousers. He embarrassed her.

"How many weeks have we known each other?" she asked in a throaty voice.

"Weeks? What do you mean?" he asked.

"It's only *weeks,* Tom."

"We have all we need for marriage."

"Tom, that's terribly naive." She said it with all the compassion she could muster; still, the hurt of her words smoothed out the skin of his face, turning him into a boy, staring wide-eyed, betrayed. Was she making a mistake? Memories of him avalanching inside her: the bus, the children clinging to him, his sweetness in bed.

"I don't want to stand in the path of your change," she offered. That sounded worse, but she had to stick with the truth. It was her only way out now. "I mean . . . people should *parallel* each other, alongside, so they can both maneuver their lives, not trip one another up."

"I must have misunderstood your reactions with me." His

confusion was metamorphosing into anger.

"I just don't want to be your reason for leaving something so important to your life as the priesthood. You're misunderstanding me."

"But you are my reason." He skimmed the sweat from his forehead. "I can't think of a better reason."

"It's too fast, Tom."

"You want me to straddle the fence until you figure out if you should say yes or no?" His voice was tough. She grabbed a string, tied back her hair toughly, and looked at him. Something was wrong.

"Is it that you're afraid to take a chance with me?" he pressed, looking at her with cold determination.

"Yes," she said, trying to match his strength. "I don't know you."

"Don't you think we're the kind of people who have the decency, the strength, to keep a promise to one another?" he asked bluntly.

"Wait. What promise are you talking about?"

"To continue to love one another, for the rest of our lives? Is that too much responsibility for you?"

She turned, resenting his sarcasm. "I don't want to hear this. This is *exactly* what I *don't* want to hear." She turned on the water and started splashing her face.

"Katelyn. For crying out loud!" His voice was a loud reprimand. "Be consistent. You're confusing me."

She grabbed a towel. "It's you who isn't being consistent. You haven't been consistent from the start. You've jerked me around about sex, about friendship. Yesterday I was an occasion of sin, today you ask me to marry you. You can't control love, that way anyhow. You can't keep it in force by a wish or a promise or a marriage. Look at your celibacy. Look at your vows. What's become of them, huh? You're standing here breaking *them* by asking me to marry you. Give me a break."

He wiped his hair back, speechless. She was right.

"Promises don't keep people together." She turned away from him sadly.

"What *does* keep people together?"

"Their goodness, their sense of fairness, the habits they get into, their sense of humor. Stubbornness. Who knows?"

"Maybe that's why the Church had to make it a sacrament."

"Well, I don't *want* any sacrament, okay? Don't confuse me with that stuff."

Her words offended. He walked aimlessly toward the palm curtains, then to the sink. He leaned against the sink, folding his arms, just looking at her. She could see new distances in his eyes, and his hurt. He was having his first hard time with love, she thought; it was inevitable.

He simply walked to the table and grabbed the handle of the toolbox, as if to leave, but he hesitated. A new silence filled the place. A sort of finality was descending. He stood frozen like an animal in the woods. She caught the way his brown hair was darker at the back of his neck. She deliberately drank in the tall strong frame of the man whom she had held in her bed, realizing that no other woman had ever had him that way. In spite of his age and his intelligence, he was so tender, so inexperienced. He had opened himself clumsily to her, embracing her with the trust of a child and the passion of an adolescent. Now she was afraid he would pull the toolbox toward him and simply walk out her door. She recalled her conversations with the ocean. The agony of loneliness sprouted in her chest again, and she begged herself not to advance her own destruction. The word *marriage* had panicked her. Yes. That was the only thing that had gone wrong.

He looked at her with eyes still cool and hard. "When I walked into this room, I had also to accept the fact that I had to go back to that rectory and tell Kruug that I'm leaving the priesthood. Do you know what it's like to place that before another priest? Especially a priest like him who is going to pull every trick in the book on me, every power he's got, and I'm steeled for it. God knows I'm ready to fight only because you mean so much to me. But . . . "

"Tom, listen . . . "

"But worse than anything, I'm going to have to resist my own . . ." He stopped short, as if something caught in his throat.

"Your own what?"

"Sentiments." He turned away. "All my old dreams are going over the waterfall, my whole life. And you talk to me like a fifteen-year-old who thinks that people get hundreds of chances every day."

"But don't you see, that's exactly why I asked if we could take *time.*"

"Katelyn, you don't understand what's involved. I couldn't linger on the cutting edge like that. I come to this from a totally different place than you do. Could it be that you're the one who is scared to plan, incapable of commitment? Tell me. I'll help you. I'm strong."

She moved toward the window, looking out again. Again, carpenters' hammers echoed down from behind the hill. His words had made her feel a certain distrust of herself, a certain rawness, as if a bandage had been ripped off an old wound. She had been sealed against this kind of talk. Her heart had nearly stopped less than a half hour ago when she thought he might have drowned, and here he was alive, *with* her, and she was acting so practical, so didactic. Maybe her hopes had become too small, and she was suffering from that strange blindness that afflicts people who grow resigned to things being less wonderful. She let out a deep breath and gave him her face.

"What do you want me to do, to say? What do you want to hear?"

"Tell me you really think we can't love one another for the rest of our lives. Just say that." She had to match his effort.

"Yes. I think we *might* be able to, and I'm willing to try. But does this mean we have to get married? I'll drive you back to the rectory. You can get your things, come back here to stay. *Live* here. But there are still questions, Tom; there must be hundreds we haven't even thought of."

"Like what?"

"What about your work?"

"I could achieve a great deal on my own."

"As a social worker?"

"No. As a human being who wants to make the world better."

"And who will subsidize you?" She folded her arms.

"Huh? I'm a fair carpenter. There's a lot of construction around here."

"Which means we would live here in Bridgehampton or Sag Harbor?"

"Can you think of a better place?"

"It's a rich man's world out here."

"Rich men need help. They hire people. Are you going to be a snob about it? We'll make a deal with your landlord and insulate this shack, or . . . or go live over a store."

"What will you do in the winter when it gets dark at four-thirty—put down your hammer and start social programs for the poor, visit the sick, hang out in those migrant shacks with a kerosene lamp?"

"I did much more once. Don't underestimate me, Katelyn."

"And what am I supposed to do throughout all this? Have dinner waiting till eleven o'clock every night? And suppose we should . . . suppose I were to become pregnant?"

"I'd love that."

"Sure. Fine. You're forty-one years old."

"We'd manage."

"God, are we set up to have problems! I don't think I want them, Tom. No." She shook her head.

He looked at her, letting that final word of hers sink in. She was a ship sailing away forever. He regretted ever having laid eyes on her. She saw the shame and the worry in his eyes. He drifted toward the screen door and stood there, looking out.

"Are you going somewhere?" she asked.

"No."

"Are you staying?"

He didn't answer. He just opened the door and shakily stepped outside, onto the cedar deck. He stood there, motionless, under the sky, looking out to the blond hill of winter wheat. He also could hear the hammering. His legs felt like marble. He couldn't run if he wanted to. Distant doubts would catch up now. They had been on his trail a long time. His adrenaline was all spent. He felt old. Behind him, the screen door slammed.

"I do love you, Tom," she said to his back, "whatever the hell that means."

"Love takes courage." He spoke to the wheat. She placed her cheek between his shoulder blades. She could hear his heart beating through his back. She threw her arms around him, locking her hands between his breasts.

"We really don't know each other well enough." She let the words out carefully. "We've shared a few unspoken thoughts; we've been to bed; but bed isn't all. Marriage is so different from all of that. Why *force* it? Don't let's go from one trap to another. There are so many things you have the right to see and do, just the ordinary things that people have been doing in this world, that you've missed. I could tell myself: Grab him, Katelyn. Don't be a fool. But you don't deserve to be grabbed at."

He heard her words, he understood them. But they didn't make him feel better. She couldn't understand that he felt like Christ in the Garden of Gethsemane, but without Peter beside him, without even Judas to give him a kiss, just a strange woman he had met on a bus a few weeks ago, whose arms wrapped around him, whose voice vibrated into his chest from behind, speaking of things he never dreamed he would be discussing.

"Say you're feeling better. Please," she asked.

"I can't."

"What're you feeling?"

"Ugly things. Strange things. Disintegration."

"Is your mind clicking away like mad?"

"Yes."

"But not over me. Is it?"

"Not over you."

"You want to be left alone?"

He answered by reaching back and grabbing her. She came around, facing him. She leaned into his embrace a little dizzily. They were getting things right now. She might have done a good thing for once in her life. She closed her eyes. She had taken a risk and she had won something for it.

"I'd like to stay tonight."

"Sure."

She had an impulse to tell him about Halifax, to invite him for Christmas, to meet Lizzie and Aunt Ency. But it was not the time. Instead, she broke away and went inside, behind the palm-printed curtains. She tried not to notice her tired eyes in the mirror as she put on her lipstick. She combed her hair, letting it flow out wide. She sighed and reached for a tampon, telling herself: *I'm going to wind up loving this guy for the rest of my life.*

Then she heard his voice from the road, coming through the cedar planks. "I'm going to the beach."

"Okay," she yelled back through the wall. When she came out from behind the curtains, she went to the window and caught him walking empty-handed down the road toward the beach. She had never seen him move that way, so stooped over. She wondered if he blamed her for killing his momentum, for chaining him to the present. It had all happened too fast.

His thoughts actually contained no specificity. His body and mind were turning into one thing, one anxiety. He wanted to reason himself into a good feeling, but his confusion was too immense, too like an ocean pressing against his door. To try to let in a drop would result in catastrophe. So he walked as blankly as he could, almost blindly, surmising it would take the rest of his life to understand what had happened in the past few hours.

It was as if that shadow figure, that gray, nude man in the bathroom mirror of Stella Maris, was walking beside him, wanting his due, a creature who believed in nothing transcendent, who never indulged in intellectual luxuries, a hostile being who saw all culture as its enemy. What word of Katelyn's had unleashed him in the past hour, the brute, walking, like his shadow, toward the flat and radiant ocean?

Tom looked down at his feet as he walked the shoreline, west, toward Water Mill, into the sun. Monarchs flirted suicidally with the waves. Many lay dead in his path. He didn't even see them as questions began to surface: *What did it mean when I subordinated my life to the life of the Church? Losing one's life in order to gain it? What is a solemn promise anyway? Holy Orders . . . Just what did I forswear? What rights did I surrender? How severe will my alienation be if I leave the priesthood? Where will I fit in? And what about a married clergy? Will I live to see it? How old will I be then? What about the people? How can I go off when I know I'm an effective priest?*

The questions came faster than the answers. *Would I constantly have to cover up my past? Will it be assumed that I've become an enemy of the Church? Will I be expected to avoid other priests? Will they avoid me?*

Questions flew at him from the dunes in rapid fire.

He walked for hours, totally unaware of time, reasoning, playing his own devil's advocate. Then, some three hundred yards out into the ocean, in a field of blue-green iridescence that was the result of the sun's rapid descent, he noticed the same little yellow light, the one he had seen from Kruug's window the night before Gene's funeral. Could Katelyn's marine flashlight have remained lit that long? The light made him sad for Gene once again: he didn't want to lose sight of it. He followed the light until it disappeared in the direction of the Chesapeake, in the probable path of fish migrations, south, where they go to spend the winter.

It was evening by the time he reached Peters Pond Road again. He must have walked five miles each way. The afternoon had been sucked out of the day.

Katelyn was waiting on the dirt road between two small dunes, her arms wrapped around herself, hugging the Irish knit afghan that had been stuffed into her straw bag the day he met her. It had actually grown cold; the sun had plunged into the dark-blue ocean.

"Let's go back and eat," she said, throwing the afghan over his shoulders. She tried not to show alarm at his face, so drained, so tired; his left eye bloodshot, both eyes strained and glassy. He was feeling cold; his shoulders lifted to warm his neck. His hands were bloodless and gray.

When Katelyn switched on the red-shaded Saturn lamp, it lifted the cabin up into the deep red sky. They sat on the bed looking out the window, leaning against pillows, drinking wine. Deeply, he kept silent, his face seemingly on fire in the red light. The clear, cold night developing outside the window was seducing his eyes. He startled her when he spoke, staring out to the strange light, as if he were seeing back to the wall of time. In a small, tranquil voice he spoke of his work, of the growing troubles of the world, of history as he understood it, of Moonghost and the teeming poor of Peru. He took her hand unconsciously, pulling her toward him.

"I have my period," she said, wondering why she felt it necessary to say that.

"Can we stay together like this?" He kicked off his shoes.

"Of course." She rested her head on his chest and brought her knees up under her skirt. He reached down and pulled the afghan up over them, and they fell asleep that way, his feet warming themselves, his mind drifting toward caverns of voices, of sighs, until his eyes left his body, to make down through his memory, like a shark diving deep, sending all his prey into hiding.

In minutes he was dreaming that he was inside under the water tornado at Stella Maris, laid out in the middle aisle looking up at the bare feet of the ascending madonna. Voices surrounded him, fingers lowering a lid, pushing velvet into his face. It was dark. Airless. He tried to call out to Katelyn, but his throat was paralyzed. He struggled, half knowing it was a dream, until finally he managed a tiny sound.

"*Kaa . . . Kaaay . . . Kaaaay uh. Kaaaay ut lllllln.*"

She stirred, surprised at first to find him there. But then, springing up and throwing the blanket away from him, she lifted him up into her arms and held him tightly. "Wake up, Tom," she ordered, shaking him. "Wake up. You're dreaming."

Suddenly panting, he was awake. "Katelyn. Don't let me go. God! Please."

"There's nothing to be afraid of. I'm here. You're all right, Tom. You're really all right." He was soaked with sweat. She rocked him until he became almost a part of her, glued to her, in her arms.

At eight in the morning he woke up and went back to the beach. The tide had left a string of very big clamshells. He collected the largest of them and picked sea lavender in the dunes, and when he got back to the shack, he quietly filled the shells with water at the sink, plucked the tiny sea lavender blossoms off their stems, and let them float in the shells. He switched off the Saturn lamp and carefully set the shells down on the bed table. When the coffee had perked for five minutes, he poured some in a cup and walked quietly to her.

"Where've you been?" she asked groggily. Then, seeing the shells, "Oh, my!" She touched the floating sea blossoms. "You feeling okay?" she asked, reaching for his hair.

"Will you drive me back to Stella Maris after the coffee?" he asked.

"Can I ask why?"

"To pick up my chalice. It's worth a lot of money."

She tilted her head. "Leaving there?"

"Leaving the priesthood." She felt pain witnessing his expression.

"I love you." She knew it was a non sequitur.

"You do?"

"Yes. And I love your courage to push out your walls. But sometimes it takes courage to hold back too."

"What do you mean?"

"Come up with a better reason for leaving the priesthood than me? Please?"

"Don't worry. Drive me back now?"

"Sure." She gulped coffee and turned herself out of bed. He walked impatiently to the screen door and waited, watching the crazily blowing wheat bend in large yellow-and-silver waves, then writhe like serpents up the hillside.

"You will come back, won't you?" she asked.

"I can't promise." His words stopped her in her tracks. "Promises don't work." He smiled teasingly. She stepped behind him and threw her arms around him sadly. "Of course I'll come back," he offered softly.

"And I promise I'll be here," she said.

"For how long?" He deliberately pressed her.

"For as long as we both need and want each other. Is that enough?"

"Yes." He turned gratefully and took her face in his hands. She pulled away to get dressed, leaving him to watch the moving hillside through the screen.

Chapter Fourteen

KRUUG AND MURIEL were left abruptly alone after Gene's funeral. He had turned off the automatic switch to the sprinkler system when the last guest left. *Let the grass burn. Let the ground be purified.* He also insisted the funeral flowers be kept on the grave. He sat for hours watching them drying, catching the offshore breeze.

"Do you hear a ringing in your ears?" he asked Muriel the next day.

"No," she replied with guilt-worn eyes. Her face surprised him. Its ravaged, worried expression sent him to his room for the day. He locked the door and sat before his window, looking out to Gene's grave. "You rendered me helpless," he whispered over and over.

By bedtime, he decided he had to rid his mind of Gene. In the dark he arranged a triangle between the ocean, himself, and heaven. There was no place for Gene in these geometrics, and yet Gene flapped noisily in his mind, like the loose part of a machine.

He fell asleep at eleven, but at midnight he sat up, suddenly unable to shake the conviction that Gene was still alive, sitting in town at John's Drive-In having a hamburger. He could no longer imagine Gene in the casket.

He had a cigarette, then tried to force sleep, but the pictures kept coming: Gene laughing with kids, Gene wiping his mouth with a paper napkin. He went into the hall and opened Gene's door, hoping the sterile room would reassure him. He found the room blue and glowing, moonlight behind the drawn shades. He smelled the product Muriel sprayed. He went back to his room, unsatisfied, and read until dawn.

After breakfast, he sipped a second cup, cautiously letting his eyes drift out his window, hoping to imagine Gene's body fixed deep in the hillside, but he couldn't. He wanted to weep but couldn't. The emotions slipped out of his grasp like wild horses over a hill, out of sight.

But when the Jesuit suddenly appeared in shirt-sleeves, coming down the pebbled drive, a sort of shocked joy got hold of Kruug's stomach. "Thank God!" he called out involuntarily. He closed his eyes and offered a silent prayer of thanksgiving. He must tell Muriel to make something light for dinner, more in keeping with Tom's tastes. He must turn on the lawn sprinklers in celebration and let them run all day and night.

"He's home, Monsignor. Father Sheehan is home." Muriel's excited voice echoed from somewhere deep beyond his door.

The Jesuit seemed much older than that awful night Kruug had caught him sprawled across the narrow bed in Granger's dark rectory. "He reminds me of myself," Kruug whispered to the glass.

"Father Sheehan is back." Muriel broke into the room without a knock, her face flushed.

"Take it easy. Tell him to come straight in here, Muriel," Kruug said calmly, "and close the door behind you."

"Yes, Monsignor." She left, and in a moment he heard her again from a distance. "Welcome back, Father Sheehan. *Father,*" she was calling from the kitchen window with such atypical shrillness that it made Kruug cringe to hear it ringing out over the lawn. Tom deliberately ignored her and continued toward the church. He pulled open the oak sacristy door, stepped inside, twirled the combination on the sacristy safe, took out his chalice in its case, relocked the safe, then pushed back out into the open air, crossing around the mound of Gene's grave, still with eyes down, pretending he didn't see Kruug at the window.

"Monsignor said you're to go straight to his room," Muriel cried out as Tom flew past her kitchen.

"Tell him I'll knock on his door in a half hour. In the meantime, I don't want to be disturbed."

"Are you in for lunch?" she yelled out.

"No, Muriel."

"Dinner?"

"No."

"There's mail for you on the hall table." He stopped and lifted the blue airmail letter from the polished table. Overseas stationery, the kind they had at the Head House in Lima. In the upper left-hand corner, in small script, was the name Rev. Philip Behan and the address:

La Misión Cristo Re
Chosica, Lima
Peru, S.A.

It had been forwarded from St. Barnabas'. He turned the thin letter over and closed his door behind him. Using the nail file from the dresser to slit it open, he was careful not to tear it in the wrong places. The fragile paper had been densely written upon in Philip's tiny hand. But then Tom wondered if reading the letter might hurt him with Katelyn, in some unforeseeable way. He put the open letter on the bed, went to the window, and lifted the shade. The sky of Montauk was not unlike the sky of Peru. Noises on the highway could have been sounds of Lima. Marta could call him from the quadrangle at any moment: *Padrecito!*

The need to know how Philip was, that perhaps worry had never been necessary, and the simple joy of the man's resurfacing at Head House, all overcame him, and he sat down immediately, took up the crisp blue letter from the bed, and unfolded it.

Dear Tom,
As I landed in Lima, I had a premonition that the two creatures whom I had loved would never again be found in Peru. The mighty condor bird, and my friend Tom Sheehan. Why did I think of the

great bird and you together? Perhaps it was that you both were driven away by a cruelty, like my own.

As the plane touched ground, a warning went through me to be ready for the loss. It seemed so fitting a punishment, because nothing would have hurt me more than not to find you here. I asked myself for the first time: Had I hurt you deliberately by not seeking you out before I left? Was I imprisoning myself to you, making you a twin in my agony? Was that my way of leaving myself to you, trapped in a stubborn puzzle that your mind could never sort out?

Sometimes I wonder if we do not steal light from our friends' souls that way, the way fish steal life from one another in order to survive. Only a great hunger could make us so evil. I ask your forgiveness if what I say has the slighest truth to it. DeSilva blames himself, but we are all at fault here, Tom.

In those last few months of work on the infant shelter, I was too embarrassed to let you know how depressed I was. It was only because I dreaded your finding yourself helpless to help me, that having to share my agony would only destroy you. I hoped to conquer it, but it was too demanding. My body started wanting sleep; that was the hardest part, and I couldn't do it. I began having nightmares in the day as I worked, talking with people, half dreams full of horrible images, worse than the terremoto. Planetary holocausts. The sun dying. Cataclysmic visions. I tried desperately to learn sleep again in order to contain them, but even when I succeeded, all the demons that had kept out all those years had piled upon the doors to my mind, pushing to get in. I was willing to accept that I was going crazy.

With that, I failed in my belief in God, irrationally, as if a chemical in my brain had altered all my prior concepts. It was a raw feeling. Nothing could comfort me, and then, my priesthood started seeming a waste of my life. I simply wanted out, to run, to leave my devastation behind.

I found a construction job in Colorado, near a Trappist monastery there, in a town called Snow Mass. And after a while I began to miss Peru. Oh, Tom, that was the healthiest emotion I'd had in a year. It was suddenly true that I had an answer to at least one of my problems, and I decided to come back to the place of the condorcito, *the* terremoto, *the Great Western Ocean, and to you, my friend.*

What is a priest without God doing in the Church? you ask. Perhaps we are only temporarily separated, God and I. Perhaps we will find one another, this time not in the sky, but in that dark monastery of silence and tranquillity called the ocean, where violence and rebirth are plentiful. Perhaps in my soul I will turn into a sea creature, a porpoise or a seal-man. I do believe the sea is the last paradise on earth. Don't let my words frighten you. You know me. Just consider that I struggle on this paper to reflect my soul. I am trying, grasping, to be your friend again with the only tools I have, my little truths.

Now, how do I ask you to forgive me this late? My embarrassment overwhelms me as I write words you don't need, words out of cadence with your life, that I throw into the air like wingless birds. Still, I must. I would hate myself worse than before if I sealed this letter without confessing the hope that I will see you again, Tom. But you know better than I if there's a chance in that. If you think not, then let this be a swift good-bye.

From wherever you go in your life, cast me a forgiving thought now and then. Forgive me when you laugh with new friends, when you say your prayers in morning and night. Forgive me when you foolishly think that no one in this world is thinking of you. Then throw this letter away, burn it, so that nothing of me remains in your memory except that I am the ghost who took you on jeep rides under the moon and who taught you to walk upon water, among the silent whales.

Philip

Tom walked up and down the tight room with the letter hanging open from his hand. While it moved him to read it, parts of it angered him. At least Philip was safe, and maybe even strong in the way that only he could be. His personality had unified in some strange way, like a John of the Cross, forced into becoming the mystic everyone believed him to be, trapped in a dark night of the soul. But in a way, Philip had made no choice; he hung suspended, like Christ nailed to a cross, and that's what angered

Tom. Or was it that Philip had cast doubt on his own choice? As Tom stepped into the shower, he felt alternatingly tender and angry toward his friend. The heat of mental anguish was turning Philip Behan into glass. He was more transparent, fragile. And though Tom sensed that the man's ego continued to be large, his honesty, his courage to hurl himself into the face of his own truth, was a kind of final conquering of himself, an immolation. He had become what everyone had always believed him to be —El Fantasma de la Luna, a ghost, a saint—and Tom resented him tenderly for it, quietly, sadly, with a feeling of terrible loss.

After his shower, he sat down and reread the letter, and as he did, he, himself, seemed from minute to minute to be moving in and out of being the person to whom it was addressed. Instinctively, he put the letter aside, stood up, working fast, packing only the most important things, because he didn't want to carry anything other than his suitcase and chalice. He hesitated about packing his cassock, deciding to leave it behind. He did pack the cincture, for the sake of memory. But he could use a suit. He decided to wear it with the collar on his way out. He put on the white collar, the rabat, trousers, and jacket. He checked the room once again. Moonghost's letter lay on the bed. He grabbed it, stuffed it into his back pocket, and whispering good-bye to the room, he grabbed his chalice case and suitcase and stepped into the hall.

It was dark as usual when Tom entered it, in spite of the glare from the glass door near Muriel's room. Tom walked a bit, put down his suitcase, and tapped his middle knuckle on the hollow plywood of Kruug's door. A click down the hall turned his head. Muriel had emerged from her room, silhouetted in the light of the glass front door. She wore so much makeup that she almost didn't appear to be herself. She didn't notice Tom. She was dressed in a navy straw pillbox hat, shaped like a small rubber tire with white netting, and white gloves. From her wrist hung a large blue leather pocketbook and an ethereal shopping sack of monofilament netting. She wore a pair of blue leather afternoon shoes with an open toe and high heels. There was the fresh-painted gleam of orange on her lips. He had never seen lipstick on her before. A white beaded cardigan sweater hung from her shoulders, its sleeves swinging lifelessly at her sides. Her dress was printed with Chinese fans, boldly scattered every which way. When she stooped to lock her door, the arms of the sweater fell forward, as if they belonged to an unconscious woman on her back. "Father," she gasped when she saw Tom, straightening up with such a jerk that the sweater fell dead to the floor.

"Come in," Kruug called, standing up. Tom pressed in. Kruug's smile dissolved as he came toward Tom, his arms awkwardly suspended, seeing the chalice case and the suitcase in the hallway. The glass front door slammed behind Muriel.

"Tom. What are you doing?"

"Monsignor, I'm here hoping you will be kind enough, understanding enough, to give me your blessing, because—"

"My blessing for what?"

"I'm leaving the priesthood."

Kruug didn't move. He held still as stone. His pulse thumped in his ears. He wanted to rush toward Tom as to a man who had accidentally shot himself in the head.

Tom only stood there calmly, listening to the ticking of Kruug's watch.

"That girl?"

"She's part of it, yes." Tom tried to catch Kruug's eyes before they turned away.

"Close the damn door," Kruug ordered. Tom brought his chalice in, placed it on the chair, and closed the door. Kruug collapsed into his chair behind his desk, swinging his back to Tom so that he could look out the window. He threw a foot up onto the radiator and picked his teeth with his thumbnail like a scared boy. "She's pushing for marriage, isn't she?"

"I asked her to. She said no. She isn't sure."

"She isn't sure." Kruug laughed with disgust. "Jesus, you have got to be the most naive man God ever put on the face of this earth!"

"Don't try to cheapen this, Monsignor. Please don't do that."

"She's not *sure*." Kruug chuckled.

Tom steeled himself for the rain of Kruug's words. He had

to pass through that rain to get out of there. He knew that. He had to keep humble to make this passage. But Kruug said nothing. He simply shrugged helplessly and smiled like a vaudevillian.

"Well, good-bye then. You leave two thousand years of struggle behind you. *Go.* Beat it." The recliner seemed to turn on its own, facing Tom. "Why are you standing here like this?" Kruug pressed dryly. Tom looked down, not answering. "Why are you wasting our time *standing* here?" Kruug repeated, his eyes looking forcefully into Tom's. "Why did you come *in* just now, anyway?" His voice softened. "Why didn't you just slip out and be gone?"

Tom shrugged. "That would justify a negative case against me in your mind. I don't want you to build me up to be a rotten apple. I know you, Monsignor."

"But you *are* a rotten apple." Kruug smiled. Tom winced in surprise. "Or else you'd have applied for a dispensation or a leave of absence."

"You know that kind of thing takes forever."

"Small price to pay for legitimacy, you who are so scrupulous."

"It takes too long, Monsignor."

"Is she impatient to leave this land of sun and fun?"

"No."

"Well, coming in here won't make you a fresh apple in my eye, Tom. As for a blessing, you've got a hell of a nerve. There's no rubric in the manual for a runaway priest and his concubine."

"It was a long shot." Tom lifted his chalice case by the leather strap, paused, then reached for the doorknob.

"Did you open Gene's casket?" Kruug's shout bounced off the blue ceiling. Tom couldn't believe what he was hearing. "Did you put that T-shirt in there?"

"Yes." Tom turned, looking at him.

"Whatever possessed you to do a weird thing like that?" Kruug's voice was strangely matter-of-fact.

"How did you find out?"

"His poor father wanted to see him before the burial."

"All right, I put it in there. It was something between me and Gene." Tom grabbed the doorknob and pulled.

"Wait." Kruug's voice snapped like a whip. He stood up. "Close that damn door. Put that chalice down," he commanded, walking around his desk. Kruug came so close Tom could smell his breath. Tom made defensive fists. A little laugh dropped out of Kruug, falling like broken pieces of glass to his red rug. "You were my unicorn," he said with self-mockery. He was trying to change gears too fast. His smile cracked his face. His fingers trembled.

"I don't understand what you're trying to tell me."

"You were *rare.*" Kruug forced a clown's smile.

"Rare?"

"A rare priest. You have to be told you were." His eyebrows arched; his forehead wrinkled; the bloodshot eyes jiggled nervously. "A *chaste* priest you were, if you'll pardon my referring to your confession that wonderful morning in Brooklyn." Kruug was smiling like a man who has just sucked a lemon, a smile full of pain and worry. "You're the last of a stubborn breed, Tom, and you don't even know it. The sweetest, most beautiful thing a man could be, a holy priest." He brought his voice low, squeezing gentleness into it. "And now, some woman's talked you into becoming common as crap at a circus. Be frank. What kind of carrot did she dangle? Sex? Or the withholding of it? Tom, you are more naive about these things than any man I ever met. Don't you think the devil is out to prey on a man like you?" Tom turned toward the door. Kruug stopped short, realizing he had gone too far. "Please wait, Tom. I'm doing the best I can, doing what I must. Please respect that." Kruug walked briskly back behind his desk, falling into his chair again, as if to let Tom know a round was over. "God help me say the right things to you." He put his face into his hands.

"Do you really think the devil brought me to this moment?" Tom asked, not concealing his hurt. "That a mere 'carrot' brought me down, and not something deeply wrong in the Church and deeply wrong with all of us? Isn't celibacy just turning us all into a bunch of hypocrites?"

Kruug picked up a pen and mechanically tapped his teeth. He put it down and blew out. "It was a mistake to bring you here. Gene was too much for you. I'm to blame."

"Gene? What has *Gene* to do with it?"

Kruug looked up, afraid he had blundered again. "I said it was my fault. Okay?" Kruug shouted. "I failed. *My* priesthood failed. Okay? Not yours. Not Gene's."

"Huh?" Tom would have sworn that Kruug was weaving a manipulation, but the raspiness in his voice, the pallor of Kruug's face, contradicted that. Kruug's eye caught light bouncing off the ocean. He spoke half-hypnotized.

"You struggle to be like the angels." He seemed to be rummaging for his feelings. "But you're just an animal like all the rest of the creatures of the world. You pee, you shit, you wake up with an erection every morning, and you wonder how God could ask you to jump across a chasm too wide for any man. What kind of cruel God does that? you ask. Then one priest comes along, you hear his confession, and lo and behold, he's done it, he's kept even the hardest of those impossible rules. God *does* give that grace to some, you say, so you hold off blaming God. But then, voluntarily, after all those years of successful striving, that very priest dives right into the chasm after all the rest of them, and you're back to wondering if God isn't just a grand deceiver."

"*Men* run the Church, Monsignor. You know it as well as I. *Men* made that chasm too wide."

"Maybe you're right." Kruug's eyebrows lifted. He straightened and reached suddenly back as if a dart had hit his spine. "Some say the Pope is fallible now. And the Blessed Mother, she's a long-lost myth. Maybe abortion isn't murder. And we're regressing to before Judaism when Cain hit Abel in the head with a log. We're sliding back into jungle disorder. And you're standing here telling me you're running, at the very moment centuries are collapsing at our heels."

"I'd rather the centuries collapsed at my heels than in front of me," Tom said, a little surprised at himself. "Maybe I'm grabbing for a branch."

Kruug's melancholy ceased abruptly. "Well, I'll go down with those years gladly," he said in an entirely new tone.

"You're older," Tom said softly.

"Don't insult me." Kruug's eyes narrowed. "It's because I made a *vow*. That's why. Because I made a promise to *stay*." Tom's audacity refreshed Kruug's powers. "I know hundreds of priests already buried in those years. Thousands. My mind sees them everywhere under the ground in their copper caskets, dressed in their white vestments, with birettas and rosaries stuck in their stiff hands: Toots McCann, Denny McCabe, dead asleep to all that's changed in the past thirty years. Thank God! May they rest in peace. I'm alive in their dead dreams, but that's a far lovelier place to be than your frontier where a nuclear bomb is about to go off any minute." Kruug turned in disgust. "Go ahead. Run away. You're an ex-priest already, as far as I'm concerned."

Tom didn't move. Again the watch ticking. Again Kruug's eyes drifted out the window, losing themselves in the ocean light. Either he wanted Tom just to leave, or he was stalling. Then unexpectedly, he spoke in the same wounded voice. "At night, I wake them out of their boxes, Toots and Denny, and we go back to Breezy Point. The dream is very alive up here, you know." He tapped his forehead. "You ex-Jesuits are heartless. You have to be to leave your own kind. But I have my class album memorized, one face sweeter than the other, young men in black." He pulled open a drawer and lifted out a gold-framed group photo of eight or nine men in bathing suits. "We took off the black for one thing only: Breezy Point. We'd change into bathing suits and go walking around, sure. But you didn't dare to drink a beer too many, or look at a woman in the wrong way. The people knew you were a priest by those angel eyes and the calluses on your knees and the miraculous medals around your neck. The people thought us lovely, above themselves, and we wouldn't betray their expectations because our one love affair was with *them* really, keeping *them* safe, keeping the dream alive, keeping their hopes fresh and clean as a Sunday morning. Not one of the men in this picture could make it across that chasm by a long shot. We knew the sad truth about one another when we were still young, but we never let the people know how weak we thought we were. We kept the dream alive for them and kept the shame and sadness for ourselves. That's a priest, Tom." His voice broke. His Adam's apple lifted and dropped. He swallowed hard. Now he faced Tom, but his eyes were not soft. "You have nightmares, don't you? I hear you groaning," he asked coldly, softly, fully aware of his cruelty. "You'll have nightmares for the rest of your life, my sweet priest."

"Thanks," Tom said, looking down at the red rug.

"It's true," Kruug shrugged in mock sympathy.

"Why?" Tom asked. "Because *I* didn't bridge that chasm? Because I didn't save you from hating God, because He made it too tough for the Breezy Point gang?"

"Huh?" Kruug blinked, surprised.

"Why didn't *you* jump the chasm? Why didn't the Grangers and the DeGroots forge the way years ago? Why didn't Toots what's-his-name and Denny McCabe and all those guys in their miraculous medals, why didn't they make it solid for me? Why didn't *you*, Kruug? All I see is a bunch of egotistical monsignors who wait for funerals to pity one another. Your picture lies."

"True. True." His voice was almost a whisper. "You, you're far, far stronger than any of us; if I were half as strong as you, I might've . . ."

Kruug squinted out the window. A faraway wave was developing, coming toward the beach. "You envy my leaving, don't you?" Tom asked so softly that his words were almost lost.

Kruug turned, letting Tom have his burning eyes. "If the priesthood is the waste of a man," Kruug said, "then yes, I do envy you."

"Is it? The waste of a man?" Tom asked.

"No." Kruug shuddered. "No. And I don't hate God." Pools broke in his eyes, at last quenching the fires. He pulled a handkerchief out from under his cassock. "I only wish I'd died twenty years ago." Kruug tried to clear his throat. "You'd better take your chalice and go, Sheehan. Seeing you standing there all packed is too much for me, though you won't have much use for that chalice where you're going."

"I may have to sell it."

"Very good. Wonderful," Kruug said sarcastically.

"Well." Tom awkwardly forced out his hand. "Do I rate a handshake?"

"No. Not that easy. This is not a win for me." Kruug shook his head.

"Whose win is it? Mine?" Tom asked, clumsily withdrawing his hand.

"It's just a waste. A tragedy, all around."

"There'll be other contests," Tom said, hurt.

"You don't need to be brittle with me now." Kruug threw him a soft look. "You've won." He stood, turned his back to Tom, and threw open his window. Sounds of air and ocean invaded. The wind caught Tom's eye as it fingered the dried flowers on Gene's grave. Birds twittered. The faraway wave finally made it to shore, booming.

"I wasn't trying to be brittle," Tom offered. "I . . . I'm sorry."

Kruug flipped a pencil wastefully into the trash basket and folded his arms before the open window. "I'll bet you don't even know why the hell you're doing this. It's not the woman; I see that now."

"I said it's her, partially."

"What's the other part?"

"My own will lacking. A certain part of me missing when I made the choice, a part that's developing now."

"Oh, come on. There's not a priest alive who doesn't feel that."

"All right. I just want to *go*. Okay? I'd rather be on my own, acting in my own name. I want to feel my own passions for once, not just the passions of the Church. I'm tired of living by creaky rules that insult my instincts *and* ridicule my body. I think celibacy is hurting me, cheating me."

"You made the vow."

"That's right."

"And now it's getting hard to keep."

"All right. Yes."

"Isn't that a little selfish?"

"Maybe."

"Admit it. It's selfish."

"All right, I admit it, for God's sake. What more do you want from me?"

Kruug felt for his temples. "Okay. Okay. Don't get excited."

"I'm sorry."

"I would chop a hand off to keep you here, and you know it." Kruug seemed surprised at how easily the words slipped out. He blushed. "You were part of a family, my family of the Church as we experienced it here together for a while. Thousands and thousands of people are losing you. I'm just the one who gets left with the aftermath. I get the cleanup work. I get to pick out the coffin again, just as I had to do for Gene, and I'm tired of that."

"In other words, this makes me dead?" Tom tried to keep the anger out of his voice.

Kruug turned back to Tom. His voice was totally controlled, cold and flat. "Gene died in body only. You're much worse off than Gene now. Surely you realize that. You'd be better off if you'd died while still at Granger's."

It took a few seconds for Tom to absorb the impact of Kruug's horrible remark. A certain trembling entered his legs. His throat tightened. He stood there, unable to defend, unable to speak. A sudden, seductive odor of earth wafted in from the open window, breaking Tom's train of thought, anesthetizing his anger. Odors of dryness, October odors, of dead flowers and fresh new earth, all confusing him, turning his trembling to chills. Lilies on the altar at Easter, wet springtimes, damp marble holy-water fonts, children in white, new holy oils, and the taste of white wine in the thin light of morning—they all invaded at once, weakening him. He would never again say mass. He would never pray the psalms on light afternoons, nor walk away from confession basking in the sweetness of the state of grace. He would miss that rare, cool loneliness, that strange privacy, of being a priest.

Katelyn flashed before him. He blinked her away, but her eyes stuck stubbornly. Tom's legs were trembling visibly now. He couldn't understand why they were trembling. It had never happened to him quite that way before. *You're worse off than Gene now*. The words must have had at least a grain of truth in them to make him feel that devastated. He was glad Kruug's back was to him, because tears began, his first tears, for the loss of his priesthood. He hated himself for not being able to prevent it. He managed to keep the sounds from escaping his throat. He hoped Kruug wouldn't turn the recliner before he could brush his eyes. But Kruug did turn slowly, shamelessly, proudly, as if he knew what he would find.

"Where do you get the gall to judge my conscience?" Tom spit the words out like small broken bones.

"From the simple fact that you made a vow," Kruug said with quiet strength. "Did you think I was going to let you steamroll over me on your way out of here? I'm not going to turn *my* conscience inside out so you can feel better about yourself. I have to live with myself after you've gone, too, you know."

"I have no guilt; why should you?"

"You have more guilt than you can stand, or else you wouldn't have come in here whimpering for a blessing. Why are you crying?"

"It's not easy for me, Monsignor."

"Of course it isn't easy." Kruug's voice was almost sympathetic. "It wasn't meant to be easy to deny the priesthood." His voice sank to the bottom of the sea. "Thou art a priest forever. You're breaking a solemn vow, a solemn promise to be faithful to God and the Church. Be a man about it."

"That's my problem. I am one." Tom wiped tears with his hand.

"Yes, Tom, you've become yet another common, groveling man, among the hordes of them. As if the world didn't have enough." Silence. Both men swallowed and looked away from one another. "Thank God Gene isn't here to see you this way."

"Don't pull that." Tom dried his hand on the leg of his trousers. "What would Gene see going on here that is so terrible?"

Kruug pointed a finger softly up at Tom's face. "A few days ago, in the middle of the night, you came into this rectory, practically on your knees, looking like you saw a ghost, calling for Gene to confess you, begging to be absolved. Did you forget that? You think you're free of him?"

"Of who?"

"*Him.* The devil." Kruug whipped the word out, raising the hairs at the back of Tom's neck.

"Muriel may be listening," Tom bolted, wondering how she suddenly came to mind.

"She's shopping. Don't avoid the question. Do you think you're free of him?"

"You are a dangerous man." Tom pointed at Kruug this time.

"The devil's name scares you? It should. It burns my mouth to even pronounce it."

"I don't believe in him."

"Tell me that till you're blue in the face, but I'm older than you, Jesuit. He'll creep into your head again, again, and again before your life is over, and you're not that young anymore, not that young."

Tom couldn't control his legs. "You're deliberately trying to scare me."

"Night after night, year after year. The devil comes in many forms."

"*Shut the fuck up!*" Tom didn't believe the scream that came out of him, the sudden rush of power to his arms. The onyx bookend on Kruug's desk—he felt the urge to lift it over Kruug's head, to let it fall with crushing strength. He forced his eyes away from the bookends, out the window. They caught on Gene's flowers shivering in the wind. "Jesus." Tom grabbed his chalice. "I've got to leave. Got to." He wanted out. He needed air.

"Look at the shaking Jesuit. Look at what he's doing now, crawling away to a lifetime of nightmares."

Tom turned, pointing a finger at the pale monsignor. "My nightmares came because it was my first time with a woman."

"So you've gotten past the first time, have you?"

"Yes, I have."

"Have you confessed those *other* times? Of course you haven't. No wonder you haven't had any more attacks of guilt. It's because you've converted. You're *his* already."

"Whose?" Tom hated Kruug for baiting him. *"No."*

Kruug turned calmly away. "You know whose you are. You're his who made you comfortable in your sin. He's given you peace. Guilt would be God's grace. But you can't even have guilt because you don't have the grace for it. Think of that."

Tom made an effort to gather his strength in his throat, but all he could cough out was a curse: "You crazy sonofabitch." Finally his voice became his own, erupting deeply and loudly. *"You crazy sonofabitch. How dare you talk about guilt?"* Now Tom felt Gene's anger spilling out of him, Gene's power, as if Gene were talking inside of him. He pointed out the window. "You turn around, Kruug, and look there at that pile of dirt," he shouted. "You should *eat* that dirt, *eat* that grave." Tom came forward. "You killed Gene," he snapped each word.

"Are you crazy?" Kruug stepped back.

"You *killed* him," Tom repeated. "I talked to Foley; he was there."

"It was *you,*" Kruug shouted back at Tom. "I brought you here to give him an example, and what did *you* give him? You messed him up more."

Tom raised his hand like a traffic cop, as if to stop Kruug's words. "Uhh-uh, no, no," Tom sang. "Don't lay that one on me, Kruug. *You* messed him up all by yourself with your quarantines, your obsessions with black suits and clerical collars. He thought you had spies following him around, and you may have, in your complete and total disrespect for his humanity, your jealousy of his youth."

"You are full of shit," Kruug yelled.

"Your jealousy of his *youth,*" Tom screamed, "because your life is over. You wasted it, like Granger, on capes and candles and Breezy Point. You haven't changed and you haven't allowed anything else to change, including Gene. You're just an ex-Navy man with a uniform fetish, isolated out here in the middle of the ocean where your actions don't affect anyone anymore. Montauk doesn't need another parish, for God's sake. Start one in Calcutta or Kenya if you want to help humanity." Tom turned toward the door. "You all had a powerful priest in Gene, but none of you wanted that kind of strength, did you? Instead of giving him room, you all dumped on him; you bowed to DeGroot. You took away his work and made him hate himself for being a priest."

"And you snubbed him when he asked you to be his friend, didn't you?" Kruug slipped in the words deftly. "Didn't you, Tom?"

"Huh? Who? Who told you I snubbed Gene?" Tom came forward. "Where did you get this information?" Tom repeated. Kruug folded his arms. Tom slammed the desk. "I'm not leaving this rectory till you tell me, Kruug."

"Stay." Kruug shrugged. "You have no right to leave anyway."

"I did not snub Gene." Tom rested his chalice case, keeping hold of the handle. "I only hesitated maybe, when he asked me to become his close friend, only because he wanted a sort of pact, which I thought was an act of self-loathing. And when I realized how sensitive he was, so distrustful of other priests, and so frustrated, I quickly reversed it. 'Fine.' I shook his hand. 'Let's be friends,' I said. 'We're in the same rectory,' I said. 'It couldn't be avoided anyway. . . . I . . .'" Tom tripped on his own words.

"Being his friend could not be avoided? You *told* Gene that?" Kruug pounced.

"C'mon, Kruug, what was wrong with that?"

"You don't *know?* And then you turn around and walk into his room to tell him you were seeing a woman?"

"So what? I asked his advice. Muriel listened at the door, didn't she? How else would you know this?"

"You were both screaming."

"Muriel told you we were screaming?"

"I don't deny she told me."

"She lied, and you probably know it. We were whispering, the way we had to constantly, with her sneaking around trying to earn the gold stars she gets for spilling the beans to you. Gene caught her outside his door. You both revolt me with your lack of shame at being so malevolent toward priests you live with."

"Malevolent?" Kruug smiled.

"Malevolent. Yes. Malevolent. *You* need help. You need a priest."

"I need a priest?" Kruug smiled even wider.

"Anyone who'll teach you an ounce of trust of other people, anything to stop you from trying to control everyone around you. You won with Gene, and there he is, planted safely in your garden. Well, that is not where I'm going to wind up, Kruug. I'm leaving here to love somebody with my body and my mind. It's not for thirty pieces of silver like you'd like me to believe. I'm going out there to work for my bread and butter, with my hands, any damned way I can. I'm not begging alms, and I'm going with a good conscience, so don't pawn off your rotten guilt on me. Don't ask me to take your garbage out with me."

Kruug waited, then spoke clearly. "I loved Gene."

"*He hated you,*" Tom screamed, hoping it would hurt. He grabbed at his white plastic collar and ripped it off, holding it in front of Kruug. "This. You made him hate this damned thing. You turned it into a noose."

"Never. I tried to make him proud to *wear* that collar."

"Proud? Did *you* wear it swimming at Breezy Point with your Toots and Denny? Huh? With your miraculous medal and your bathing suit?"

"Gene wasn't on vacation here."

"*He wasn't here to be executed either.*" Kruug's eyes widened at Tom's words. "You clean the rotten flowers off his grave. But me, I'm on my way out. I'm saving my skin, Kruug. I'm grabbing that branch quick as I can, because you scare me. Yes. Oh, you terrify me with your fetishes and your hellfire devil bullshit. Here." Tom ripped off his jacket. "Here." He tore at his black rabat, revealing his tan arms. "Take your black stuff, take it in your face." He threw the bib and jacket at Kruug. "Priest Doctor, you keep it, you mourn. I don't want it, won't wear it ever, ever again. You wear it; you're the executioner."

Kruug came straight at Tom, lifted his hand, and landed a slap so flat into Tom's face that it made his ear ring. Kruug reached back for a second slap.

"Executioner," Tom screamed. *Slap. Slap.* Kruug landed several slaps. "Killer," Tom repeated with each slap. Kruug's eyes burned crazily as he raised his hand again and again. Tom was spitting into Kruug's face in between the slaps: "Killer, killer, tchilllllllller . . ."

The gray, exhausted face of Kruug backed away, trembling, toward his recliner. He shakily pulled out a white handkerchief from his trouser pocket through the slit in his cassock and brought it to his nose, almost dropping it. Tom's face burned from the slaps, but the trembling in his legs had ceased completely. The heat of his face drained into his chest, calming him.

Kruug's breathing was much heavier now. "Never . . . never . . ." Kruug couldn't even finish the sentence. He let Tom have his eyes. There was cruel honesty there, no hidden rage anymore, no sweetness, no camouflage. "Never did I once want Gene to die. Never." Kruug let himself collapse backward into his chair, his face white as death. His breath was definitely not coming right. Tom watched worriedly as Kruug turned the chair to the window.

"Okay, I'll split the guilt with you," Tom said impulsively.

"The guilt for what?"

"Gene's suicide." Kruug turned the chair back to Tom.

"Suicide?" His mouth dropped in horror.

"It *was* suicide," Tom said quietly. "Neither of us knew what to do for him."

"It was an accident."

"God, Kruug! Why still pretend? We both know it was suicide. It was. And now I'm not brave enough to stay here. I'm just not brave enough to wait for what never came to Gene. I'm scared. Do you understand? I don't want your life. Let me go, for God's sake."

The monsignor stared. "I? Let *you* go? Do you really think I have that power?"

"Yes," Tom whispered in a voice he could hardly hear himself.

Another wave had arrived. The sound of its boom filled the room, a sizzling noise, then silence. A breeze made a song around the telephone wire at the open window. Beyond, it lifted the petals of Gene's flowers, flowing downward, fingering the grass, which was lying flat, combed northward by the ocean winds.

Kruug blew his nose into his handkerchief, put it away under his cassock, and spoke to the horizon.

"What about the poor in the cities, stacked on top of one another, whom you accused Granger of betraying? Who is betraying them now?"

Tom looked away. "I won't stop helping people just because I'm not a priest anymore."

"May I make a suggestion?" Kruug bit his lip.

"What?"

"Stay here. See her twice a week until you get it out of your system. I'll close my eyes."

"Huh?"

"You'll save your priesthood."

"And what about my self-respect?"

"Well, you lose that either way, don't you?"

Tom looked at him with shock. "Please, no more. You tried, Kruug, you really did. Let me go now."

A child's expression came over Kruug's face. He let his hands fall on either side of him to his rug. He spoke through a stuffed nose, dreamily, out the window. "You know, before I was old enough to go to school, I wanted to be a priest," he said. "No TV in those days. We lived over a barber shop, windows facing the el, trains making a racket day and night. Five of us sleeping in two rooms. No father. Sewing machine going in the kitchen all night. But two blocks away was St. Monica's. Like a planetarium: saints floating way up from niches, vigil lights twinkling. They sang in Latin on Sunday. Then up, into this sort of rocket ship, the priest would climb, up and up, and suddenly, he'd appear all in white, close enough for everybody to see the color of his eyes. He looked like a man in the pulpit, but you knew he was more. Nobody heard of astronauts in those days. So, I'd make a visit after school and talk to the floating saints. Never locked;

nobody'd dare steal from the house of God in those days. 'Cause that's what it really was then, the house of God." Kruug looked ten years older.

"It still is the house of God," Tom offered.

"Is it?" Kruug choked back a sob and turned back to Tom.

"Why not?" Tom shrugged.

"We know better, don't we?" The intended sarcasm didn't make it into his voice. Tom heard a watch ticking again. He looked down as Kruug pretended to blow his nose. Then Kruug stuffed his handkerchief through the slit in his cassock, into his pocket, and stood up, sweating. He pulled open the buttons at his collar on his way to his bathroom, leaving Tom standing there, in black trousers and T-shirt, wondering if it was his cue to leave. Kruug turned on the bathroom light as if Tom were not there.

"Dear Jesus!" he exclaimed to the mirror, seeing his tired face. He turned on the faucet and stooped to splash up water. He straightened, dried his face with a towel, then reentered the room and headed for his clothes closet. He opened the door, reached in, and pulled a blue-and-red plaid shirt off its hanger. "I never wear this thing. It's made of Viyella," he said. "I got it from my niece for golf. I hate golf." He coughed as he held the shirt out to Tom. "It should fit you."

Tom cautiously lifted the shirt off Kruug's fingers.

"Try it on," Kruug urged.

Tom put one arm into the shirt, then the other, not quite trusting what might be in Kruug's mind, looking down, pretending to be lost in buttoning. Kruug helped.

"Fits fine," Tom said, still not secure enough to look into Kruug's face.

"Good," Kruug said. "It was going to waste in there."

"Well, thank you." Tom looked up now, firmly. Kruug looked back.

"Now kneel," the monsignor ordered. Tom sank beneath Kruug's tired eyes, down the line of purple cassock buttons till his knees touched the red rug and he was staring at the old-style black cordovan shoes and the little fringe at the hem of his cassock. Kruug made the sign of the cross over Tom's head and pronounced the words the old way, in Latin: *"Benedicat vos omnipotens, Deus, Pater et Filius . . ."* When he finished, he gave Tom his hands to help him up.

Tom stood awkwardly, and Kruug simply turned away with a tired face and walked back into the bathroom. He flicked on the overhead light and started to close himself inside the white tile room. "That's all, Tom. You can go now," he said softly. "Please go, Son. Good-bye." The door clicked closed.

Kruug found his bloodshot eyes in the mirror, the disgrace of his weepiness, his wrinkled, clownlike grief, all there in one fast glance. Why was this pain so different from anything he had ever imagined, or felt, worse than a parent dying, worse than anything? The man was really only a stranger.

He sat on the closed lid of the john, grabbed onto the sink, and rested his head in the hammock of his arm. Other issues would tumble into the void Tom Sheehan had caused.

Tom waited outside the bathroom door, as if something more was to happen in the room, but when he realized it was all over, he unbuckled his belt and unzipped his pants, stuffing the plaid shirt down inside. Then, zipping up and tightening the belt, he took his black jacket from Kruug's desk, where it had landed inside out. He straightened out the sleeves and put the jacket on over Kruug's shirt, letting out the plaid collar. He hooked into the leather strap of his chalice case and opened Kruug's door, pausing for a few seconds to look back.

Suddenly he came forward, back into the room, grabbed a pencil and paper from Kruug's desk, and wrote: "Find a priest who needs this chalice. Give it to him for me." He spun around and made for the hall. His stomach felt as if he were falling out of a plane. "God help me," he whispered, and, pulling Kruug's door closed, he dropped into the hallway, lifted the suitcase, and made his way toward the glaring glass door, then out into the light of day under the moaning telephone wire. "Good-bye, Gene," he whispered toward the mound in the cemetery. He walked up the pebbled driveway to the chain gate, unhooked the latch, and stepped out onto the asphalt road.

A tall old bakery truck pulled over as he walked. It was brush-painted silver, like an old radiator.

"I kin take ya far as Southampin'," a creaky voice called out. Tom jumped up onto the platform, standing inside the high doorway. The driver seemed almost too old to be driving. The vehicle was lined with metal bread shelves on both sides. The truck was so tall that a man could walk down the middle aisle without bending over. But there was no place for Tom to sit.

" 'Fraid you'll have to stand right there," the old gentleman apologized.

"Do you know the yellow blinking light at the crossroads in Sagaponac?" Tom asked.

"Oh, sure." The old fellow put the truck into gear and took off slowly. "Don't fall out now. Jes' grab that there pipe over the door."

"I can walk from the blinking light."

"Goin' toward the ocean?"

"Yes."

"That'll make a pretty walk through them horse farms."

"Yes."

"Very pretty that way."

"Yes, I look forward to it."

"Too bad it ain't sunnier for ya."

"I don't mind it." Tom liked the old man's twinkling blue eyes. They were silent as the truck took each little hill and curve of the old Montauk road.

"We've had a fair share of sun this summer," the old fellow said with seriousness.

"Have we?"

"Oh, yes. In comparison, yes."

"Then how can we complain?" Tom asked with a grin.

"Well, we just *can't*." The old man laughed. "We don't have hardly the right, do we?"

The truck bounced up a rise and dropped sharply down, curving smoothly through the cavernous low pines. The ocean below was jade in color, except where some sun came through the clouds, making translucent lakes in the dark sea. The cloudiness made the trees seem more dazzling green. Tom reached into his back pocket and pulled out Moonghost's letter. He turned it over, then held it with one hand to the open door frame, spreading it out so he could read the last few lines.

. . . I am the ghost who took you on jeep rides under the moon and who taught you to walk upon water, among the silent whales.

Tom looked away from the letter, letting the wind, the sky, and the trees enter through his eyes as they did the day he painted the world with Katelyn. His fingers tingled; his groin and knees tingled. He looked up at the telephone wires awkwardly zigzagging against the velvety gray sky which filtered the sun, making the green buzz and shudder the more. "Mother of God, help me in this strange new place," he said under his breath.

As the foliage jumped, electric, olive and emerald, except where traces of autumnal red and yellow were distracting his eye, Moonghost's letter, pinned under his thumb near the open door, was rattling loudly in the wind. Suddenly, almost capriciously, Tom reached for the overhead bar, letting the letter fly out behind the truck, not as if to discard it, but lovingly as Philip had asked, giving it back to God, to the earth, hoping at least that the sky would adopt it, as a leaf, to be rained upon and bleached dry, over and over, until it became no different from the world itself.

Tom buttoned the top of Kruug's plaid shirt at his neck, letting his nostrils fill up with wind. He thought of that night long ago in Peru, his first ride to the windy Pacific with Moonghost, their cassocks snapping at their legs, flapping like flags around their bodies.

But he felt bare now. A chill ran down his back. Cold weather was certainly coming. He needed to get himself a work coat, a jacket, or maybe one of those goose-down things. He would have to drive the van to the beach for firewood before nightfall, and tomorrow he would have to talk to some local contractors about work. But for the moment, he closed his eyes, letting the wind pick the worries off his face. And he imagined the landscapes turning white. Snow coming, flake after flake, day after day, winter upon winter.